SINFUL

FR

Also by Victor McGlothin

Down On My Knees

Borrow Trouble (with Mary Monroe)

Ms. Etta's Fast House

Sleep Don't Come Easy (with J.D. Mason)

SINFUL

VICTOR McGLOTHIN

Kensington Publishing Corp.
http://www.kensingtonbooks.com

DAFINA BOOKS are published by

Kensington Publishing Corp.
119 West 40th Street
New York, NY 10018

All Kensington Titles, Imprints, and Distributed Lines are available at special quantity discounts for bulk purchases for sales promotions, premiums, fund-raising, and educational or institutional use. Special book excerpts or customized printings can also be created to fit specific needs. For details, write or phone the office of the Kensington special sales manager: Kensington Publishing Corp., 119 West 40th Street, New York, NY 10018, attn: Special Sales Department. Phone: 1-800-221-2647.

Dafina and the Dafina logo Reg. U.S. Pat. & TM Off.

ISBN-13: 978-0-7582-1349-5
ISBN-10: 0-7582-1349-2

First trade paperback printing: April 2007
First mass market printing: August 2009

10 9 8 7 6 5 4 3 2

Printed in the United States of America

Acknowledgments

A special thanks to Victoria Christopher Murray and Kim Lawson Roby. Y'all started something great for the rest of us.

Amanda 'Star' Halton and Gloria Mays, two of the best real-estate agents in Texas. Thanks for showing me the ropes.

Karen Thomas, a queen among editors, thanks for keeping me on point and reshaping my career. I still owe you.

To every book club, discussion group, bookstore, and reader who has added my work to their bestseller or favorites list, I am very thankful. Without you, there would be no me.

And most of all, thank you God for blessing me and my family every step of the way. Your love knows no bounds.

Prologue

"Everybody's got a weakness," was Dior's quiet proclamation. Sighing wearily, she stared at her ragged reflection captured by the dusty hanging wall mirror inside of the tiny room at the Happy Horizons mental care facility where she'd been sentenced for psychiatric evaluation. *The difference with me is,* Dior continued to herself, *I claim mine and ain't never tried to put it off on nobody else.*

After sweeping hair in desperate need of professional attention underneath the baseball cap her favorite cousin Chandelle had brought along, Dior smirked at her tired expression. Her eyes seemed darker, murkier, than she remembered them, but her flawless cinnamon brown complexion and attractive features hadn't waned one iota. She was still just as fine as she was when they checked her in and took her belt and shoelaces away.

"You're a Wicker, too, Chandelle," Dior spouted adamantly. "Or else you used to be. Deep down, where it makes every bit of difference, you still are, so don't go thinking

that swooping me from this giggle factory on my early release day makes you any better than me."

Dior sighed again, turning away from the image of a
troubled 25-year-old with a pretty face. She placed the
last of her personal belongings into a stolen designer
travel bag and then snapped her fingers in a snooty chop-
chop fashion. "Get that bag for me, Chandelle, before
they try to hold me for the full two-week bid. I wasn't
loony when that stupid judge sent me here, but I swear I
ain't wrapped too tight now. Go ahead on and get that
bag off the bed; it's checkout time."

"Humph, you ain't that crazy," Chandelle chuckled
under her breath as Dior paused to sneak another glimpse
of her tightly fitted low-rise jeans in the filthy mirror.
"Look, Dior, you're my girl as well as my blood, but you'd
have to be up in here a lot longer than eleven days for me
to feel sorry enough to be your personal valet. I don't
even carry my own bags."

Dior's attempt to obtain her closest friend's pity didn't
go over well because Chandelle was one of two people
who often knew her better than she did herself. The other
person was Dior's fraternal twin, Dooney.

"I know you have issues but they have nothing to do
with me," Chandelle contended. "You're the one who . . ."
she began to say before realizing her own words waxed
judgmental. "You right about one thing. It is way past time
to get you out of here." Chandelle, the color of ginger
peach and fashion model tall, with the looks to match,
stood up from the cloth-covered chair placed by the door.
Although she tried mightily to avoid the inevitable, it was
utterly impossible. She found herself primping the chic,
angular hairstyle framing her face in the same dirty mirror. Chandelle's stunning beauty, beset by round brown
eyes and anchored by full voluptuous lips, beamed back
at her with a brilliant approving smile. "Yes, just as I suspected. Beauty knows no bounds."

"If you ask me, they had the wrong one locked up," Dior heckled from the hallway. "Come on, cuz, let's get out of here. I'm hungry for some real food. Something dumped in grease."

"Ooh, Dee. That's the sanest thing I've heard all day. Let me get your bag."

1

Exodus

The brisk fall Dallas air brushed against Chandelle's cheeks. "It's too cold to be early October," she shrieked. The mink jacket she slid out of a slick plastic covering from the trunk of her car, the one she'd sufficiently convinced herself that she couldn't live without, hugged her shoulders as they approached the front doors of the Alley Cat'n Restaurant parking lot.

Dior caught the hint. She peered over the hood of the car at the dark brown collection of expensive pelt and escalating debt. Chandelle sashayed casually in the ridiculously overpriced fur as if the hefty bill, including a truckload of finance charges, wouldn't be arriving in her mailbox within the week. "Look at what the cat drug in," Dior howled. "That's a nice coat." She stepped around the front of Chandelle's two-year-old Volvo to run her fingers along the velvety sleeves. "Uh-huh, soft as cotton too. Who boosted it for you?"

Highly offended, Chandelle was outdone. "Boosted? Don't get the way I do business mixed up with how you handle yours. I don't get my hands dirty like that anymore, and if I did, I wouldn't appreciate you putting it out there like that."

After Dior smacked her lips, she turned her nose up at Chandelle's refusal to pay the drastically discounted prices for stolen goods like she had done in the past. "I's just saying, I know Marvin didn't let you run up his credit cards with no department store mink. Even I'm smarter than that."

Chandelle flipped the collar over her ears and huffed. *Shows how little you do know. Marvin didn't let me because he doesn't know about it yet*, she thought. "Let me deal with my husband. He doesn't tell me what I can buy with my own money," she contended in an irritated tone.

Still fuming over having been chastised by a street-wise headache after their entrées were delivered, Chandelle quietly picked over a deep-fried fish basket while Dior dove into hers face–first. Instead of listening to her cousin recount the events that landed her inside of the county-funded facility for observation, she was having second thoughts of treating herself to the exotic jacket now saturated with oily catfish odors. It was all right, Dior explained only what she was willing to share, there were always incriminating details she'd purposely leave out. And despite how often Dior managed to get herself caught up in a web, it was never, under any circumstances, her fault.

"See, what had happened was, that trick of a store manager couldn't hold off long enough to see things from my standpoint. It would've been cool if he'd have just listened to me and then let me bounce. Besides, it was a victimless crime anyhow. After being poked and pinched in that loony bin they put me in, I'm the victim." With a half-eaten hush puppy in one hand, Dior used the other to illustrate how she'd been wronged yet again by the system, although she was caught dead to rights shoplifting in the department store restroom. Fourteen sets of lingerie items, in assorted sizes, were stuffed inside her jogging suit when an employee began pounding on the door. Dior's eyes had bugged out as the realization of serving jail time popped into her head. That was a fate worse than death as far as she was concerned. Knowing that the jig was up, she worked feverishly at pulling the bunched undergarments out of her pants while reattaching them to hangers scattered about on the floor. "Just one minute," she pleaded, before a large, brooding white man opened the door with his master key. When Dior heard him warn that he was coming in, she acted fast. She snatched her jogging pants down past her knees and plopped down on the toilet seat. The scream she hurled at him reverberated throughout the women's clothing section of the store. "Get out!" she shrieked. "Police! Police!"

Immediately detained in the manager's office, Dior readily explained how she'd never felt so violated before and that she'd never intended on stealing a single garment, but rather how she'd innocently taken the items to the restroom during the fleeting hours of a "once a year" sale because she couldn't risk losing her great finds to other shoppers with similar taste. Soon enough, the police arrived, heard Dior's outrageous story, and as quickly as they appeared, sped away with her handcuffed in the backseat of their squad car. She pled her case vehemently while traveling downtown for central booking. "I'm serious, officers!" she clamored loudly. "I couldn't wait for a store employee to come and watch the clothes for me because I got a condition, uh-huh, a weak bladder." After being reassured that the officers had no plans for letting her go, the cagey criminal decided to build a case for insanity by leaving a urine sample on the vinyl seats of their squad car.

"You know what, Chandelle? I ought to sue," Dior contemplated, from the other side of a forkful of fries. "I just might win, too. You know I can lie real good. Humph, I can make a stupid bunch of jurors believe me like I fooled that judge who signed my crazy papers instead of sending me to county."

Chandelle sat across the table. She stared at Dior as if she had been released too soon. "Don't tell me you thought you could pee your way out of that too?"

"Why wouldn't I?" she questioned. Wetting her pants had gotten Dior out of numerous tight spots before, and it still worked.

"How many times are you going to use that stupid defense as a 'get out of jail free' card?"

"Until they take it away," Dior answered quickly. "That pill-popping palace they call Happy Horizons is the closest I've ever gotten to doing real time. Well, except for that one night, when I almost get snatched up. That cop caught me behind that night club trying to get back in good with Kevlin. Girl, I had my skirt hiked up when he shined the light on us. Shoot, I squatted so fast it nearly ruined the officer's shoes. Sure did, told the law how Kevlin was back there to keep a lookout so nobody would bother me. Uh-huh, the same bad bladder scheme was on and popping then too."

"You're getting too old to be showing out like that with Kevlin."

"That's what you think," Dior smarted back. "I'll never be too old to hike my skirt up whenever I feel like it."

"You are too old to be doing it in back alleys with some brotha who won't half call you afterward. And all of the scheming you're so stuck on has gotten you tossed into that asylum. Dior, nobody even knew where you were until you called today begging for me to pick you up."

"That's why I had to go about the schizted route. I couldn't risk you or Dooney showing up there talking about 'she ain't crazy, just too sinful.' That's been the bad rap all of my life, and I don't deserve it. I'm just misunderstood."

"You mean misdiagnosed."

"Whatever. You say po-tay-to. I say to-may-to."

Chandelle glanced up when she replayed Dior's mishandling of the common cliché. "You mean po-tay-to, po-tah-to?"

"Why would I say the same thing twice? That's stupid."

"Yeah, and so is this conversation," Chandelle replied, realizing it about thirty minutes too late. She massaged her temples with all ten fingers, agonizing over the slim chances of returning a mink coat that reeked of deep-fried fish. Since Dior didn't elaborate on how she'd successfully proved to clinically trained psychologists that she wasn't harmful to herself or others but not likely to harbor the propensity for shoplifting either, Chandelle assumed she'd pulled off yet another ruse whereby urinating her way out of it. Unfortunately, this time around, Happy Horizons was only the beginning.

Chandelle fought with further attacking her cousin's dirty deeds while maneuvering through the streets of Dallas. She wondered if beating a dead horse would have amounted to much, if anything, in the way of setting the mixed-up sister straight. When Dior insisted that Chandelle zoom past her apartment, she didn't question it until they were speeding off in the other direction. "What's gotten into you?" she yelled, feverishly glancing in the rearview mirror.

"Just keep driving!" Dior cried out, whipping her head around to see if they were being followed. "Make a left up there at the corner." Chandelle did just that; she kept her foot on the gas pedal and followed directions until entering a drug-infested neighborhood off the interstate. On the outer ring of a densely cluttered assortment of aging apartment complexes, commonly referred to as "Crack City" by the local police, Chandelle pulled her car into a convenience store parking lot, and then slammed on the brakes.

"I've been quiet long enough, Dee. This is as far as I go until you tell me what's got you too scared to set foot into your own spot and has me all jacked up and ready to jet from this one. I'm trying not to end up on the news, gunned down in a drug bust gone bad."

"It's not that serious, Chandelle," Dior argued, although reluctant to face her. With her head down, she fiddled with the suede tassels hanging from her Navajo Indian–style purse. "You wouldn't understand if I told you, so I won't even try."

Now, Chandelle was seething too much to lay eyes on her salty passenger. "So that's it? I just fled the scene like some kind of fugitive from justice and that's the best you can come up with to justify it? I'm not moving another inch unless you tell me what you're running from and why you've chosen this crack alley of all places to hide."

"You're lucky, Chandelle, always have been. You might no longer be what you used to be, but I am. This thing hanging over me ain't up for discussion. Feel me on this, pop . . . pop . . . bang. It's dead and buried. Trying to go home again was my fourth mistake of the day, so please let it rest in peace."

Chandelle lips pursed into a firm pucker. "Fine, if you want to go at your demons alone, then so be it. I'll drop you off, but don't come beating down my door when Kevlin decides to throw you out with tomorrow's trash." When Dior's eyes widened, Chandelle laughed. "Huh, sure I knew you've been creeping back to him every chance you got. Your never-agains don't hold any weight with me, baby girl. I'm still slicker than you'll ever be without even breaking a sweat, so save it. All I needed was one time for a man to paint me stupid and then go upside my head because I called him on it. That grew me up quick, fast, and in a hurry. We'll play it your way, but this is where I get off of your constant collision with catastrophe. You need to grow up, too, and get your head on straight before Kevlin knocks a hole in it."

A sigh escaped from Dior's lips, making it apparent to Chandelle that the words she spoke were ignored. Dior's eyes gradually rose to meet Chandelle's icy glare. "What makes you think I want to grow up, huh? What makes you think that just because you made college and marriage work, that I want the same things? Besides, ain't no guarantees, Chandelle, not for a sistah like me. What, am I supposed to grow up and get shackled down to some brotha selling toasters for a living while trying to make a slave outta me? I already know I don't look cute chained to a stove."

"You just keep on pressing your luck, trying to get over without putting the work in," Chandelle said, before issuing a stern warning. "And you got one more time to criticize my man."

"You're right, my bad going there about Marvin, but don't forget I've *done* the nine-to-five thing and it didn't suit me. My heels were too long, my lunch breaks were too short, folks didn't like my clothes being too tight, and somebody was always complaining about something I was doing wrong. Listen to me close, I can't do the square life and can't use no square love."

Caught between a hard head and her better judgment, Chandelle refused to let Dior's difficulties in the workplace go unchallenged. "That may be so, but every black woman deals with the same issues until they realize it's not always about us. I wasn't gonna say anything, but you know who you sound like talking all pitiful and woe-is-me?"

"I know who you bet' not be thinking of," Dior spat ferociously. "Leave her out of this. I'm not going to end up like Billie." Her mother was doing a ten-year bid in the state penitentiary on a welfare food stamp charge. Dior had yet to forgive her for getting caught. Hustling was a way of life she'd grown accustomed to, but a woman leaving her family behind was unacceptable under any circumstances.

"Dior, you might not plan to but that's where the road

you're headed down leads. Me, I love being a *square*. Need I remind you that you're in my whip? My square job and my square husband help to keep me rolling in it. Thank God."

"Whatever, I'm just saying . . . can't do the square thing."

"Here's a note for you, cousin, we all have to grow up sooner or later."

"I hear you, just ain't ready yet. Anyways, all that stuntin' I do, it's cool because it's like I've heard you say, that God of yours knows my heart."

"Listen at you. *He knows your heart*. That's another reason for you to check yourself because He does know about the stuff you're too ashamed to tell me." After Chandelle got her dig in, she backed out of the small parking lot and proceeded toward the apartment she'd sworn never to revisit, Kevlin's den. "I can't believe I'm doing this," she huffed. "Nothing good can come from getting mixed up with him again. He's a snake, poison."

"Bump that, Chandelle. Kevlin said he was sorry, and that's what's up. Let me out so I can get what I've been dreaming about for almost two weeks." Dior hopped out and wrestled her bag down the walkway to an open gazebo-style beige-colored brick building with three doors on either side. She knocked at the nearest door on the right. When a yellow-toned, muscle-bound man wearing a long gangster perm and sagging blue jeans opened it, Dior's eyes floated up in a begging-please-take-me-in manner. Chandelle, looking on from the street, shook her head disapprovingly. Kevlin's expression was undecipherable to Chandelle as he stared at Dior and her bag resting at his doorstep. Then he leaned out to clock whoever was watching their reunion from the red Volvo idling in the road.

Yeah, I'm the one who told Dooney you were putting hands on his twin. Uh-huh, the same one who's responsible for him posting you up at the car wash and had you crying like a li'l punk, Chandelle thought, as she rolled down the window so he could see her face clearly, displaying her unmistakable contempt for him and men like him. *Yeah, the stitches and the lumpy hospital bed, that was all on me*.

After mean-mugging Chandelle like he wanted to return the favor, Kevlin nodded his head respectfully instead, pecked Dior on the lips, and then ushered her inside.

"That's what I thought," Chandelle mouthed triumphantly, before making a fast U-turn to get out of the area as quickly as possible. Although Dior was willing to brave the climate of the low-rent apartment district, she wasn't in the mood to reminisce on the life she led before leaving it all where it belonged, in the past.

2

At the Job

Appliance World, a second-rate retail operation, thrived in the midst of mammoth-sized chain stores dwarfing it on both sides. When the owner, Larry Mercer, learned that two appliance giants wanted his location near the busy freeway, he held out for more money. Unfortunately, his plan backfired. Instead of making another lofty offer to purchase his property, each built stores on either side and squeezed him in the middle.

Weeks before Mr. Mercer was forced to pull the plug on his family business, Chandelle's husband, Marvin, walked through the front door to price a blender. The salesmen on duty had neither salesmanship skills nor an appreciation for customers. After overhearing Marvin explain how that was a leading reason most people were reluctant to do business with African Americans (who expected to succeed simply because their doors were opened), Mr. Mercer took a good look at the attractive medium brown shopper and quickly offered him an assistant manager's position on the spot. Marvin's first order of business was scheduling training classes for all eight of the slacker salespeople.

Three years later, Mr. Mercer was happily making money hand over fist because of Marvin's diligence and training techniques. The fact that he still held the same position, at the same salary grade, both made Chandelle very unhappy. She wanted him to be more of a corporate mogul instead of an aspiring store manager of Appliance World. She also kept after him to trade in his khaki pants and navy short sleeve pullover uniform for a sleek designer suit. Marvin's business degree hadn't produced much in the way of options, but Chandelle didn't give up hope. Her husband would be important some day, she'd see to that. Oddly enough, Marvin was the type to fight sudden change head on. Although he loved Chandelle, it was her constant bouts of impulsivity and ongoing propensity to own a lot more than she could afford that he couldn't stand.

At 7:05 P.M., Marvin's cell phone rang. With a semiannual sale running at top speed, he was glad to have a moment to himself. He lay down the remnants of a half-eaten baloney sandwich, his third of the day, in order to wrestle the tiny handheld from his belt holster. "Hello, this is Marvin," he answered, wiping crumbs from his thin mustache as if the caller could see him in disarray. "Uh, yeah, Kim, I have a minute. Thanks for returning my page."

The empty break room at the rear of the store watched him smile. Nearly twenty years had lapsed since he'd seen her, Kim Hightower, but he couldn't shake the indelible image of a beautiful 18-year-old prom queen he'd carried a serious torch for, along with over a thousand other mannish boys at John Quinn High. Now an accomplished realtor, Kim was back in his life to help him and Chandelle find their first dream house. The thought of his lovely wife catching a glimpse of him gushing over another woman pushed that eager grin from his lips.

"Good," Kim replied. "I'm very excited to be working with an old schoolmate, but I'll have to be honest, Marvin, I can't seem to remember you. Anyhoo," Kim continued, "we can catch up tomorrow. And just so you know, I have selected six very nice properties for you and the Mrs. to view. Based on your e-mails, there should be something she likes in the bunch. If not, we'll keep going until we stumble onto something that she does."

"You found six *very nice* houses in our price range," Marvin asked, somewhat surprised. "I thought Chandelle's list of 'must-haves' would have sent you running in the other direction."

"A lesser realtor might have, but that's why you were referred to me. Like you, I have a reputation for exceeding expectations. Finding a home with the perfect amenities is the key." When Kim sensed Marvin was blushing with pride, she laid it on a little thicker. "Oh, you're not the only one who does their homework. Mr. Mercer is lucky to have you running the store from what I hear. Just make sure you have that pretty wife of yours at my office around nine in the morning so I can show you how I do my thing."

"Confident, I like that," he said, nodding his head assuredly. "We'll be there." Marvin closed his flip phone, tossed the brown lunch bag into the trash can, and then exited the break room feeling ten feet tall. He was not only looking forward to being the first man in his family to purchase a home, he also wanted to give Chandelle what she'd wanted all of her life: a castle fit for a queen.

While easing through the long dimly lit corridor, separating the warehouse from the showroom floor, Marvin stopped. Something moved a heavy refrigerator wrapped inside an upright box. He circled around, expecting to offer extra muscle to an employee carrying it to the delivery dock. He knew it was a mistake when a full pair of breasts greeted him instead. "Ooh-ooh," he hooted, embarrassed for himself as well as the woman whose dress Mr. Mercer had his hands rummaging beneath. "My bad, y'all," Marvin apologized, although reluctant to turn away from the erotic scene. "Mr. Mercer, I had no idea you were back here with . . ."

"Well, now that you do know," the store owner barked, "get up to the front and make sure everybody is selling something on the floor!"

Marvin stared at his boss, a raisin shade of brown and smaller than him in size. But the man was determined to prove his manhood before granting the full-figured female his usual half-off discount in exchange for her services rendered.

"Don't make me say it again, Marvin," Mr. Mercer grunted quietly.

Looks like you're about to get into something that might get you cut by Mrs. Mercer, Marvin thought. "Yes, sir, I see, and please believe me, I ain't saying nothing to nobody. It's like they say? Don't ask, don't tell."

Mr. Mercer glared at Marvin viciously. "Just say it walking."

Marvin did what his boss demanded, like he'd done too many times before to count. Although sneaking another peek at the woman's impressive half-off coupons, he went on about his business trying to forget the owner's best attempt to handle his.

Customers looking for deals, scurried throughout the showroom like ants at a picnic. Marvin loved a busy store because of the opportunity to make higher commissions. He noticed a familiar face among the crowd, one that always made him glad he married Chandelle. The face belonged to her cousin Dooney. He couldn't wait to visit with his favorite customer, who never bought a single thing. But first he had to make a slick managerial maneuver, he thought as he saw Lem, a young salesman in training, was headed out back to check inventory. Marvin placed his hand on the young man's shoulder to stop him. "What's up, Lem?"

"Just hustling to make another sale, just like you

taught me," he answered proudly. "I'm going to see if we have any more of those stainless steel side by sides, the big unit."

It's a big unit back there, but not the one you're looking for. "That's gonna have to wait. Mr. Mercer is doing inventory in the warehouse," he lied. "And he doesn't want to be disturbed. It shouldn't take too long, though. He's pretty fast at this sort of thing."

Lem, a lanky twenty-year-old kid, looked up at Marvin and then smirked. "Please don't tell me ol' man Mercer's in the hole again pushing up on another customer to get him some discount booty?"

"That's not what I said, but you can't interrupt him and you do need to respect the man's need for privacy."

"Whatever, Marvin, that's a dirty old dude and you know it. Let me know when he's done. I *need* this sale."

"Cool, I'll page you on the intercom to the warehouse when I see him come out. Stall the customer until then. Show the new business office Executive Cooler line. Nobody wants to pop for it but everybody likes the presentation. If you need me to jump in, I'll be around."

Lem dashed off to locate the customers he'd left with their faces shoved inside a lift-top deep freezer. Marvin struck out in the other direction. He wasn't up for standing guard over Mercer's evening rendezvous. If another associate busted him like he had, that was just too bad.

"I'll take two of everything," Dooney hollered, when he saw Marvin approaching. He was the same shade of cinnamon as his sister Dior, handsome, nearly six feet, slight of build but wiry. Always dressed in starched jeans, pressed button up shirts worn outside of them, and neatly polished hard-soled shoes, Dooney's cornrows seemed out of place until he opened his mouth. Then, rock-solid evidence of the hard streets that helped mold him came pouring out. "What you know, good Kinfolk?"

"Lying," Marvin replied, while shaking his friend's hand.

"Hey, hold on, we'll get back to that," Dooney said, putting off the conversation he planned on spinning with Marvin. He returned to the one he'd started with a curvy, thick-hipped employee with her nose in the air. "Back to you," he continued, flirting vehemently. "You say your name is Reeka? For real? Is that like Eureka? 'Cause I'm on time for that whole sweating-digging-getting-dirty thing."

"Funny, you don't look as foolish as you sound. Don't waste your dreams on me. Whatever you think this is, it ain't," she spat, crossing her arms. "Marvin, get your cousin. Call his parole officer or something."

"He's harmless, Reeka," Marvin chuckled. "But I'll hip him to the news for you."

The young woman swung her hips in his face, then sashayed away, to offer him a lengthy gaze at what she'd determined was out of his league. Dooney's eyes locked on to her behind like a guided missile. "Man, that's all to the good. *Reeka*, I've got to remember that."

"Naw, you can forget that," argued Marvin. "Reeka's got her college papers, feeling herself, and she's too up-tight to give a brotha like you a swat at it."

"All I'd need was one, I know that much," he laughed. "Whewww-wee. She's fully grown like a bison, one of them buffalos on the western movie channel." After amusing himself with the buffalo analogy, Dooney recalled what Marvin insinuated in his last comment. "Hey, man, what you mean . . . a brotha like me?" When his question was returned with a we-both-know-you've-been-locked-up sneer, he digressed. "Okay, I see what you're screamin', but she don't know that. Not necessarily."

"Dooney, what exactly are you rolling through on the busiest day of the year to do?"

"Who me? I'm browsing. I figure with the sale and

your friends and family fifteen percent off the back end, it's got to be something up in here I can splurge on."

"All right then, get at me if you come up with whatever that something might be."

"Straight up, I'll do that. Right after I get back into this hunting expedition I was on when you crept up." The associate he was smitten with sauntered near with a stack of DVDs to reshelf. "Wait, Reeka, you dropped this . . . It's your ghetto pass. They won't let you back into the projects without it."

"Marvin, get him!" she shrieked.

"Dooney, let the girl work now. She's on the clock."

"And I'm on time for that, Marvin. I'm just gonna bend her ear a minute and see what snaps back."

Marvin saw that look in his eyes, the one insinuating he was in a hurry to see Reeka getting undressed. "Dooney? Dooney!"

3

Hers over His

"I thought you were tired," Chandelle cooed beneath Marvin's heaving chest. It was three in the morning. She was married, happily, and at the moment extremely satisfied. "Okay . . . okay. You got me that time. I'll admit it. You won," her voice confessed softly in his ear. "Good game, baby."

"Yeah, it was kinda intense," Marvin replied, rolling off to rest, spooning behind her. "Let me know if you want to run it back. I'll just need a minute to . . ." he said, with his words fading into the darkness of their bedroom.

Still basking in the afterglow, Chandelle purred seductively at the mere thought of another lengthy session with her husband. "You know I can't say no to you . . . never could. Remember how I used to rush home from work, Marvin? Marvin? Marvin?" He answered her with a chorus of light snores and deep sighs. Chandelle chuckled and pulled his arm tighter around her waist. "Go 'head on and rest, baby. Lord knows you deserve it."

* * *

Marvin continued his after-lovemaking anthem until the alarm clock interrupted him at eight in the morning. Reluctantly, he cracked his eyelids to peek at the red blinking numbers that flashed atop his nightstand. After he slapped at the digital clock, the insistent buzzing ceased. "It cannot be eight already."

"Hmmm," Chandelle sang, her voice tired and dry. "Come on, let's get up. My house is out there waiting on me to find it."

"My?" he questioned. "You said my."

"What's mine is yours; you proved that again last night," she said, sitting up to meet the morning, as a back-arching stretch and yawn greeted her.

"Why don't you get the shower going, I'll be in . . . in a minute," Marvin suggested halfheartedly.

"I used to fall for that, baby, but I caught on a long time ago. Get up now. We've got to get started."

At Chandelle's prodding, Marvin swung one leg over the side of the bed but held his position under the covers. "Yeah, you fell for that one a lot," he laughed. "Every now and then it took a hard sell, but I used to pull it off. Remember how you'd come stumping out of the restroom in a cloud of steam like Diana Ross in *Mahogany? Marvin, you get your big head out of that bed,*" he mimicked. *"Had me waiting on you. Should've known you'd go back to sleep as soon as my back was turned."*

"Yep, I was so gullible then, but you couldn't blame me for being a newlywed and wanting to be with my husband every moment of the day. That hasn't changed, but I learned to recognize when I was being conned. Besides, we both can't stay shacked up in the bedroom all day."

"It's a wonderful thought, though. We could get a flat screen TV put in right over the bed, replace the nightstands with miniature refrigerators, and have food delivered three times a day."

"Marvin?" Chandelle cooed like she had a few hours before.

"Yes, sweetheart?" he answered, with both eyes still tightly closed.

"Stop stalling, stop trying to con me, and get your big head out of that bed."

"Busted."

Once up and out of their two-bedroom apartment, Chandelle pulled a set of keys from her jeans pocket and tossed them to Marvin. "Let's take my car, I need some gas." She knew he would use his debit card to fill her tank. Not that he would mind, but Chandelle was already envisioning thirty-five dollars' worth of bath gels and body oils she'd rather spend her private slush funds on. Marvin had no idea that she'd opened a secret bank account with a high-interest credit card after they had been approved for a mortgage loan, but he was wise to the "let's take my car when the tank is low" gimmick when opening the passenger side door to escort her into the car.

Chandelle was giddy as all get out when they pulled into the service station. She was still humming while strutting inside for coffee.

"I'm so hyped about this," Chandelle chuckled, after returning to the car with two cups of butterscotch cappuccino and a bag of glazed donuts. "It's taken three years but we're finally doing it. It feels good."

Marvin folded the gas receipt, then shoved it into the back pocket of his jeans. "You know, it took some doing to save up for that down payment, but we stayed on it. Had to get the money right," he said, looking both ways before veering out on to Skillman Avenue. "We should have been further along, but everything has its own schedule, I guess."

He didn't have to state the obvious, the cause of one argument and heated disagreement after the next. Chandelle's frivolous spending habits along with the unnecessary items she purchased without regard to their budget were their main issues. Chandelle was accustomed to the finer things of life that shopping outside of her means provided. She refused to accept the grim reality that her salary hadn't begun to measure up to her expensive taste. Although Marvin's take-home pay barely rivaled hers, he rarely purchased anything over one hundred dollars unless he absolutely had to. Chandelle would dip into their savings to broaden her shopping expedition. When Marvin threatened to remove her from their "down payment" account, she promised to stay out of it and curtail her spending. Unfortunately, that was easier said than done.

On their way to meet with the realtor, Chandelle flipped through a stack of *Home & Garden* magazines she'd collected over the past four months. Bubbling with anticipation, her head was filled with decorating ideas, grand archways, and spiral staircases. Whether any of those came with homes within their price range had yet to be revealed. One hundred and eighty thousand dollars provided several options for a young couple seeking a four-bedroom property in north Dallas. The realtor had confirmed it beforehand. "Honey, you think we'll find something today?" asked Chandelle, when they parked in front of Hightower Realty.

Marvin shrugged his shoulders and stepped out of the car. "Maybe, I told Kim what you wanted and she said it was doable."

"Doable?" *And who's Kim?*

The realty office door opened as they walked up. A petite white brunette sauntered out, wearing a pinstriped skirt and blue ruffled blouse. She held a leather binder tucked beneath her arm. "Good morning," she announced as if it were her name.

Chandelle returned the pleasantries immediately. "Are you Kim?"

"No, but she is," answered the brunette, when a striking milk chocolate-colored woman appeared from behind the wheel of a shiny crème-colored Cadillac Escalade.

Initially, Chandelle was ecstatic that they'd be working with an African American and then she saw it: the effervescent grin plastered onto Marvin's lips. He was actually grinning, too hard for his wife's liking. As far as Chandelle knew, this Kim person was simply a voice on the other end of the telephone before that day, but Marvin's ridiculously overbearing smile had her thinking otherwise. *I thought you said you'd never met,* was keenly transmitted through the five-fingernail death grip Chandelle covertly administered. Marvin didn't understand what he'd done to deserve the sharp pain shooting up his right arm or if the beautiful realtor had witnessed him being assaulted. Marvin was caught between the awestruck boy he used to be and the man he'd become, fearful that Chandelle would clamp down even harder and draw blood.

"Hello, I'm Kim Hightower," she said cordially, extending her right hand.

Marvin shook Chandelle's talons from his in order to accept it. He opened his mouth to speak, but Chandelle cut him off at the pass.

"Hi, Kim, I'm Chandelle Hutchins . . . Marvin's *wife,*" she said, fake smiling all the way. She'd appraised sister girl's ensemble from head to toe in one millisecond. *Hair, long but not overdone, nicely woven, no track lines, and professionally coifed: two points for that. Eggshell designer jacket and skirt cut above the knee, most likely by St. John: three points because it has obviously been tailored to fit just so. Slender, toned legs: A one-point deduction because I'm hating. Hosiery, oomph, DKNY business fishnets . . . the same ones I buy: gotta give up four points for that. Shoes, uh-uh-uh, the shoes just have to be the classic Stuart Weitzman leather pumps: five points for finding them in that shade of bone and walking like they don't hurt your feet. Score: thirteen points total. Uh-uh, she's put together too well to be showing my man anything but the spot I'm standing on.*

"Glad to meet you, Chandelle," Kim replied, her Pepsodent smile intact. "And, Marvin, finally we meet. It's good to put a name with a face. I talked to my younger brother, Felton, and you were right, you both failed ninth-grade algebra together."

"Kim, it's great seeing you," Marvin said, snapping back to reality. "Yeah, me and Felton had lots of fun flunking that class. Second time around was serious biz, though. Mom wasn't having it."

"With such a pretty lady, it's apparent you made out all right. I can't say the same for that hardheaded brother of mine."

Chandelle noticed that Kim looked him over but didn't spend too much energy or time in any one place, which was cool with Chandelle, feeling better about the situation by the moment.

Marvin massaged his arm casually when it occurred to him that a further explanation was warranted. "Sweetheart, Kim was three grades ahead of me at John Quinn High. She was voted . . . let's see, Most Beautiful, Class Fav', Student Council President," he recited from memory.

"And a whole list of other honors, I'm sure," Chandelle snapped. "Not that I'm complaining."

"Girl, I know that's right," Kim seconded. "Don't get me wrong, Marvin, but all that school days stuff happened a long time ago. If I have to hear how popular I used to be one more time, I might scream. Come on, y'all, let's go check out some properties."

"Yes, come—come, Marvin," Chandelle prodded gleefully while climbing into the realtor's dazzling SUV. The sixteen-year-old-crush her husband savored for far too long had suddenly drawn up and blown away. "Let's go with Kim, to see some *properties*." *And if I ever catch you looking at another woman like you want to see her naked, you'll be wearing three shoes, yours plus one of my size nines hanging out of your behind.* "Hurry up, baby, time's a-wasting," she insisted dutifully.

From where Marvin sat, in the backseat of that whale-like vehicle, it appeared he'd dodged a bullet. Chandelle was in her element, discussing expensive concepts and digging every minute of it. Marvin knew that Kim High-tower was a whiz with numbers and her business savvy rated top-notch too, but she had already begun to exceed his expectations in the interpersonal department. In short order, Kim had cast a spell over Chandelle. She had some-how created a nonthreatening and accommodating atmos-phere where an attractive woman felt at ease immediately. Like an accomplished salesperson, Kim allowed Chan-delle to direct their conversation, while she listened atten-tively. Marvin used a similar technique when displaying appliances on the showroom floor. He always said, "Let a customer talk long enough, they'll eventually say some-thing you can use to earn a bigger commission."

Chandelle didn't realize it, but she'd raised several red flags for Kim before they pulled into the driveway of the first home. Even though Kim predicted that it was likely to be a very long day, she proceeded to show the homes, preselected based on the Hutchins's financing and Chan-delle's list of must-haves.

"Come on in," Kim beckoned, when Chandelle only jutted her head inside of the front door. "It's impossible to see the good stuff from out on the porch."

"Chandelle, what's wrong with you?" Marvin whis-pered in her ear. "Are you that nervous?"

"No, this house is that small," she whispered back to him.

"Is there a problem?" Kim asked. She knew precisely what the problem was when Chandelle went "oh" instead of "ooh" when she first laid eyes on it, the two-story red brick with an oversized backyard. Most new home buyers experience delusions of grandeur. The palace they had in mind didn't exist for the money they had in the bank. Kim had seen it a thousand times. This was her 1,001 chance to coach yet another of them through the realization process of separating what moved them and what they could afford to move into.

"Honestly, I was expecting something . . . bigger," Chandelle admitted, now standing in the front doorway. Marvin was at a loss. To him, it appeared to be four times bigger than their apartment.

"Okay, but that's the beauty of looking, it's free," Kim chuckled. "It's very important to check things out, look around to see if there is anything you do like about it. Every house has different qualities, like men. Let's take a few minutes getting to know this one."

"Yeah, I'm with that," Marvin said, with his eyes roaming throughout the front room.

"I was never interested in getting to know a single thing about little men," Chandelle huffed. "I'll be waiting outside."

"It shouldn't take us too long, huh, Kim?" Marvin asked, loud enough for Chandelle to hear and become jealous. The realtor caught on fast. She played it up at the husband's behest.

"Uhh, yes," she agreed. "Giving you the ten-cent tour shouldn't take more than ten, fifteen minutes tops."

I know they don't think I'm gullible to the point of being tricked into getting to know this tiny little bread box, Chandelle thought. "Well, if it only takes a few minutes, maybe I should look it over and you know, see what's what," she said, easing off her leather mule slip-ons. *I ain't trusting to the point of letting my man traipse from room to room with that former prom queen either.*

"This house is a charming three-bedroom with a study," Kim began, once Chandelle followed. "Marvin said you only wanted to see two-story properties, with spacious master bedrooms, a garden tub, and kitchen upgrades," she said to Chandelle, who strategically paced between the realtor and Marvin. "As you can see, the ceramic floors are practically new and very nicely maintained."

They don't look that new, Chandelle thought.

"There are two food pantries, a particular upgrade because there's also a breakfast nook. Usually there isn't room for both," Kim pointed out.

"Two pantries?" Chandelle replied. "And a breakfast nook?" *This bassinet is too cramped for an extra trash can*, she almost said aloud. She was already glancing at her trusty Movado timepiece and this was only the first home on their list to view.

"Note the vaulted ceilings, two full baths upstairs," Kim politely explained. "This closet has a custom finish, see the his/hers built-in shoe racks and hat coves; a distinctive difference."

Chandelle wasn't even slightly interested in the walk-in closet. *This isn't a closet, it's a hutch,* she thought, *a tiny one at that. I couldn't even turn around good inside of it, much less stroll through trying to decide on outfits and shoes. And what do hats need with some coves in the first place?"*

With the second house, it was even more charming than the first. Chandelle understood then that *charming* must have been an industry code word for very, very tiny. The vibrant chatter that had accompanied them before the tour began dwindled each time they exited another of Kim's wonderful finds and piled back into her fancy vehicle. Marvin was increasingly embarrassed each step of the way. Chandelle was just plain through. Not at all impressed by the finely manicured lawns, charming four-bedroom split levels, updated kitchens, and fresh paint, she couldn't envision moving her royal throne into either of them.

During the ride back to the realty office, not one single word was uttered. Marvin gazed out of the back window in a cloud of frustration. Chandelle flipped through pages of her magazines, silently wondering where the photographer who'd found them officed because that's who she wanted on her house-hunting team. Kim wasn't in the least bit surprised. For most young couples, agreeing on their first home was one of the toughest decisions they'd ever have to face. She'd seen marriages implode because of it. Hopefully, Marvin and Chandelle's wouldn't become one of them.

With the wind taken out of his sails, Marvin exited the SUV and opened the door for Chandelle even though he couldn't muster anything to say.

Kim thanked them for choosing her, asked that they talk things over and openly share ideas before planning another trip around the block. When neither Marvin nor Chandelle offered much in the way of an endorsement, she handed business cards to them and excused herself.

Marvin blew out a laborious sigh, the one he'd held in for hours. Chandelle stood near him in the parking lot, with her mind on dissolving their relationship with Hightower Realty. Both of them were frayed at the edges with great measures of disappointment.

"Marvin, I didn't want to say anything because you and Kim's brother go way back, but she isn't doing it for me. Maybe we need to get another realtor with better taste. Maybe that white chick we saw coming out earlier, maybe she can come up with something. If I have another day like this one, I'd be willing to keep the apartment."

Scratching at the nape of his neck, Marvin put on his

business hat after removing the one that said, "Husband."
"You didn't have to tell me you weren't feeling any of the
places we saw today. It was written all over your face.
Kim noticed, too, but didn't trip on it. If you really want
to be honest, the problem isn't with her."

"What, you trying to say she's right and I'm wrong?"
Chandelle challenged.

"Now you're tripping. Listen to what I've been thinking before jumping on me about it. I know people. I'm a
salesman. It's my job to figure out what they want before
they do and I'm good at it. Kim went out and located
what we, I said *we* were looking for based on the financing we got from the bank and the stuff you put down as
'deal makers.' Let's give her another shot and see if we
can't stretch our money."

"Ooh, baby, you think we could?" Chandelle moaned
heartily, like she had when they were in bed.

"Yeah, it'll work out fine. I just don't want you to get
discouraged. Home buying is a big deal. We'll talk to
Kim about it and see if she can work on another group of
properties."

When the seasoned realtor saw them exchange tender
lip smacks from her desk, she headed out of the door on
cue with briefcase in hand. "What are y'all still doing
here?" she questioned, believably surprised. "I was on the
way out."

"Kim, do you have another client today?" Marvin
asked, behind an eager grin.

"Actually, I do, my favorite one," she answered with a
gleam in her eyes. "I'm booked all afternoon with my
four-year-old Danni. She's with a sitter now and I'm sure
watching the clock. What was I thinking, teaching her
how to tell time?"

"It was just a thought but we'd hate to keep you from her," Marvin said, his eyes exhibiting a glint of defeat.

"Is there something you wanted to discuss? I do have a minute."

He tossed a smile at Chandelle, then slid both hands inside his front pockets. "It's obvious that we need to reevaluate a few things."

Watching as Chandelle's eyes flickered, Kim nodded that she fully understood. "Sure, let's step inside a few minutes. I know exactly what you mean. Chandelle would like more house than you've qualified for."

"Yes!" Chandelle answered for him.

"It happens all the time," Kim admitted. "And it won't take but a sec to run some numbers. Hopefully, our next outing will sustain that smile on Mrs. Hutchins's face."

"*Mr. Hutchins* would like that very much," Marvin replied, with a sinking feeling in the pit of his stomach. He was also secretly hoping that their credit line didn't end where Chandelle's happiness began. What he hadn't considered at all was his own state of mind.

4

Dooney Does It

Saturday afternoon, Marvin showed up at Appliance World even though he was scheduled to be off. Mr. Mercer was happy to see him. The store was packed to the gills with potential shoppers who'd missed the big sale the day before. Since the newspaper mistakenly ran the same ad for a second day, he felt compelled to honor their requests and extend his cost-cutting sale throughout the evening.

"Didn't think I'd have a chance to breathe today," Mercer told him. "Now that you're here, I can roam around and check on things."

Marvin knew what that implied. It wouldn't be long before the unscrupulous owner found another willing female who wanted something from the showroom she'd have to pay only pennies on the dollar to work out a back-door deal. Since it was none of Marvin's business, he decided once again to mind his own.

"Lem, where's Rodney?" Marvin questioned the energetic salesman. Rodney was the weekend only part-timer who sat in an office Monday through Friday. He was a natural, thirty years old and liked the buzz he got from closing deals. Marvin often wished he was still just as enthusiastic about moving metal, one difficult customer at a time. Lem, in desperate need of a break, shook his head while searching a microwave for the serial number. "I don't know," he grunted, utterly dismayed. "Rodney has been displaying dishwashers all day. He's probably sold ten of them by hisself."

"That's what's up. I'll make a sweep to see if Reeka and Thomas need a break. Knock off and take a thirty after your next sale. I'm covering today."

Lem seemed puzzled. "What about Mr. Mercer? He said nobody gets to leave until the showroom closes down at seven."

"Don't worry about him. He'll be too busy working his own magic." Marvin knew it was against state laws to enslave employees by refusing them time for lunch. When the younger man glared at him, regarding Mr. Mercer's overly aggressive sales tactics, Marvin changed the subject. "By the way, the serial numbers on General Electrics are always stamped on the door . . . right under your thumb." Lem slowly lifted his hand, discovering what had him steaming for over five minutes. Marvin was right, but then he always was when it came to products sold in the store. He should have been promoted to manager years ago, but Mr. Mercer wasn't about to relinquish that kind of power. His "say so" was all that mattered unless his wife superseded his authority, which she did every now and again.

Grinning wildly, Lem thanked Marvin as he jotted down the serial number on an order and pay pad. "Go get 'em, Lem," Marvin cheered.

Rodney marched down the aisle between televisions and high-end stereos. Rodney was almost as tall as Marvin, a dusky shade of brown, twenty pounds heavier, and often complained about losing his boyish physique because of fifty-hour work weeks tied to a desk. They were alike in many respects, both of them shared the same disrespect for the way the boss pimped merchandise and cheated on his wife. "Hey, Marvin, where's Mr. Mercer?" he asked anxiously, slapping Marvin's right palm homeboy style. "I need to get something to eat before I fall out. Reeka's starving too. She's getting mean."

"Getting?" Marvin said, suggesting that was her most notable personality trait. He craned his head to peer over the tall shelves. "Naw, I don't see him. Tell you what, though, take Lem with you and dash out. He's wrapping up something and I've talked to him already. I'll get Reeka's back while y'all skate. She's a selling machine when she's hungry. I'll slide her some lunch money and make it cool with her. Now, beat it before the old man gets done with one of his . . . meetings."

"Oh, Mercer's in freak mode? It figures. He's been cracking a whip until you showed up. I just want to be around when wifey rolls up on him like she did last week. I ain't gonna tell you who he had bent over the sink in the restroom because I don't like to gossip, but Lem's mama left with a crook in her back and something in her sack, no charge, no tax."

"Ahh, man, I could've lived my whole life without knowing that," Marvin whispered regretfully. "A single momma don't stand a chance around him."

"Humph, not if she wants something nice for baby boy's twenty-first birthday, on the house. Yep, Lem's legal on Friday. I'm taking him out for a few. See if you can get a hall pass from Chandelle."

"Man, I don't need a pass," Marvin huffed adamantly. "Shoot, I'm running things at my house."

"That's what I thought," Rodney chuckled. "See you in a minute. Bring you something back?"

"Naw, I'm straight. Just don't get lost out there. Reeka's on the prowl." Rodney headed left as she stormed in from the right. "Hey, Reeka," Marvin greeted, with a manufactured grin. "Here's twenty dollars on your lunch, but first I want to see who can rack up the most sales in a half hour. If you can beat me, I'll make it forty." Of course she bit, made an immediate U-turn, and shot off in the other direction. Within the first ten minutes Marvin had arrived, he'd arranged a workable lunch schedule to spell valuable associates he cared about, learned more than he ever wanted to about Lem's mother, a mere sixteen years older than her son, and he convinced Reeka to shine brighter than she thought probable on an empty stomach. Marvin was talented like that. His uncanny ability to spot a dilemma and resolve it with little effort was invaluable. But for the time being, he was proving that no one could match his prowess on the sales floor, including Reeka on her best day while hyperfunctioning on fumes.

When the doors closed, Appliance World had amassed a record sales day. Mr. Mercer didn't give a flip who took a break after seeing the cash register printouts. All he could see was money rolling in, more than ever before, and he had a dedicated team to thank for it.

At Dooney Does It barber shop, chatter resonated in the five-chair salon. During his last eighteen-month stretch in the state pen for check kiting and credit card fraud, Dooney learned a trade. His skills with shears were legendary by the time he made parole. With a dream and a barber starter kit from Wal-Mart, he began cutting neighborhood heads in his tiny apartment bathroom. When the booming traffic sent the police to his door, they expected to make a drug bust. Although none were found, Dooney was forced to become a legitimate operator and find a place to accommodate his loyal clientele. Blessed with friends in low places, a city councilman persuaded him to throw every cent he had into an abandoned storefront, to access the city's revitalization program in impoverished neighborhoods. Within two years of barely making ends meet, Dooney was awarded the deed to the building free and clear. He'd been living that dream and laughing about his good fortune each and every day since.

This Saturday night was no different. The shop was humming with hip-hop music and black men catching up on old news and discussing current events. Children were not allowed to hang around after seven o'clock because there was no telling what topic might have jumped off once the sun set.

Dooney howled loudly when his seven-thirty appointment strolled in with a dinner box from Maylee's soul food down the street. "That's what's up! Rocky, you came through." Dooney snatched the box, wrapped in a plastic bag, from the tough-looking customer. He pulled out a roll of money and passed a crisp ten-dollar bill to the man for his trouble, and then held the package up to his nose. "Did they put the extra syrup on my yams?" he asked, hoping they did. "Oh man, I'm on time for this! All y'all got to wait. My man Rocky is next." To a chorus of complaints from those who'd waited longer than anyone should have, Dooney held his arms outstretched. "What? Did any one of y'all cut for a brotha? That's what I thought. Then quit your yapping. Rocky, go 'head on and get in the chair. This here is gonna feed me like two fat females. Ain't nothing like yams and big women. Ooh!"

"I know you gonna let me sample some of that baked chicken," Tim, the grossly overweight barber standing nearest to him, suggested, rubbing his pot belly that appeared to be more than full as it was.

"Huh? Did somebody say something?" Dooney smarted. "Brotha, you's gonna have to get your own."

"Come on, Dooney, don't be like that. I'd run on over to Maylee's myself but my feet hurt."

"Your feet hurt? So!" he shouted dispassionately to a

roaring herd of customers who saw not a war of words but of wit whereby to the winner went the spoils. "You think bad feet, bunions, and corns got anything on what I have to deal with. You don't want to get started. Can't no man up in here out-complain me."

"Put that hot plate on it, then," Tim chided. "I got more stuff wrong with me than going to war with them Iraqis."

"If y'all's going at it, I want in too," asserted yet another busy barber, two chairs down.

"Uh-uh, this is between me and Tiny Tim," Dooney objected. "Please believe, you don't want this."

"But I do want that," Tim replied, staring down Dooney's meal.

"All right, then, there's only one rule, no cussing 'cause I'm tryna quit. You cool with that?"

"It's on, then," Tiny agreed. "Do your thing."

Suddenly the shop fell silent with anticipation.

"Okay, you said your feet hurt. Yeah, but . . . my dogs are barking and I got a hitch in my back from standing all day."

Tim's stomach shook as he chuckled. "Too easy," he smirked. "Okay then, my feet hurt . . . my back is tight, and my momma told me last night that I was adopted." A quiet band of "oohs" rose into the air.

"Okay, okay, my feet hurt, my momma told me I was adopted, and I woke up this morning missing a kidney."

"I still got you beat, my feet still hurt, my back is so tight I can't stand up straight, this morning my kidney just fell out, before I came to work I watched *Brokeback Mountain* thirty-seven times, and I cried because two grown men who love one another can't just do their thing and be left alone."

Once again silence played loudly over Tim's daring offering.

Dooney stared at the barber, gritted his teeth, grunted loudly, and then reluctantly handed over the sack of food in defeat. "Here you go, man. I just lost my appetite and now my stomach hurt."

The assortment of customers clowned Dooney noisily as Tim raised his short stubby paws in the air triumphantly. "And once again the challenger goes down, down, down," he cheered.

Dooney waved his friend off dismissively. "Naw, podner, that'd be you and them two white cowboys going down, down, down."

Everyone in the shop was rolling when Marvin entered through the front door.

Gazing over the boisterous clamor, he inquired, "What'd I miss?"

Dooney snatched a pack of Newport cigarettes from his black barber smock and headed for the door. "Nothing but Tim coming out of the closet, butt naked in cowboy boots."

"You lost to him again, didn't you?" Marvin surmised.

"Yeah, how you know that?"

"Because he's the one licking syrup off his fingers." Marvin watched the big man gloat through the large-paned window. "Turn around, it's all running down those thick wrists of his."

"Kinfolk, I can't even much watch. He got me out here hungrier than a hostage and working on getting past losing my vittles."

"Talk about getting over, Chandelle had me all house shopping today. She didn't like a doggone thing." When Dooney blew smoke into the air and then cut his eyes sharply at Marvin, he sneered in disgust. "You don't even have to ask. She punked me into raising the stakes. We can get a handle on it, though, but it won't be easy."

"Serves you right for marrying my cousin," Dooney joked. "She's been pimping egos since we was kids. Now she got you caught up. Didn't you know she's a thorough-bred? High minded, high stepping, high maintenance.

You'd better yank on the reins or rope her in before it's too late. That's why I don't ease outside the hood. You let a woman see too much, sooner or late she'll want it all. That's the cost of doing business, I guess." After a sidewalk philosophy session, Dooney flicked a lit cigarette into the street. "I hope Tim done finished with them yams by now 'cause I might have to clock him."

"Yeah, you have a full house. I'll come by for a cut early next week. Want me to swing by Maylee's for you?"

"You got enough on your own plate with house gazing and whatnot. Tell Chandelle I said what's up."

"I will," Marvin said, slapping palms as a parting salutation. "Oh yeah, I haven't seen Dior in a while."

"And you won't neither until she needs something," Dooney answered knowingly. "You can bank on that."

5

She's a Crowd

"What do you mean I need to find some other place to be?" Dior yelled, waving her finger in Kevlin's face. "After I've been cooking for your sorry butt and cleaning this nasty apartment for you, now I'm supposed to gladly accept my walking papers and bounce? Man, you're crazier than you look."

Dior had been on her best behavior since arriving unannounced at Kevlin's door. After playing house over the weekend, he was merely conducting himself the way he always had before, and in the same manner Chandelle had predicted. That was the worst part of it, Dior reasoned, as she stared at the furious Kevlin. "My cousin told me you'd be stuntin' like this, but I told her she was wrong about you. Well, you're not making a fool out of me. I ain't going nowhere," she'd concluded firmly.

Danger, was the expression Kevlin wore when he pushed the mute button on the remote control to silence the football pregame show on the stolen big-screen television, much too large to be in a living room that small. "I let you lay up for free. I even took you to the city pound to get your ride, so that ought to cover the cooking and cleaning, since you're making a big deal about it. Humph, like you didn't have to eat too. If I say you're leaving, that's it," he told her, his voice thickening with contempt. "I didn't ask you to come here; you just showed up and like a friend I took you in, but this ain't no rest haven for hoochies."

"You can't be squawking at me because I ain't hooch," Dior argued, before sucking her teeth. She swung her behind in his face and then snapped her fingers. "You wasn't calling me that when breaking your neck to get all up in this." Kevlin tried to look away but the way those tight workout shorts hugged Dior's thighs held his gaze in check. "Uh-huh, that's what I thought," she challenged. "You can't say no to this, never could."

"Watch me!" he snapped, leaping from the sofa. He darted past her toward the bedroom. "Get your purse, you're leaving," Kevlin barked. "I've got company coming and there's some things I need to get a handle on before that."

Dior smirked at him defiantly when he returned with an armful of her clothes stuffed in the only luggage she owned. "Wait a minute!" she screamed. "You bet' not throw my stuff out, Kevlin. Why you doing this to me?" Dior hustled behind him as he headed for the front door, dug in her house slippers, and wrestled the bag away from his hands. She recoiled like a frightened child when he raised his fist. Suddenly, he caught himself and lowered it. The beating Dooney put on him was still fresh in his mind. Dior was not worth going through that again, he'd decided.

Slowly, her eyelids fluttered. Dior squinted nervously, then fully opened them. The look she saw on Kevlin's face didn't fit. He was scared, not of Dior directly but what trouble she could bring to his door.

"Well, well," she said slyly, realizing a change in his demeanor. "I guess the mad dog done got his shots because he ain't so bad no more. Yeah, this is what's up. I like the way you checked yourself like a smart little doggie. You didn't like what happened when that man from animal control rolled up on you at the car wash. See, I tried to protect you, but Chandelle wasn't having it. Now, you get the chance to protect me. Feel me?"

There was a time when he'd have popped her across the face for such insolence, but times had changed. Dior laughed at Kevlin, huffing mad and doing nothing about it. He simply stood there, glaring and wishing she was gone.

"Naw, not quite," he answered, wearing a mask of resolve. "See, you will leave or I'll have you put out."

"What? You're threatening to call the police? That's a laugh. With all the dope you got stashed around this tacky place? Huh, go on and dial them up."

Kevlin rubbed his hands together, playing the card he'd hidden up his sleeve. "That's where you're wrong again. All I have to do is pick up the phone and tell that lady where you are. Who knows, animal control might sneak up on you too."

Now it was Dior's turn to shudder. Her prideful eyes dimmed the moment she believed Kevlin might follow through on his threats. Oddly enough, she dealt with it better when he intimidated her with violence. At least that was something she understood. "You're really making me go?" she asked, with a single tear staining her cheek. "Knowing what I'm up against, I got to get out?"

Kevlin was hard but nowhere near as sinister as Dior was when she had the upper hand. "It's like I said, we kicked it. That was well and good, but I've got company coming."

Assuming he was trying to make room for a gaggle of beer-guzzling homeboys to watch the football game, Dior pleaded with him. "You know I hate to beg, Kev, but please don't do this to me. I'll help you entertain the fellas. I can put some hot wings on if they'd rather have that than the roast in the oven, and . . . and . . . there's brew in the fridge and . . ." she rambled, in a feverish attempt to grasp at straws. A faint knock at the door brought her back to reality. "Wow, look at me," Dior heard herself say. "This ain't it . . . not even close. What was I thinking that you'd have my back and stand up for me?" As if nothing happened at all, Dior glanced at the door before walking over to the bar area to retrieve her purse and car keys. "You should keep an eye on the meat before it overcooks. It'll dry out if you don't watch it. The cornbread is ready and on the stove. I hope you and the boys have a good time."

Kevlin's face softened, but he was unwilling to change his mind or his ways. "You need to put on a coat," he said as she reached for the doorknob. "It's cold out."

"Yeah, but it can't be no colder out there than it is in here. You don't have to worry about me coming back, I won't. Bye, Kevlin." Dior lowered her head and opened the door. The young woman, fair-skinned and pretty who looked to be about 24, standing on the other side smiled politely when their eyes met. Dior turned back to look at Kevlin, finally realizing that he wasn't expecting a crowd of friends to watch the game and that he'd pushed her out to make room for a replacement, someone who would soon be stuffing her mouth with the roast she'd prepared. Dior hauled off and slapped the taste out of his mouth, exhaled her frustration, and then stared down the woman she hadn't seen before. "Sooner or later, he's gonna hurt you too," she asserted thoughtfully and without malice.

"Yeah, I know," the woman replied, sidestepping Dior to get in through the doorway. "Something sure smells good, baby," she sang to Kevlin before he closed the door and locked it.

Dior's stomach growled as she hoisted the bag from the ground. Her arms and legs sprouted goose bumps when the winds scraped against her skin. "Shoot, I was wrong. It's just as cold out here." She scurried down the sidewalk to her Ford Escort and jiggled the key until the lock tumbled. While waiting for the car heater to manufacture warmth, Dior winced and growled. She dug into the bag, flinging clothes about until running across a pair of sweatpants. Her teeth chattered as she pulled them up past her hips. "It's cold," she yelled, "too cold to be out here without a coat." Before Dior knew it, Kevlin's visitor was strutting down the path toward her car, waving the jacket that she'd been too proud to go back for and carrying something covered in aluminum foil in her other hand. Dior lowered the window, having no idea what to think then.

"Hey, girl, you forgot this," the woman said, handing it to her. "Sorry how things went down back there. Oh, here's a plate to take with you. Kevlin said you were hungry too. It's the least . . . you know."

Dior imagined a thousand vile things she could have said after Kevlin had his new plaything deliver a mere portion of her dinner curbside but "Thank you" came rolling out instead. Dior raised the window and shrugged on her leathered sleeves, all the time watching the woman rushing back to Kevlin like she had done all the times before. "So that's what a fool looks like from behind," she said, thinking of herself.

Twenty blocks and a world away, the choir at Fellowship Union belted out a final number from behind the pulpit. Chandelle gazed at Marvin and squeezed his hand. She smiled thank you at him, then leaned against his broad shoulder as if she wasn't sitting close enough.

Chandelle's immediate boss and mentor, Grace Peters, who was sitting with her husband in the next pew, caught a glimpse of their tender moment. She had a lot to be thankful for as well, a wonderful marriage to Wallace, a wardrobe of designer maternity clothes, and a baby growing inside of her. It was Chandelle's brainchild that had inspired Grace to take stock in her life and envision it with a husband. Dating woes, men's lies, and alibis plagued her throughout a tumultuous journey. However, she stumbled onto something great and subsequently had been enjoying it.

"I almost passed you a note suggesting that you two get a room," Grace whispered in Chandelle's ear, once the church services concluded. "It was hard paying attention with all of that body checking going on."

"I didn't know it was that obvious," Chandelle said, her face all aglow. "Marvin and I met with the realtor yesterday. As soon as we find a house we like, we'll have plenty of rooms to choose from."

"Ooh, Chandelle, I should have known better than to bring up married folks' business around you. I'm surprised you're not standing here with your belly stretching out like mine."

"We've been practicing, that's for sure," Chandelle chuckled. "But we decided to wait so the baby would have a real nursery. Now it won't be long," she said, slightly envious of Grace's good fortune. "It'll be nice for our kids to come up together. You'd make a wonderful godmother, Grace. That'd make it harder for you to fire me, then."

"Job security isn't a bad thing nowadays, is it?"

"No, it isn't," Chandelle agreed. "Speaking of that, when is Wallace going back to teach?"

"He decided to let it go for now. His father's been leaning on him pretty heavy to join the family firm. Since I'm not interested in moving to Austin, he'll probably run a satellite office here. Oh, there he is flagging me down from the back door. See you tomorrow."

"See you, Grace," Chandelle hailed, very glad to have a friend whom she could look up to and receive a paycheck from at the same time. Marvin eased up behind her, slyly brushing his hand against the back of her dress. "Oops," she stammered. "Boy, don't be sneaking up on me in public like that. I didn't know who that was trying to cop a feel."

"It'd better be only me, in public or otherwise," Marvin said, with a raised brow. "I almost had to break down the water cooler in the pastor's office. He didn't opt for the delivery service like I recommended. Now I'm the one he expects to change out the bottles and keep it running."

"So, what did you do?"

"I changed out the bottles," he admitted, laughing at his predicament. "And I'm waiting on the call I know is coming to keep it running too. Let's get out of here before something does go on the blink. I'm picking up an extra shift today."

Chandelle wrinkled her nose at Marvin's latest news flash. "I thought you got Mr. Mercer straight last year about working on Sundays?"

"I did, but this was my idea," he confessed, knowing that an argument was imminent. "We'll talk about it on the way home."

We most certainly will talk about it, Chandelle thought, while dragging her feet all the way out to the parking lot. "Have a good week, Sistah Kolislaw," she spoke pleasantly to one of the mothers of the congregation. Once inside the car, it was another story. "Now, what's this about you wanting to work on Sunday? We both decided that Sundays were family-me-and-you-chill days. Why didn't you confer with me about it?"

"I didn't want to get into it because I knew we'd be right here doing this, fussing about it. Sometimes I hate being right."

"What's right about you living at the job, Marvin? If you'd taken a regular office position by now, this wouldn't even be an issue."

Marvin huffed as he turned the wheel to exit the lot. "If you didn't have to have a more expensive house, it wouldn't be an issue either. Chandelle, there's a cost that goes with moving upstream." When she didn't have words to combat his, Marvin assumed the discussion was over, but his wife was only catching her breath.

Chandelle gathered her thoughts and chose her words. No matter how she planned on using them, they seemed to backfire in her mind every time. When Marvin parked her car outside of their apartment building, Chandelle was positive she had an airtight argument to keep him home. Then the unthinkable happened: He pushed the trunk release button from the inside.

As the lid sprang upward, she screamed but nothing came out. She had forgotten to return the mink coat. Ready to take her punishment for breaking their agreement on purchases above one hundred dollars, Chandelle held her breath and winced.

"Are you too mad at me to get out of the car?" he asked, fiddling around in the side wells for a music CD. "Ahh, there it is," he mumbled to himself, before slamming the trunk shut. Chandelle was afraid to face him until he forced her hand. "Aren't you getting out? Don't tell me you're hot enough at me to sit out here in the cold?"

"No, no, I'm not mad," she whimpered. *I just got a pardon from the governor.*

"Cool, because we'll need some extra money and I don't like fighting with my woman," he said, softly kissing her on the cheek. "Let's go in and make up. I've got an hour before I punch in."

"Ohhh, yeah," she flirted seductively. "I've got something you can punch right here."

"I'll bet you do. Let me put on this CD, then you can show it to me," Marvin growled softly.

Chandelle tossed her eyes up at the sky and thanked her lucky stars, though she wasn't sure God had anything to do with her having gotten away with deceiving her husband. No sooner than she felt confident that the stars had aligned in her favor, the doorbell sounded. Chandelle was half dressed and almost deeply into an afternoon rendezvous with Marvin when the doorbell rang again. "Let it ring, baby," she said, when he hesitated with the business at hand, pleasing her. "It's probably somebody selling something."

"No, no, it's Sunday," he said, grabbing a handful of Chandelle's hair.

"That's my point," she answered cunningly.

The doorbell rang for a third time with an intermittent rally of bothersome raps thrown in. "I'll get it," Marvin grunted, though not nearly in the intimate manner he'd laid on Chandelle to put her in the mood. "Don't you move an inch," he said, slipping on his robe and house shoes.

Chandelle gestured at the rise in his robe. "I won't if you won't."

"I'm coming," he yelled in the direction of the door. "Hold on a minute." One quick glance through the peephole deflated his hopes of finishing what he'd started. There were no peddlers bidding for a shot to make a sales pitch. As far as he was concerned, it was worse than that, much worse.

6

Damned If You Do

"Hey, Marvin," Dior said as quietly as a church mouse. She wanted to barge in like she'd always done, but Marvin was purposely blocking the door with his body. "Can I come in?" she whined.

Reluctantly, Marvin pulled the door open wider so Dior could enter. "What's with the bag?" he asked, flicking a quick glance toward the taupe-colored duffel.

"I saw Chandelle's car out front so I knew y'all was back from church service. I hope I didn't interrupt nothing," she said, scanning his legs and anything else she could see pushing against the thin navy-hued silk robe.

"Nothing that won't keep," he answered, casting another suspicious eye at her luggage. He didn't know what was happening, but he was sure he wouldn't like the outcome. "I'll go tell Chandelle you *stopped by*. You may as well go on and have a seat," Marvin offered finally.

Oh, I plan to. "Thank you so much, Marvin. I'm sorry for showing up without calling first. I know how you hate that."

Marvin grumbled as he headed down the short hallway

to the master bedroom at the end of it. He closed the door behind him, and then sat on the edge of the bed. He'd been gone so long that Chandelle had dozed off. "Your girl came by," Marvin informed her, smirking his displeasure. "And she brought some clothes with her too."

Squirming beneath the warm sheets, Chandelle sighed seductively. "So that's what took you so long? Hmmm, I'll call her later. Get back in the bed, baby," she said in a noticeably faint tone.

After looking at his beautiful wife over his shoulder, he realized that she hadn't comprehended what he said. "Chandelle . . . she's still out there. Said she needs to talk to you."

"Dior's still out there?" she asked, raising her sleepy head. "You left her out in the cold?"

"Nah, she's in the living room, probably cooking up a scheme to get in your pockets. You know, the usual," he added, as if Chandelle wasn't already well aware of Dior's long-term bouts of mischievous behavior and her lack of funds. As she climbed out of bed, Marvin watched her nude body glide across the room. His expression conveyed how he'd rather she stayed to perform some of the intimate pleasures of life, but after Chandelle had cloaked herself in the woman's version of his stylish robe, his hopes up and fluttered away.

"Dior? Are you all right?" Chandelle whispered, with remnants of pleasure deferred in her voice.

Dior, possessing the inexhaustible ability to drum up nifty lies at a moment's notice, reached deep down inside her soul and came off with a world-class doozy. "Ohhh, Chandelle," she moaned. "I didn't want to bother y'all, but I need some money."

"Dior, you've got to be kidding me. I have some business of my own to sort out, too, and it was about to click so . . . Can't this wait? And anyway, what happened between you and Kevlin? Did he get rough with you?"

"Chandelle, I wouldn't even be here but I ain't got nowhere else to turn. I'm late on my rent, again, and now they done went and locked me out." She had been summoned with a pending eviction and her locks had been changed, so that much was true. "Please, don't be that way. You don't know what I've been through. Kevlin kicked me curbside last night just like you said he would. He had some freak coming over and cussed me until I felt so bad I ran out of there. After my key didn't work at the apartment, I used my fist to bust the bedroom window to climb in and get some necessary stuff. When the mean old lady who lives upstairs heard me, she said she was calling the police. She didn't even care that it was my own stuff I was taking." Merely for effect, Dior lowered her head in shame before continuing her onslaught. "I ain't never felt so alone so I drove around until I got too tired to drive. If the dollar movies weren't open until midnight, I don't know what I'd have done."

Chandelle was cautious, but Dior's words came from that place she once knew too well herself: desperation. "If you put your hand through the window, why isn't it all cut up?" she challenged.

"I wrapped my hand in my coat like they do on TV, or else I'd have one more thing I couldn't afford to fix," she babbled. "Please, just give me a couple of days to get something cracking. I can't take nobody else flipping on me. When I fell asleep on the back row at the movies, two men woke me up and one of 'em called me a crack head, and you know I don't get down like that, but still this manager and another man, they started loud talking me and then told me I had to go. Kevlin done dogged me. I ran the streets all night, and . . . now you're looking at me like I'm lying. Chandelle, I'm not lying," she lied most assuredly, with misty eyes to help further her cause. "If I could, I'd do the same and look out for you. You know I would."

"Oomph, this is too much," Chandelle said, massaging both of her temples with outstretched fingertips. "Sit down, girl, I won't trip. Besides, your mother was there for us when mine got laid off. Blood is thicker than tears," she'd determined.

"Thank you, Chandelle, thank you so much," Dior sighed, while celebrating quietly so as not to disturb Marvin. "What about him?" she asked, gazing toward the closed bedroom door.

"You let me worry about that. Put your things in the other room. But this is not a permanent situation. You will look for a job tomorrow and every other day until someone's willing to pay you for something."

"I will, Chandelle," Dior agreed, although with reservations. "I'll come out of this on top, you'll see. Uh-uh, you won't regret this, not one bit."

I'm already regretting it, Chandelle thought, while turning the doorknob and praying that Marvin had somehow fallen asleep. Unfortunately, Marvin was fully dressed in the Appliance World uniform, khaki slacks and top. Feverishly lacing up his shoes, he was visibly consumed with getting away from there. "Do you have a minute before you leave?" she said, secretly wishing he didn't. "We should talk."

"No, and no we shouldn't," he replied rudely. "I don't want to discuss it and I don't like the idea of Dior crashing here because she's always putting in work on some scam."

"For someone who *don't* want to discuss it, your mouth sure is moving overtime," Chandelle fired back, louder than she meant to. Dior's dilemma had her in a rough spot. She'd given her word to help, and that was that. "I've . . . already told her I would. I should have talked it over with you first, but it wouldn't have changed anything. She's busted, tired, and probably hungry too. How can we turn our noses up at that?"

Marvin snatched a thin jacket off the bed. "Watch me!" he yelled, brushing by her like she was a hat rack. "She's trouble, Chandelle, trouble."

"What family member isn't? Look," she debated, extending her hands to summon a calmer spirit. "Honey, today's sermon was meant to address this exact issue. It's like a sign or something. What does the Bible say, 'I was hungry and you gave me meat. I was thirsty and you gave me drink. I was a stranger and you took me in,'" she recited as best she could from Matthew 25:35–36. "Now, Dior isn't a stranger, but we should do our best to feed her and provide a warm place to lay her head as best we can. That's the Scripture. We said we would always strive to have a Christian home, not just when it suits us."

Marvin stroked at his chin. Having heard the same sermon, he took his analysis to another level. "Feed her and take her in, huh? Don't forget the Bible also says to clothe the naked and look in on the sick. Well that cousin of yours is twisted all the way to the bone, and there ain't no cure for that."

"Don't be so short-sighted," Chandelle argued.

"And don't you get all *'What would Jesus do'* on me. Dior doesn't know Him and He probably forgot about her a long time ago."

"Watch what you say, Marvin. Neither one of us is in any position to judge or to be trying to guess who Jesus is pulling for or is still down with. Me and Dior, we've got a good understanding, and she'll be on her best behavior or I'll toss her out myself. You have my word on that."

"Your word?" Marvin huffed. "It doesn't mean as much to me when you've already given it to her."

Dior had been listening attentively with her ear pressed against the bedroom door. Marvin nearly stumbled over her when he darted out. *Slow down, dude, it ain't that serious,* she thought. *But ooh, isn't it cozy to have y'all fighting over me? Warm fuzzies.* Dior realized then that Marvin was not even remotely happy with her being there. An array of mischievous ideas crossed her mind immediately. She was determined, willing to stop at nothing, to manipulate Marvin's attitude toward her.

Once the door slammed behind Marvin, Dior sighed as she plopped down on the sofa, she was relieved to have slid in just under the wire. Chandelle exhaled, too, although for a different reason entirely. Her man was not happy, her home had been upset by an unannounced visitor whom he didn't much care for, and trouble was brewing inside of him. She felt that the one saving grace was making it through the weekend without having had her expensive purchase detected by him.

Then there was a knock at the door. Chandelle shrugged her shoulders. When she looked out of the peephole, her eyes found Marvin's face scowling back at hers. Chandelle wasn't sure what to make of it when she twisted the doorknob. "What is it, Marvin, did you forget your keys?" she asked.

"No, but you forgot to tell me about this," he smarted. Before Chandelle had the chance to explain what a six-thousand-dollar fur was doing in the trunk of her car, Marvin iced her with a damaging assessment of their commitment to fiscal responsibilities. "I've been munching on pimp steak for a month now, saving every dime I could so that we wouldn't be strapped over buying a decent home, and you've been out there behind my back running through the mall and running up our credit. It's going back, Chandelle, today!" Without as much as another word, Marvin handed the garment bag to his wife, turned, and walked away.

"I never told you because I'd already planned on returning it," she said to the closed door. "Besides, nobody asked you to eat all that baloney."

"I told you he was gonna trip," Dior chuckled, with her head in her hands. "Baloney? For a whole month? I ain't ever had a man love me that much," she added as an afterthought. "And I hate baloney, even if it does have a first name."

"So does Marvin," Chandelle whispered, recognizing just how lucky she had been while being carelessly frivolous at the same time. "Give me a minute," she said, before heading for the backroom. "We've got to go."

"Go? Go where?"

"Where a woman should steer clear of when her man is sacrificing for their future by living on pimp steak. Girl, we're going to the Galleria."

7

Two Kinds of Crazy

"I am so blessed to have Marvin," Chandelle admitted fondly, while patrolling the mall parking lot for an available space not too far from the entrance. "It's still hard to do what I'm supposed to, though. It's like they say, I shop, therefore I am." She glanced at Dior, who was frowning curiously.

"I saw that on a swap meet T-shirt before," she said, with her lips pursed momentarily. "Almost copped one, too, but it sounded like something a white chick would flow with so I put it back."

"Uh-uh, white women don't have a lock on blowing money. That's always an equal-opportunity situation. Oh, here's a good spot." Chandelle guided her car in and killed the engine. She turned toward her cousin and glared.

"What?" Dior said with the same curious frown as before.

"Don't what me. I want you to be on your best behavior in there," Chandelle demanded. "Not that you would, but I don't need to get jammed up behind some stolen goods misunderstanding, and I'm certainly not in the mood to watch you try and urinate your way out of a shoplifting beef."

"Chandelle, I wouldn't do that to you," she answered, lowering her head in shame. "Anyways, I ain't even got to pee. Let's go." Dior hopped out of the car like it was on fire. "Hurr' up, cuz, the quicker we can shake you loose from that funky coat, the quicker we can scout around for sales."

"I thought you couldn't make rent," Chandelle asked, as they stepped inside the entrance doors.

"I can't, but what does that have to do with anything?" Dior reasoned, despite her bleak financial predicament. "I left one of my favorite dresses at the apartment. Might not get it back after they find that window I smashed."

"And if you had taken care of business like I suggested, instead of dashing over to Kevlin's, you might not be in this mess," Chandelle told her. "Why don't you like normal men who want to treat you right?"

Dior's impulsive and sometimes carefree attitude was legendary. She had no use for *normal* men who actually were interested in working on more than merely perfecting various sexual positions. Dior craved drama and men who could deliver it by the bus load. Pure and simple, she was known in certain circles as a *jump off*, the kind of woman who committed men often kept on the side for quick hits and cheap tricks. While stumbling through life and searching for her place in it, Dior had grown accustomed to being the other woman. She preferred things that way. Her biggest weakness was a yearning to acquire without exerting the effort and energy required to do it honestly. After she continually managed to come up short, the same questions traced her lips: *Why does it take the wrong men a hot minute to love me while the right ones never seem to want to?*

"I don't have time to sort through normal brothas trying to figure out why they don't already have a woman and what they did to chase the last one off. And I don't have room in my life for misfits. One's plenty, and I'm it."

Inside of the glassed-in elevator, Chandelle pushed the button going up. She allowed Dior's flawed logic to play around in her head until she became dizzy. "Your way of thinking missed me. It almost sounds like you couldn't be interested in a man unless he has at least one woman in his life to start."

"At least one," she answered matter-of-factly. "Take Marvin, for instance. My friends think he's so cute, but they love the fact that he has a real pretty wife. Don't ask me, but that's the way it is, coming from where I'm from. His stock went way up when he married you."

"Dior, promise me you won't tell anyone else what you just told me? That's two kinds of crazy." Chandelle asked Dior to take a seat on a bench outside of the furrier's. She didn't need another dose of *ghetto rationale* to show itself while she was conducting business. It was a good thing because the saleswoman initially refused to accept the expensive fur that she deemed as a slightly used, nonreturnable item until Chandelle articulately argued that the coat not only possessed a peculiarly foul odor, but that her husband didn't like the looks of it whatsoever. After she threatened to complain to the platinum card company, the snotty saleslady reluctantly complied. With a signed chargeback receipt in hand, Chandelle strutted out of the store with a sigh of relief and a zero balance on her brand-new credit card. "Come on, Dior," she said, grinning gleefully. "We have an hour to see what's what."

"That's what I'm talking about," Dior agreed. "Let's hit that boutique you like so much. I think they carry the Marc Jacobs bags everybody's packing, the real ones." Through the specialty shop window, Chandelle remembered admiring that designer's line of purses as well.

"Yeah, I've seen those, the soft leather with the gold buckle. Uh-huh, real cute but not my style. Well, more like not in my budget since I've decided to do better." She entered the shop, ogling the sales racks. "Dolce and Gabbana dresses, ohhh . . . that's hot," marveled Chandelle, until she flipped the price tag over. "Humph, unfortunately the cost is not." She craned her neck in search of the clerk who typically assisted her. The thin redhead sauntered closer, and then smiled brightly when she recognized one of her favorite customers.

"Chandelle, I didn't see you come in. And I probably wouldn't have recognized you over here at the sales rack."

"Hey, Sally, I thought I'd luck up and find a steal. My man's watching my money, if you know what I mean."

"Huh, that's why I can't afford to shop here unless it hits the clearance rack first."

Chandelle laughed. "So you feel my pain? Does this red tag mean twenty percent off the sales price?"

Sally glanced at the sales tag she'd altered earlier in the day and nodded. "Yep, gotta make room for the latest stuff coming in on Tuesday. Hold on a minute, I'll get the catalog so you can check out all the cool winter skirts." When Sally found what she'd gone after, she waved for Chandelle to meet her at the counter. "Here it is. Find what you like and I'll put back a few pieces of it in your size."

"*Miss 60*?" Chandelle moaned excitedly, while perusing the pages thoroughly. "These are really nice."

Back in the fitting area, an ugly incident had taken shape. "Mrs. Jennings, how'd you know where to find me?" Dior yelped.

The blond woman, wearing a ritzy jogging suit and a crazed stare, held her right index finger to Dior's mouth to silence her.

Rosalind Jennings, a former employer and severely

unstable 42-year-old socialite, used her other hand to caress Dior's face.

"Uh-uh, I ain't with that no more," Dior said. "You got to get out of here."

"Shush now, Dior. Now that we can talk face to face, it'll all be okay," she answered in a hushed tone. "Be quiet and no one will get hurt." There was something extremely unnerving going on behind the white woman's pale blue glassy eyes. If she meant to frighten the pants off Dior with her deranged-white-lady-in-the-fitting-room routine, it worked. "Oh, sweetie, why haven't you returned my calls? You should have. I left tons of messages. And the letters I sent, it wasn't very nice of you to ignore them. I've spent too much time following you, staking out the little apartment of yours and that other place on Britstone. It took some doing, but I had to find you again."

Britstone, Dior repeated, although silently, *that's Chandelle and Marvin's place.* Throwing down in the small booth occurred to her more than once. However, Mrs. Jennings didn't appear to be in her right mind while seemingly capable of anything. Dior had only played the part when it suited her. She'd seen her share of textbook fixations during her stint at Happy Horizons, and this was the real thing, a bona fide psychosis. Dior cowered against the mirrored wall then. "Mrs. Jennings, you need to see somebody—"

"I said to keep quiet," the woman interrupted her through gritted teeth. "I would really like you to come by the house," she offered pleasantly as if another personality had superseded the last. "I, we want you to work for us again. Wasn't it a mutually rewarding situation? We went out of our way to take care of you. You must know that. The sex was good and we paid you well for it."

Dior had no idea what to think. Visibly shaken, she became more withdrawn as if succumbing to a fearful alternative. Dior had hired herself out before getting arrested.

She was employed by the wealthy white couple to play with the kids during the day and then later entertain the parents after hours for $500 a week and another $500 for her nightly duties. After two months, the Jennings introduced Dior to other couples and things were getting increasingly more aggressive. They were heavily into bondage, role-playing, and other kinky sexploits. Dior received bonuses when performing the parts of strippers and prostitutes, but she charged double for playing the role of a plantation wench being taken advantage of by the overbearing white master. Incidentally, Rosalind Jennings became jealous when catching her husband, Paul, in Dior's room without having been invited to join them. When Rosalind discovered them, she displayed mere hints of the frantic behavior unleashed in the fitting room. After Dior sneaked out in the dead of night, Rosalind grew verbally abusive over the phone. The threatening notes she posted on Dior's car windshield intensified. She was petrified to be home alone. All of that had culminated into Dior being held hostage.

What if I have to kill her to end this? Dior contemplated nervously. *I could end up in jail just like Billie. Huh, I'd be better off if she killed me.*

Near the front of the store, the mood wasn't nearly so tumultuous. "Uh-oh, Sally, you were right. There might be trouble over Tuesday's shipment. Sale or no sale, I want one of everything." Chandelle continued thumbing through the magazine until a cold chill ran down her spine. *Speaking of trouble, where's Dior?* she thought. "Sally, have you seen another black woman in here? I came in with my cousin."

"There was one, a minute ago, shorter than you and real cute," answered the clerk. "She was taking a few things into the fitting room last I looked." The telephone rang near the cash register. "Excuse me, Chandelle, I have to get that."

And I have to get back there to see if Dior is going back on her promise, Chandelle thought. *Lord help her if she's ripping off the boutique and using me to run interference.* Chandelle tipped into the fitting area of the store, whispering her cousin's name. "Dior? If you're back here, you'd better speak up," she demanded finally when rustling noises from the rear stall drew her attention. "Dior, bring your butt out of there or I'm coming in to do it for you," Chandelle threatened. Cautiously, she shoved on the swinging door. "What the . . ." was all she could get out before her eyes told her to shut up. She gawked at the white woman holding her hand over Dior's mouth, like a 7-year-old playing a quiet game. Chandelle gave the odd scene a once over, then lowered her purse to the floor. She called Dior's name, this time with disbelief written all over her face. "Uhm, what are y'all doing back here?" she asked the both of them at once, although her stern tone was directed at the woman she hadn't seen before. Neither of them moved, so Chandelle motioned with her hand for Dior to come forth. The piecing stare she shot at Rosalind held her at bay for the time being. "What's this about?"

"Mrs. Rosalind Jennings," answered Dior, humiliated by Chandelle's presence but thankful for it simultaneously. "She's the lady I was working for as a nanny, only she didn't like it that I quit."

"Who're you supposed to be, Dior's girlfriend?" Rosalind huffed, as she made a sudden move to exit the stall.

"Naw, you got me messed up," Chandelle replied, refusing to let her pass. "See, I'm the cousin about to break you down." She glanced at Dior to question why she allowed another woman to play her weak. "Dee, tell me why you're afraid of her? What's she holding over you?"

Dior exhaled like she'd rather not say, but Chandelle

had sufficiently taken over the situation leaving her no choice. "She's been leaving messages on my phone and on my car saying if I don't come back to work she'll make life hard on me or worse. That's why I wouldn't let you drop me by the apartment. Chandelle, she won't let me out."

"Won't let you?" Chandelle barked heatedly. "You're a grown-up, Dior.

"Please tell her I don't want to be a nanny no more," Dior whined.

"You tell her yourself, once and for all. Here and now."

"Mrs. Jennings, you can tell your husband that I'm through with that life and I mean it," she spouted with a renewed assurance.

"We'll just see about that," Rosalind challenged, with both arms folded. She talked tough but at no time did she try to run over Chandelle the same way she'd manipulated Dior.

"Want to see about it now?" Chandelle offered boldly. "Right now, we can iron out any misunderstandings you might have concerning ever coming around my family again. I'm not above breaking the law to end this if I have to. Believe you me, there're lots of us, and we don't scare so easy. You can bet your life on that." Chandelle felt Sally standing behind her. She raised her hand, signaling that she had a handle on things. "Mrs. Robinson or whatever you call yourself, I will not entertain having this discussion again. You can go now." As soon as Chandelle stepped aside, the disgruntled socialite stormed away before experiencing firsthand the willful woes of a South Dallas "breakdown."

Sally made sure that Rosalind left the store before calling off the dogs. She didn't know Chandelle possessed street savvy beneath her polished veneer. "Wow, I'm impressed," she ranted upon returning. "The sistah's got skills," she joked. "Call me on Tuesday. I'll have a package waiting for you."

Chandelle was so angry with Dior that she could spit nails. "Yeah, thanks, Sally," she groaned, while catching her breath. "But right now someone's got a lot of explaining to do."

After Chandelle literally dragged her to the car by the nape of her neck, Dior did explain, as best she could, how she managed to get her life jammed up in lustful, triangular vice. "I know you're mad at me, Chandelle, but you didn't have to pull me out here like I was a stupid kid. I never planned on getting involved with the Jennings past looking after their two children. When Rosalind's husband, Paul, started peeping the way I walked, it was kinda cute. I mean, he is rich and fine for his age. As white boys go, he's even a little sexy."

"Rich, fine, and sexy?" Chandelle shouted. "It sounds like you were feeling this man. No wonder his loony wife went ballistic on you and kicked your butt out of her house."

Dior's eyes drifted toward the floorboard. She drew her lips together and pouted. "Shoot, if you're gonna stay on me for something I'm not into anymore, then you can forget talking about it."

"Nah, that ain't even it," argued Chandelle. "You're going to spill it all so I'll know exactly what you've snatched me into."

When Dior continued brooding, Chandelle squinted furiously, then popped her on the back of the head with an open hand.

"Oouch, girl," Dior whined. "Why'd you hit me?"

"Because somebody needed to tell you to stop acting like the stupid kid you claim that you're not," Chandelle barked sternly. "Don't make me tell you twice."

Dior flinched when Chandelle's eyes narrowed again.

"Okay, I get it. I—I got it. Humph, that's why I kept all of this from you, because I knew you'd snap. Sure, I like being watched and it felt good that the man treated me like I was somebody. Rosalind was extra nice to me too," Dior said, thinking back. "It was a trip when she came to me that first night, in my room off the kitchen. I just figured she was trying to check on me at first, talking about how handsome her man was and how he could go on for hours in the sheets. I laughed because it was funny imagining them two slapping skins, all off rhythm and bumping into each other like two whack dancers looking for the perfect beat. Then she asked me what I thought about him, you know, if I was attracted to white men and stuff like that. I told him he was all right and real sweet when he wanted to be." Dior glanced up at Chandelle, who was peering straight ahead with the car running. "That's when he started buying me things, like shoes and blouses and other little trinkets. Rosalind was cool with it because she's the one who brought them to me. One evening, she poured two glasses of wine and then said that she was going on up to bed early. I told her she was forgetting her glass, but she just kept on going up the steps to the second floor. I was ready to chill with the TV and get my drink on alone . . . didn't matter to me. A few minutes later, Paul comes floating downstairs in some silk pj's. He was fresh from the shower because his hair was still wet." Dior looked up at Chandelle again, this time she was looking back at her, attentive and disturbed.

"I think I've heard enough," she said softly, deciding to forego hearing whatever happened next.

"There's not too much more to it anyway. We drank on a few bottles, told jokes we knew, and then started kissing. Paul told me that Rosalind was cool with it as long as we didn't sneak, and how her leaving the wine was the signal. Humph, I didn't know anything about rich folks' freak games, but it seemed all right so I went with it. They doubled my pay and Rosalind started pouring three glasses of wine." Dior didn't have the guts to glance up to see what kind of face Chandelle was making then, neither did she have the stomach to share how their private episodes eventually included other adventurous couples from within their gated community. Before Dior knew it, she was in way over her head.

Chandelle found it difficult to string two words together. Her riddled emotions came out in a labored groan. "Don't hate me," Dior said, uncharacteristically solemn and still like a repentant sinner who had eased her burdened soul.

Chandelle knew what feeling alone could do to a woman lost and seeking something to hold on to, even if it was morally appalling to others. She fully related. "I could never hate you, Dior, you're family," she told her. "Although I do feel sorry for you . . . for the hole you're carrying around inside. You need to be around your people and you need to find a way to fill it."

8

Devil's Got a Hold

During the two weeks since Dior made herself at home in the Hutchins's small apartment, she had been on her best behavior. She also took pride in tidying up, and helping Chandelle with dinner and the dishes. Other than the tedious chore of riffling through the job classifieds every morning in the newspaper and following up on leads every afternoon, Dior was comfortable with her duties in the household and her status as the "unemployed third wheel" in their relationship. However, comfort took a backseat to Dior's personal aspirations when she got it in her mind that she was due for a promotion. With Chandelle spending half of her leisure time running back and forth to the home design stores searching for items to jazz up the new home she and Marvin had been approved for and the other half running down Marvin for pulling extra shifts and then subsequently hanging out with his coworkers after that, it allowed an opportunity for evil intent to creep in and shake up an otherwise manageable living condition.

Chandelle climbed out of bed, after having had the

most difficult time understanding why Marvin all of a sudden decided that it was so important to go out palling around with the boys more than he had in the past. "Marvin, wake up," she snapped angrily, nudging him in the ribs with the palm of her hand. "Marvin, you know you hear me. We need to talk."

"Not now, I'm trying to sleep," he grunted irritably.

"Get up and talk to me," Chandelle demanded. "Is there something bothering you, something you want to tell me?" she prodded. "You're changing on me and I don't like it. I also don't see why all of the dudes you run with are single," she argued, while getting dressed for work. "Single dogs are always on the prowl behind the nastiest tail they can find."

"You need to stall all that, Chandelle," Marvin mumbled, with the covers pulled over his head to mute the overhead light she'd flicked on for the sole purpose of annoying him.

"You need to start coming home at a decent hour," she fired back.

"Keep your voice down," he ordered, poking his head out to exhibit his displeasure to her sharing their business with the neighbors, as well as giving their houseguest an earful. "'Sides, I know way more married dogs on the hunt than the dudes I hang with."

"And that's another thing," Chandelle said, refusing to rein in the volume. "I can't come up with a single reason why you have to hang out with *the dudes* in the first place. They're not putting any money in your pocket, and don't get me to talking about what else they can't do for you." She folded her arms and threw her head back in utter disdain of the way he'd been carrying on lately. When she felt the old cantankerous Chandelle fighting its way to the surface, she swallowed hard to stifle it. "I'm tired, Marvin, tired of watching the clock and wondering what time you're gonna come stumbling in. Ever since we found the perfect house, you've been tripping. Sometimes I'm not so sure I still want to jump into a thirty-year commitment with someone who's acting like he'd rather be out there, single and free." Marvin pretended to have dozed off on his side of the bed once Chandelle had finished her tirade. "I'm tired, Marvin," she huffed heatedly to the back of his head. After she'd rolled her eyes, slipped on her favorite leather pumps, and then stomped away, Marvin's eyes fluttered, then opened.

"You're tired, too, huh?" he replied. "That makes two of us."

It was the third Friday in October when the inevitable happened. The tension in Marvin and Chandelle's bedroom became thick enough to slice. Marvin's sex drive had maneuvered a fast getaway. He'd grown exasperated over Chandelle's backhanded insinuations. Simultaneously, Dior's self-esteem suffered a major setback. Marvin wasn't sure how to handle the divide widening between him and his wife, but Dior did the first thing that came to mind to ease her anxiety, she started fishing for compliments in Chandelle's pond. Dior couldn't have predicted that compliments wouldn't be nearly enough to satisfy her.

"Marvin, as soon as I'm finished making a few calls, I'll take care of your dishes," Dior offered eagerly. She was cloaked in a thick pastel-colored terrycloth housecoat, but her scheme wasn't hidden too far beneath the exterior. "Just leave it there, I'll get it. Need something to do with my hands anyway," she added. "Shoot, I'ma have to do something drastic if I can't talk up on a decent interview soon."

"Don't worry about it," said Marvin, chomping on a sausage link that Dior had whipped up before Chandelle left for work. "You'll make out all right. A hustler and a smart woman like you gets her share of breaks in life. The next time it comes around, make the best of it. Keep at it. Everything will work out in due time."

"Hey, now, that's got to be the nicest props you ever hit me with," Dior gushed. "Thanks, I really needed that." *You have no idea what else I need*, she considered telling him before catching herself. "Chandelle is so lucky to have you, Marvin. You're a good brotha."

"You don't know just how much *I* needed that," he replied, wearing a tired expression. "I hope you get what you really want."

"Me too," she whispered seductively, a bit louder than she intended.

"What was that?" he asked, believing he probably heard wrong.

"Oh, nothing, just thinking out loud," Dior answered, while backpedalling to her bedroom. "I know you need to leave for work. I'll see you later."

Marvin sensed that Dior had something else on her mind, other than the words she had breathed life into, but he figured it was better not to pry. He'd heard stories of in-law incest and didn't want his name added to the other men stupid enough to entertain a tryst that should never have happened. Besides, Dior wasn't the type of woman he'd look at twice, even if he was still single. He knew better than anyone how her life was peppered with troubled episodes and one bad decision after another. Actually, he'd grown hopeful that Dior would strike out in the right direction and eventually find her way.

Before leaving for the store, he read over the mortgage papers Kimberly forwarded to him from her brokerage firm. An angry collection of knots tightened in the pit of his stomach as he pored over the selling price of the home Chandelle had fallen in love with at first sight. She'd whined hysterically over the house with a corner lot until Marvin acquiesced. Begrudgingly, he signed the loan documents, which exceeded their previously agreed purchase amount by $50,000. He was in too deep and couldn't sleep for worrying about the hefty obligation.

After he exhaled and stuffed the folded copies back into his business portfolio, he wandered into the master bathroom to run cold water over his face. The coolness seemed to lessen his woes. The bath towel draped over his head offered a false sense of relief as he stretched his developed arms. Unfortunately, it was merely a momentary reprieve. While Marvin searched the living room to gather his keys and cell phone, Dior sauntered down the hallway into plain view, wearing a pair of provocative high heels, a snugly fitting pair of pink low-rise panties, and a matching tank top.

Marvin's mouth popped opened when he realized two things at the same time: He wasn't dreaming, and he couldn't force himself to look away. The sight of Dior's toned brown thighs made his mouth water. The way her hips swayed rhythmically to and fro caused him to shudder. Her firm breasts pushed against the revealing top. And his commitment to his wife made him wish he hadn't seen Chandelle's cousin practically naked.

Dior waggled her behind as she poked around in the refrigerator. She began to hum casually as if alone and amusing herself to pass the time. Marvin, genuinely ashamed to have been extremely excited by what he watched, cleared his throat when he reasoned Dior didn't know that he was observing her. "Huh-hmm," he coughed, uncertain how to explain his presence and the potentially embarrassing incident. When Dior's hips continued to bounce with the music going on in her head, Marvin coughed louder.

Like a deer in the forest hearing a strange sound, Dior pulled her head out of the refrigerator and jutted back.

"Marvin?" she said, swinging her breasts in his direction. "Shouldn't you be gone by now? I thought I had the place to myself," she lied, and not too convincingly. Marvin was still gazing at her, now through guilty eyes. After two solid weeks of being a good girl, Dior enjoyed witnessing the helpless expression that had subdued him. It confirmed what she already knew about human nature. Even a good man had to struggle against a tempting can't-miss opportunity staring him in the face. "What's wrong with you?" she teased him, with both hands riding on her hips. "You see something you like?"

"I . . . uh . . . I'm sorry," Marvin stammered nervously. "I shouldn't be here. I should go." His better judgment warned him to run, not walk, to the nearest exit, but his feet listened to another part of him and neglected to move an inch.

"Suit yourself, if that's what you'd rather do," she answered disappointedly. "Just let me get some juice and I'll climb back in my bed," Dior cooed. Her sultry purrs were accompanied by a sensual grin. "I'd hate to make you feel like you couldn't come and go as you please . . . when you please. I mean, with this being your place and all."

Why can't I stop looking at her? Marvin asked himself. "Oops, did I say that out loud?" Dior's schoolgirl giggles confirmed that he had. "Okay, now I'm really out of line."

"Yeah, and you're sweating too," she informed him. "I can't say that I blame you, though. I'm here, you're here. We're alone."

"But nothing's gonna happen," he spouted hurriedly, with an uneasy frown on his lips.

"Who are you trying to convince, me or you?" asked Dior in a straightforward manner that sent a chill through Marvin.

"Huh? Oh, naw, I'm straight," he said, mostly to reassure

himself. "Ain't nothing going down. Uh-uh . . . nope . . . nothing."

"You tryna tell me you don't want it to?" Dior questioned brazenly.

"That doesn't really matter, does it? You are my wife's cousin, who she took in, who's living here in her home, and who she trusts me being around," was Marvin's politically correct response. "You're wrong for putting it in my face like this, Dior. You know you're wrong." She twisted her lips and tossed him a smirk after hearing his lopsided declaration condemning solely her. Marvin quickly agreed that he wasn't entirely sound in his assessment of the sticky situation, which had lingered for far too long. "Okay, I see your point. I don't have any business sizing you up either. There, are you happy?"

"Not even . . . but you'd better break out now because I'm a woman without a man, I'm in heat, and about three seconds away from stepping into a long, hot shower to take matters into my own hands so . . ."

"All right, all right," Marvin yelled in his own defense. "I'm going. I'm out. Just promise that this won't happen again so Chandelle won't be forced to kill the both of us."

"There's nothing to tell, Marvin," Dior decided. "It was a harmless mistake. I didn't know where you stood and you didn't know how good I looked in my private party uniform. That makes us even. No harm, no foul. Now, about that shower, one, two . . ." she counted.

"Uh-uh, you ain't even gotta . . . I'm gone!" he shouted, with one foot out the door.

Yeah, but you'll be back, she thought, *and now that you've seen what I got, that's gonna sit on your mind until you're begging me to sit on your lap.* Life was all a game to Dior. She often rolled the dice and glided along the spaces with various strategies at her disposal. Winning didn't motivate her actions. Playing against the odds offered all the intrigue she needed, and pure adrenaline propelled her forward. It was the uncertainty of risk and reward that moved her. Plain and simple, Dior was in it for the rush.

9

I Didn't Mean To

Chandelle spent the entire day moping at her desk. The stack of home redecorating magazines she'd studied copiously were of no interest. Something was wrong with her man, but she couldn't put her finger on it. The symptoms were obvious. Marvin was working more than Chandelle felt he needed to, he had become prone to staying out even later, and the healthy romantic jaunts she could always count on in the past weren't nearly as likely with his hectic schedule. Those were the symptoms, what caused them were considerably more difficult to detect.

When Chandelle's phone rang, she glanced at the caller ID. A very caring friend and the junior partner of a successful marketing company had beckoned her. "Hey, Grace," she said, after holding the cold receiver to her ear. "No, I haven't gotten to the Dream Creams file yet. I'm sorry. I'll get right on it. Yes, Grace, you'll have it by four." When Chandelle sighed unwittingly, she was summoned into the boss' office. "Right this minute?" she asked, alarmed at Grace's managerial tone. "Yes, ma'am."

In the eighteen seconds that it took Chandelle to reach Grace's doorway, she didn't figure that dragging her feet while prepping a client's chart for an upcoming meeting would land her in the doghouse. Although she'd taken her job seriously, and was rewarded a promotion because of it, Chandelle knew Grace didn't allow for sloughing at any turn. Since it had been fourteen years since she'd been pregnant the first time, Grace wasn't in the mood for any foolishness. Depending on how that baby was treating her, she'd been known to run hot and cold at a moment's notice. Chandelle was hoping for a plane of emotional stability landing somewhere in between the two.

Standing at the mouth of Grace's office, Chandelle cautiously poked her head inside. "Yes, Mrs. Peters," she said, just above a whisper.

"*Mrs. Peters?* Maybe you ought to come in and have a seat," answered Grace, as she studied her younger associate arduously. That hitch in Chandelle's voice she'd heard on the phone didn't stop there. Now it was leading her around by the nose. "Chandelle, you're going to tell me what's gotten you moving slower than molasses, because my feet hurt too much to also have my head hurting as a result of trying to guess."

Chandelle, wide-eyed, snickered uncontrollably at Grace's grumpy tirade. "Please, I'm sorry, Grace. Working full time in your condition must be challenging. I'd hate to add to the stress."

"Good, then don't. Hurry up and get to telling me why the client's file isn't complete and on my desk?" When Chandelle acted as if she might balk at the idea of sharing her business, Grace groaned and leaned back in her leather chair. "Come on now, I've already told you about my feet."

"Right, you have," Chandelle replied, shifting her

weight to the front of her chair. "I don't know what it is really, but something is up with Marvin. He hasn't been himself lately."

"And what about Chandelle, has she been herself lately?"

"You know me," replied Chandelle, suggesting she was never off-kilter.

"Yes, and that's why I asked," Graced offered honestly. "See, there's often three sides to every story: his, hers, and the truth."

"It's not like that, Grace, not this time," Chandelle explained. "It's something I don't understand. Marvin has not been the type to run with the fellas or work himself into a coma. We don't ever seem to . . ." she started to say before remembering Grace was still her boss after all. "Well, let's just say I'm sleeping alone more now than when I was single and auditioning, know what I'm saying?"

"Uh-huh, but do *you* know what you're saying. Look, Chandelle, from what you've told me, I'm sensing that Marvin is running himself ragged and avoiding you for the same reason."

Chandelle eased back into the chair and crossed all ten fingers beneath her chin. "My spirit is telling me that he's sneakin'."

"Has he given you any real reason to think that, or is your loneliness overriding your intuition? Marvin is a good man, we both know that. We also know how much he loves Chandelle. Perhaps this is a good time to sit him down and get to the root of the problem. Marvin's sensible, get him to talking about things and it'll play itself out. I agree that something is keeping him away from you, but trust me on this one, for people who love one another more than they want to be alone, it always does work out."

The words Grace planted in Chandelle's mind made a

promising impact. She hustled throughout the afternoon and delivered the file with time to spare. Chandelle drove home for the weekend thinking that if only manipulating her husband to come clean were that easy, getting him to come home on time would have been a cinch.

After taking Grace's words to heart, she waited for a perfect time to have that "getting him to open up" chat, but it appeared by Sunday evening that it would never arrive. Even with Dior chasing cocktail waitress gigs for the last two days, Marvin wasn't at home and awake for three minutes at a time. Chandelle just kept telling herself that her husband was crazy about her and that they were very fortunate to be moving upstream with a new home. *Build bridges, not walls*, she kept reminding herself, although her quick temper made that easier said than done. *Just get him to open up about what's got him acting all distant and love will take care of the rest.*

Chandelle stood in the kitchen of their small apartment, wrapping flatware in old newspaper. She was so excited when their mortgage loan for the house on Brass Spoon was approved two weeks before. Marvin had been sulking, ever since then. Although she tried to overlook it, the increasing long hours at the job had only intensified, and so did the anemic paychecks he'd been bringing home despite busting his rump for an unappreciative owner. After being married for three years, Chandelle thought she knew her husband. In short order, she had to learn the hard way how little she knew herself.

"Marvin, do we have any more old newspapers?" she yelled, standing over a stack of china plates yet to be wrapped. "Marvin!" she shouted, when he didn't answer.

"Yeah, I'm watching the game. Cowboys about to get a touchdown," he said finally.

Chandelle rolled her eyes, and then pretended she wasn't bothered that he didn't jump into action the way he used to when they first married. Back then, he was all about her and she missed that. To make matters worse, seemingly he'd become all about himself, and that was unacceptable. "Marvin! I need you to get some more newspaper. I'm out already and I haven't even done the china from our wedding yet. Marvin!" When Chandelle stepped around the corner into the tiny den area, Marvin's eyes were fastened to the expensive flat screen as if he were sitting in the stadium on the fifty yard line. "Ah-hmm," Chandelle uttered, as if clearing her throat. "Forget it, I'll run to the corner store myself," she said, starting to collect her purse and coat.

"Good, now I can finish watching The Boys put it on them rusty-butt Redskins," Marvin said, louder than he should have.

Chandelle cocked her head to the side, smirked her displeasure, and began to fume over the way her husband had blown her off for a stupid football game. "So, you really are gonna let me go out into the cold while you sit on your behind watching those scrubs lose another game?"

"Chandelle, don't start," Marvin barked, dismissing her.

"Don't start? That doesn't sound like a man who cherishes his wife's safe being."

"Hey, didn't you say you were going? Who am I to stop you?" Marvin argued. "Wait 'til halftime, and then I'll go. Otherwise, pick me up some pork skins and I'll see you when you get back."

Yes, something had definitely changed. There was a time, not so long ago, when Marvin wouldn't have thought of sending his wife out into the elements. Chandelle didn't understand how it happened or when exactly, but she felt compelled to get at the root of it without wasting another minute. "Marvin, I want to talk," she announced, while standing directly in front of the television. "So you need to turn that off."

"Move, Chandelle," he fussed, trying to shoo her away. "Move, girl, quit playing now."

Defiantly, she refused to relinquish her position. Instead, she crossed her arms and flashed Marvin a hardened stare. "I'm not moving, so you can either watch the TV through me or you can talk to me. It's up to you. You can either misssss . . . !" she screamed when he leaped off the sofa, gently scooped her up, and moved her from blocking his view of the tube. "Oh, it's like that now, huh?" Chandelle ranted. "You just gon' resort to putting your hands on me. Uh-huh, that's the way it always starts with playful nonaggressive manhandling, but before long the pushing, shoving, and slapping starts! Is that what you want to do, Marvin? You want to beat on me?" Although Chandelle wasn't serious about Marvin hurting her, she was willing to say just about anything to get a rise out of him. It had been a while since he orchestrated one in the sack.

Marvin frowned at her, vehemently objecting to her unwarranted outburst. "Whutever, Chandelle. If that's what you call me putting my hands on you, you're slippin'." When her bothered expression didn't change in the least, Marvin marched past her. He snatched up a thin jacket off the wooden coat rack near the door. He wrestled it on quickly and felt his pants pocket for the car keys. "Okay, since you want to put on a show. I'ma go watch the rest of the game at Duper's where ain't nobody gonna be silly enough to jump up in front of the TV."

"Ohhh, so now I'm silly!" she sassed. "So, how long have you had that opinion of me? You didn't used to think I was so silly when you begged me to marry you. *Chandelle, I love you, I need you*," she mocked. "Now look at you. All I wanted to do was talk, but you'd rather send me out into the cold so you can watch some stupid team that ain't worth a bent nickel anyway."

"Everybody's entitled to their own opinion," Marvin said casually, as he searched around the den for his keys. When Chandelle spotted them first, she dashed over to the end table and grabbed them. "Cool, give 'em to me and I'll head back after the game."

"Ain't giving you nothing until you tell me what's wrong with you. Lately you been hanging out with the boys, and that's not like you, Marvin. We hardly say two words to each other when you do come home, and that's not like us."

"Chandelle, we can talk about this when I get back from the bar. Stop playing and give me the keys," he demanded, getting more annoyed by his overdramatic wife.

"Uh-uh, not until you tell me what's so important out there that you can't seem to stay away from it. What's at the club that you don't have here? Drink, we got that. Music?" Chandelle asked, turning up the stereo system loud enough to upset the neighbors. "What? Sounds like music to me. Oh, can it be sex you're out there hunting for? Nah, I know it can't be that, because you don't even want the good stuff going to waste up in here." Chandelle was exasperated. She'd used everything she could to make Marvin argue with her, but still he refused. He simply stood there with a bothered look on his face that made her want to fight even more.

"Are you through now?" he asked finally. "Can I go or are you not finished with the theatrics?"

"Why not, it's obvious that you don't care about us anymore. I don't know why we're moving into the house on Friday. What we have here isn't much of a home; three thousand square feet won't change that," Chandelle concluded loudly.

"Now you're talking," said Marvin excitedly. "I'm still not sold on buying that big of a house to begin with."

"Negro, please! The way you were running behind that

real-estate agent, you'd have said yes to every house she showed us if I wasn't there to stop you."

"Well, she was a hard worker and I appreciated that," he answered. "It's hard dealing with people who don't know what they want. I ought to know. Down at Appliance World, I spend most of my time breaking down my extensive product knowledge, per the salesman handbook, and explaining the differences between the benefits only to have the customers either go with the cheapest appliance or the one that matches what they already got at home. I'm just saying Kimberly's a hard worker is all."

"Yeah, I see she did a number on you. Since when did you start calling her Kimberly, Marvin? Have you been talking to her when I'm not around? Y'all got a little thing going on?" Chandelle interrogated.

"Now I know I need to bounce. Give me the keys, Chandelle," he ordered, sticking out his hand to receive them. "Chandelle, quit stalling and give them to me!"

Instead of complying, she grabbed the waistband of her sweatpants and dropped the keys down inside. "How bad do you want them," she goaded, "bad enough to take them from me?"

As soon as she smarted off, Marvin lunged toward her. Chandelle shrieked at the top of her lungs, laughing as she skirted around the small room to avoid capture. Marvin chased and Chandelle cackled wildly until he caught up to her. Unfortunately, Marvin stumbled over the sofa ottoman and came crashing down on the coat rack, knocking her against his beloved flat screen. She tried to brace herself but couldn't. Chandelle and the television slammed hard against the floor. Both she and Marvin watched as a big puff of smoke rose from the expensive television.

"It's ruined!" he shouted. "Twenty-five hundred dollars down the drain because you wanted some attention! I'm tired of you acting up when you don't get your way. Look at what you made me do!" Marvin was hot. Admittedly, he hadn't been as thoughtful as when they initially married, and he did not fully understand why. He still loved Chandelle more than his actions conveyed. He wondered sometimes if she should have married one of the ball players she'd dated before meeting him. Maybe then Chandelle would be happy now. And as a result, maybe so would Marvin. After brooding over the television, smashed beyond repair, he went over to check on Chandelle when it appeared she was actually injured. "You okay, baby?" he asked, sincerely concerned.

"No, I'm not okay, and when are you gonna check on that stupid thing before coming to see about me!" she replied, more salty than hurt. "Maybe now we can talk like I wanted to in the beginning."

Before Marvin had the time to process Chandelle's complaints, there were three hard knocks at the door. When no one answered fast enough, they beat on it again.

"What!" Marvin yelled, as he opened the door to find two police officers, one black and the other as white as a snowy day. Neither appeared too happy about being shouted at. "Well, what y'all want?" Marvin asked rudely. "Ain't nobody selling drugs here, so you might want to go and harass somebody else."

They took one look inside the apartment, discovering a knocked-over television set, a hole in the wall caused when Marvin went flying into the coat rack that stood next to it, and Chandelle limping over to rest on the sofa. Both cops stepped inside of the apartment then and backed Marvin against the wall. "Miss, we're answering a public disturbance call. One of your neighbors reported loud screaming and fighting," the taller white officer stated.

The black cop had positioned himself between Marvin and the very attractive woman who was adequately filling out those sweatpants in a way that got him extremely interested. "Sistah," the black one called out to get her attention. "This your husband?"

Chandelle winced while rubbing her hip. "Yeah, we're married," she said softly.

"That don't give him the right to get physical with you, though," he told her in a comforting voice that Marvin found offensive.

"Say, man! What do you think you're doing?" Marvin heaved, objecting to the officer using the situation to flirt with his wife.

"Shut up!" the black officer asserted. "I bet that's one of your problems, you don't want to listen." Again, he eyed Chandelle for her approval.

"Man, this ain't even cool," Marvin barked. "Y'all just can't run up in here like this and talk to me like I don't have any rights."

"And you can't go slapping your wife around anytime you feel like it," the white cop replied.

"Sistah, did he hit you?" the black officer asked Chandelle.

"No, he didn't," she answered. "It wasn't even like that. Besides, it was partially my fault."

"Yeah, that's what all battered women say," the black officer contended. "And I guess that flat screen just tossed itself on the ground 'cause it got tired of working?" His countenance had quickly undergone a sudden shift when Chandelle seemed to be protecting Marvin.

"Look, officers, this is a misunderstanding," Marvin tried to explain before the black cop shut him up by placing his hand on the holstered department-issue revolver.

"No, I understand real good how this sorta thing goes," he said. "Miss, you say he didn't hit you, but it's obvious you're shaken up and have been manhandled. How do you expect us to believe he didn't put his hands on you?"

"Well, yeah, he did, but it wasn't . . ." Chandelle uttered before she realized those were the magic words the cops were waiting on. "Hey, hold on," she hissed, when they charged Marvin with handcuffs dangling from their mitts.

"It's too late for that, ma'am," argued the pale one as his partner took great pleasure in doing the honors.

"Homeboy, you picked the wrong day to jump on your girl, and as fine as she is, you deserve to go down," the other whispered to Marvin, while tightening the cuffs behind his back. "You have the right to remain silent . . ."

"Ahhh, man. Y'all taking me to jail?" Marvin asked, as he dug his heels into the carpet. "This ain't right. Chandelle, please tell them I didn't mean to hurt you."

"She already told us all we needed hear to lock you up for spousal abuse." That was the white dude backing up his partner. "Anything you *or your wife* says can be used in a court of law," he continued sarcastically, as he evil-eyed Chandelle like a jerk who had just been rejected at a nightclub. "That means you oughtta shut up and ole girl should have kept her trap closed too." He shoved Marvin in the small of the back with his nightstick to prod him along when he saw that there might be a struggle in the making.

"Man, you ain't got to be pushing that thing in my back," Marvin snapped, as he exited the small apartment. "Y'all know this ain't right!"

Chandelle was mortified. It was all happening too fast for her to grasp. One minute they were horse playing, and the next he was in the midst of being hauled off. "I told y'all he wasn't trying to hurt me. I told you that. Hey! Where are you taking him?" She chased down the stairs behind them, barefoot and beside herself. "Wait. Marvin, I didn't mean for this to happen."

"Go back in the house, Chandelle, you've said enough already," he answered, as they shoved him into the back of the police squad car.

She backed up onto the curb and watched as they drove away, wondering how something so innocent turned out to be so bad.

10

Jailhouse Blues

When the patrol car glided into the underground garage downtown, all Marvin could think of was how improbable the chances were that such a simple misunderstanding turned out so terribly wrong. One minute he was watching a football game in the comfort of his quaint apartment, without Dior lurking about to put more of a strain on his morality. Then, as if someone was playing a cruel joke at his expense, his coveted flat-screen television was sizzling on the floor and two determined cops appeared out of nowhere threatening to beat him for something he hadn't done. Unlike most of the inmates he was destined to cross paths with during his stint in the Dallas County lockup, it wasn't he who happened to be in the wrong place at the wrong time, that dubious honor belonged to the men who'd plucked him like a low-hanging fruit from the confines of his own backyard. There had to be someone who'd listen to Marvin explain his misfortune, he reasoned, someone in charge, someone who cared that he was actually an innocent man caught in a net of lies. He was innocent. Innocent.

The black officer, the angrier of the two, who thoroughly enjoyed roughing him up while Chandelle looked on, sneered at Marvin from the front seat of the police cruiser before his white partner opened the back door to usher him out, with steel cuffs tightly binding his wrists. "I hope the ride over was to your liking, Mr. Hutchins," the angry officer said, feigning a momentary bout of sincerity. "Because there will be a lot of fellas in there who'd just love to ride a big, strong, good-looking buck like you."

Marvin hadn't allowed himself to contemplate what potentially inhumane and most assuredly dangerous tribulations awaited his arrival. He had been hyperfocused on the unfortunate circumstances that led him to that point. Now, he would be forced to shift his attention forward while shelving his tragic afternoon in the recesses of his mind.

"Yeah, he'll be real popular when he hits the pit and the lights go out," seconded the white cop. "Pretty boys make great slow dancers inside."

"Whatever," Marvin replied, adding an extra measure of swagger to his long stride. Having no idea what to expect, he was more nervous than he dared admit. Cops and criminals were a lot alike in one regard, each of them sensed fear like a mad dog. "Ain't no man gonna turn me anyway I don't wanna be turned, including neither one of y'all."

"Did you hear that, Ted?" the black officer growled, as he shoved his baton in the center of Marvin's back for smarting off. "We'll find out how hard you are when the night gets cold and mean. Better get your dancing shoes laced up nice and tight, twinkle toes."

"If you didn't have that badge and gun, I'd beat you right out of your shoes," Marvin would have said, but he'd never been mistaken for stupid. There was no sense in making a bad situation ridiculous, so he wisely kept his comments to himself.

"What? Did I hear you say something, twinkle toes?" The officer glared up at Marvin, just as he did earlier when showing off for Chandelle. There was no doubt that the harsh officer wished Marvin had given him cause to use his discretion and his fists.

"No," Marvin answered quickly, "I'm done."

"You're doggone right about that. Come on, step through the door and into my world," he said with a sinister chuckle.

Upon entering the long corridor where the drafty parking garage met with the justice department intake area, Marvin felt the hair on the back of his neck stand on end. The walls were fashioned with a sound brick construction, six by twelve-inch blocks, covered with several coats of white latex paint. Other than police personnel passing along the hall, it could have been a pathway to any office building in the city, but Marvin wasn't so lucky. The ugly looks he received from uniformed passersby reminded him of that.

As the hallway opened into a larger area, Marvin listened to voices coming from every direction at once. He tried to lean in closer in order to get a handle on things when ordered to state his name to a hefty, flat-footed police veteran who appeared to have little love for his job and less regard for the spare tire that collected around his waist. "Louder!" the dumpy man shouted. "If you hadn't noticed, this is a 'no whisper' zone. State your name, last first, first next, and middle last."

"Hutchins. Marvin. Bernard," answered Marvin, with sharp, concise woofs. His words came out louder than he predicted, but no one seemed bothered in the least. If those jailhouse walls could talk, he'd have understood why his spirited barks didn't draw a single wrinkled brow. He had been delivered to a bad place, one with bad people who did bad things. When slapped with harsh reality that he was going to be booked and processed like one of those bad men, a common criminal, Marvin felt hollow inside. His parents would have died of utter shame if they hadn't passed on already. It was the first time in his life that he was relieved about it.

The policemen who arrested Marvin stood guard until he had been fingerprinted. Another man, a county detention officer dressed in a royal blue uniform, approached him from a glassed-in office while holding a black slate with tiny white lettering aligned in three different rows. When that fellow hung the slated sign around Marvin's neck, he felt like a rabid dog that nobody wanted and would rather have locked away instead of roaming the streets. Marvin glared at the first county officer he'd encountered, the shouter who also served as the mug shot photographer instructing him to hold the slate straight and turn from side to side between poses.

"We'll be seeing you," the black cop heckled, as two other detention goons entered through a steel door to take Marvin away.

You'd better hope I don't see you first, Marvin thought to himself, while looking back over his shoulder to exhibit the sentiment in his heart with a menacing jeer. *If I catch you off the clock and in your civvies, it's on.* The police officer's confused expression almost put a rewarding grin on Marvin's lips, almost, until the steel door slammed behind him. On the inside now, there wasn't one thing to smile about.

"Empty your pockets on the table and take out your shoelaces," demanded a seasoned gruff-talking man from the opposite side of a stout wooden table, which was old and unfinished, splintered and rough like the gruff talker. Both had undoubtedly outlasted their welcome.

Marvin did as he was instructed, flipping his pants pockets inside out, followed by the tedious task of wrestling shoestrings from his leather high-top sneakers. "What, y'all think I might hurt myself with these?" he said, merely as an audible thought and nothing else.

"Probably not," answered the senior officer standing at the table. "But there's always the outside chance somebody might decide to use them *to hurt you*. And that fancy timepiece of yours, you might want to hand that over too. Some folks will fight over anything when they get bored." Upon hearing that, Marvin's leisurely pace increased to the point of breakneck speed. In the blink of an eye, he quickly complied, thus completing his check-in to what many called the "gray bar motel."

The cell he was shown to wasn't accommodating, to him or the other fifteen or so men camped on the bolted-down bench and dirty cement floors. The only toilet they had access to was a stainless steel bowl, filthy, reeked of urine and bile, and was positioned out in the open against the furthest wall. Privacy was not an offered amenity for a kennel packed with stray mutts. Marvin's temper flared then, feeling helpless and enslaved. He grabbed the nearest bench to the cell door and plopped down on it.

Not fifteen seconds had passed before a country mouse scurried across the floor. Two young white men, who both appeared to be around nineteen, darted after it, swiping at the frightened animal with their rolled up T-shirts.

"Grab it!" one of them yelped. Trap that thing with your shoe!"

"Then what?" the other hollered back. "Let it bite me?"

"Don't worry, it won't put its mouth on your funky butt."

"Why not? Your sister did last night, twice!" his companion quipped. As quick as that, their focus on catching the rodent disappeared. A real live Texas Cage wrestling match broke out between them. Several of the men looking on began hollering helpful suggestions. Marvin was one of the few not at all interested in the free floor show.

Two skinny teenagers scrapping for the heck of it wasn't his idea of entertainment. Before either had sustained a single bruise, the corrections officer swaggered down the block to take a look.

"Uh-huh, just what I thought," the broad, muscle-bound black man grunted through the cell bars. "If y'all want to wear yourselves out, be my guests, but if one of you gets hurt, I'll have to fill out a report, and believe me, you do not want me to put down my newspaper to fill out a report." Before he turned and marched off in the same direction he came from, the scrawny young men had clothed themselves and found a quiet place not far from Marvin's feet.

"You better be glad the CO saved you," one said to the other.

"Whatever, if that's what you want to think," his partner replied. "Know what? I'm hungry."

Now that was something Marvin agreed with. "Hey, when do they get around to feeding us?" he asked the harmless scrappers in particular, hoping that anyone with knowledge of the dining schedule would answer.

"I don't know," they said in unison, before chuckling about it like boys in a gymnasium. "We only just got here 'bout two hours ago."

"And they haven't learned jack yet," offered a heftily built man, raisin brown, waking from a nap. "See, I done told them once to sit down and be still. If I have to say it again, 'the man' is gonna be writing two reports, serious injury reports." Both teenagers huddled up closer to each other. Marvin had no reason to discount his gripes, the scrappers didn't chance it. There wasn't another peep out of them for hours.

During that time, the cell had evolved into a mini-community with separate factions debating sports trivia and which female movie stars they'd get into bed if the opportunity ever presented itself. Although Marvin refused to join in and toss another worthless opinion on the heap along with theirs, it did get his mind off of the fix that held him in check like a school yard bully. He even noticed laughter pouring out of his mouth when the mountainous raisin called dibs on Halle Berry after Vivica Fox's name had been passed through too many lips. Like the giant ever had a chance with either of the screen sirens, Marvin mused quietly, until he realized that he had actually entertained sleeping with a woman other than Chandelle. Then he was angry with her all over again.

The squeaky wheels of the dining cart caused him to salivate. He couldn't remember having been so ravenous. Whatever they were handing out, he was determined to wolf it down without wasting a crumb. Unfortunately, his determination and appetite waned as soon as the trustee handed out styrofoam cups of watered-down Tang, and then tossed out ziplock baggies stuffed with sandwiches, every last one of which was baloney.

Marvin didn't know it, but he was being watched, observed. Several of the men sharing the den with him noted how he passed on the entrée of the evening. They had previously discussed the fact that he'd been standoffish and reluctant to become a functioning part of the group.

Eventually, he was forced to account for his presence among them. Minutes after the remnants of their meals had been collected, Marvin smelled the most rancid odor brushing by his face. He groaned sorely, holding his hand over his mouth and nose. Tears filled his eyes when they began to burn. Both of the young men sat closely together, glaring at the man on the toilet, the one who'd taken their sandwiches for his own as a penalty for disturbing his rest. It was the strangest thing, Marvin thought, when they were summoned to the raisin's throne to provide amusement while he used the facilities.

"Go on and make me laugh now that I done ate," he

commanded them with a broad, majestic gesture. They didn't have the energy or nerve to defy him, despite his cruel and unusual request. Incredibly, they belted out the lyrics of one rap song after the next, while holding their noses. Marvin, viewing the spectacle, was opposed to the way both men had been degraded for sport. It was just plain wrong he reasoned, and he'd be willing to risk his health before giving in like them.

"Hey, you!" the big man yelled in his direction. Marvin didn't look his way so he yelled a second time. "Hey, you, college boy! Yeah, I can tell 'cause you think you're too good for pimp steak! Come over here."

Marvin looked at the man with his pants gathered around his ankles, then at the others betting he'd do as he was told. "What you want with me, man?" he shouted back, buying time more than anything else. He'd already decided he was going all right, but he had to make it appear that he had a choice in the matter.

"Right now, I just want to rap with you," the big man answered, with his words trailing off at the end. Before he'd explained what might be up for discussion later on, Marvin dragged his feet across the cell floor.

Avoiding eye contact, Marvin coughed and sputtered. "Hmmm . . . What is it, man?"

"I've been wondering something every since you got put in here with us. What'd did they get you for? I mean, a clean-cut fella like you couldn't have been doing too much of nothing to get locked up on a Sunday afternoon." The begrudging frown Marvin wore then caused the "king for a day" to chuckle. "Man, don't be shame. They got all of us in here for something. You the onliest one we don't know what for."

Marvin ran down the giant's rationale, thinking why he should tell them anything about this private life; then he factored in the ridiculousness of his current plight. He was in midst of a pantless terror-wielding tyrant and his court, all awaiting his response. Marvin couldn't see himself still standing there once the man finished his business and then proceeded to get up, so he answered, although with an ounce of trepidation, "Man, they picked me up on some bull—"

"Yeah, you and me too. So, what did they bust you on?" he asked, his patience wearing thin.

"Domestic abuse," Marvin sighed, so quietly no one was sure what he said.

"Come again, college boy?"

"I said they brought me in on domestic abuse." No one made a sound for a few seconds, then as if on cue, the entire cell erupted into riotous clamor. Marvin didn't understand it until the laughter subsided.

"No disrespect, college boy, it's just that we all thought you said you got popped for beating on your old lady."

"Uh-huh, some bull—"

"Move back, college boy," his majesty huffed finally. "I figured you for a meth' dealer out in the suburbs. We already got three of those, two armed robberies, a whole bunch of grand-theft autos, and one assault with a deadly weapon." The way everyone was staring at Marvin, he knew who the most serious crime belonged to before the tyrant claimed it. "I'll be sent up tomorrow if that dude I shanked don't make it out of surgery. He should have kept to mail handling instead of trying to backdoor my old lady. She's got us both facing life now. Mine for his." Marvin's eyes dimmed when he heard the bully gasp to keep from bawling. He waved Marvin away, dismissing him once and for all.

Three detention officers appeared just after midnight. They came to segregate the tyrant for early transportation when his victim died on the operating table. He didn't fuss when they shackled his hands and feet with chains, but he did take a minute to say his good-byes. "Don't ever let your love for no female get your freedom papers revoked, college boy," he said jokingly to Marvin, who stood instinctively as a salute.

"All right, then," he answered solemnly. "Take care up there." Not that Marvin knew exactly where up there happened to be, but it seemed like the appropriate thing to say.

Not another word was spoken throughout the night. Those who couldn't sleep traded uncomfortable glances and an unexplainable level of sadness for the man who intimidated them. A death row inmate was hailed as a man among boys in the joint, and they were there to witness his rise into the big time, an honor that no one aspired to.

11

Somebody's Lying

As soon as the breakfast wagon made its run, Marvin gobbled up a runny egg sandwich and cold sausage patties, which he was glad to have. He didn't even mind it when some of the other men teased how "college boy" had found his appetite. Marvin's stomach was satisfied, but his nerves had worn thin. Having Chandelle come and bail him out wasn't an option as far as he could see. She was the reason he'd been incarcerated among felons and murderers. There had to be another way to turn.

The long line for telephone privileges provided him time to think. Who could he call to help him, he wondered, with enough money to make a difference? Five minutes before his turn came, so did his answer. Marvin discovered a piece of paper stuffed in his back right pocket. He hated to put someone in an extremely awkward position, but having to deal with Chandelle before he was ready weighed in as an ugly alternative. After flicking the small rectangular card over and over again in his hand, he lifted the phone receiver and made a collect call that changed his life.

With a long line of inmates stacked behind him, Marvin punched the numbers in a slow, methodical manner. He didn't think he'd get an answer, but the third ring proved him wrong. "Marvin," he announced, when prompted by the automated operator to do so. Suddenly, his face softened when he heard her voice. "Who, Felton?"

"No, it's Marvin Hutchins this time. I don't know why I'm here, but I am. No, I've never been locked up before. Huh?" he said, turning to glance at the men trying to listen in. "It's hard to go into right now. So, you know I don't have a lot of time on this phone, but you're gonna make me come out with it."

Marvin had no choice if he wanted a shot getting her assistance. It was a discussion worth having despite its disparaging nature. "Okay, me and Chandelle got into it over me working so much and hanging out to blow off a little steam. Playing around got out of hand and the neighbors called the law. No, I didn't hit her," he explained fervently. "I've never hit a woman and I'm not trying to start now. I don't know what to do. We have about three grand in savings after the down payment on the house, but that won't get a decent lawyer." There was an interruption on the line, a beep signaling there were only ten seconds left before the call terminated. "Look, they're saying I gotta get off, but thanks for accepting the charge. I didn't know who else to call. Bye, Kim."

Marvin stepped back from the phone, turned, and walked way. He'd learned from the attending CO that his case wasn't due to go before the judge to be arraigned until later that evening or on the morning of the following day because the men arrested ahead of him were awarded earlier appearance slots. Prepared to sit and wait, Marvin was surprised when an officer walked up to the cell door before lunch and called his name.

"Marvin Hutchins, you're up."

"Whaaaat?" came from every direction at once from

the others booked before Marvin. "I've been here since Friday night," one of the men protested.

"And me since Saturday morning," another yelled.

"He's on the fast track," the detention office said, guessing mostly. "And you're not. So shut up and move back," he warned when they crowded behind Marvin.

At a loss for words, Marvin shrugged his shoulders. "Sorry, fellas," he muttered.

"Yeah right, *college boy*," someone heckled from the pack of usual suspects.

Marvin walked in front of the man who'd arrived just ahead of the baloney sandwiches. "Hey, man, can a brotha get a toothbrush before I see the judge?" he asked.

"What, are you trying to get a date? This is jail, homie. Funky breath comes with the territory."

"I'll take that as a no," Marvin concluded. When the officer scoffed at his question, Marvin felt foolish for asking it. "Thought so."

"When we get inside, keep your mouth shut and don't do anything unless you're told. I'll hitch you to the chain and someone will unhook you to go in front of the judge." Marvin nodded that he'd understood. "They told me a lady pulled some strings to get you kicked this soon. You must be somebody."

Marvin entered the cluttered courtroom thinking how insignificant he had become in such a short time. Then he remembered how Chandelle's boss Grace was married to a high-priced lawyer. Wallace was likely his ace in the hole. Who else had the clout to get him pushed up in the chain gang wading pool? After Marvin had taken three steps toward the pew of detainees, all connected to a metal wire running through their handcuffs, he caught a glimpse of a familiar face in the rear of the room. Kim Hightower was sitting in the last row near the door. Chandelle wasn't there, blubbering like the remorseful wife he wanted her to be. There were no "please, let my man come home" theatrics like he'd imagined a million times throughout the night. Chandelle wasn't anywhere to be seen. On the other hand, Kim's hopeful smile warmed Marvin's heart.

Thirty minutes later, after hearing one defendant after the other plead not guilty for a myriad of crimes, it was Marvin's turn to add his as well. "I'm innocent, your honor," he said, to the chagrin of the judge. Marvin's public defender, an overworked 28-year-old-almost giggled. The arraignment segment of the process had been the most boring and uneventful, so his comment was actually funny.

"We have a habit of letting juries decide that, Mr. Hutchins," replied the balding man behind the broad bench. "A simple plea of guilty or not guilty are your options this morning, your only options."

"Not guilty, sir," Marvin said, as assuredly as he could.

"I figured as much," replied the judge. "Mr. Hutchins's bail has been procured, I take it?"

A uniformed bailiff flipped pages on a clipboard before speaking up. "Yes, your honor. His papers are in order."

"Good, we'll set a trial date and get back to you, Mr. Hutchins. You can come back then and meet the jury," he joked. "Next case, Houston Escobar come on down."

"Your judgeship, I'm innocent too," the defendant shouted, as soon as he faced the judge's bench.

"Yeah, us too," the row of chained inmates cackled like an off-key choir.

"Thank you, Mr. Hutchins," the judge said sarcastically, as Marvin eased out of the side door with an armed guard trailing him.

The checkout process took less than fifteen minutes. Marvin signed some documents promising to appear for trial; then he had his wallet and keys returned to him in a manila envelope. Kim was pacing in the hall when he exited through the inmate release doors. "I don't know what to say," Marvin told her.

"You've already said thank you over the phone," she replied.

"No, not for this. I mean, I wasn't even supposed to be in court until maybe tomorrow. How did you pull that off?"

"You've forgotten." Kim blushed, with a soft smile. "My brother Felton, remember. I've met a lot of good people down here. Some of them owe me."

"Now I do, too. How can I pay you back?" he asked, calculating a payment plan in his mind. "Hold up, how does a bond work anyway?"

"You don't belong in here, do you?"

"God, I hope not. I've seen some things that I'm ashamed of."

"Then I don't want to know anything about them," Kim said, passing on the chance to play catch up. "I have a long day ahead of me, but I can make time to take you home."

"I'm not ready to go there yet, but I could use a decent meal and a bath."

"And . . . a tooth brush," Kim quickly informed him. "Yep, kinda stale."

Shamed, Marvin placed his hand over his mouth. "I know I'm busted right now, but I'm going to prove myself worthy of your trust and all you've done for me. Besides, you must have believed I was innocent or you wouldn't have stood up for me."

"For one, it's not guilty. Two, you didn't strike me as the wife- beater type. I can usually spot those. Three, you sounded like you really needed a friend. And four, you and Chandelle seem like a happy couple. Despite whatever happened, and it's none of my business, you should get a real lawyer and patch things up with your woman."

Again, Marvin found himself speechless and nodding his agreement. Only this time he wasn't so sure he really agreed. Chandelle's carelessness was the cause of his troubles, he reasoned. Her thoughtlessness put him face-to-face with a killer and in the debt of another woman. As far as he was concerned, his wife was zero-for-three. In no hurry to fight it out with Chandelle, Marvin called the apartment to see if she was there. "Hello," Dior answered, groggily. She told him that her cousin went to work, then asked a barrage of questions. "Marvin, tell me how it went down? Did those police jack you up? You know Chandelle can't ever get no story right. Anyway, what are you doing already out of jail? Who bailed you this quick? Your boss? Was it your boss?" she asked repeatedly until he hung up the phone.

Dior was at it again when Kim's Escalade dropped him off at the apartment. She met him at the door with a shrewd leer. "Who's this?" she snapped, like a jealous lover.

"Nobody," Marvin sighed, waving good-bye to Kim from his doorway.

"Then why are you waving bye-bye while *Nobody* is pushing her twenty-inch rims down the block?"

"Dior, I am not trying to have this conversation with you right now," he argued, after closing the door.

"We'll see how much conversatin' Chandelle is going to be about having when I tell her about *Miss Nobody*."

"Mind your own, Dior. This is married folks' business."

"Yeah, I see, and it looks like *Nobody* has her nose stuck in it, too," she challenged.

Marvin pitched a look so brazenly spiteful at Dior that she cowered back on the sofa. His brow wrinkled after she slinked against the cushions. "Oh, you're scared of me now."

"I don't know Marvin," Dior pouted. "I ain't never seen you like this and you did just get out of the clink for smacking Chandelle."

"But I didn't . . . !" he yelled, before calming his voice. "This whole mess has got me twisted. I'm not sure what to think of me either. Tell Chandelle that I'm getting some clothes and staying in a hotel for a few days." Dior nodded her head slowly, confirming that she'd pass the information on. "Sorry Dior," Marvin apologized, for frightening her.

"I'm sorry too," she whispered, as Marvin marched into the master bedroom and closed the door. "I didn't get to tell you that I got a job. You said I would land on my feet and I did. I came up on some money to get my place back too." If she did have the chance to run it down to him, Dior would have omitted the part about her new gig being illegal. She wouldn't have received any "atta-girl" points for that, not from Marvin. He hated the idea of anyone going to jail. It was his worst nightmare, haunting him during the daytime, so he did what made sense in his head. He got a room at the Holiday Inn and fell into a very deep sleep on rented sheets far away from his misery.

Meanwhile, Chandelle spent all morning at her desk dialing extensions at the Dallas County Courthouse. "What do you mean he's not in the system?" Chandelle hollered. "I know he's in the . . . system because I'm the one who got him arrested. What? I'm his wife. I'm calling now to get him out," she explained bitterly. "Yeah I'll hold. I don't see why not, I've been holding all day."

"Chandelle, in my office now," Grace ordered, after overhearing her phone conversation.

"Yes, Ma'am," she said, while ending the call that'd taken several hours to land. She was close to finding Marvin and learning the particulars of his case, she thought, if she hadn't been discovered while doing it.

"Why didn't you tell me Marvin was in jail?" Grace fussed. "Ahh, why didn't you tell me you had him arrested? Ahh, what did he do that made you call the police on him? Ahh, why did you come into work when your husband is locked up in God knows where?"

Chandelle was afraid to speak, fearing that the company's junior partner had another question loaded to spring on her if she did. "I . . . I . . ."

"Speak up Chandelle, we've got to fix this."

"I'mmmm so sorry!" Chandelle whined with tears flowing effortlessly from her eyes. "I didn't mean for anything like this to happen. I made a mistake." Grace handed a box of tissues to Chandelle while she described how the episode began and ended with the police taking Marvin downtown to the county lockup, although she couldn't say for certain because no one knew exactly where he was. The group in his cell had yet to go before the judge but he wasn't on any of the afternoon or following day dockets.

Grace had heard enough. She slipped on her comfortable flats and called her husband's cell number. "Wallace, this is an emergency. Yes, I'm fine, Andre's fine and the baby's fine. We're all fine. However, I've just learned that Chandelle and Marvin are not fine. No violence was involved in what they'd gotten into, but the neighbors sent the police over to see about the noise. What? No, she told them that Marvin did cause the bruise on her leg, but not intentionally. Yep, that's when they took him." Grace watched Chandelle knotting up into a ball of guilt. "Uh-uh, you stop feeling sorry for yourself. People make mistakes everyday. Let's just hope this is one we can unmake. No, honey, I wasn't talking to you. I was fussing at Chandelle. Okay, I'll have my phone with me. We're going there now to see about getting him out. What do you mean *be nice*. Of course I'll be nice." Chandelle recognized the tight expression on Grace's face. It said loud and clear, "Chile, get your purse because I'm about to raise some Cain."

No sooner than the first county clerk had informed them that Marvin had been misplaced, Grace blew her stack. She was a whirlwind of commotion until an assistant District Attorney and a good friend of her son's deceased biological father noticed it was her going smooth off. Geoffrey Diggs jumped in to save the clerk, invited them up to his private office, and then personally took over the investigation. After checking the usual places, the county hospital and morgue, the assistant D.A. dialed the Chief Detention Office. Diggs held for a minute while some queries were made, then hung up the phone with an uneasy look shrouding his embarrassment that soon wouldn't be his alone. "That certainly does explain it all right. Thanks for the scoop, Charlie. Yeah, I know, I owe you."

"What certainly explains it, Geoffrey?" asked Grace, much quieter than she'd spoken in the last hour.

"Ma'am, your husband has already been bailed out," he said to Chandelle, "that's why the clerk couldn't find him. Looks like he made it out in record time, too."

"What do you mean Marvin has already been bailed out?" Chandelle growled suspiciously. "When? By who?"

"Just before noon by the sounds of it, and by a woman, a Kimberly Hightower bonded him out."

Grace was lost in the fog, but Chandelle was blinded by rage.

"What it is, Chandelle?" Grace questioned when it appeared her girlfriend was about to explode.

Chandelle sat speechless in the chair until she grabbed hold of her emotions. "How could I have been so stupid?" she said eventually. "That realtor lady who found the house we just bought, she's Kim Hightower. My antenna went up the first time I saw her. I'll bet they've been tipping behind my back the whole time. And to think, he's got me down here crying over him and he's been running around sneakin'. My spirit was on to something."

"Maybe your intuition antenna is off a bit about Marvin. You've told me earlier that he hadn't given you any reason to think he knew that woman before she signed on as your real-estate agent."

"That may be true. Marvin told me he knew her in high school but that she was three years ahead of him. I know I wasn't interested in li'l boys during my senior year."

"See there, case closed," Grace said, thanking Geoffrey for his hospitality and the use of his office. "Marvin had always struck me as an honest person regardless of what your intuition has to say about him."

Chandelle thanked the assistant DA as well; then she stared at the carpet near the door for the longest time. "Marvin flat out told me he didn't have some other woman and my spirit says different. Well, somebody's lying."

12

Oh Yeah, You're Fired!

Chandelle dialed Marvin's cell phone number repeatedly while racing home to have it out with him for two-timing her with Kim Hightower. Dior's exaggerated account didn't do her any favors either. She met Chandelle at the door with her arms folded.

"He ain't here, you know," Dior said, eager to pile it on thick. "This real pretty dark-skinned chick rolled up in her Caddy SUV and brought him home. Uh-huh, she was hugging all on him, blowing kisses and everything," she lied. "I tried to talk to Marvin, but he went off on me. Huh, I tried, but I'm not up for all this madness. Matter of fact, I got a new job that pays a little money, so I'm out of your hair. My apartment manager told me to see him about getting my place back too." Dior watched Chandelle's lip quiver. That excited her. "Sorry, cuz, I didn't think it would play out like this for you. Oh yeah, Marvin said he would be chilling at a hotel for a while." When that tidbit of news didn't yield the reaction Dior predicted, she tried again. "Chandelle, you don't think Marvin's posted up at a hotel with that chick in the Escalade, do you? I mean because if he is . . ."

"Shut up, Dior!" Chandelle screamed. "Didn't you say you were leaving?" Exasperated and boiling over with fury, she thumbed through the yellow pages. Chandelle made two calls: The first one scheduling an emergency Salvation Army furniture pickup impressed Dior with its deviousness, and the next call sent Dior scrambling with her personal belongings to the car. She did not want to be around when that world of Marvin's came crashing down. This time, Chandelle had overplayed her hand. Even Dior knew that she had gone too far.

Chandelle hurried the movers along, offering an extra $100 if they cleared everything out by five. She had some pressing business to attend to, and it all had to go according to plan so that Marvin would feel the full extent of her bitter scorn. "Hurr' up!" she yelled, when the workers appeared to be slacking with the bedroom furniture. "I've got some corners to turn and y'all are slowing me down."

Chandelle packed her clothes into suitcases, and once they were full she began tossing clothes and shoes into the backseat of her car. "We'll see who's fooling who," she muttered, between trips in and out of what used to be their love nest. "You wanna show your tail? You'll get to see me work mine. I can't believe you, Marvin," she moaned. "I know you're mad at me, but what you're out there doing just ain't right."

"Ma'am, are you okay?" asked one of the burly movers, observing her babbling.

Chandelle whipped her head around so fast that he recoiled backward as if he'd mistakenly walked up on a snake. "Mister, I've got a cheating man to deal with and a skank who's probably bodychecking him right now. What do you think?" Even though he was twice her size, the mover didn't stick around to answer.

"You just wait," she repeated, as her Volvo glided toward Hightower Realty. She barged into the building looking for Kim and breathing fire with every step. "Where is she?" she yelled, going from office to office. "Where's Kim? I know she's here somewhere. She'd better hide."

The small brunette Chandelle encountered the first time they met Kim together hung up the phone when she heard someone shouting.

"Hey, I know you," Chandelle hissed, with her finger pointed in the woman's face. "Where's Kim? Tell her she's got trouble and I want the keys to my new house. I want them now!"

"Okay, Mrs. Hutchins, I don't know what's got you so upset, but I'll get the keys for you. Ms. Hightower isn't in. She's out in the field."

"In the field? Is that some kind of code for sleeping with another woman's man on the low-low?"

"Uh, on the low-low? I'm sorry," the brunette answered, with a failure to comprehend Chandelle's streetwise insinuations.

"Yeah, *the low-low*," Chandelle reiterated. "Ask Kim to explain it to you. I'll bet she's got lots of practice." She snatched two sets of keys from the distraught woman's hands and headed for the door. "Tell your boss lady I said it ain't over. She can have Marvin, but she's got it with me now."

"Got what with you, Mrs. Hutchins? What are you talking about?"

Chandelle gave her the same stinging glare she'd flung at the gargantuan mover. "Just tell her that I know what I know."

The brunette stood in the doorway as Chandelle burned rubber out of the parking lot.

* * *

The following afternoon, Marvin exited the hotel refreshed and looking forward to getting back to his life. Dressed for his Tuesday shift, he tried to hash out everything that happened to him over the past two days, but it all ran together with each attempt. When Marvin entered Appliance World, an hour late, Lem, greeted him at the door.

"Marvin, what are you doing here?" he asked. "It's messed up what happened to you." Before Marvin had the chance to discuss how the associate learned of his brief incarceration, another surprise hopped out of the box.

"What's up, convict?" Dooney joked gleefully. He was gleaming with a handful of DVDs that Marvin knew would quickly be dubbed and hawked in the back of the barber shop for ten dollars a pop.

"Not now, Dooney, I've got business," he answered dismissively. "Let me see the man first and I'll holler at you in a minute."

"Cool, I'll be right here handling my own with Reeka."

Marvin dreaded the conversation whereby he'd have to explain himself, not as the wife beater, but rather as a man trapped beneath a heap of circumstances. "Mr. Mercer, I'm innocent and I'm sorry for not calling in late," he rehearsed quietly. "I don't know why I'm getting all worked up. I'm practically running this store, anyway. Yeah, it'll be cool. I'll tell him what happened and that'll be that, just like nothing ever happened."

Marvin tapped on the door before entering. "Hey, Mr. Mercer, you got a second?" he asked, uncomfortable about putting his business on the table to be dissected by an unscrupulous owner with a sex addiction.

"Have a seat, Marvin," the owner offered reluctantly. "How are you making out?" The way Mr. Mercer phrased his salutation told Marvin he had already caught wind of his arrest somehow.

"It's all a misunderstanding, but I'll be all right. Look, I know I missed the sales meeting, but I can explain all that."

Mercer leaned back in his chair and eyed Marvin peculiarly. "No need for any explanations," he sighed.

"Good, then I'll clock in and hit the floor."

"No, not that fast. We've got to set good examples for the other employees. I'm gonna have to fire you."

Marvin's eyes grew wide. His chest swelled. "You're letting me go?" he wailed loudly. "For what, because I missed a sales meeting and came in an hour late?"

"No, Marvin. I'm terminating you over the incident that caused your arrest."

"Incident, what incident?" he asked.

"See, you signed a morality clause on the back of your application. We can't let your arrest go that easy. Now, if it was up to me, I'd let it slide pending the outcome of the trial, but my wife holds fifty-one percent of the company and she ain't having it. Spousal abuse is a serious offense. I should know, had a little issue back in the day myself. I don't want to can my best salesman, but you know, my wife heard about you getting pinched for knocking some sense into yours. While it's none of my business, I have to do it."

"You're right it isn't any of your business, just like who you're screwing in the warehouse, kicking it with after closing hours, or the fact that three of your former cashiers got babies who look exactly like you, isn't any of mine," Marvin smarted back.

"Hey, keep it down. Now you're getting personal."

"Don't fool yourself, Mr. Mercer, it don't get no more personal than not being able to pay the bills."

"I'm sorry you feel that way, and that's why I've added a special lawyer's appropriations bonus to your last paycheck." The stumpy little man slid a white envelope across the desk. "I was shocked when Chandelle called and told me you probably wouldn't be in today because of all the drama."

"Chandelle, she's the one who told you?" Marvin asked, almost as surprised as he was wounded. "Just when I thought it couldn't get any worse." He stood up from the chair, folded the envelope, and then stuffed it into his pocket. "I understand, Mr. Mercer. We all have to do what we gotta do, huh?"

"I'm afraid so, Marvin. Sorry."

All traces of hope that accompanied Marvin when he trekked through the corridor to Mr. Mercer's office had all but vanished into thin air. He found it difficult when Dooney took time off from macking on Reeka to accost him near the front registers.

"Convict, Chandelle called and told me you did the fool and got yoked up by Starsky and Hutch."

Reeka smirked at him. "You should talk. When'd they let *you* out?" she asked Dooney. Marvin would have laughed on any other day but that was impossible at the moment.

"What I want to know is when are you gonna let me in?" Dooney fired at her, with a cocky grin. He'd been imagining how she looked without the khakis and blue pullover, how she looked in nothing at all.

"Tell you what," Reeka said, swinging her hips from right to left with a gang of attitude. "Come over to the house and holla at me, the day after *never.*"

"*Never?*" Dooney's confident grin faded briefly before returning with more exuberance than before. "Girl, quit playin'."

"Who's playing?" Reeka snapped harshly.

"Yeah, it's a game, you acting all stuck-up," Dooney concluded. He saddled her with a thorough once over, licking his lips in the process. "You got to be stuntin'. Ain't no sistah from the west side ever been that saditty."

Reeka rolled her eyes. "It's been a long time since the west side sun went down on me."

Dooney flashed an impish grin. "Who were you doing it with when it did? I might know him."

"Never mind. Why do I even bother?"

" 'Cause you miss the hood and I'm Dooney from the block . . . and then some. Sit down and tell Doo-doo all about it."

Reeka's lip twisted as if she smelled something rank. "Security!"

Marvin shuffled his feet toward the exit doors when Dooney pulled on his elbow from behind. "Hold on, Kinfolk. Where are you going? You just got here and I need a new microwave."

"Mr. Mercer let me go, fired me on the spot."

"Awe, Marvin, that's jacked up. How am I gonna get that friends and family discount now?" Dooney couldn't see past his own dilemma to recognize Marvin's plight. He headed back inside the store looking for option two. "Reeeka!"

13

His Clothes and Her Wrath

Marvin drove the city streets for hours. He'd lost his job and was at a dangerous crossroad in his marriage. Chandelle had become the enemy, without rhyme or reason as far as Marvin was concerned. There was only one person he felt comfortable enough with to discuss the shambles that had become his existence.

Marvin killed the engine in front of a second-rate bar and grill on the south side of town. Duper's was the pride and joy of Dave Headley, the longtime best friend of Marvin's father. Although he never married himself, the seasoned ex-high school basketball legend had seen his share of bad ones to lend a good ear. Marvin was lucky because it was too early in the day for the after-work crowd to swarm the small tavern and start licking their wounds.

"Super-duper Dave," Marvin hailed as he plopped down on a bar stool.

The older man—tall, lanky, clean shaven, gray hair covered partially with a black dye rinse—was dressed in a dated long-sleeved sweater and faded jeans. For a man in his sixties, his soft brown skin was unlined.

Dave had been reading the newspaper when he heard a familiar voice with a tired chord running through it. He peered up from the sports section and shook his head. His eyes found Marvin sitting there with trouble painted all over his face. "Uh-oh, I've seen that look before, just not on you. How bad is it?"

Before Marvin answered, he turned his head to see if anyone was within earshot of his voice. Two retired firemen, who were always there when the doors opened, argued about checkers from one of the back tables. Other than a middle-aged woman singing along with a jukebox, they had the place to themselves.

"Real bad," Marvin replied eventually. "My marriage is over, Dave. Chandelle called my boss and got me fired right after she had the law put the cuffs on me."

While brushing against his chin with the back of his skinny fingers, the barkeeper sighed. "Yep, that's pretty bad all right. You didn't let her catch you with another woman, did you? It was a woman, I hope?" he asked, wide-eyed and wondering. "You're not one of those *Oprah Winfrey Show* tell-all types. They say it can be mighty hard to spot 'em nowadays."

"Come on, Dave, you know me better than that. I love women, women only. Besides, I've been on lockdown, not on the down-low."

Laughing, Dave nodded as he slapped Marvin on the shoulder. "Juuuust checking," he teased. "Your daddy would be spinning in his grave if he knew the son he raised was acting like a daughter." After he opened a can of soda and poured half of it in a drinking glass over ice, Dave tossed a questioning glance at Marvin. "Since you're in it waist deep, you could probably use something stronger than this I'd imagine?"

"Bartender's choice," Marvin told him. He stared at the dusty bottle retrieved from a special place beneath the bar.

"This is a li'l something I keep for especially hard times. Me and your dad, we used to pour a taste when him and your momma were going through it," he explained.

"For real? I never heard a harsh word between them. So even the perfect couple had a rough go at keeping peace in paradise?"

"Your folks were smart at being married, Marvin. They knew that a tiny bit of time apart could calm the waters enough to get back to smooth sailing, that's why your daddy would come here and rest his bony butt right there on the same spot you're occupying now. Uh-huh, Silas would come dragging in after a fight with Margaret doing the Married Man's March like his shoes weighed thirty pounds apiece."

"Super-Dup', I didn't have any of this drama when I was single. I could always up and bounce if things got stupid."

"Yeah, but you're grown now and living a grown man's reality. Marvin, you have a beautiful wife who'd love you funky, broke or bald. For that alone, you are truly blessed and should be thinking on patching things up instead of seeing yourself without her. I was there when you stood in front of all those people saying how you was gonna love her through thick and thin, in good and bad times. Well, this here is one of those thin and bad times."

"Come on, Dave, whose side you on?"

"Can't you tell? Both of yours. I thought you knew, young brotha."

"You don't know how it is. Even before this, Chandelle spent too much money and she was always twisting my words."

"Name me one woman who doesn't do a world of both? That's part of the package deal, son. Listen close on this one because I ran it down to your old man over thirty years ago, when you were just a gleam in his eye. Marvin, having a wife is a wonderful thing when matrimony is working right. You get to touch it, squeeze it, hug and love it, but then every now and then, you also got to listen to it. It's not that bad a deal when you read the fine print."

Marvin hadn't listened attentively until that point. "Hold on, *fine print?*"

"Sure, you know every contract has a gob of fine print at the bottom that nobody gives a care about until things get rocky and they want out of it. Working it out when it appears all is lost is that important because there's nothing better than seeing the other side of a mountain once you've managed to climb it together. That is what you signed your name to, isn't it?"

"For a man who has never gotten close to signing his own contract, you sure do know a lot about it," Marvin challenged, with a renewed smile.

"Young buck, my constitution is too weak. Those who can, do, and those who can't, talk about it. The conversation is on the house, but you owe me seven-fifty for the drink."

Marvin laid a twenty dollar bill on the bar. "Keep the tip. That's the best drink I've ever had. It was very sobering. Thanks, Dave, and thank you for helping my folks stay together too."

Dave raised the bill above his head to examine its authenticity. "Juuuust checking," he laughed.

Marvin couldn't wait to get back to the apartment and sit down with Chandelle, hash things out, and share how much she meant to him and how he couldn't envision life without her. He was also anxious to put his pride in check and tell her why he'd been distant—how he'd been terrified of a home mortgage far and above their means. All of that was behind him, he thought, as he looked forward to climbing his mountain with her by his side.

When Marvin turned the doorknob, he expected to find Chandelle sitting on the sofa, waiting for him to come home and begin patching up the holes in their relationship. The moment he flicked on the light switch inside the apartment, surprise hijacked him and slapped him with a dose of a new reality. There'd be no dutiful wife waiting on his arrival, no immediate patchwork or makeup sex to smooth things over. The havoc-ridden apartment was filled with mere remnants of what Chandelle left behind, his clothes and her wrath.

14

Somebody Slap Me

If there was ever a day to avoid work and call in *tired*, Thursday was it. Chandelle had been up all night putting away her belongings in the new house. She sorted out her dress clothes and shoes in the massive walk-in closet. It was easy to say how pleasant it was to have a 3,500-square foot, five-bedroom home all to herself, but it was another thing altogether believing it. Posh carpeting and a state-of-the-art alarm system didn't nearly offer the comfort and security she enjoyed in the small apartment with Marvin. But Chandelle kept on telling herself that she was better off regardless. The hardwood floor on the lower level, crafted in an expensive parquet arrangement, each of the three full baths exquisitely decorated by the past owner, and the covered patio were all on her must-have list. However, a loving husband to share it with didn't appear on it anywhere. She was living in her own prison without bars or guards. One she'd created unwittingly with Dior's devious assistance. One she'd grown to despise and stand a good chance of losing.

In the noon hour, the first of many delivery trucks

rolled in front of Chandelle's lavish abode. Steinman's Furniture arrived with her order as promised. She was once again ordering strong men around like a circus elephant trainer. "Put that there," she instructed. "No! On second thought, move the sofa and love seat to the other living room," she yelled, unsteady on all of her directives. By the time the delivery men escaped, Chandelle was just as exhausted as they were. She'd never seen three men drive away so fast. After the television satellite installer showed up, a half hour late, she berated him until he completed the job and took off like a shot too. When a set of major appliances arrived, Chandelle threw a fit. The side-by-side refrigerator was too large and the dishwasher didn't match her kitchen décor. "Well, I don't care what I ordered," she spat viciously. "It doesn't look like the one in the catalog, the color is wrong and I'm not paying for it, so y'all can take it back to wherever you got it from." Reluctantly, the men carried the heavy machines back onto the truck. Neither of them had the nerve to hang around for a tip.

Alone again and hating it, Chandelle couldn't stand the expanse of space. She pulled a cell phone out of her purse and stared at the screen. "Shoot, no messages," she growled. "I don't know why I would even think Marvin tried to reach me. He's probably working too hard selling people the right size appliances and in the right color." Just as a trace of a smile tickled her lips, she grabbed her jacket and keys off the brand new beveled glass coffee table and struck out to feed her curiosity. "I know another place they sell what I need."

Chandelle was off to Appliance World with two goals in mind. First, she wanted to get a reaction from Marvin when she sashayed into the store. She'd planned on purchasing replacements for the fridge and dishwasher she had returned, and then rub Marvin's nose in it. If he caused a scene and acted up, she was prepared for that too. Under no circumstances would she fly off the handle. Chandelle was above that, she'd convinced herself, since becoming a responsible homeowner. Her other goal was one she wouldn't readily admit because it was harder than she'd imagined being away from Marvin. The love she'd held for him wasn't as easy to replace as the kitchen appliances. Her husband used to fit perfectly and he came in her favorite color.

With an extra order of wiggle in her stride, Chandelle entered Marvin's former workplace like she owned it. Her spirits were riding high while her intentions scraped the bottom. "Hey, Reeka," she said, greeting one of the only female sales staff members. "Where's . . . I mean, it looks a little slow today." Chandelle craned her neck and peered past Reeka so often that the employee began looking over her shoulder as well.

"What . . . are we looking for, Chandelle?" Reeka asked, knowing it couldn't have been Marvin, seeing as how she was the cause of his termination.

"Nothing, girl, I was just trying to see where y'all's kitchen display was," she said, continuing to scan the showroom.

"You're shopping here?" Reeka queried suspiciously. "Okay, I guess I can ask Mr. Mercer if he'll still let you have the friends and family discount."

Suddenly, Chandelle was more interested in one of Reeka's words than all off the gadgets in the entire store. "Excuse me, but you said *still*. What did you mean by *still*? Marvin is *still* my husband, so I'm *still* entitled."

"Huh, you act as if you don't know Marvin was fired the day after you put your little call in and dimed him out to Mr. Mercer," was Reeka's catty response. When Chandelle's face hit the floor she realized the news hadn't made it home. "Oops," Reeka added as an exclamation point to Chandelle's befuddlement, "I thought you knew."

"Obviously I should have," was Chandelle's humble reply. She had just begun to regret making a lot of decisions. She looked around, noticing that each of the associates was mean-mugging her. "Okay, that explains the dirty looks."

"What we want to know is why the dirty tricks? I mean Marvin is a good guy. You can't make us believe he jumped on you."

Chandelle lowered her head and cinched the zipper on her Chloe handbag. "I don't care what you believe and care less about how you feel about me," she offered assertively. "I guess I'm in the wrong place. There's nothing here I want."

"I could have told you that before you strutted up in here," Reeka told her plainly. "Girl, you've got a good one. Get your business straight."

"You need to manage your own," Chandelle warned.

Reeka smirked. "That's funny," she answered, "coming from you."

"I think this is a good time for you to leave, Chandelle," the owner strongly suggested, stepping in front of Reeka. "We're extremely busy today."

Chandelle bolted through the parking lot in a royal huff. "Who does Reeka think she is," she vented. "Trying to tell me about my husband and all up in my biz. I ought to go back in there and turn it out. That's what I ought to do. They don't know about me." Her handbag rang as she seethed in the parking lot. "What?" she answered rudely.

"Ooh, see I was about to hip you to something, but I don't need ugliness in my afternoon," Dior fussed playfully. "I've had an ugly-free day 'til now so don't jack it up."

"What do you want, Dior? I'm fresh out of money."

"So," she hissed, "I've got plenty of cheese, but thanks

for offering. I was calling to ask you to dinner when I stopped by this cute wine boutique they opened next to the grocery store on Skillman and Whitehurst, then before me very eyes, who do I see?"

"I'm not trying to play any games, so you'll have to tell me," Chandelle stated quickly.

"You'll ruin the suspense, but here's the lick. I saw Marvin go in. Yeah, I was about to run over and speak to him, you know, and see how my cousin-in-law is making out, but then I saw that chick who dropped him off from jail go in right behind him, like they wasn't together, together. You know I want y'all to work things out, but somebody needs to get some answers about their *affiliation* because they're getting way too chummy for my taste." Dior held the phone. She could hear Chandelle fuming on the other end.

Honestly enough, Dior had seen Marvin enter the grocery and Kim did enter the same store five minutes later; but it was pure coincidence and nothing like it was presented. However, Dior was ready to whip up additional lies to sabotage their sinking love boat if necessary. She had jotted down several of them while following Marvin that afternoon.

"Yeah, it's way past chummy for me too," Chandelle said, venom dripping from her lips. "Stay there. If they leave together, call me back. I'm on my way."

15

Fools in Love

After four days of questioning every aspect of his life and how it could have turned on him so viciously, Marvin found himself wandering through the aisles at the supermarket. With two arms full of perishables to restock his barren pantry, a smile came over Marvin, when he literally bumped into Kim and her precious 4-year-old, Danni. "Ahh, I'm sorry, Miss," he apologized, when turning directly into their shopping cart. Packages of chips and microwavable pasta dishes flew from his hands to litter the aisle.

Danni squealed with delight. "Yay, tell him to do it again, mommy."

"I don't think that's a good idea, sweetheart," Kim said to her daughter as well as to *him*. "Marvin's having a bad enough week as it is."

"Kim, I really am . . ." he started to say before she waggled her finger in his face.

"No need for another sorry." Actually, she was growing weary of apologies from a man who appeared to have it together before agreeing to house shop. "But did you honestly think that you'd make it to the checkout stand with all that?"

Marvin chuckled. "Yeah, actually, I did. I figured, you know, that shopping for one might not require a cart."

Kim wrinkled her brow while Marvin collected his groceries off the floor. "Shopping for one?" she asked, as if it were a huge piece of a bigger puzzle.

"That's right. You couldn't know what postjail has been like for me."

"Why don't you put your things in my cart, in front of the boxes of Frosted Flakes," she offered, "and I'll let you in on a thing or two." Much to the chagrin of an excitable child looking forward to another loaf of bread to go whizzing by her face, Marvin carefully placed his items inside of the wire cart, with big boxes of cold cereal separating his things from theirs. "Did Chandelle tell you that she came to see me earlier this week?" Kim inquired cautiously.

"No, I haven't spoken with her at all," Marvin said with regret. "I'm not sure there's anything we'd agree on discussing."

"Uh-huh, I thought that was about the size of it," Kim said. "I got a call that Chandelle showed up at the office, huffing and puffing and accusing me of being on the down-down with you."

"Down-down?"

"Yeah, that's what Kristy called it, but I think she got the message confused. I'm sure Chandelle thought there was something between us. Obviously she found out I paid your bail and drew her own conclusions from there. Take it from me, not knowing about your husband is a monster to deal with."

Marvin grabbed the cart handle with both hands. Kim accompanied him, stopping to make additional selections as he tried to make sense of things in his scrambled mind. Danni, with her little legs swinging from the seat, glared at Marvin with her arms folded. "Kim, you wouldn't know it, but I do not handle my affairs like this. I can't take all the credit for the jacked-up state of things, but I wish it would stop."

"I can understand how she'd be upset, coming to find out her man has been released on another woman's dime. You should have predicted at least that."

"Maybe so," he admitted, "but there wasn't any way to predict getting fired and all of the furniture looted from the apartment. Chandelle has taken things too far."

Kim cleared her throat as she placed a liter of grape juice in the cart. "Uh, did you bother talking to her before calling me? Ah-ha, thought not."

"I couldn't get by at being your man either," he jested. "You're hard on a brotha."

"My man wouldn't have to call anyone else if he found himself in trouble, and besides, it pays to be hard on occasion. Some women like it rough. Me, I like it hard." After Kim witnessed Marvin's mouth pop open, she took one calculated step back. "Now I'm apologizing. That came out wrong and sounded despicable." *Actually, it came out just as I thought it would, with some heat on it,* Kim thought to herself. "Okay, let's pump the brakes. Chandelle's decision to pack up and move into the house alone is one thing that has nothing to do with me. However, you having no way to pay me back, now that's a Kim and Marvin problem."

While studying the price of dry spaghetti noodles and sauce, Marvin agreed. "Yes, true. I still can't believe after being the top salesman for four years that the owner of a store just up and let me go after Chandelle complained to him. Mr. Mercer said he didn't want to but his wife wasn't having 'no wife beater' working at the family business. I wonder what she'd have to say about the cashiers' kids who look just like him."

"She won't hear it from you because that's not your concern," Kim answered near the toiletries. "He lost a valuable employee but the question is, what are you going to do about it?"

Marvin reached for the bath soap Chandelle liked before it occurred to him that she wouldn't be around to use it. He picked up a three-pack of Irish Spring instead. "Well, until I figure it out, I'm going to hibernate in my empty cave."

Kim found it difficult not to laugh in Marvin's pitiful face. "She really took everything?"

"Everything that wasn't nailed down and a few things that were," he answered jokingly. "I'll swing by and pick up a bag of apples and meet you at the register to divvy up the goods if that's okay with you."

"No, I have some produce on my list too," Kim offered, not ready to part ways just yet. "Who knows, maybe you can make another mess over there. Danni would love that."

"Yay, do it again," the giggling little girl cooed with optimum zeal. "Do it again."

Chandelle considered it good fortune that she was a few minutes away from the grocery store when receiving the call from Dior. Her intuition was working overtime yet again. The chance that she would have the perfect vantage point to see Marvin and Kim together was a divine coincidence. On the short drive over, she prepared for one heck of a fight. "I'ma set this right," she heard herself say, in a tone that reeked with unbridled insolence. "Humph, I'll see what Marvin has to say about running around with that freak in sheep's clothing and in public like he's single. Ain't nobody

gonna shame me like this. Just wait 'til I roll up on 'em.
I'ma set it off!"

Chandelle flew down the streets of Dallas weaving in
and out of traffic like a NASCAR driver zooming toward a
checkered flag. "Move!" she screamed at an elderly driver
teetering down the avenue below the speed limit. "Come
on . . . come on . . . move!" With reckless abandon, Chandelle cut off a pickup truck to make her turn into the supermarket parking lot. "Whatever!" she howled, when the
truck driver cursed at her for putting his life in danger.
"Yeah, then you're another one." Circling the collection
of parked cars, Chandelle spotted Dior waving her hands
near the front of the store. "Uh-huh, I see you, cuz. It's
about to be on now. I should have brought my pepper
spray." She rolled into a handicap parking space and
hopped out with her pricey handbag dangling from her
clenched fist.

Dior drew in a deep breath as Chandelle stomped in
her direction. "Hold on a tick," Dior said, grabbing the
human tornado by the arm. "I said wait!" Dior exhaled
slowly, then positioned herself so that Chandelle couldn't
dismiss her grave expression and exacting plea.

"What, why are you holding me?" Chandelle asked,
with her heart beating like a college drum line. "Come on
so you can hold my purse."

"Uh-uh, Marvin and them ain't going nowhere, but I
need to be straight on something. I don't want to be in
y'all's mix so you cannot tell Marvin I was the one who
ratted on him."

Chandelle squinted. Her eyes narrowed into thin slits
as she tried to understand why Dior was adamant about
being discharged from duty before the confrontation en-
sued. *Something isn't on the level here*, she thought. *Dior's
usually up for a fight, especially if she's the one watching
it*. "Okay, I'll keep it to myself, but we're going to speak

on this later," Chandelle told her, while pulling off her earrings. "It's time to be about mine." She left Dior standing alone and determined to ruin a successful marriage.

While stalking the grocery store aisles, Chandelle was fuelled by what Dior had put in her mind. What she did discover in the produce section made her nauseous. Marvin was pushing a grocery cart with a little girl aboard. Chandelle couldn't believe it. *Has he already jumped into a fling and started playing baby-daddy?* she feared, before staring up at the ceiling. "Lord, please forgive me for what I might say in front of this child, but I'm about to go slap off on her momma," she said. Her life was spiraling downward and nothing on earth could stop it, including her desire to save face.

"I knew it!" Chandelle spat as she hurled herself toward them. "I knew you were up to some mess when I carried my behind downtown to see about getting you out of jail. So, how long you've been tapping her, Marvin? Huh, tell me how long you and this Single-Momma *Barbie* been getting all chummy like this? Okay, I can admit to jamming you up. That was on me, but this, *this* is unacceptable. Imagine me losing sleep over you in the county. Now that you got street cred' for being locked up, yellow women ain't good enough for you no more, Marvin?" Chandelle was talking so fast and furiously that she didn't notice how her tirade drew attention from other shoppers. Danni covered both ears with her tiny hands, then buried her face in Marvin's chest. He laid his hand over her head and glanced down.

"As for you," Chandelle said, sneering at Kim from head to toe as if sickened by every inch of her, "you thought you were slick, smiling in my face while creeping around my back door."

"Chandelle, you need to lower your voice and calm yourself," Marvin asserted, while heeding his own advice.

"You don't have any reason showing up and talking about what is and isn't acceptable. I'm the one with a felony charge hanging over me. Me, not you! I'm the one who went in to work to find out my wife had a hand in getting that twisted too." When he realized his voice had elevated, Marvin backed down for the sake of Danni. "The only thing between me and Kim is her generosity. Yeah, I called her and she came through. Whatever crazy ideas you got in that hard head of yours have nothing to do with me."

Kim was poised while taking in the spectacle. She'd been involved in a scene like this one previously, although it caught her on the other end as her ex-husband's mistress confronted her for messing up an extramarital affair when the rent was due. Kim saw through Chandelle's paper-thin bravado for what it truly was, a desperate plea to be heard. As her eyes darted back and forth from Danni to Chandelle's finger pointing, she decided it was more prudent not to offer an opinion since she hadn't been asked for any.

"You need to back off and go back to *your* new house," Marvin huffed. "At least you have something to sit on while you give some thought on how we got crossways."

"Shows just how little you know about me," Chandelle debated smugly. "I'm sure your girlfriend told you about my early move-in arrangements, but here's something you didn't know. I put our furniture out on the street for the Salvation Army to swoop up. And another thing, I'm living all to the good with a whole 'slew of new.' Uh-huh, that's what's up. I pimped out the house and still have the tags hanging off every piece of furniture I ordered. That's right, I'm upscale now and digging it."

"You didn't?" was Marvin startled reply. "While I'm dealing with all this, you threw out our stuff and went on a shopping spree?"

"Why not?" Chandelle fired back. "I'm living single just like you."

"Forget that nonsense," he countered, "where's all this new money of yours coming from? I'm scrappin' and you're buying out the mall?" Marvin raised Danni out of the shopping cart and gingerly passed her to Kim before directing his utter shock toward his wife. "Chandelle, keep playing games like this . . . you're gonna fool around and get yourself hurt."

"Well, you already took care of that by nuzzling up to her," she snarled viciously. "So, I decided to get even." Chandelle cast a nasty scowl at Kim, who hadn't seemed all that concerned over the woman's rants.

"You'd better check your step, Chandelle," Kim warned finally, as the store manager came tramping up behind their war of words.

"Too bad you're in my step," Chandelle answered hastily. "You don't have anything on me. I'm his first love, his first!"

"Whoa, hold on!" the manager shouted. He approached the scene like a crossing guard who had taken his small amount of authority with a bit of overexuberance. With his hands spread apart, he wedged himself in the middle. "Ma'am, sir, I don't know anything about who's first or last, but I don't want it discussed further in here. Please figure out a way to settle this or somebody's got to go."

"No stress," Chandelle sighed. "I'm already gone." She turned to walk away, mad at herself, mad at Marvin, and mad at the world in general. She exited the supermarket with less than she entered with, her shortage of self-respect was only the half of it. Chandelle predicted Marvin had no choice other than to outright hate her when he did attempt to use his debit card for the groceries. She'd cleaned out both bank accounts and their savings the day before.

Back in the produce jungle, Kim held her daughter tightly, beginning to have second thoughts about stepping out on a limb for Marvin. In a matter of days, his wife had run out on him, he'd found himself unemployed, and she aptly recognized what was invisible to Marvin and Chandelle—they were still madly in love with each other but didn't know what to do about it.

16

Good Move, Wrong Game

Friday night at eight o'clock, a herd of wadded tissue paper huddled on the angular beveled glass coffee table in Chandelle's second living room. Dior listened attentively, taking mental notes, as her cousin recounted the past twenty-six hours and how they seemed to pile on one another to build a monstrous hedge around what used to be love. Chandelle drew both sock-covered feet up from the floor and tucked them under her housecoat like a teenager turning inward for comfort. "Yeah, it was just like you said, Dior. I searched every aisle in that grocery store until running upon them in the produce section. I got so angry it was hard not to march up and knock Marvin upside his head. If I hadn't promised not to, I'd hate to think how I might have played myself."

"And they were actually together, I mean, when you caught them . . . together?" Dior prodded.

"Uhhh-huh," Chandelle answered, wiping her nose with another fistful of tissues. "Just like you said they'd be. Marvin was pushing a shopping cart, with Kim's daughter in it. That hurt me, too, but I refused to let them know. It was bad enough seeing him with that chick and playing Unca' Marvin on the side. There's no telling how long they've been hooking up. It didn't seem brand new because the little girl was so attached to Marvin. You should have seen the way she threw herself into him when I cracked the case."

Ooh, this is better than I'd hoped for, Dior thought. *That lady was probably using her daughter to snag Marvin, knowing men are such suckers for baby girls. Good move, if I have to say so myself.* "Chandelle, do you really think Marvin's been creeping on you with her?" she asked, doubting that he could have pulled that off while she'd been tailing him during the daytime. Although Dior couldn't be sure because her late-night moneymaking enterprises kept her tired after dark. "I mean, she don't strike me as the type he'd try to get at. I mean, she's even older than him."

Chandelle sniffled again and nodded her agreement. "Kim is old, probably thirty-five. She is fly, though in a midthirty-something sort of way, but come on, you saw her. I can't figure out what she has on me or what she's doing to my husband that I wasn't doing."

Chandelle stared into space for the longest time. She didn't want to believe that Marvin was the kind of man to put up an extra piece on the side, but nothing seemed clear. "Want to hear the strangest thing, cuz?" Chandelle said, after a lengthy stream of silence. "A week ago, I would have killed for my man. And I'm talking about digging a hole to hide the body. Now, I'm not so sure I'd cross the street to save his life. I know how it looks, but I thought Marvin was better than this."

Dior was presented with another opportunity to cast further confusion, so she took it. "Listen to me, Chandelle, Marvin had me fooled too. I always thought the best of him because of how good he treated you, but now he's moved on to sampling some dark meat." When Chandelle's chest began to swell with grief at the thought of him sampling anything Kim had to offer, Dior tried to backpedal as quickly as possible to appear neutral. "Wait a minute, I didn't mean to imply that Marvin's been freaking, I mean, slapping skins with someone else. No, that's not what I meant either. Okay, look, you are a married woman who's got to figure some things out for herself, that's all I'm saying. There is a lot of cool in Marvin, let's not forget that."

"That is true," Chandelle whined softly, as a single tear ran from her face. "Before all the drama started, he would have breathed for me if I asked him to. He's probably breathing for Kim now."

He'd better not be, Dior thought. *If anyone's gonna be sharing his breath, It'll be me.* "Now that's hard to imagine," she said resentfully. "I can't see it going down like that. Uh-uh, not even a little bit."

"Wow, Dee, that's sweet of you to stick up for Marvin. Maybe I should believe in him as strongly as you do?"

"Huh, well, uh, I was only saying how it would be hard for me to accept him putting it to another woman is all," she replied uneasily, careful not to push Chandelle back over the hedge dividing them. "I'm not feeling that." Instinctively, Dior's jaws clenched against the backdrop of mere discussions of Marvin's infidelity, considering how it didn't involve her like she wanted. The game she'd initiated with other people's lives was in full swing despite the next move by an unsuspected player. A knock at the door sent her reeling. "Who—who's that?" Dior stammered.

"It's probably just Dooney," Chandelle answered, getting up to answer the door.

"Dooney?" Dior repeated anxiously, as if he were the black plague wanting to get in. "Why is he here?"

"I asked him to come by for a man's perspective. He

might act like he doesn't know better, but I know different. Dooney's here to help, and Lord knows I could use all I can get."

That's what I'm afraid of, Dior admitted silently. *That's just what I need, a meddling know-it-all, and Dooney's the worst.* Dior sank deeper against the sofa cushion, wishing she could disappear altogether. She and her fraternal twin brother were separated by a few minutes at birth, but he'd been locked on and looking into her soul since she could remember. Dior felt sick to her stomach with mounting apprehensions that Dooney would gaze into her eyes and somehow see that she had been working her scheming and conniving angle like a part-time job. If Chandelle said too much, he'd throw two and two together and then quickly throw her under that bus of hers. More often than not, he knew her better than she knew herself.

"Nice house you got here, Chandelle," Dooney said, while offering a warm, brotherly embrace. He surveyed the foyer, porcelain tile, Chandelle's exquisite taste in furniture, and then her dubious choice in houseguests. The moment his eyes landed on Dior, he shook his head. "Yeah, nice place, except for the ornery smudge on your couch. You'd better get to scrubbing now or it might not ever come out. What's up, Gemini?" he said to his sister, using the two-faced nickname he felt best suited her.

"Dooney," said Dior dismissively. She pouted and avoided eye contact as best she could without making it obvious.

"It's a mighty fine palace, cuz," Dooney reiterated to set the bait. "Funny, it looks kinda empty, though. Yeah, the word is out on you, stunting and whatnot. Before you dialed me up, I'd already heard you done ran your husband off." Dooney assumed the same paternal role Chandelle had always counted on in the past. Somewhere down the line, Dooney developed an unrivaled ability to grasp a situation and hammer out the details in no time flat. Dior found his talent unnerving when unsolicited, but valuable when called upon. This was a good time to keep her mouth shut before saying something Dooney could rip apart and turn inside out until shaking the truth from it. It worked when they were younger and even though he'd spent two years in prison his skills were sharp as ever. The power of discernment is the term their mother pinned to it. Spotting a lie wrapped around the truth is what Dior reasoned. Looking beyond the deception, that was Dooney's gift.

After Chandelle returned to her perch beside Dior, she cleared her throat. "I don't care what the word on the street is," she spat irritably. "I didn't run him off."

"What the . . ." he shouted, before sliding both hands inside front pockets of his starched jeans. "Okay, hold on, y'all. I said I was gonna stop cussing." The ladies observed as he counted backward from ten to five slowly per the instructions in the last anger management self-help book he read. "There . . . That's much better, Dooney," he said, speaking to himself. "Now then, Chandelle, your man is gone, agreed?" Reluctantly, she nodded her head. "Can I get a word up?" he asked, to elicit genuine emotion from Chandelle.

"Aghhh, Dooney, I hate when you do it this way," she fussed. "Why can't I just tell you what happened and you tell me what you think about it?"

"Because this is the 'Dooney Show'," he told her, "and I, like Oprah–Dr. Phil-and-'em, get to run things as I see fit. I could come right out and ask you what you did to the dude to make him bolt, but then I'd only get your side of the story. What has that gotten you so far?" He raised his brow to ward off any unwarranted comments from Dior, who despised this form of relationship interrogation more than Chandelle did.

"I'll start by telling you what I know about the situation, and then you can lay your hands on it," he finished.

"Why should you go first?" Chandelle complained.

"'Cause this fool loves to hear himself philosophize, that's why," answered Dior.

"Okay, your first mistake, Chandelle, was eliciting the advice of a woman concerning how to keep a man, when she is chronically without one to call her own."

Chandelle hadn't thought of that.

"Next, I am certain that Marvin was chased away against his will because I have never, ever, met such a sappy brotha so in love with his woman," Dooney continued. "Chandelle, Marvin is driving an old SUV that I wouldn't be caught dead in so that he could save for a house that he doesn't have keys to, he's pulled double shifts so that y'all wouldn't be broke and hungry when you moved in here, and he loves you so much that he went to work on time day after day. Now, if that ain't love, you can cancel my program and pull my sponsorship."

Chandelle smiled for the first time all day. "I'll admit it, that makes me feel a smidge better," she said, with her lips tightening after that. "But, what about Marvin letting another woman bail him out of jail? Huh? What about that?"

"Uh-huh! What about that?" Dior chimed in.

"Listen to my answer to that. So?" he blasted them. "If a three-ton transvestite wanted to spring for my freedom papers, I'd let him, depending on how it was dressed at the time, you understand. Marvin was in jail. Jail! His wife gave the cops the go-ahead to take him, although it was a mistake. And then, when his feet did hit the concrete, his woman done called the job and got him eliminated."

"Terminated," Chandelle corrected him.

"Yeah, just making sure you're paying attention," he joked, behind a straight face. "And now, for the coup de grâce with the cherry on top. From what I understand, Marvin came home after sleeping off his time in the clink to a house full of nothing. All that is very odd because I don't see one thing I recognize but somebody sprinkling discontentment around somebody else's back door."

Dior leaped from the sofa in a heated fury. "You can't be talking about me, Dooney. I only reported to Chandelle what I saw, Marvin and that Kim Hightower chick when she dropped him by the apartment in her fancy whip," she explained before he interrupted her.

"Hightower, did you say Kim Hightower?"

"Yeah, why?" Dior hissed.

"See, 'cause she's something special. I used to be sprung on her. She taught at the school when she finished college, and boy I can't tell you what she used to do to me by just coming into the room."

"Well, now she's doing it to Marvin?" Chandelle heckled.

Dooney began pacing back and forth before resuming his role a shade-tree swami. "Dior, you told Chandelle that Marvin was kicking it with Kim Hightower?"

"Yes!"

"How do you know that for a fact?" he challenged.

"I saw her dropping him off at the apartment and then later at the grocery store," she boasted proudly.

"You saw them doing what at the store, shopping for groceries?"

"Wait a minute, Dooney," Chandelle spoke up. "Dior called me and I went into the store and caught them."

"Hmm, this is interesting. You caught them doing what exactly?" he asked, preparing to start picking at the lie he was then certain had come from the dramatic stylings of Dior Wicker.

Chandelle wrinkled her nose as she played back the scenario in her head. "Since you think you know everything, *Dr. Dooney,* I shouldn't tell you jack, but I will. They were in a close-faced discussion when I *caught* them," she said, recounting the scene.

"Okay, let's see, Kim's baby was in the shopping basket and Marvin was behind it."

"Was he kissing on Kim?"

"No, but . . ."

"Was he kissing on Kim's baby like he'd been spending a lot of time around her?"

"No, but I got you there," Chandelle hollered. "The little girl placed her hands over her ears and shoved her head into Marvin's chest when I . . . went . . . smooth . . . off and probably scared the daylight out of her." Suddenly, Chandelle didn't feel so good. It occurred to her that she might have taken everything too far too fast.

"I'm amazed at you, Chandelle. I never would have expected to see you working so hard to prove Marvin doesn't love you. If you ask me, he's better off where he is. I'm not so sure you still deserve a man like him. Maybe you ought to go on over to the apartment and see for yourself. Oh, and a few words of wisdom, don't take Dior with you."

"Forget you, Dooney!" Dior groaned. "You make me sick."

"I love you, too, Gemini," he said, "and Billie would love to hear from you sometime. You can't stay mad at her forever, and you'd better not try either. People make mistakes; you more than most. Don't forget that while you're sitting in judgment." After touring the rest of the house and taking his bows, Dooney wished Chandelle good luck and better common sense going forward. As for Dior, he checked her on his way out. "Don't leave here thinking I don't know what's going on with you running interference between Chandelle and Marvin. Keep it up and I'll lay it all out on the table so everybody can read it, line for line." Dior didn't dare go up against him, instead, she pursed her lips and pouted.

"Next time you won't find out what I'm up to," she whispered after he was gone. "I'll break out the slick kit on the next go around. This isn't nearly over, not by a long shot."

17

The Bed I Made

Chandelle sent Dior away so she could think. She put on her tightest jeans, the low-rise Apple Bottoms that Marvin bought for her last birthday. After she slipped into a fresh-out-the-box pair of black suede pumps to accentuate a long-haired jacket she saved three months to treat herself to, Chandelle walked a path in her thick eggshell-colored carpet. Rehearsing, she wrung her hands over and over trying to find the right words to make things right again. There had to be something she could tell Marvin to make him feel about her the way he had before the ill-fated Sunday when the love they shared quit on them like an old secondhand car along a stretch of bad road. Of all the speeches and practical one-liners she practiced repeatedly, "Baby, I'm sorry" wasn't one of them. Still unable to woman-up and concede her part in the tragic scene playing out on the main stage of their lives, Chandelle was holding back. She had to learn how a halfhearted apology didn't amount to much when her back was against the wall, just before it went tumbling down.

"All right, Chandelle, you're ready for this," she told

herself on the drive over to Marvin's place. "Just tell him how you feel and get him back. He loves you, girl; that's gotta be worth something. Humph, I sure hope it's enough." As she pulled into the parking space next to his vehicle, Chandelle remembered what Dooney said about Marvin sacrificing for the greater good of their future when she had always assumed that he was being a cheapskate. She took a deep breath and knocked at the door, wondering what else she'd overlooked and misunderstood about her husband. Becoming nervous to the point of running away, Chandelle's hands trembled when the doorknob twisted to open.

"What?" was Marvin's cold salutation. Every light in the house was off because he hadn't paid the electric bill, which was formally paid for via automatic draft. Since Chandelle took the money and broke camp, Marvin sat in the dark during the night and slept as much as he could in the daytime. His whole world had flipped on him.

"Hey," she replied uneasily as she stared at the ground, expecting him to pull the door wider and let her inside. When he blocked the opening with his bare chest, Chandelle's eyes filled with sadness. "You're going to make me stay out here? I came to talk, not shout, accuse you of anything, or pick another fight, just talk." It seemed like an eternity for Marvin to decide how he'd proceed. "I could just come back if you're in the middle of something," she said, hoping he didn't have someone in his apartment, the love nest they shared for three years. A long train of moments crawled by until he answered.

"You can come on in, but it's late," he said, sounding more bothered than upset with her.

Perhaps he was genuinely too tired to make a fuss, she pondered, or maybe he'd simply given up on himself and on them. "Thank you," Chandelle mouthed humbly. *At least he hasn't gotten on with his life without me yet*, she thought. After seeing the bare walls of the apartment with the aid of the streetlights from the outside, Chandelle caught a telling glimpse of what she'd left Marvin to work with. There was a plastic lawn chair placed in the middle of the room, facing the window. On the other side of the room was a pile of clothes, more than likely dirty from the stale smell permeating the living room. Another whiff backed Chandelle up a step. "Do you mind if I open the blinds and crack a window?" she asked, praying he'd say yes.

"Oh, I got it," he said, chuckling on the inside. "Too funky for your taste, huh?" Marvin grabbed the first shirt off the pile and slipped in on over his head. He pulled the cord to raise the blinds, then eased the window open an inch.

Come on, Marvin, I know you smell yourself, she wanted to say but thought better of it. This was the man's home, after all. *If he can stand it, so can I,* she concluded with great difficulty.

"So," he said, with both hands shoved deep down into his front pockets. "What'd you forget? That is why you came by? I'm sorry but the lady who used to live here gave away all that she couldn't carry."

Chandelle shifted her weight while gazing at Marvin. Through muted light, the apartment appeared abandoned. She could tell he hadn't shaved in days, bathed either, and if she had to guess, he probably hadn't left the apartment since his grocery store run the day before. "Marvin, I didn't forget anything," she said quietly. "That's not why I'm here." She kicked playfully with her boot at a candybar wrapper lying on the floor. "On second thought, that's exactly why I came back. Somehow I forgot how much we've meant to each other, how much I love you. If I had remembered, there would have been no reason for me to leave and no place for me to go, not without you." *Wow, that came out better than I rehearsed it.* "Believe it or not, I also came by to see about you. I'd like to know what you've been up to . . . what you've been thinking."

"You really don't want to go there because every place I've been, you've sent me," he answered calmly. "Jail, you did that. The unemployment line, you. Me ending up dang near homeless . . . you again. You took me to another place I never expected to see, at a time when I'd be ashamed to have you as my wife."

"Okay, I accept using poor judgment when the police came beating on the door, but you turned your back on me when inviting Kim into our marriage," Chandelle countered. "Another woman had no place, no business getting involved. It's always been me and you, Marvin, no matter how rough we had it, *me and you*," she reiterated to make her point. "I didn't know what to do after they took you away, but when I tried to figure something out to fix the mistake I'd made, your friend had beat me to it." Chandelle hadn't rehearsed that part. It came from the heart, unabridged and real.

"Is that it?" Marvin asked, looking past her.

"I don't have anything else to say except that I still love you and hope you won't throw that away. We can get past Kim, me calling your boss, and me letting my emotions get in the way of us. Can't you see how torn up I am over this? I can't focus at work and I can't sleep a wink in that big house by myself." Suddenly, Chandelle went to a place she hadn't expected to find herself, groveling at his rusty feet. "Come on, Marvin," she pleaded, while collecting his dirty clothing from the floor. "Baby, get your things and come home. They have 'Connected Couples' counseling at the church on Wednesday nights and . . . you know, for people like us. I've found other groups to help too." Chandelle thought her idea to get assistance with their struggling marriage sounded like a great beginning to move from the rough spot in their relationship.

"Put those things down," he ordered curtly.

"What, baby? We can come back tomorrow and get the rest if you want."

"No, put it all back on the floor," he said somberly. "This is home. This is where and how I live now. The only thing I'll have time for is finding a job to pay for a lawyer. I don't need some messed-up couples trying to get into my business. Besides, you've helped us enough already. Matter of fact, I can't hardly stand to look at you. Get out of what's left of my house before you jack up something else."

"Marvin, no!" she objected. "I said I was sorry."

"Oops, wrong again. Until now that's never come out of your mouth. You've gotten me confused with the old Marvin, the one who put you ahead of him. That dude doesn't live here anymore." He began backing Chandelle toward the door. She pressed her hands against his chest and clenched her fists to hold on to him. "You need to bounce now. I've got things to do."

"Marvin, honey. I understand why you're upset but please don't do this. I've never been good at apologies and you know that. It's not an excuse but when I saw you at the store with that lady, that realtor, I lost it. It's not going to last between y'all Marvin. It can't." Chandelle dug her heels into the carpet until one of them snapped in half. Marvin continually nudged her in the other direction until she was clearly through the door. "It's that woman, Marvin," Chandelle panted hysterically. "She's got you treating me like this. You belong with me. Don't push me away."

"Get out!" he insisted.

Chandelle scuffled feverishly to get back inside as Marvin's stiff arms prevailed. "I won't let it end like this. What about us?"

"You must be crazy. I'm living with what you thought about us. You showed your tail enough for a lifetime. You wanted it, you got it. There is no us."

"Marvin, please don't. You're gonna want me back!" she screamed from the parking lot, crying and waving her broken shoe at him like a vicious vendetta. "You'll see, Marvin. You're gonna want me back!"

Marvin hesitated a moment before slamming the door. His next five words hurt Chandelle more than she imagined mere words could have.

"I don't want you now."

Tears stained Chandelle's cheeks as she hobbled on one heel to her car. She searched her purse for keys that seemed to be hiding from her. "You'll see. I'm better for you," she muttered pitifully. "I'm your wife, Marvin, and I came back on my hands and knees. Through all that, you couldn't find it in your heart to call me by my name, not once." Just then she slid into the car, wiped runny mascara on her coat sleeve, and pressed the power window button to lower it. "Chandelle Hutchins, that's my name," she belted, with her head sticking out. "*Hutchins,* and I ain't about to give it up. You hear me? I'm not about to let you quit me. Not like this." Chandelle wiped at her face again to clear her eyes as she barreled out of the parking lot with several of Marvin's neighbors sneering at her.

Unnoticed, Dior was hidden in a car across the street and had heard every word. She wanted to run to Marvin, offer comfort or whatever else he'd have been willing to accept from her, but duty called. Dior was scheduled to perform at a private birthday party for an exclusive client and she was running behind. "Don't worry about that, Marvin," she said, as if he could hear her voice. "I'll be around to see about you. Don't worry."

18

No She Didn't!

One week ago, Dior deemed it necessary to take her game to appalling new heights and all-time lows after spending several hours a day pleading with hiring managers to grant her interviews. But because her employment history read like a collection of unfinished short stories, not one of them complied. In a moment of desperation, she adorned herself in the most lascivious outfit she owned and hit the boulevards, visiting several topless clubs to exploit her best assets. She mingled with the exotic dancers, ran into some acquaintances she'd grown up with, and seriously contemplated a career change that involved deviant behavior and cash-paying customers. Although the thought of working in darkened smoke-filled rooms with men who'd most certainly drink too much didn't appeal to her, lonely men dishing out twenty dollars per lap dance to ogle and grope her shapely curves gave her an idea she couldn't pass up.

After spotting the very same woman who'd replaced her at Kevlin's apartment, she quickly resolved that the occurrence was water under the bridge. Isis was the professional name Dior's newest friend had been given when entering the realm of dirty dancing eighteen months ago. Since she obviously didn't mind taking her clothes off for perfect strangers, Dior decided to share her latest brainchild. In a matter of minutes, a scandalous partnership called *Ladies DI 4 Rent* was formed. Isis thought the company moniker was catchy, encompassing both of their initials in a promising joint venture. Dior almost laughed at the woman's gullibility, because to her it stood for "Ladies Doing It for the Rent." She wasn't sure if Isis was down for "doing it" as easily as she appeared eager to act it out on the main stage, but all of Kevlin's girls were super freaky so she didn't doubt it. Determined to hire themselves out as late-night entertainment for high-powered men who had everything including money to burn, Dior and Isis placed a provocative ad in the leading swinger rags about town. From the time the periodicals hit the shelves, their phone line was ringing off the hook.

Experiencing extreme difficulty keeping up with the overwhelming demand at $500 an hour, they increased their fees 100 percent and scaled back the clientele to the wealthiest thrill seekers in Dallas. Money was coming in so fast that Dior had a hard time believing it was real. And in the midst of it all, she had begun to slip farther away from reality. She hadn't considered the ramifications of sin for profit and the dangers that accompanied it. None of that occurred to her as she scooped up Isis and sped across town to make their ten-thirty date in Highland Park, the city's most exclusive community where blue bloods and old money held hands like lovers on a slow stroll.

The rendezvous point was a 2.5-million-dollar mansion, with eight bedrooms, six full baths, and two kitchens. As Dior read the handwritten address from her appointment book, Isis's eyes almost fell out of her head. "Ooh, girl, this is a lot of house," she marveled, gawking at the grandiose estate from the street.

"I know, it is big, huh?" Dior contended as well. She cruised past the main entrance and puttered her Escort around to the rear driveway.

"Why did you come all the way back here?" Isis asked, wearing a peculiar frown.

"Because the woman who called in the date said to be sure to use the servant's entrance. Heck, I didn't care. We're both getting a grand for this."

"At least a thousand dollars?" she said, her voice rising with excitement. "Each?"

"At least," Dior informed her. "Work your magic right and we might come out with a lot more paper than that."

Isis's smile returned with lingering vigor. "Let's be about our magic, then. Ladies DI is on the job," she said sensually, while gazing at her fresh makeup in the flip-down vanity mirror. "I had my eye on this bad Missoni dress at the mall. Uh-huh, it's over two grand, but I know a dude who'll boost it for one, and he don't have a lay-away plan." Both of them chuckled, primped another minute, then called the cell phone number that came with the address.

The same woman's voice that left the directions answered and instructed them to enter at the back door inside the courtyard. Dior strutted past an oval fountain with her game face on, painted and poised, and wearing a tailored business suit, with a skirt cut above mid thigh.

Isis, wrestling with the hem of her golden nylon gown, done up in an Egyptian motif, struggled to keep pace. "Wait up, Dior, shoot. This material is caught on my heel."

"Keep up, then," Dior whispered urgently. "I told you about overdoing it on the costume. These people pay to see it come off, anyway."

Isis paused as she passed by the fountain several paces behind Dior. Her eyes widened as she glanced into the water. "There's real fish swimming around in there. Uhm, what rich people won't do to throw their money away. Those fish aren't even big enough to eat."

"Hush, Isis, somebody's coming to the door," Dior warned. "Get your act-right ready."

Isis morphed into her Egyptian queen role and reeled off a shot of attitude. "I already got my act-right on and popping."

A stately platinum-blond woman in her sixties opened the side door and invited them into the house. Dior observed every inch of the white lady from her poofy over-permed hairdo to the expensive black heels she wore and the glitzy designer cocktail dress that didn't look like much of nothing, but she was sure it had been purchased at a posh boutique with a French-sounding name. For her age, the woman was attractive with a tight alabaster complexion due to a number of plastic surgeries, nips, and tucks. The flirty leer tossed at the Ladies DI by the lady of the house didn't go unnoticed either. *Yeah, you want some,* Dior surmised correctly. *Hopefully you won't be sticking around once the meter gets to ticking. Wrinkled old men are bad enough.*

"I'm Princess," the lady said, as if it were a title. "Thank you for coming. My husband is in the den, call him Pistol Pete. He'd like that."

Dior almost laughed. *Pistol Pete, huh? I bet he would.*

"All that's cool, but what about the money?" Isis asked, getting rather impatient with Missoni on her mind. Dior hit her with a stinging glare that should have knocked her over.

"Ah, yes, your fee," answered Princess. "I've met your demands and you'll find an envelope on the sofa table in the foyer, *on your way out.* Although you're new to my circle of friends, you've come highly recommended. Make sure that the birthday boy has a great time." When Isis looked at Dior with a question on her face, Princess answered that one too. "I'll be out enjoying Pete's birthday in my own special way. I've purchased two hours of your time and I don't expect to find you here when I return."

"Yes, ma'am," Dior replied, more in agreement to the curt directive than to the woman herself. "He'll have the time of his life."

"And so shall I," Princess alluded. "Do lock up on your way out. Good night."

Isis waited until Princess left the room before she exhaled. "She was trippin'. Why would a man with all this money keep her around?"

"'Cause it might be all *her* money, not his."

"Whose ever it is, let's go and get broke off some."

"Yes, my dear, let's," Dior said, in her own manufactured stuck-up version to make fun of Princess's highbrow diction.

Their high heels click-clacked against the marble floor when entering the massive common area. Exquisite paintings and porcelain vases were placed throughout the room. Casual but tasteful furniture had been pushed back against the walls. That, along with the soft music piped in from an entertainment center, insinuated that the birthday boy enjoyed dancing as an appetizer. Dior scanned the trappings as Isis discovered a well-dressed, stout, white man mixing cocktail at a wet bar.

"Humph," she grunted to get Dior's attention. "Get a load of the li'l Pistol."

Peter was a pistol of sorts, balding and as round as he was tall, a firecracker in his younger days and still one to raise the roof on special occasions. He and Princess had an understanding allowing them to feed their demons as long as the other knew about them. Their agreement for over thirty years of marriage could have been summed up in two words: *No Surprises*.

"He's kinda cute," Dior laughed, watching him dance along to music she'd only heard when watching old black and white movies on a busted TV set when she was a kid. Peter was having a grand time without them, but it was show time nonetheless. "Come on, Isis. Let's meet the man of the hour."

"But she paid for two hours," Isis said, clueless of the cliché.

Dior put on her best smile and struck out in Peter's direction.

When they approached the bar area, Peter raised his head and cheered as if he were a small boy at a backyard children's party. "Hail, hail, the gang's all here," he applauded. "Hot times in the city, ladies, and I've got just the thing." He handed them umbrella drinks to get the evening under way.

"Pistol Pete, I'm Dior and it's a pleasure to meet you," she said, pecking him on the cheek. "And this is my friend Isis."

"Hello, ladies, two real pretty gals," he said, giving them the once over. "I like, I like. So let's crank up the music, get down and boogie."

And boogie they did. Dior was impressed that a man of his age and girth had the moves to keep step with them. During the first hour, Peter taught the girls to jitterbug, swing, and other famous dances he'd perfected in lavish country club ballrooms. After their lesson was completed, the *Ladies DI* taught ol' Pistol Pete what they'd learned during less noble activities in the hood. Needless to say, the birthday boy enjoyed his tutelage tremendously. For their participation in the "Birthday Threesome," Dior and Isis danced away with $2,000 apiece.

19

Second Slice

Saturday morning, Dior slid into her sexiest pink man-catching sweat suit and darted out as early as she could. She didn't know for certain whether the jitterbug antics of the previous evening had worn on her more than she would have predicted, or whether that Viagra pill-popping Pistol Pete's bedroom aerobics caused her to feel like a high-performance vehicle stuck in first gear. Whichever happened to be the case, Dior was dragging. It was already half past ten when she stopped by the Java Hut, the trendy breakfast nook that Marvin preferred above any other in the city. With the pressing conversation she intended to have on her mind and closer proximity to Marvin in her sights, Dior practically floated into the restaurant on a cloud. Since she'd heard him rave about their omelets before, it seemed like a safe bet to order one of each. Surely, he'd be thankful and honored she went to such great lengths to put something in his stomach. With any luck, she hoped getting the chance to put something else on him, namely, herself.

Two white "to go" bags filled with tasty entrees rested

on Dior's front passenger seat. The gratitude she expected when Marvin laid his eyes on her bounty made her blush; what she'd planned on doing with his gratitude made her hot. *He can't do nothing but feel me on all of this,* she thought, patting the boxes as if they were obedient pets. *We'll fall into his spot, get him good and full so he'll want to lay down and talk about a few things. Huh, after he told Chandelle to kick dust last night, it'll be hard to pass up on us.*

Dior was still convincing herself that she'd done the right thing by giving Marvin another opportunity to see what he was missing. Deflated doesn't begin to describe how foolish she felt after turning into the apartment complex and not finding his severely used Four Runner anywhere. "You got to be kidding me," she groaned sullenly. "I went through all this trouble and he ain't even home." Dior contemplated leaving the collection of omelets on his doorstep but figured neighborhood cats would beat him to them. *I'm leaving a note to let Marvin know I came by to look in on him. Maybe he'll call to see what I wanted; then I can chat him up about a friendly dinner. Yeah, then I'll have a better shot at putting in work.*

Dior did leave a note on Marvin's door; then she tossed her useless ammunition in the trash bin before striking out for a full day of pampering and planning. As long as she could keep Chandelle on the outside, she assumed getting in Marvin's bed was a cinch. Making sure things remained gummed up between them required engineering a crafty trail of deceit and a devilish inside influence. Dior was an eager candidate and well suited for both.

Marvin's head was still spinning from the night before as he put his name on the waiting list at Java Hut, not five minutes after Dior slithered out of it. He flipped through the business section, made himself comfortable in the waiting area, and then tugged at the bill of his baseball cap to shield all extemporaneous stimuli. Where to initiate his job-hunting expedition on Monday was weighing on him heavily. Never having been fired before, it was not going to be easy for him. He dreaded telling men who he needed to impress how he'd been terminated because of a pending "spousal abuse" charge. *Yes, sir, I'm extremely qualified, but I'm currently awaiting trial,* he thought to himself. *Oh no, sir, nothing as serious as armed robbery. My violent crimes only involved an arrest for beating my wife. So, when do I start? Never!* Marvin folded the newspaper over his knees and exhaled. *Look at me. I'm already thinking like a criminal and more than ready to lie on employment applications. Marvin Hutchins, you're a bad liar and a real trip.*

He left the paper for others waiting when he heard his name called from the hostess stand. A pleasant-looking freckle-faced girl smiled when she instructed him to follow. "Excuse me, but I thought you said the wait was at least thirty minutes?"

"Yes, it is," she answered amiably.

Marvin stared at her peculiarly, then did as directed. He traced the hostess's steps deep into the nonsmoking area of the busy eatery. Just as he reached out to ask where she was leading him, the young girl stopped on a dime.

"Is this the one you were talking about, ma'am?" she asked the attractive woman coloring a cartoon hamburger and French fries with complimentary crayons.

"Yes, Sherry, he's the one all right," Kim Hightower replied. "Could you ask our waiter to get him something to drink and another silverware setting? Thanks a lot."

"Uh, hey, Kim," was all he managed to say after accepting a seat and her hospitality.

"Hey yourself," she jested, with a brilliant smile. "Rough night?"

Marvin cast his eyes down, imagining how scraggly he

must have appeared to her before answering. "How'd you guess?"

"I saw you climb out of your truck like a man with no place in particular to be and you look like something the cat dragged in."

"More like something the cat spit out," he mused, laughing at himself.

"That too," Kim agreed. "Regardless, you know we have to stop meeting like this. A certain someone might pounce up again and get another wrong idea about us."

Marvin bit his bottom lip playfully. "I don't think she cares that much anymore. Last night was rough, remember?"

"Hmm," Kim uttered, as if to let that one go. She'd seen more of her share of men in troubled marriages and wasn't prepared to help him carry that baggage any further. "Has the owner at your last job reconsidered?" she asked with a grin.

"Oh, I see," Marvin chuckled. "You sent the hostess to fetch me like a Mob boss ready to make an offer I can't refuse?"

"No, it's not that serious," she said, after taking a sip of tea from her mug. "But, you do know that the judge will not look favorably at your case if you come across as another unemployed thug with a bad temper." Marvin suspected that Kim was going somewhere with her line of conversation but didn't see it clearly yet, so he just nodded and listened. "Let's not even talk about your being in my pocket at this point."

"Ahh, you gonna go there on me?" he debated half-heartedly.

"Yes, I am, Marvin," Kim said, making no bones about it when she did. "Look, I understand you're having a bad stretch, but that's all it is at this point. If you let it take you under, believe me, it will. When I spoke to you over the phone the first time, I thought, this brotha has a lot on the ball. Unless I'm mistaken, that hasn't changed. You're still a very smart man, Marvin, and extremely good with customers."

Kim's compliment made him sit up straight and pay closer attention. "Yes, I'd like to think so," he agreed. "And you're right. I'd better make the best of it before going back to court. Never thought I'd be out there hitting the bricks, but everybody's gotta door-to-door it some time. I can handle that."

"Can you handle working for a woman, a black woman?" she stated seriously, with a noticeable shift in her demeanor.

"Yes, of course I can," he responded before realizing what he'd walked into. "Hey, you don't mean come to work for you as an indentured servant until my bail is paid off?"

"Yeah, you catch on quick," Kim said, laughing at his concerned expression. "I told you you'd go far. But I'm not proposing any work release program. I'm always keeping an eye out for talent. You have it, and what you lack in the way of real estate savvy, I'll teach you."

"Real estate?" he said, as if those words flew right out of her behind.

"Yes, do you have problem with what I do?" she hissed defensively. "Don't forget that's what got your butt out of jail."

"No, no," he sputtered, backpedalling all the way. "Kim, don't get me wrong. You're excellent at what you do; *muy, muy excellente,* but I don't know a thing about that industry. I'd be a bull in a china shop trying to move houses."

"Well, if you're scared to learn something new, they're always hiring at Appliance World. Oops, you can't go back there, can you?"

Marvin slumped in his chair and tugged at his hat again. "I'd bet you can sell ice to Eskimos."

"If I put my mind to it," she replied most assuredly.

"Yeah, I'd bet you could at that," Marvin said, smiling softly. "Tell me what it takes to get started and I'll see about putting my mind to that. One other question," he said, as the waiter finally appeared with a menu, "what are you coloring and why?"

"That's two questions," Kim corrected him before answering. "When I come here without my munchkin, Danni, I try to remind myself why I work so hard and how much she misses me when I do." It was Kim's turn to lower her eyes then. She was not accustomed to showing her vulnerable side, but Marvin was not in any position to judge. Secretly, she hoped he wouldn't become the type once his life was back on track. A blind man could have seen that they shared a great deal more than tea and orange juice between them. Kim wanted to trust him. Marvin had no choice but to trust her.

He exited the restaurant long after Kim left to meet with her next client of the day. Marvin's mind motored a hundred miles an hour. Kim had explained in detail what he'd need to do in order to get his realtor's license and get on her award-winning sales team. Fate caused them to cross paths, he concluded, and who was he to battle against it? *Making room for a new career and a fresh start will be easy without Chandelle throwing drama in my face*, he thought. *I've got to start living for Marvin, and Marvin only,* were the words resonating in his head. His heart was singing another song, but he refused to listen.

As Marvin's future and fortune called out to him, he spent the better part of the day chasing after his past. He opened an individual checking account at the banking center inside of the grocery store. That so-called lawyer-

appropriation bonus from Mr. Mercer came in handy.
Marvin deposited the $3,700 check, and then mapped out
a budget for the next two months. After covering the rent,
phone, and electricity bills, he had enough to live on but
not nearly the fee to pay a reputable attorney. If he burned
the midnight oil and studied for the real estate exam with
every waking hour, he stood a better chance at making
ends meet and retaining his freedom. The compass Marvin used to lean on for guidance and the light he counted
on illuminating his path hadn't abandoned him, he just
had to be reminded where to look.

In the meanwhile, Marvin used his time to run errands.
He picked up a study package from the Hightower Realty
Group, equipped with manuals, mission statements, pretest
kits, applications, and a book of realtor terms. It felt like
college exams again, and that brought an unexpected smile
to his face.

There were two more stops on his checklist for the day.
The thrift store located near his old job sold refurbished
furniture so he wandered into the warehouse to see what,
if anything, he could get with $100. He pulled his SUV
away from the back loading dock thirty minutes later with
the love seat Chandelle had begged them to haul off
crammed inside and the reclining chair tied on top. Marvin
was lucky to get them back. He was blessed to get them
back for $75. By the end of the day, he met with Dooney
as he closed the shop early.

"Thanks, man, I really appreciate you squeezing me in
this evening," Marvin told him in earnest. Dooney flicked
off the red neon OPEN sign in the window.

"No sweat, Kinfolk, but I thought you decided to pass
on stopping by." Dooney glanced at his watch and
laughed as if there was an inside joke. "A couple of more
seconds and you would have had to keep on going."

"My bad, Dooney," Marvin apologized. "I know I'm

late and on your time so go ahead hook me up, then I'll jet out."

Dooney glared at him playfully, then gestured toward his barber chair for Marvin to sit. "By the looks of it you need to cop a squat anyway. I wouldn't be walking around like this if I were you."

"Oh, you're cracking on me? I know I need a cut, that's why I'm here."

"Who said I was talking about your head?" Marvin, facing the broad mirror, glanced up to note Dooney's expression. "That's right. I'm talking about you and Chandelle. She called me. I put the Dooney Show on her and did what I do. Man, I even got her to look you up and get back in the ring."

Marvin began to replay the last interaction he shared with estranged wife while Dooney worked the clippers around the edges of his hairline. "I should have known she needed some convincing to come back begging."

"She was beggin'?" Dooney asked in an elevated tone. "And you still booted her out?"

"Don't mix it up, Dooney; it wasn't even like that," Marvin explained. "I wasn't in any mood to have her knocking on my door and I haven't been myself in a while."

"Marvin, we're cool like the other side of the pillow, you know that. I respect you and what you feel necessary to maintain peace of mind, but sometimes us brothas get our hearts stepped on and forget that we could use some convincing too." When Dooney saw Marvin's jaws tighten, he stopped cutting and turned the chair around. "Kinfolk, I ain't never told nobody this, but it's the God's honest truth. There's a curse on the women in my family that goes all the way back to slavery. Not one of them can keep a man."

Marvin squinted at Dooney, trying to read him. "You're joking, right?"

"I wish I was," he answered, with a grave expression.

"Dooney, you play too much," Marvin said, figuring it had to be a ruse.

"Marvin, I'm as serious as a stroke. There's a curse on the Wicker women. None of our ancestors on my momma's side could hold down a man longer than a few years, not my momma, not Chandelle's, nor any of the ones who came before them." When Dooney was sure he had Marvin's undivided attention, he lowered the guilt boom appropriately. "Everybody was rooting for Chandelle to break the hex and now this. Marvin, you're gonna fool around and set the sistahs in my family back six generations."

"That's heavy," Marvin uttered, with his head hung low. "Why didn't Chandelle say something about this curse before?"

"Would you? I mean be real about it, if y'all can't hold it together, we got to depend on Dior, and she can't even keep a gig six months. Hold down a man . . . dude, please."

"I see what you mean," Marvin said, as the magnitude of Chandelle's family history weighed on him. "I'd hate to keep the bad luck going, but I'm concentrating on some other things right now."

"Just thought I'd lay it on you for size," Dooney told him, as he started up the electric clippers again to resume the trim.

True enough, Marvin had a lot on his plate as it was. It was too much to heap on the future and respectability of an entire family tree. He tried to shrug off the conversation but couldn't, so he did the next best thing, pretended not to be affected by it. It was a man thing, right, wrong, or in between, a man thing. "You put that on me for size, huh?" Marvin said finally.

Once again, Dooney had stepped up to help facilitate a meeting of the minds. Although he didn't think twice about enduring the struggles of a committed relationship, personally he believed that Marvin and Chandelle belonged together. Ironically, Dooney was working both ends against the middle in direct opposition to Dior's plan. He and his twin sister had many characteristics in common, but they were as different as two sides of the same coin. Dooney wanted to give his favorite cousin every possible chance to retain the one thing he couldn't conceive putting his name on.

After finishing with Marvin's haircut, Dooney ushered him out of the door quickly. "All right, Marvin, I know where you live. Do right by Chandelle," he suggested firmly. "Or at least say you'll think about it?"

"I'll get at you later, Doo'," was Marvin's noncommittal answer. "Keep it tight." He was halfway to his vehicle when he snagged a fleeting thought from midair. All the lights inside the barber shop were shut off. Marvin remembered that Dooney lived above the first floor in a crammed one-bedroom apartment.

While climbing the apartment's back stairs, Marvin intended to ask Dooney if he'd be just as helpful by passing out his business cards after he passed the real estate exam. His first group of knocks went unanswered, but Marvin knew he had to be in there. He beat on the door a second time. "Dooney, open up!" he yelled, and banged insistently. He stumbled backward when Dooney snatched the door open, already stripped down to his boxers.

"What is it with you, Kinfolk?" he barked. "You don't want your woman so you're gonna jinx what I got going on with one of mine?"

Marvin looked past Dooney's narrow shoulders. Sure enough, there was a woman in the bed, hiding beneath the covers. One glimpse of her long dreads exposed who she was. "Reeka?" Marvin mouthed quietly, in utter surprise. "Go head on, you dirty dog."

"Told you I needed a new microwave," Dooney replied in a similar tone. "How else am I gonna get that store discount? Oh, and Marvin, don't come back tonight. I'm putting in work for an Executive beer cooler. Reeka said they got one left and I want it for the shop. Ooh, this is gon' be fun. Told you she was a freak," Dooney added before slamming his door in Marvin's face.

"Yeah, you told me."

20

What About Us?

Chandelle spent her first Saturday on Brass Spoon Drive alone, rearranging furniture. She started by moving the canisters she'd purchased from Bed, Bath & Beyond back and forth from the counter near the black range oven to the one nearest the breakfast table. When she grew tired of looking at a neatly decorated kitchen, done in a colorful southwestern theme, Chandelle busied herself in the master bathroom.

The bathroom's crème-colored ceramic tile floor with a rectangular border done in a tan-hued pattern beneath her brown leather house shoes is what caught her eye at first glance. The Jacuzzi-style sunken bathtub took her breath away. When signing the loan documents, Chandelle imagined long, lazy soaks in it with her husband. Now that seemed like a lifetime ago, so she went back to rearranging.

Shortly after finding in her walk-in closet a shoe box filled with vacation photos, she began sorting through them one by one with the intention of placing them in an album. The memories captured on Kodak paper caused

Chandelle to pause and search deep within her soul. Saturday night saw her toss and turn. Sunday morning rolled in just in time to gloat.

Chandelle drew her legs over the side of the bed, stretched, and yawned. There were at least four hours of sleep still languishing between the sheets, but they would have to stay there if making it to church service on time still meant anything. Exhausted, Chandelle closed her eyes. She wanted to scream. Mentally and spiritually drained, she found it hard to deny that everything about her seemed tragically out of place.

While selecting an outfit for church, Chandelle cried. After she'd gotten dressed and realized there would be no pleasant compliments forthcoming to tell her how beautiful she looked before leaving the house, she cried. When Chandelle strolled through the church parking lot without her husband by her side, she hurried into the women's lounge and fell apart again.

Several concerned sisters tried to console her as she sobbed uncontrollably. Moments before service began, Grace overheard women gossiping about Chandelle's nervous breakdown. She whispered to her husband, "Wallace, Chandelle is coming undone in the ladies' room. That poor thing is in a very bad place with Marvin and I've got to go and see about her."

"Go on, sweetheart, and keep the hens away," he wisely suggested. Wallace knew church folk well enough to spot a few busybodies among them. Not everyone who peeped in to witness Chandelle at her worst was interested in helping her get over it.

Grace could have hardly been confused with a coddling "there-there" type. However, her heart poured out when she discovered Chandelle being tended by two of the biggest gossips in the congregation. "Thank you, sisters," Grace announced, as if the cavalry had ridden in on white horses. She shooed the women away from Chandelle, who was huddled on the lounge sofa. "Dear God," she sighed, holding in her reaction. Seeing her young, sassy friend in tears saddened her.

Rushing to aid Chandelle, Grace joined her on the sofa and hugged her. "Chandelle," she cooed. "You're going to have to pull together, sweetie. Married people go through things all the time, that's part of the process to make it great. It'll be all right. There . . . there, now. I know it's rough right now, but you're strong and Marvin will come to his senses. It will be all right in due time," Grace assured her.

Chandelle raised her head slowly as if it weighed a ton; then she shook it disagreeably. "You don't understand, Grace. Marvin hates me. I deserve it."

"He does no such thing," Grace sang tenderly.

"Yes, I'm right about this. Marvin's gone. He does— doesn't want it anymore," cried Chandelle. "He told me so the other night." She also revealed what else Marvin told her before shutting her out of his life. Once Grace had heard and seen enough, she stormed out of the women's room on a mission to make something good happen but fast.

Marvin had crept in the church and taken a seat on the back pew. He hadn't been there long when Grace sent one of the ushers to "fetch his behind" for her. Marvin didn't question when he was summoned.

"Grace Peters said your wife is in a bad way," the man whispered. "Said you need to come quick."

Marvin excused himself from service. He pushed through the exit doors wearing a bewildered look, fearing Chandelle had been terribly hurt in an accident. Oddly enough, that much was true. "Grace, what happened to Chandelle?" he asked frantically. "Is she going to be okay? Brother Clement said she was bad off. She sick?"

Grace placed both hands on her hips and tilted her head back. "She'll live, but I'm the one who's sick. Yeah,

I said it. I'm sick of y'all showing out when you have better things to do with your time."

"What?" Marvin said, totally lost. "Where is Chandelle?"

"Come on, you need to see this," answered Grace, as she pulled him by the arm into the women's lounge.

Marvin protested heartily. "Whoa, Grace, this is the women's room. I can't come in here . . . Hey, y'all got a couch?"

"Shut up and look!" she grunted insistently.

Marvin's knees weakened when his eyes fell on Chandelle's condition. "Thank you, Grace," he whispered softly. "You mind? I need to be alone with her."

Smiling pleasantly, Grace nodded her head. "You're very welcome. No, I don't. And, yes, you do," she answered him. Grace stood outside, guarding the door until her feet began to hurt; then she grabbed two chairs, sat down, and propped them up.

Inside of the lounge, Marvin held his wife tightly with his muscular arms. "I never wanted to see you like this, Chandelle," he confessed.

"I didn't want you to see me crying," she sobbed, hiding her face in her hands. Marvin moved her hands aside so he could get a better look. Chandelle's eyes were puffy and red. "I must look a mess," she said, turning her face away from him.

"No, you're as pretty as ever," he replied with utmost sincerity.

"Marvin, tell me you still love me."

"Yes, I do, but—" he started to say before she interrupted him.

"Then why aren't we together?"

"After the worst week of my life, I don't know what to do about us anymore," Marvin replied honestly.

"We could get someone to help us fix it," she suggested, while allowing her tear-filled eyelashes to brush against Marvin's suit coat. "You could also stop seeing that lady and come home," Chandelle threw in as a Hail Mary, figuring it was worth going for it all. Marvin remained silent on both accounts. One of them was strictly off limits: his extreme opposition to counseling and opening himself up to criticism. Like too many men in rocky marriages, his heart was in the right place but his pride was getting in the way.

Over the next week, Marvin took the required real-estate courses twice. He studied marketing, buying, and selling trends into the wee hours of the morning. With each call he received from Chandelle inquiring when he planned on joining her sessions with a professional relationship psychologist, he balked, citing that his busy schedule wouldn't allow it. Time, he said, is what he needed, more time.

Kim had taken Marvin under her wing, teaching him strategies to become successful and a method of doing business to help facilitate it. "Pull interest rate sheets every morning, first thing," she told him. "Review client applications and search the Web for the most recent home-lending products. If you stay on top of loan products and what your customers' needs are, you'll make a very good living and your client list will grow because of it. This isn't rocket science, Marvin, but doing it the right way makes the difference between a lot of commas in your bank account and being forced to find other ways to keep your lights on." Marvin took Kim at her word, especially after learning how she'd started a small company on her kitchen table and it grew into a million-dollar business in less than four years. He estimated that she worked sixty to eighty hours a week and cleared around seven hundred thousand a year.

The morning of Marvin's trial, Kim arrived at the office

at seven-thirty. Marvin had used his key to open up. With the envelope containing his exam scores placed beneath a stack of home listings he intended to walk through to get his feet wet before doing it with real live clients, Marvin spoke to Kim calmly. That struck her as odd, considering how her brother was always a bundle of nerves on the days of his trials.

"Good morning, Kim. I was just pulling the daily rates sheets, but some of our banks haven't posted theirs yet. Maybe I could review the listings in quad four and see if anything new in the three hundred thousand dollar price range pops up. The McClellans said they wanted a suburban-style build job in north Dallas. I've heard you say a million times that you'd have to knock a house over to do a construction job on the north side because there are no available lots to build on. Remember I sat in on the interview you did with them. I'm almost positive that the *Mrs.* wants fresh paint near a good elementary school in the suburbs. Mr. McClellan is thinking more about the miles he's logging to and from work." Kim listened attentively to Marvin. "So, if I can find a recent new construction with a lot of add-ons and a sizeable back yard . . . ahhh, see what I'm getting at. I think you can sell the McClellans on an *almost* new home within the city limits."

Kim was impressed because difficult home buyers were challenging to reason with. "Not bad, Marvin, not bad at all. However, there's only a fifteen-minute drive time difference in the area from where Mrs. McClellan wants to raise her kids and Mr. McClellan's office is located."

"Not during peak traffic hours," he replied in ah-ha fashion. "You've taught me that married home buyers have two needs, hers and his. Let's present them with some options to satisfy both. If they start shopping in the 'burbs, it'll be harder to keep them on our leash. You taught me that too."

"Bravo," Kim applauded. "You must have ice water flowing through your veins," she joked. "I know you're committed, but enough is enough."

Marvin assumed she was getting at his tireless desire to soak in the industry culture. "Oh this, I'm beginning to figure out better ways to spin the news."

"No, that's not what I meant. My brother is usually hanging over the edge on the days he's gone to trial."

"Trial? Today is the twelfth?" he asked, flipping through his desk calendar. "How did I forget? Kim, I've got a couple of hours to get downtown and hire a lawyer to beg for a continuance." He grabbed his suit coat off the back of the chair and sprinted for the door. "Oh, my test scores came yesterday. They're on my desk."

Kim watched Marvin leap into his vehicle and tear out of the lot. She wouldn't allow herself to imagine his trial going against him. Because she presumed that Chandelle would be on hand as a testifying witness, Kim decided to steer clear of the proceedings. What she did instead made her happy. After locating the exam scores Marvin alluded to, she pulled them out of the envelope. "Ninety-eight percent?" she said to herself. "Huh, almost as good as mine. He's definitely got potential."

21

In for It

Marvin zoomed down the avenue until the morning traffic slowed his progress to a crawl near the highway on
ramp. While speeding south toward the criminal justice
district, he remembered how playful roughhousing with
Chandelle had spun out of control in the blink of an eye.
He recalled how worthless he felt when the cops dragged
him from his home, berated him, and threw him into a
cell. Then he kept in mind that truth was on his side, the
fact that he didn't mean to harm his wife, and that she
didn't intend to get him arrested afterward. His biggest
concern was the court's plans for his future. That had him
shaking down to his shoes.

He carried the overbearing anxiety into the Dallas
County Courthouse. His palms sweated profusely as he
emptied his pockets, then passed through the metal detec-
tors. He asked the registration desk attendant where to
find Judge Spicer's office. While hustling up to the third
floor, Marvin felt like a man on the run against time. "Excuse me, I need to speak with the judge about my trial,"
Marvin said hurriedly to a middle-aged Latino woman

dressed in tight gray slacks and a white button-down blouse with a tin badge attached on the left side.

"Slow down, sir," she replied, without looking up from a log book. "What's your name, and when is your case slated to begin?"

"I'm Marvin Hutchins, and it's supposed to start this morning. I just need to ask Judge Spicer if I can request a continuance."

"A continuance before the trial begins?" she asked, peering up at him like he was eye candy. "I'm sorry, sir, but a continuance is usually requested by the attorney. Why don't you tell me what it is you're trying to do?"

Marvin's chest tightened with exasperation. He blew out a dense huff of apprehension and tried to put his words together. "Okay, I am not ready today. I haven't hired a lawyer to defend me because I'm flat broke."

The woman's countenance had changed since he showed up babbling about his trial. She ran her thin finger down the first page and stopped at the bottom. "You said Hutchins, right? No, sir, your trial can't be today. I've checked and your name isn't on the court docket. An attorney from the public defender's office could file a pretrial motion to postpone the proceedings."

"But I know it's today," he contradicted her. "Maybe I'm in the wrong place. If you just let me talk to the judge, I'll work this out myself."

"That won't be necessary," Wallace interjected, as he approached the woman's desk. "I'm Mr. Hutchins's attorney of record as of yesterday. Marvin, it's good to see you. Sorry it has to be under these circumstances."

The county clerk was staring Grace's husband down like she was happy to see him and her day had gotten off to a roaring start. Wallace, the shade of maple syrup and just as sweet, had more going for him than charisma and male-model features. He was a hotshot litigator before taking a break from the grind to teach high school. Now his clients counted on his savvy to defend their wealth. He'd traded in his battles with the DA's office to fight with major entertainment corporations when crawfishing on movie and music contracts with those he represented. Chandelle worried Grace until she convinced her husband to reschedule his meetings in south Florida to aid a Christian brother in dire straits. After she'd leaned on the cross to bring about a successful outcome, Wallace caught the next flight home. He reviewed the arrest reports, then made substantial inquiries regarding the arresting officers' records to see if his hunch was correct. His investigation uncovered several disturbing coincidences, none of them good.

Since Wallace appeared out of nowhere, Marvin had been staring at him, too, but for another reason. He couldn't shake the surprise from his face when shaking the attorney's hand vigorously. "Wallace? What's a big-timer like you doing down here?" he asked.

"I'm here to get you out of something you shouldn't have been in from the start."

"I'm innocent," Marvin said solemnly.

Wallace patted him on the shoulder and grinned. "I know. That's what makes my job so easy. You didn't need to be here for this, but it is good you came. Judge Spicer moved your trial from his docket per my request. The DA's office didn't like it, but we won't concern ourselves with them."

No, let's not be the least bit concerned about the people who could send me up the river on the next boat, Marvin thought, wishing he had the nerve to be as smug about the state of affairs. Because he wasn't sure what Wallace was up to, he found a seat in the judge's chambers, wisely kept his mouth shut, and waited for the show to begin.

Soon enough the same two crooked cops who arrested him trailed in behind a thin, clean-shaven white man wearing a knockoff of a Brooks Brothers suit. His dark brown hair was cut in a neat ultraconservative style. Everything about him screamed Young Republican Association, Marvin thought. Then he noticed something he hadn't seen before, both of the police officers seemed uneasy. A closer look confirmed it; they were scared. Marvin sat up a bit straighter in the chair, staring them down like they had done to him. Although he had one foot in the justice system, their worried expressions gave him the confidence to face the moment with a stiff upper lip.

The judge waddled in underneath a black robe. Wallace got to his feet so Marvin did likewise until his attorney gestured for him to return to his seat. The cops glanced at one another like two naughty little boys dreading the school principal's corporal punishment. That brief Kodak moment was worth a million words, all of them satisfying. Marvin almost laughed out loud, but he wasn't out of hot water yet.

"Wallace, it's been a long time," the judge said, while unzipping his black robe.

"I can't complain, judge," Wallace answered casually, as if speaking to an old friend.

The pudgy arbitrator hadn't addressed the other men in the room or paid them any mind. "I don't have to ask you how the private practice is faring. Yes, sir, I've heard that you're wasting away while making a name for yourself in contract law. We miss your talent around here, but who's going to say no to bundles of money? Not everyone is lucky enough to marry into a fortune, I guess." After sharing niceties with Wallace, Judge Spicer finally perused the papers on his desk to refamiliarize himself with the finer points. "Oh boy, this is going to be good," he said to no one in particular. "It might even leave a mark." Suddenly, he raised his fat head, then looked over the uniformed officers with sympathy-stained eyes. "If you fellows haven't figured it out by now, somebody's in for it," he informed them. "After reading your brief, Wallace, I don't need to hear your arguments, but some things need to be said. Plus, I like a good story."

Assistant DA Tad Fogerty cleared his throat before speaking. "Judge Spicer, I've read Attorney Peters's motion for dismissal as well, and may I say I was not as impressed as your honor, with all due respect."

"Save your all due respect and sit down, Mr. Fogerty," the judge barked. "Wallace, make it good. I'm missing a *Judge Judy* marathon."

All eyes were trained on Grace's husband as he straightened his silk necktie and flipped pages in a document he'd been holding. "Judge, as you've read in the motion before you, my client Mr. Marvin Hutchins is a victim of at least one overzealous police officer. In addition to a poorly written arrest report, my client's accuser continually claims that she was coerced into making a false allegation due to the egregious acts of two men who went out of their way to make a collar. I have also included an affidavit signed by the accuser stating that one of the arresting officers openly flirted with her."

"Your honor, this is merely a tactic to avoid having a jury hear the case against the accused," belted Assistant DA Fogerty.

"Some people just don't learn," Judge Spicer chuckled. "Obviously, you didn't read all of your mail this morning, Tad. Wallace, tell him what a scraggly pair of malcontents he's fighting to put on the stand."

Marvin was interested in hearing all about the scraggly pair as well.

"Yes, sir," Wallace replied, with a twinkle in his eye. "Mr. Fogerty, the first three pages you probably should have read before taking this meeting include a litany of complaints regarding arrests involving your witnesses for the prosecution. Did you know that one third of their arrests for domestic violence, where attractive women are concerned, are currently under police Internal Affairs investigation? I could have a private detective interview all twelve of them at length, but we know what they'll say. Officers Pitts and Dumas here have a long outstanding well to dig themselves out of, notwithstanding the countercharges my client is contemplating against the city of Dallas."

Marvin hadn't discussed suing the city, but it sounded great when Wallace presented it as an option.

The black officer was squirming in his seat. His partner remained motionless during Wallace's browbeating. Neither of them had any of the crass comments they leveled Marvin with on the day in question. They were both quiet as church mice now.

"What have you to say, Mr. Fogerty?" asked the judge, when the time it took for the Assistant DA to sort through Wallace's paperwork outlasted his patience.

"Uh, your honor, I wasn't aware of these outstanding allegations against my witnesses," he said, uncomfortably upstaged. "I'll need to speak with these officers in private and—"

"No, sir, Mr. Fogerty," objected Judge Spicer. "All you need to do is read the last paragraph on the bottom of page five. As you can see, I did read my mail."

"Page five, your honor?" he uttered, flipping as fast as his fingers could manage. His eyes closed briefly at the end of the last paragraph. "I have no other choice but to dismiss the charges against Mr. Hutchins at this time," he said reluctantly.

Judge Spicer smiled at Marvin. "*Now* you're innocent," he ruled, beyond a shadow of a doubt. He shook hands with Wallace, who seemed a whole foot taller. "It was great seeing you again, counselor. Next time let him up off the mat once or twice before burying your knee in his chest." The judge's smile faded when he pointed his stubby finger in the DA's direction. "You should be hung by your feet for putting up such a weak fight. And as for you two," he added, casting a disapproving scowl at the policemen, "I have a very distinct feeling that you're going to get everything that's coming to you. Case dismissed. Good day, gentlemen."

Marvin pounced to his feet in jubilation. The officers bolted from the room in fast order. It would have been wrong to heckle them despite how badly Marvin wanted to. "Thank you, Wallace. Brother, that was beautiful," he asserted with an exuberant embrace. "I could never repay you, but I'll try. I'm free. I can't believe it. I'm free."

"Grace and Chandelle are to thank for it," Wallace informed him. "They leaned on me pretty hard after singing your praises. "I understand that all of it was a mistake until the police got involved. Then it became a miscarriage of justice."

"I'll let you ride with that one since I don't know what all of the legal-speak means," Marvin chuckled.

Wallace closed his leather briefcase and laughed. "Well, a little snooping paid off big. I learned that both partners have some serious problems and pending paternity suits in the works. It appears that some of the women whose men they carted away on flaky spousal abuse allegations are now pregnant."

"So they tricked women into giving false statements, and then doubled back after getting their men locked up?"

"Unfortunately, that does appear to be the case," said Wallace.

"And that was what the DA neglected to read on page five, the last paragraph?"

"Yeah, that and the fact that Chandelle saved a message from Officer Dumas, who'd been asking her out to dinner repeatedly. *Conduct Unbecoming* can unravel any criminal case."

"Conduct Unbecoming an Officer?" Marvin guessed.

"No," Wallace corrected him, "conduct unbecoming a decent man."

22

Wait a Minute

Chandelle watched the telephone as if it were about to hatch. She'd been on pins and needles all morning awaiting a call from Marvin thanking her for undoing a grievous mistake that sent their relationship spiraling downward. At ten of twelve, it finally came. "Pinnacle-Marketing-this-is-Chandelle," she said all in one fast breath.

"Hey, you," a familiar voice replied. "I owe you for putting Wallace on those cops. I had no idea what you'd been going through, I mean with that snake calling and trying to get with you."

Chandelle's smile lit up the room as she worked diligently to conceal her excitement from her coworkers. "I've been hoping and praying that it would go well for you, Marvin. You deserve to get your life back to the way it was."

"Yeah, I've been meaning to talk to you about that," he said, his voice filled with trepidation. "I'm busting my behind with this new business, but give me a minute and if you want, then we'll sit down and try to get our minds wrapped around where we are now."

"Okay," Chandelle replied. There were so many things she wanted to say, but his tone pushed those desires into a corner. "Are we going to make it?" she asked, with a folder in front of her face to muffle her words.

"We'll talk about that soon," Marvin answered. "I have a meeting to attend to, but thank you for today."

"You're welcome," she said, her voice trembling. "Have a good afternoon."

"You, too, I'll call you later."

"Honey, I love you," Chandelle whispered to a cold dial tone. Marvin had hung up before she managed to force those words from her lips. The phone conversation left her with more questions burning a hole in her chest. It wasn't so much what he said or even how Marvin said it. Chandelle placed the phone receiver in its cradle and stared at it. Hearing what hadn't been said, she pondered if he still loved her. That question had been tearing her apart for weeks. He wouldn't readily return the calls she'd left him concerning insurance and maintenance issues with the house, things he'd set up and those she'd expected him to handle once they took possession of it. Marvin had not once picked up the phone to ask how her day was going or if she needed something from the store, like he'd done from the very beginning. For the first time that Chandelle could remember, she felt empty and alone.

Blaming herself was the easy part, living with it was extremely challenging. She'd laughed at herself the night before as Marvin's favorite movie ran on the cable channel. So many times she lay on the sofa propped up against his chest while they recited the dialogue to *Love Jones* in unison with the actors on the screen. Ten minutes into the movie she had to turn it off. Something was missing so bad it hurt. It reminded her of the days her husband worked his fingers to the bone, then came home dog tired and happy to see her. Marvin always made a concerted effort to stay awake as Chandelle recapped her day, what great deals she'd found while shopping and other trivial ramblings she wanted to talk about. What she had on her heart to share wasn't that important, it was him thinking enough of her to listen that touched her in places words could never penetrate. She didn't have to ask if he loved her then, his actions exhibited it 100-fold. Chandelle talked herself into getting back to work with two continual thoughts zigzagging through her head: *Can I love my man if he doesn't love me back? Can I love him if he doesn't love me enough?* Chandelle's mother told her as soon as she came of age, "Don't cry over nothing that don't cry over you." Obviously, that was never suggested by anyone who was deeply afraid of losing the best thing they ever had at the time. Chandelle would have bet her life on that.

As the remainder of the workday crept by, Chandelle glanced at the phone often. She began kicking herself for what she called "a momentary lapse of fortitude," but it nagged at her like a bad habit begging for a fix. She'd stopped in Grace's office to discuss Marvin's call and what he didn't say, how glad she was to have that dreadful arrest and subsequent harassment over and done with, and to show off the spectacular flower arrangement that was hand-delivered to her desk. The card read, *Love is. Marvin.*

"It's not exactly *I love you with eternal and unrivaled devotion*," Chandelle commented, "but it'll do."

Grace smelled the flowers and sneezed violently. "Whew, I hope so because my pregnancy and my allergies are acting up. If Marvin sends any more, just call and tell me about it."

Chandelle chuckled, reading the card again. "Yes, ma'am, I will."

"Good, now get back to your desk and take that vase with you. I think I just busted something." Chandelle studied Grace to see if she was joking. Fluids streaming down Grace's legs confirmed that she wasn't. Right in the middle of her plush office, Grace's water broke. "Call the ambulance," she instructed calmly, "and then call Wallace and tell him that he's having a baby today."

"Ooh, okay, okay," Chandelle muttered frantically. "Sit down and breathe. I'll handle it." Grace, the mother of a 14-year-old son, had undergone the mysteries and miracles of childbirth before. She watched as Chandelle darted from place to place, trying to make her more comfortable until the paramedics came. "Hello, Wallace? Grace is going to have the baby. She said today. Uh-huh, uh-huh, uhhh-uh. She's still sitting at her desk waiting on the ambulance. Okay, I'll see if she wants to talk."

"Chandelle, give me that phone," Grace howled as a contraction coursed through her body. "Wallace, you're going to have to excuse Chandelle. She's not right in the head this afternoon. Yes, dear, it's going to be today, maybe in the next five minutes. I have to go. The baby can't wait to meet you. Ask for me at Presbyterian Hospital; they'll know where to find us." Grace didn't hang up the phone: instead, she tossed it on her desk and let it slide onto the floor on the other side. "Somebody had better get here fast, or I'm going to turn this place into a maternity ward. Chandelle, you and the ladies might have to help deliver my child—ohhhh!" Grace yelped hysterically. "Umm, that was a big one. Help me get cleaned up. It's coming quicker than I thought." Chandelle grabbed a roll of paper towels from her boss's credenza and swabbed Grace's legs. "Thank you. On second thought, I'm not in the mood to have everybody looking up my tail. Now, get my purse, you're driving me to the hospital. Come on. Let's go."

Chandelle began to hyperventilate. There was no possible way she'd remain calm under the pressure of motoring her good friend and employer to a hospital several blocks away. "Grace, Grace, Grace," she gasped. "I can't . . . can't drive you." The loud noises coming from outside of Grace's office sounded as if they were slow-pitched into

Chandelle's ears. She was halfway to the floor when a stocky paramedic caught her.

"Bring her with us," Grace barked assertively when the other emergency medic struggled to bring Chandelle back around. "What's this world coming to, grown folks acting like they've never seen a baby trying to push its way into the world? This baby doesn't have the patience to stick around here fooling with her. Go ahead on and snatch her up."

The men followed Grace's instructions to the letter. Chandelle sat in the back of the ambulance with a capsule of smelling salts in her face, while Grace complained about waiting fourteen years to do what she said she'd never do again in a million. Grace was acting a fool when they reached the hospital ambulance dock. "I'm not letting that man talk me into anything else, Chandelle. Tell Wallace this is all his fault!" she screamed, as they wheeled her inside the emergency department doors for admittance.

Chandelle followed in close step, grinning like a schoolgirl with a brand-new secret. *I'll bet you were not complaining when your fine husband was doing more than talking,* she wanted to say. *And I'll also bet this isn't all his fault.* She waved good-bye holding Grace's purse and wishing her a safe delivery.

Later that evening, Chandelle scrubbed a perfectly clean shower and recapped the afternoon's activities as Dior painted her toenails nearby on the floor. "Yeah, it was something to see. Grace, as tough as nails, clutching the gurney rails with her uterus about to pop," Chandelle chuckled. "She had the cutest little girl on the maternity wing, you hear me, the cutest. Nicole Andrea Peters is off to a good start. It's like the song says, 'Her daddy's rich and her ma is good looking.'"

"Whuut, I'm on time for that," Dior agreed. "Nowadays I'd settle for the rich daddy and make out the rest on my own."

"Huh, money ain't never hurt nobody," said Chandelle, snapping off an oversized pair of yellow rubber gloves. "At least not this body," she added, with stiff slap on her faded jeans.

"Hey, uh . . . You heard from Marvin?" Dior asked, changing the subject to suit her itching ears. "I've been here 'bout an hour and you haven't brought him up once." Dior was bursting at the seams. She could barely contain the dirt she thought might be a nail in Chandelle's matrimonial coffin. Besides, it would be only a matter of seconds before she broke out her book, chapter and verse, after taking copious notes about what went on in Marvin's day.

"I talked to him briefly," Chandelle replied while blushing. "We're not back together, together, but he's coming around."

"You think so?" Dior said, baiting her cousin to bite the hook.

"Well, I did get a sweet phone call and that flower arrangement," she answered, pointing at the extravagant assortment of daisies, daffodils, and peonies in the tall indigo vase on the bathroom counter.

"Yes, they're very pretty, Chandelle." *Good for you*, she thought. "Once again, there's this thing I been fighting with. See, it would be easier if you knew where you stood with Marvin. If you thought y'all were on the mend, well . . ." she said, letting the end of her sentence trail off like she wouldn't dream of getting any deeper involved in married folks' business.

"I've got no other reason to think any different. Why? And don't tell me you've lucked up on another bit of information you think I should know?"

Dior blew on her nails before answering, knowing how that would infuriate Chandelle's well-documented shortage of patience. "Whew, I like this color. Mango, it's tight."

"Dior, don't play with me. Unless you want me to shove that bottle of polish . . ."

"Okay, shoot. I was just admiring the color," Dior stalled. "Look, just like the last time. I'm not telling you if Marvin is going to be mad at me."

"I didn't tell him then, and I won't this time either," Chandelle proclaimed.

"I saw them together again today," Dior answered finally. "Marvin and that dark sistah." When Chandelle's eyes drifted toward the floor, Dior predicted that her story filled with half truths and outright lies would sink in like a rattlesnake's fangs. All she had to do then was supply the venom. "Marvin rode with her to this post office place, the kind you rent by the month. Chandelle, look, it's not easy for me to be telling you this, but I don't feel good letting it ride. I probably would have left it alone, but when I saw them leaving the movies," she lied, "and then tiptoe into Boscoe's after that for some dinner, I had to come here and blab it all."

Chandelle bit on the inside of her bottom lip. The report she'd received from Dior was incriminating and hard to argue with, so Chandelle did the only thing she could, she turned her anger on the messenger. "What did you do, follow them?" she asked boldly.

"Well, yeah. I had to give you a full report. Somebody has to look out for their favorite cousin. You know I love you fam', too much to let Marvin make a fool of you all out in the open." Dior studied Chandelle's face, searching for signs of acceptance. A long sigh confirmed her calculations in a well-formulated scheme to defraud a woman she cared about of the husband she wanted for herself.

With nothing else to clean, Chandelle lifted the bucket from the floor. "Thanks, girl. What would I do without you?"

"We need each other," Dior asserted quickly. "You've always looked out for me. Now it's my turn to put time in for you. I'll always be around to lift you up." Dior's sentiment flowed so smoothly she partially believed it herself. "I'll say this and then mind my own business. The little girl they had with them looked to be mighty attached to Marvin. I'd hate to think she might even be his daughter seeing as how we can't tell how long they've been close."

Chandelle pushed the shower door closed and scanned the spotless bathroom. There were numerous thoughts multiplying in her head, all of them too hurtful to voice. Instead, she stared at her down-trodden reflection in the mirror and frowned sorrowfully. "Nothing would surprise me anymore, nothing."

23

No More Surprises

Chandelle sat at her desk for the umpteenth day in a row, sneering at the telephone. At quitting time, she poked her tongue out at it. "Traitor!" she heckled, while waggling her finger. "You used to come through for a sistah." When one of her female coworkers asked if she was talking to the telephone, Chandelle offered three cold words to ward off any discussion, "Mind your business." She had begun to build a hedge around her private life, afraid others would see into her potpourri of despair and pity her—or worse, laugh.

With Grace out on maternity leave for who knew how long, Chandelle's workload increased immediately. In for a long night, she collected a stack of files and headed to the house. Hoards of motorists edged along the freeway with her. There were no magic words to make all of them disappear, or Chandelle would have been screaming at them at the top of her lungs. "Come on," she grunted when the woman in front of her slammed on the brakes to avoid hitting the car farther ahead. She craned her neck to see if there had actually been an accident, which she'd immediately refuse to get involved with. *Next time, stay off the cell phone, lady. Have you ever heard of Bluetooth? They even sell them at Wal-Mart, and there's one of those on every corner*, she thought. When Chandelle's stomach growled, she rubbed on it as if that would sooth her hunger somehow. *Good grief, I shouldn't have pushed paper all through lunch. I'll never get anything done at home running on empty, and this traffic isn't going anywhere. Come on, people, you can't go any faster than the person in the front of you; it's simple physics.* Just as she ragged on other drivers for potentially dangerous maneuvers, Chandelle observed the one next to her punching numbers into his cell. She watched the brake lights on the car before her and gunned the motor. Her Volvo surged forward as she wrestled the steering wheel to the right, then to the right again. *Two lanes in under two seconds*, she thought. *That wasn't bad. Now, if I can make it in front of this truck, I can take the next exit.* Chandelle put on her right blinker, assuming she'd find at least one friendly driver, if not another one slipping enough to get by. She made eye contact with five people in a row, all blowing her off. The last guy flipped her off to boot. Chandelle grimaced at him and would probably have done something she'd have to repent of later, but there was a task at hand, a hazardous task at that. She stopped the vehicle until cars began piling up behind her. Horns blared endlessly, but she was relentless. Eventually, someone pulled beside her to offer assistance. When the flirty white man idled his Porsche and lowered his window, Chandelle winked at him and then mashed the gas pedal to shoot over in his lane, then off the highway she went. "Sorry, but I need to get at some nutrients to feed me, preferably extra greasy," she sang along with the hip-hop beat cranked up a notch on her stereo. "Louder . . . turn it up. Louder . . . turn it up. Louder . . . oh yeah. Don't stop, I'm almost there."

It hadn't occurred to Chandelle as she parked the car next to the curb down the street from Boscoe's that it was the restaurant Dior said she'd seen Marvin and Kim having dinner in after a trip to the movies. Nor did it come to mind when she entered, but the second she bumped into Kim coming out of the ladies' room, it hit her like a sneaky right cross.

"Oh, you again," Chandelle huffed.

"Hello, Chandelle," Kim replied cordially. "We could stand a conversation, you and me, woman to woman."

"I'm in and out, Kim, and much too busy to waste time talking about something that doesn't matter anymore. Marvin's . . ." she began saying until her eyes landed on him at the bar with a whole slew of people she didn't recognize, save one, the brunette from Kim's office. "I see, I assumed it was over between you and him. This isn't the first time I've been wrong today and I'm sure it won't be the last."

"How many times do I have to tell you that Marvin isn't with me, well, not like that," Kim clarified, because of the way things might have appeared. .

When Chandelle and Marvin's eyes met, he froze, froze like a man who'd seen his wife and his other woman chatting. "Right, and I'm Debbie Donut with a hole in my head?" Chandelle remarked, choosing to believe her eyes over Kim's adamant denial. Hastily, Chandelle ended the conversation with a stern revelation from her vantage point before ducking into the women's room. "If you ask me, it looks like you're with him, *just like that.*"

Inside the restroom, she strutted around with both hands over her eyes until she heard Marvin standing at the door pleading for her to come out and talk it over. "In my mind, he'd only have me to love him," she whispered to herself. "He'd only let me inside. Silly of me, I know, so silly." Positive that Marvin had moved on whether or not Kim was willing to admit it to her face, Chandelle tried to outrun a complicated situation by fleeing the scene. She pushed past Marvin and kept right on stepping. He took out after her, tugging at her coat on the sidewalk out front.

"Chandelle, wait up! Wait! The least you could do is let me explain."

"Explain what?" she asked. "Why you're cocked up at the bar with ol' girl, drinking and having one big party? I've seen too much to be trying to hear all about it."

"No, I mean slow down. I want to talk, but you just bolted right by me. What's up with that? Where is all this hostility coming from?"

"Oh, so now you want *me* to explain? Negro, please! All I did was cruise into the spot to get some dinner to go and what do I find, you and the very source of our problems schmoozing over fruity drinks? I was not and am not going to sit up in Boscoe's with you and your lady like nothing's wrong with that. You should know me better."

"Let's clear this up once and for all. Kim is not my lady. She's my boss. I needed work, and we don't have to go into why because everybody is well aware of the dynamics leading to my termination. Kim owns an agency and various other companies. She agreed to take me under her wing."

"And then under what else?" Chandelle quipped curtly.

"Nothing else. She's mentoring me," he answered proudly. "Kim's good people, Chandelle."

"By the way you're sticking up for her, I can tell she's good at something. Kim's *mentoring* you, humph! I see, so that's what they're calling it now?"

"I'm getting real bent on begging you to believe me," Marvin said, his tone low and hardened. "For the very last time, my relationship with her is strictly professional. Read my lips, baby: Kim is my em-ploy-er. If that's not a good enough answer, then we do have a major problem, and you can't put it on her." Chandelle twisted her lips in opposition, but she remained quiet to check his next move. "Tell you what, stay right here. I'm going back in for a minute to tell the fellas I'm leaving with you."

"The fellas?" Chandelle remarked.

"You could come and join us. You're already here and you've admitted to being hungry."

"No, thank you. I've suddenly lost my appetite. But there is something I'm starving to know, Marvin," Chandelle said, noting that he was wearing his wedding ring. "I see you still consider yourself married, but are you still my man?"

Marvin smiled instead of answering and then hustled inside toward the bar. He apologized for cutting out early and rolled off a few bills for his tab. To a crowd of playful boos and jesting, he excused himself nonetheless. Wearing a reasonable facsimile of the smile he took into the restaurant, Marvin returned to discuss in full detail exactly what he considered himself, but Chandelle was gone. He searched up and down the street to no avail. Confused, he dialed her cell phone to find out what happened.

Chandelle answered on the first ring and in no uncertain terms blasted him for what she deemed another of his transgressions. "I might not be the woman I want to be yet, but I won't ever become the kind to stand outside on the sidewalk while my husband asks his mistress for permission to leave." Before Marvin had a chance to argue the point, Chandelle had hung up in his face.

"Hello? Chandelle . . . ? Hello?" Marvin hollered into the phone. Further from understanding his wife than ever before, he wandered back into Boscoe's like a disenfranchised man without a clue. "Bartender, another beer, please," Marvin ordered, as he stood near Kim and the crew.

"Back so soon?" Kim asked, with a raised brow. "I sent

you out there to patch up things with Chandelle. Lo and behold, you come traipsing back in scratching your head."

Kim raised her wineglass for a toast. "Here's one for the man, our newest associate at Hightower Realty, Marvin Hutchins. He almost single-handedly closed a deal with impossible clients in forty-eight hours. To Marvin's first!"

"Marvin's first!" the crowd applauded in unison.

"Not a bad way to get your career off the ground either," Kim whispered softly in his ear. "I'll have your commission check in a few days. You get to keep the first one all to yourself, no splits," she informed him.

After calculating the three percent fee in his mind, Marvin wanted to wrap his arms around her and squeeze. "Nine thousand dollars?" he mouthed in her direction.

"And you deserve every penny. The McClellans were on their way to another agency. Your ideas and presentation saved the deal. I'll do all right on the loan side. It pays to run a brokerage firm, too. A girl's gotta eat."

"And you've taught me to fish. Thank you, Kim, for everything you've done." Marvin was feeling ambivalent. Accepting a great deal of money from her seemed out of line when she'd shown him the ropes, among several other random acts of kindness. On the other hand, he'd displayed an immense aptitude for the business and an unwavering desire to think outside the box. He reminded himself that Kim was correct, he did deserve his first commission check.

On the fifth floor of Presbyterian Hospital, Chandelle stepped off the elevator. She followed the thick green stripe on the floor all the way to the maternity wing. A hefty nurse supervisor greeted her at the reception area.

"Yes, may I help you?" the older white woman asked, with a small pair of bifocals resting on the end of her nose.

Chandelle smiled pleasantly at the nurse, who was graying around the temples. "Yes, ma'am, I'm looking for Grace Peters. I believe she's on this hall."

"Ohhh, yes, Mrs. Peters," she replied, glaring over the top of her glasses. "You'll find her in Room 568, that's at the end of the corridor behind you."

Snickering, Chandelle thanked the woman. She headed in the other direction wondering what Grace had done to warrant such a cold response from the nurse. After pushing the door open, she had a pretty good idea. Grace had a microwave brought in and a miniature refrigerator, a DVD player, and a personal fax machine. Chandelle laughed at all of Grace's comforts of home and office. "Wow, Grace, you're holding it down. I'm guessing that none of this is hospital issue."

"Humph, I wish," she answered, while rolling her eyes. "Then I wouldn't have had the office courier them over. You should have seen the head nurse's face when I told her to see my attorney if she had a problem with the way I roll." Grace pressed a button on a handheld remote to raise the upper portion of her bed. "Whew, I feel like a fat toad and I probably look just like one too." She waited on Chandelle to argue with her, but she didn't. "Hey, are you all right? You don't look any better than me and I pushed out a seven-pound dependent yesterday."

"Huh? Oh, I'm sorry, Grace. You look great, like always," Chandelle responded evenly, with a wall behind her words. "Where's the baby?"

"Where's your husband?" Grace smarted back. She chuckled when that didn't cause her visitor to stir either. "Chandelle!" she hollered.

"Huh? Yeah, what is it, Grace? Do you need anything?" she answered, wide-eyed and attentive. "I'm not all here."

"Ask me, most of you is someplace else. And, no, I don't need another thing. Truth be told, I feel claustrophobic as it is."

Chandelle plopped down in a chair next to the bed. "What do you mean? I didn't say a thing about me."

"You didn't have to, Chandelle. I read your mind the second you tiptoed through the door. Let me guess, you haven't talked to Marvin yet?"

"Yeah, I talked to him all right, just didn't like what he had to say," she answered coolly. "Anyway, I did not come way over here to spend time yapping about me. Where are they hiding Miss Nicole?" On cue, a young blond tapped at the door, then entered quietly with a squirming blanket. "Ooh, lemme see her," Chandelle cooed. This nurse maneuvered around to Grace and peeled back the corner of the cloth covering the infant's face. Chandelle gawked at her full head of dark black hair. "Grace, you know she's going to be a heartbreaker," she complimented. "Can I hold her?"

"Let me give that baby what she came for first," Grace snarled playfully, as she extended her arms to receive her bundle of joy. "She's a junior diva in training already with her fussy self. Yes, you are," she whispered. "And you can eat, too, huh, Nicole? Your big brother's got nothing on this sugar's appetite."

Gushing with admiration, Chandelle politely dismissed the nurse and then poured her friend a glass of ice water from a plastic pitcher. "Here you go, Grace; your lips are a little ashy and we cannot let mommy set a bad example for Nicole."

"Thank you so much, I'm usually too worn-out to move once this child's latched on." Grace held her daughter close to her chest. Chandelle watched as she swung her legs over the side of the bed. "Here, take her for a minute, I've got to pay a water bill."

"A what?" Chandelle asked, making sure to place one hand beneath the baby's head.

"I've got to pee, girl. Hold her and come over by the door in case I fall in," Grace joked. "I may need a hand getting out."

Chandelle marveled at the newborn like she'd never done before, imagining one for herself. "Grace, she's so tiny," Chandelle said from the other side of a cracked bathroom door.

"They all get bigger and poop on everything," she hollered back. "But that's part of the package. Andre's almost fifteen, a good son, but he has his moments too. Wait 'til you and Marvin get past your differences, you'll find out firsthand then and, no, I'm not babysitting, so don't call me every Friday trying to unload y'all's children with Auntie Gee. I'll be trying to get my groove on like you. Just keep on praying for good things to come with Marvin and He'll handle the rest."

"Grace, you are too much. Where do you keep the bottles?" she asked, changing the subject. "Nicole is trying to nuzzle up on me and I'm bone dry." Chandelle paced the floor to give the child something to think about other than milk until Grace returned.

"She'll live," Grace replied the moment she exited the restroom. "Bring her to me. I'm responsible for fulfilling her needs like God's vigilantly seeing to yours." Again, Chandelle balked at the topic. "Let me get comfortable a minute so I can multitask. Don't tell me you haven't been taking your worries to the Lord?" Chandelle couldn't lie so she refused to say anything. "Uh . . . uh . . . uh, you haven't gone to God but you expect Him to drop what He's doing to step in on your behalf?"

"He knows my struggles and my pain," answered Chandelle in her own defense.

Grace unfastened the top button of her hospital gown before she shifted her baby to her left side. "Listen to yourself. He knows my struggles and . . . you ought to be shamed. Yes, He knows your pain. You can say the same for me, but notice how I didn't go to Wallace and have him get Marvin's bogus charges thrown out until you came and asked me to, did I? Chandelle, prop this pillow under Nicole for me," she said, interrupting herself. "Thanks. Now, don't be the kind of Christian who talks the talk but sits on her behind when it's your turn to prove your faith by doing some walking." Chandelle lowered her head and stared at a small cloth diaper folded across her lap as Grace hit her with another dose of faith-based reality. "It's no wonder you keep taking backward steps, trying to be tough enough to carry it on your own narrow shoulders. Well, has it worked?"

"Not even," she answered, peering up to face Grace's spiritual spanking.

"Chandelle, you can bet your life on what I'm about to tell you. God can speak to Marvin in ways you can't. Humble yourself and ask Him to talk to your husband's heart. He'll listen and so will Marvin." Grace unfastened the flap on her gown to breast-feed. Chandelle turned away from her boss's exposed engorged breast.

"Whoa, heyyy, I'm in the way," she exclaimed awkwardly grabbing toward the floor for her purse with both eyes tightly closed.

"Don't be silly," Grace griped. "If it were Wallace in the bed with me trying to tap the jug, then you'd be in the way." Grace laughed heartily while Chandelle's lips parted. She revealed a reluctant smile hiding behind them.

"I know you're right, though, about my dumb idea to

carry my own load. I had my mind made up but my heart wouldn't listen to me anyway."

"That makes sense because hearts don't have ears, never did," Grace teased.

"Isn't it something how a woman's heart does what it wants, when it wants? I'm way past tired of doing without and being without my man."

"You don't want to know how tired I've been having to see you sad and sorry without your man. Does Marvin know you still want him back, that your feelings haven't changed for him?"

"I don't know. After my accusations, it's a toss-up if he'll take me seriously again," Chandelle reasoned.

"Seems to me a woman in love ought to at least be sure what she's about to throw away."

"Who said anything about throwing it away? I'm going to get prayed up and then let the Lord sort it out. I've been getting in my own way long enough. From now on, I'm going to do what a child is supposed to do, sit down and be still."

"That's the spirit, Chandelle. Let Him lead you. He's had a lot more practice." Grace tugged at the sheet to cover herself when someone knocked at the door. Wallace eased in, bearing a bouquet of balloons, blankets, and an armful of barbecue hot wings from Boscoe's.

"Hello, Wallace," Chandelle greeted him with a cordial embrace. "Nicole is a stunner. You did good, brother."

"Thanks, Chandelle, I didn't think you'd be here. I just saw Marvin at the wing place," Wallace said, unaware that she'd seen him too.

"Yeah, I'll catch up with him later. Got some things to talk over with my daddy," Chandelle said, openly sharing her intentions. She thanked Wallace for the circus act he performed with the rogue cops and Marvin's case, winked at Grace, and then excused herself from their family reunion. Chandelle's stride was noticeably loftier when she strutted past the frumpy nurse supervisor.

"That's a first," the nurse stated sarcastically to Chandelle. "I hadn't seen anyone come out of there grinning."

"Better watch what you say. That lady is most likely on God's A-list, that's what all the extra equipment is for."

24

Speaking of Hot

Over the next two days, Marvin worked at putting his last conversation with Chandelle to bed. She had her mind made up that he was involved intimately with Kim, despite his numerous attempts at squashing it. Although Marvin could understand how her jealous notions sprang up, he couldn't figure out how she sprung up, time after time it seemed, when he was with Kim. Chandelle wasn't the type to snoop, so it was inconceivable to think she'd have someone on his tail. Suspicions had him jumpy, looking over his shoulder and acting guilty as charged by Chandelle.

Deciding that his time and energies were better spent on growing his clientele, Marvin called Dooney and Super Dave to get them interested in fully utilizing their hard-earned money. After putting it like that, both men agreed to set meetings.

"What's wrong with you, Kinfolk?" asked Dooney, when Marvin met him in front of the barber shop at closing time. "I thought you kicked that wife-beatin' rap."

"I did, but it wasn't even like that," Marvin answered,

keeping an eye on each car that rolled by. "That charge was trumped up and you know it. I'm innocent," he protested.

"Yeah, okay, but calm down. You're acting *not innocent* and you should probably let me in on who you're hiding from. Got me tripping too." Dooney fired up a Newport cigarette, glared at Marvin suspiciously, and then tossed a glance up the street for good measure. "Is it that other woman?" he asked eventually. "Is that who you're ducking?"

"What other woman?"

"Kimberly Hightower," Dooney said knowingly. "I heard you might be sniffing behind her these days. I wouldn't blame you if you did, because she is a dime. If you got pictures with her clothes off, let me hold them for a minute."

"I can see Chandelle has gotten to you," Marvin suspected. "Have I ever been one to roam?"

"Well, lemme think." Dooney smiled at him. "All right, I'm just messing with you. You have been on the straight and narrow, I'll give you that."

"Thank you, Dooney. Finally, some common sense coming from out your mouth," he sighed, staring into the distance. Marvin's shaky behavior caused Dooney to turn around and watch his back.

"I done told you, Marvin, I've got two strikes already. The way you're carrying on, the po-po could pick me up on acting like I'm up to something."

"My bad, I'm working too much and sleeping too little," Marvin explained. "My bad."

"That's what's up," Dooney said, chuckling under his breath. "You're riding on fumes, the po' man's pick me up, No Doze and coffee." Dooney slapped Marvin on the shoulder like he felt sorry for him. "Just say no, cuz. Pork is the other white meat and caffeine is the other white drug. Leave both of them alone." He peeked around Marvin and moved him aside so he could get a clear view of two people approaching on the sidewalk. "See, now I don't trust my own people. I can't live down here being scared of young brothas like these." They observed two young black males casually passing a marijuana joint back and forth. "Hold on, Marvin. Hey!" he called out to the shorter one puffing away.

"Yeah, you, li'l dude. You look mighty familiar. Don't I know you? Ain't you Stamina Jenkins's oldest boy? That's what I thought. It's too late for you to be out here toking blunts like can't nobody smell that sticky-icky. Git on home." When the young man leered at Dooney as if he was crazy, the barber turned up the volume to match his stern warning. "You heard me. Git! Ain't nobody ever told you it's disrespectful to be eyeballing your elders? Shoot, I might be your daddy." Dooney chased him off, yelling after him. "And tell yo' mama to call Dooney! She still got the number!"

"Dooney, you for real?" Marvin asked, watching the boys flip obscene gestures once out of harm's way. "You and Stamina hooked up that long ago?"

"Naw, she was already pregnant with two little dudes in diapers when I got with her. Good thing, too; she can drop one or two a year, no lie."

"Whuuut?" Marvin said, laughing at Dooney's sophomoric antics.

"She had a nice run back in the eighties and early nineties." Dooney contended. "Six kids in five years. Every time I saw her, somebody had planted another ram in the bush."

"It's hard to argue with the math, but I wanted to pitch some other numbers to you, this proposition I got," Marvin said, using terms to pique Dooney's curiosity.

"A moneymaking proposition?" he asked between puffs.

"Is there any other kind?"

"Yep, but I don't get down like that with dudes, though. So, what is it and what's in it for me?"

"Cool, that's what I like to hear from a sharp business-man." Marvin laid out a quick and easy explanation why Dooney should become a home owner and leave his small apartment. The tax benefits were substantial, because Dooney was a sole proprietor and he owned the building he operated in. The thought of having a nice spot to enter-tain female guests appealed to him as well. It had been years since he actually had a bath, because his loft came equipped with only a shower, and it wasn't long before the pros of home ownership overtook his apprehensions of taking on a thirty-year commitment. After Marvin broke down the financial benefits of making accelerated payments to the mortgage principle to satisfy the loan years ahead of schedule, Dooney was all in.

Marvin promised him that he wouldn't regret taking the steps to solidify a stronger portfolio. Dooney didn't fully comprehend that one, but it sure did have a nice sound to it. They slapped palms and parted ways. Dooney locked up the shop and contemplated having a room ded-icated to his true love, music.

Marvin hopped in his vehicle and pushed on to the next stop, Duper's Bar & Grill. When he arrived, the place was packed. Super Dave Headley stood behind the bar pouring drinks at his usual pace, as slow as he wanted to. Patrons waved money at him, pleading for faster service.

Dave spotted Marvin at the end of the bar, gawking with a smile on his face. The bartender hollered at every-one. "Shut up! My best friend's son is here and he's next."

Marvin wanted to sprint out of the front door before the thirsty mob turned their hostility on him. Dave was unflappable. Twenty plus years in the service industry taught him one thing: His customers were always willing to wait. He sold alcohol and attitude. People expected a lot of both from him. Dave wasn't one to disappoint.

"Marvin, what can I get you?" he asked above the manic crowd.

Realizing then that he couldn't get a word in edgewise until he quenched the crowd's thirst, Marvin hopped over the bar and strapped on an apron. He winked at Dave and then rang the bar bell to get everyone's attention. "I'm serving beer only! If you want beer, I got it!" As the last three words flew from his mouth, a third of the customers pushed toward his end of the bar. "One Michelob?" Marvin shouted across the wooden bar top. "You've been in line all this time and all you want is one?" After the man thought about it, he changed his order. "That's what I thought, three Michelobs coming up. Don't push, we've got plenty. Two beers at a time, I don't have change!" Marvin shouted, racing past Dave to snatch a second rack of frosted mugs.

"Just like old times, Marvin," Dave shouted, his chest stuck out like the proud godfather that he was. "Shoot, I forgot how much I missed your summers home from college."

Marvin filled in for the next hour. Rubbing shoulders with Dave felt just as good to him. It was as close as he could get to being around his deceased father. The older man had always been in Marvin's life, as a father figure, a voice of reason, and a great friend. Marvin was reminded of that the night he helped restore order in the busy tavern. Dave wouldn't have asked for his help, too prideful mostly, but he was glad Marvin stepped in on his own. Friends shouldn't have to ask, his dad taught him when he was a kid, and he'd never forgotten it. Not that Marvin was asking anything major of Dave, all he needed was a few minutes to ask a few questions. He was surprised to learn that the shop owner currently dabbled in real estate, living a cash-poor life while investing heavily in his retirement. Dave enjoyed speaking with a college graduate about his money, without having to open another banking account or pay consultation fees with one of the many money-minding firms. Marvin struck a gold mine when Dave reported owning six rental properties, all of which he showed interest in liquidating right away. Acting as the listing and selling agents for those homes meant that Marvin stood a chance to earn six percent commissions on each deal. He calculated potential dividends based on $100,000 property values. Overwhelmed with good fortune, Marvin threw his arms around Dave and squeezed until the older man coughed.

"You can't help me sell my houses if you choke me to death," Dave jested. "I need a vacation, ain't had one in fifteen years. Thanks for looking in on me, Marvin. Your daddy would be proud of you. I know I am." Dave went on talking about Marvin's parents, funny anecdotes and stories that Marvin had heard a million times over the years, but that didn't stop him from being thoroughly entertained by each and every one.

While driving back to his apartment, Marvin received a call on his cell phone. He lowered the volume on his car stereo and answered. "Kim, it's almost ten o'clock, I thought you were the 'early to bed early to rise' type?"

"I am when I haven't been stood up," she said, as if he should have realized what she was getting at. "So you did forget?"

"Kim, I can hear it in your voice that I was supposed to have done something that I didn't." Marvin cringed while bracing himself for the fallout.

"It's Thursday and you were supposed to come by and look at my dishwasher. You know how long it takes to get a serviceman out and how they make you stick around the house all day waiting on them. Never mind, it's too late to drag you out," she said, hoping he'd sense the insincerity in her voice. She grinned when he did.

"Cool, you got me. I was on the way home after two

spectacular meetings with my warm market like you suggested in the last sales meeting."

"If you can't do business with people you know, why
should other people do business with you? Good, you
were paying attention. The question is, were you as attentive that time you stopped by here for the Hightower
Cares charity brochures?"

"Yeah, I remember the way. See you in a minute."

Marvin's mind was on cloud nine. He'd convinced
Dooney to purchase a starter home. Dave owned six of
them in his price range. All he had to do was find five
more qualified buyers, preferably young couples starting
out, singles wanting to make astute business moves, or
clients who needed to downsize their expenses. It was all
very peculiar the way his life was panning out—without
Chandelle in it. He wore that new reality on his face like
a tailored suit when Kim answered the door, in her fluffy
housecoat.

"Hey, you found me all right," she said, welcoming
him inside. "And you smell like a brewery."

"I helped a good friend of my pop's serve beers at his
bar tonight. Sorry."

"No, I'm not complaining. It was just an observation,"
she replied, as the upbeat voice on the telephone seemingly pulled a disappearing act. "The kitchen is this way,
Marvin, but if you'd rather skip it, I can make other
arrangements."

"I'm straight. Something just crossed my mind, but I'll
deal with that later. Where's the tool box and I know you
have one because you're a new millennium sistah."

Kim smiled brightly. "I'll get it from the garage."

"No, I'll get it," Marvin said cunningly. "I'm still an
old-school kind of brotha."

"My favorite kind," she answered, moving aside to let
him exercise his old-school values.

* * *

Kim sipped hot tea as Marvin lay sprawled out on the floor, fiddling with her dishwasher. She listened to him recount his discussions with Dooney and Super Dave and the pitches he made to each of them. Offering Marvin a position with her company was the right thing to do. His determination and persuasiveness were already paying off, for him and her.

In practically no time at all, Marvin's handiwork was completed. Kim was slightly disappointed that the show was over so soon. She couldn't help but delight as he writhed on his back to manipulate the inside of her appliance. It was easy to imagine Marvin's waist duplicating those motions in her bedroom, although she fought those naughty thoughts as best she could.

"It's running smooth as a top now," he told her, after returning the tool box to her garage. "Your timer was off by a few degrees. That's why it wouldn't get hot enough to dry the dishes." *Speaking of hot*, he thought, looking at the way Kim's robe hugged the rest of her. When his eyes floated up to meet hers, Kim's mouth opened in an ultra-sensual manner. She wanted to kiss him, he was sure of that as much as he'd been sure of anything in his whole life. Marvin took a deep breath, attempting to calculate a romantic night with her just as he'd done with potential business deals, but this was different, very different. *There would be no turning back if you cross into the unknown, Marvin*, he thought to himself, with Kim gazing into his eyes. *Then, there is always the possibility that I would really dig the other side.*

"A penny for your thoughts," Kim whispered.

"Don't look at me like that," he said. "It makes me . . . nervous."

"Like what, Marvin?" Kim replied, moving closer to him.

"Like I wished Chandelle would."

"Then you'd probably want to stop looking at me . . . like that," she countered.

Marvin licked his lips and swallowed hard before continuing in their dangerous game. "And how is that exactly?" he groaned softly.

"Like you were wishing I were her. It really makes me . . . well . . . I think you'd better go. Good night, Marvin."

"I'll see you at the office," he said, exhaling heartily over what almost jumped off with his boss. "Are we still cool?"

"Very, let's keep it that way."

"Agreed," he answered with a shining new resolve. "Good night, Kim."

Surveying their long good-bye at the door, Dior glanced down at her watch. She didn't believe that they got into anything that required getting undressed, because she knew that Marvin typically had Chandelle going twice as long as he'd been on the inside of Kim's home. Since it appeared that her trickery with Marvin hadn't worked in her favor, Dior decided to work it from the other end. If Chandelle didn't break up with Marvin over the hint of infidelity, she'd have to see to it that he found himself on the bad end of a good tryst.

25

Webs and Woes

"I'm coming," Marvin shouted from the kitchen in his apartment. He noted that his cupboards were bare again, although his bank account was swelling like the mumps. Dooney had viewed three of Dave's rental properties at lunch that day and wanted to look at financing another one. Marvin instructed him to relax until he'd seen them all before making applications to Kim's brokerage service for the mortgage loans. Marvin also planned a marketing strategy to reel in more clients like the McClellans, mature buyers with salaries equaling their aspirations and taste. He was clicking on all cylinders and it seemed that nothing could stand in his way. "I said I was coming," Marvin reiterated, as he hustled to answer the door when the knocks grew louder. A quick look into the peephole put a curious sneer on his face. *What is she doing here?* he thought.

"Come on, Marvin, open up!" she complained. "I brought you something nice and I can hear you breathing. Come on, I've got to pee." Reluctantly, Marvin unlocked the door and invited her in.

"Hey, Dior," he said, looking her over like a nightclub bouncer who was wise to keep his eyes on a seedy character. Marvin stood in front of her, contemplating whether he should allow her in past the living room area, remembering that whenever she just popped up he always regretted it later on.

"Whew, thanks a lot," Dior sighed, handing him a gift box with expensive cognac and two crystal glasses. "Here, this is for you. I've heard how hard you've been working and thought maybe you'd want to chill a minute and reflect on your success." When Marvin cradled the wooden box, still eyeing her suspiciously, Dior held her cheek toward him so he would feel obligated to plant a kiss on it. Marvin smirked, objected initially, then thought it ridiculous to be standoffish with Chandelle's cousin, who probably for once in her life meant well. "You're welcome. Now, can I use the restroom, or should I drop my pants and let her rip right here on the carpet?"

"Sure, Dior, go on back and do your thing."

"Ooh, my coat," she said, slipping a brown leather jacket off her shoulders. She darted past him with her handbag in tow.

When she laid it on the sofa, Marvin caught himself clocking the way her dress swayed effortlessly with her curvy hips. *Yeah, that's Chandelle's cousin all right*, he thought. *They've got the same moves.*

Behind closed doors, Dior stuffed something in a black nylon bag underneath the cabinet, camouflaged it with a stack of bath towels, then flushed the toilet in case Marvin was listening. After washing up and primping her new hairstyle, with longer weave tracks cascading past her shoulders, she smiled to her reflection in the mirror. "You are something else," she said to herself, "and then some." She exited the restroom much in same way she'd sashayed down the hall to enter it, with both hips slow dancing in perfect rhythm. "I'm about to bounce," she announced, as if he cared what she did. "I have a hot date and it might last all night, if you know what I mean."

"Huh, I'd be surprised if it didn't," he smarted back. "Thanks for the gift, Dior. I have been doing nothing but putting in work. It'll be nice to kick back and take a pinch out for myself."

"Well, what are you waiting on?" she asked. "Pour me a swig so I can kick back too." Dior begun unwrapping Marvin's gift.

"I thought you had to roll out," he said, with a nervous hitch in his voice. He couldn't help thinking about the last time she pranced through the kitchen, wearing nearly next to nothing.

"I do, and don't worry, I'm not gonna drink it all. There's just something about popping a cork that appeals to me." She let her comment hang in the air momentarily for full effect. "So, here is a li'l for me and, of course, two fingers for Marvin Hutchins, the real-estate tycoon." Dior tossed a mouthful of sipping liquor down the back of her throat like an old pro. "Ahhhhh, that was smooth," she gurgled with her mouth on fire. "Very smooth."

"You're getting too big for your britches," Marvin joked, as he sampled a measure as well. "Yes, this is smooth. You did good, Dior."

"Cool, now it's time to do some good for myself. Help me with my coat," she prodded, when he purposely stood a safe distance from her. "Come on, boy, I don't bite . . . no more."

Marvin sat his glass down on the counter and obliged, holding the jacket behind her so she could easily slide her arms in the sleeves, in the same way he'd done for Chandelle too many times to count. "This is a very expensive jacket," he said, noting the quality and design.

"My new gig is paying well. I've already started treating myself to some of this and that." *I can't wait to treat myself to some of you*, she thought, with him located mere inches away. "Be careful if you can't be good," Dior told him on her way to the door.

"You should take your own advice," Marvin replied.

"I have been. I do. And I will. Enjoy," she said with a carefree flip of her wrist, an indication that her good deed for the day was done. As soon as she jumped in the car, her trusty Ford Escort with a fresh paint job and shiny rims to set it off, Dior called Chandelle to orchestrate the back end of her covert operation. "Hey, Cuz," she said, loudly and jubilantly, "I'm on my way to swoop you. Get something on so we can step out tonight. Naw, I'm not going to drag you to some hole in the wall with rough-necks pulling all on you. I don't go there anymore. Besides, the police raided that joint the night after we fell up in it. Hush and get dressed. I'll be there in about fifteen minutes. Bye."

Dior didn't ask Chandelle to join her for an evening out on the town, nor did she allow her to decline the offer, she couldn't afford to. After weeks of surveillance, plotting, and engaging herself as a provocateur, Dior had her stars aligned and devilment mapped out to the letter. She had devised a stunt so devious that no one would see it coming.

"Ooh, girl, look at you," Dior squealed with excitement when Chandelle answered the door fully dressed. She fussed over her cousin's navy wool jumpsuit that would undoubtedly turn heads. "You know I gots to get me one of those."

"Hey, Dior, I knew you'd be superfly so I shrugged on something cute." Chandelle took in Dior's burnt-colored cocktail dress and matching animal print shawl. "That dress is hot." Although she couldn't remember the last time Dior adorned herself in anything other than tight pants, this was a great change of pace. "Oh, hold on. I'll get my car, then come through the garage."

"No way am I letting you push your whip tonight. This is a girl's night out and I'm the designated driver. Lock the door and let's be out." Again, Dior's fast-talking theatrics negated the opportunity for Chandelle to think for herself, just like Dior intended.

"Why not," Chandelle agreed. "I can drink what I want and relax too. I hope they have some crab claws where we're going. I'm in the mood for seafood." She sauntered toward Dior's pimped-out ride in her high heels, admiring the racy metallic custom makeover. "Sweet paint job, but these rims are gonna fool around and get us jacked," she predicted.

"Just get in," Dior grumbled. "Ain't nobody gonna jack me up for these, they only look choice. I don't part with my pennies that easy."

Chandelle turned the radio on, then cranked it up louder. "So says you, new sounds, rims that bling, and tight polish to turn it out. Appears you've been tossing pennies all over the place."

"Not any that I'll miss," Dior said, dismissing the talk about her frivolous spending. "What I have missed is sharing *we* time, Chandelle and me time. Promise me that you'll loosen up and ride with me tonight, nothing wild but super chilled."

"True be told, I could use some we time too. Since Marvin . . ."

"Ahh-nah-nah, no Marvin talk," Dior whined. "One minute into our *we* time and you're already bringing a man into it. It must be difficult to have him on your mind, but for one night, just one, could you please . . . hold it down on the *y'all*? Thank you very much."

Chandelle laughed at Dior's insistence, feeling like she was a young girl, footloose and fancy free, hitting the strip for some fun times and carefree laughs. That was pre-Marvin; of course, she'd begun to reminisce until Dior's orders chased those renegade thoughts away. One night, without the mention of Marvin coming out of her mouth, that would take some doing no matter who was opposed to it. That man was still her heart. "Okaaay," Chandelle acquiesced after pretending it pained her to do so. "That gives us plenty of time to discuss where all of your new pennies are coming from?"

Dior glanced at Chandelle from the corner of her eye. She was salty over the question but played it off. "So, how is Marvin doing these days?" Both of them howled over her witty stay-out-of-mine comeback.

The valet attendant at Café Bleu, an ultraposh restaurant and bar, grinned when he saw two very attractive women inching forward in a candy-painted Ford. He straightened his red jacket as they approached. "Good Lawd," he exclaimed through clenched teeth. "Welcome to Café Bleu where heaven must be missing two angels."

"Isn't he a sweet little boy?" said Dior, to back him off her. "Didn't me and your mama go to school together?" The young man took his ribbing in good fashion as she handed him the keys.

"My bad, that's an angel and another somebody from the other place," he said to himself, thinking they were out of earshot.

"I heard that!" Dior spat over her shoulder.

"So, I hope you did," he replied with a wicked smile. "I bet my mama didn't like you either."

Chandelle doubled over laughing at his retort. "He got you there, Dior. Should have quit while you were ahead."

"And you should have had my back. I can't let some goofy valet clown me. I've got a rep' to protect. I'm known on these streets," she testified proudly.

"Oh, I don't know you," said a burly doorkeeper when she tried to stroll past him. "IDs please."

"I thought this was a restaurant," Chandelle contested, while fishing in her purse. "Y'all got a cover charge too?"

"No cover tonight," the doorman grumbled. He checked the birthday on each of their driver's licenses. "We don't like drama at the Café. Cool, go on in," he decided, with one eye tracing the snug fit of Chandelle's jumper.

"Some people take their jobs too seriously," Chandelle snapped. She held her wallet opened to insert her ID. "I thought he was going to strip-search us."

"In his dreams," Dior quipped. "Fat boy already pictured you naked on a plate with a scoop of grits and a hot-buttered biscuit to sop up the juices."

Dior flagged a waitress down, then asked for a table for two. She was rudely told to find herself an available table and she'd be over to serve them. "I hope that means I get the tip too," was Dior's response. "That's what I figured," she said when the waitress recanted her earlier statement. After sitting down, Dior appraised the talent in the room. "Hmm, hmm, hmm, it's raining men and I forgot my bucket."

"I'm glad we came for some *we* time," Chandelle reminded her, "because there are a lot of handsome distractions."

Dior rolled her eyes until she saw that same lazy waitress beckoning to them. "Ooh, come on, our table is ready."

Several single men ogled while they trekked across the restaurant. It had been a number of years since Chandelle felt like she'd forgotten to put on any clothing before leaving the house. Men with female dates were the worst, undressing her with their eyes.

Dior wasn't fazed in the least by the overwhelming attention; she was accustomed to being around horny grown men with their objectives written on their faces. "Men are so transparent," she mocked, making eye contact with a well-dressed gentleman near the end of the bar. When she winked at him, he headed over toward their table. Dior quickly held the dinner menu in front of her face. Chandelle blushed unexpectedly after recognizing him. His name was Tony Jones, Chandelle's last ex-boyfriend.

"Tony?" she said, standing to give him a cordial hug. Tony was Marvin's age, near the same size, and drop-dead gorgeous. At thirty-one he was a perfect picture of health and masculinity. "Wow, look, Dior, it's Tony Jones."

Dior lowered the menu slowly, like it was a bother to speak. "Hey, Tony," she spat hurriedly, faking her enthusiasm.

"Hey, Chandelle, Dior. Thank you for supporting a brotha. It's a treat having y'all dine with us."

"Us?" Dior repeated, manufacturing her surprise with a broad, open-handed gesture.

Tony blushed, attempting to shield his modesty, a character trait Chandelle admired about him in the past. "Actually, us is me. I bought this place about eighteen months ago."

"All of this at Café Bleu belongs to you?" She tossed a phony "I'm very impressed" smile his way, but it was meant to smack Chandelle upside her head to get her thinking the same thing.

"Jeez, Tony, I remember you talking about leaving the corporate arena and doing it your way, but what a leap," Chandelle said, marveling at his success. *Jeez,Tony*? she thought to herself in retrospect. *Where did that come from? I'm not twenty-three anymore. How silly was that?*

Tony's black pinstriped suit and white cotton shirt set off his perfect teeth and thin dark mustache. His neatly trimmed wavy hair over golden bronzed skin was the icing on the cake. She loved the way he kept up his appearance, and had kept her up late at night, too. Oddly enough, Chandelle had begun to conjure up images of that, against her better judgment.

Tony and Dior pretended not to notice how Chandelle failed to stop examining him from his manicured fingertips to his wide, kissable lips. Dior almost laughed but managed to keep it inside. "Tony Jones, this is quite a surprise. You're doing well for yourself. Everybody's talking about Café Bleu and it's packed, so the food must be banging."

"We're proud of the menu, but hey, I didn't come over here to talk shop with the one who got away, and y'all didn't come here to listen to me talk. Eat, drink, and have a great time. It's on me."

"Tony, we can't accept your generosity," Chandelle said, while shaking her head adamantly.

"Yes, we can and we will," argued Dior. "It's not every day that a fine man offers dinner and drinks without somebody expecting me to get undressed for dessert."

Chandelle was appalled at her crass statement. "Dior, please!" she said, just about as embarrassed as if she'd said it herself. ·

"It's all right, Chandelle," Tony said, chuckling lightly. "Dior's got a point. Enjoy yourselves, no strings attached. It was great seeing you again," he told Chandelle in parting.

"Yeah, it was," she replied. "It was real cool."

"What's cool is that the food is free," Dior offered, with her finger pointing to the priciest items on the menu. "I want one of everything. Then I want three slices of bread pudding with extra syrup."

"I'd like crab claws and sautéed shrimp over angel hair pasta, asparagus spears with those cute little potatoes on the side," Chandelle recited, as she looked over the dinner selections for anything sounding remotely similar. The waitress, who appeared to be too consumed with herself to seat them initially, returned with a splendid personality fresh out of the box.

"Mr. Jones says you're special guests of his, so I'll see to it your dining experience is a pleasant one."

Dior looked at Chandelle peculiarly. She was trying to

guess whether the woman had read that line off the back of a notecard or had simply practiced being that plastic.

"My girl was wondering if y'all can make her something that's not on the menu?" Dior said, suggesting that special guests of Mr. Jones should get whatever they wanted and served however they wanted it. The waitress must have felt the same because she wrote down exactly what Chandelle had a taste for, down to the little potatoes on the side. However, she experienced a difficult challenge explaining to the chef why someone would order ribs, fried chicken, and catfish on the same platter, to go along with the French fries that Dior said she couldn't do without. The bottle of Cristal Tony had sent over served well as a decadent complement to Chandelle's seafood hors d'oeuvre. Dior declined to fiddle with an appetizer, she said, while real food was cooking in the kitchen.

26

Evil Is as Evil Does

Chandelle felt as if she were in heaven when dinner hit the table. Her entrée smelled divine and the presentation reminded her of fancy dishes displayed in food and beverage magazines. "Oh, I'm going to bust if I eat another bite," she groaned, stuffing herself with the most memorable meal of the year. "Dior, you've hardly touched your plate. What's the matter?"

Dior picked at the catfish, took a tiny sip from her champagne flute, and then smirked uncomfortably. "I don't know, cuz, but something has my stomach knotted up."

"It isn't the food?" Chandelle asked, patting her own stomach.

"No, it was tasty, but I have a friend who's not been doing well. He's kinda sick, chest pains and such," she answered, talking about Marvin. "Problems at the job had him down for a minute, but things are looking up."

"I hope you're not running behind Kevlin anymore. He can't do a thing but waste your time."

Dior placed a cold French fry in her mouth and chewed on it slowly.

Chandelle could tell something was on her mind, something she didn't want to talk about readily. "What's gotten you staring into space all of a sudden?"

"Just thinking I should have ordered the steak," she answered nonchalantly. That lie came out as easy as breathing. "But we'd better hurry up and finish. I heard they move the tables back and open up the dance floor at ten o'clock."

Chandelle read her watch at nine-fifty. "I didn't see a dance floor when we came in."

"That's because you're sitting on it," Dior answered quickly. "Let's find the waitress so she can take these plates away. Maybe I can find her on the way to the restroom." She left Chandelle with her third glass of alcohol, one more than she was used to, and champagne always went straight to her head. Dior had mapped out every detail of the evening. Now it was time to spring the second trap.

Tony's office was down the hall from the restrooms. Dior flew past them and hooked a left. When she approached the waitress who had been attending them, Dior overheard her complaining about ungrateful customers. Dior pulled two twenties from the thick roll in her clutch handbag. "Here's your tip," she offered, with the discourteous intent to drive the waitress away. "Now see what you can do to earn it." Backing away timidly, the woman studied the money, then stuffed it inside of a small black portfolio.

"Thank . . ." was all Dior heard before she slammed the door shut. "Tony, where have you been? Chandelle's been asking about you," she lied. "And you act like what y'all had doesn't mean anything to you. I saw you, Tony, I saw how you looked at Chandelle when we came in, and I saw her getting goofy over you."

"Dior, I have a bad feeling about this. Yes, I still care for Chandelle and probably will forever, but none of this seems on the level to me. Not to mention your being rude to my staff."

"The meal was complimentary and that silly waitress has forty dollars to pocket. Trust me, she will make out okay. Back to you and Chandelle, though, her and Marvin are about done. There's poison between them. I wasn't supposed to tell you this but he got arrested for beating her. You know there's no way she's gonna bring it up. She's too proud to admit putting up with an abusive husband." Dior was on a roll. She didn't mind stretching the truth on an ordinary lark. That night, she had a lot riding on Tony buying her story. "Look, she deserves better than him, than that. Chandelle bought her own home to get away from him and she deserves to be happy with a good brotha like you." Dior hit the main vein with that one.

Tony shrugged his broad shoulders and stood up behind his desk. He envisioned himself as Chandelle's would-be savior from a violent spouse, and he liked the way it made him feel. "I would like to see her happy, but I imagined she was with what's-his-name," he said with a soft smile on his lips.

"His name's not important," Dior said. "What is important is you getting back out there with your charming self and show our girl the time of her life. Oh, and she can't handle her liquor, so I suggest you order her one more to get her good and loose." Dior pulled a piece of paper from her purse and pushed it into Tony's hand. "You might need this," she informed him. "See you at Chandelle's divorce party." She opened the door, checked the hallway, and then scooted into the ladies' room before Chandelle came searching for her.

"What did you say to the waitress?" Chandelle asked, when Dior returned to the table.

"Why, what did she say I said?" she answered venomously.

"Just that you took care of her and something about

you being off of your meds," Chandelle revealed, behind a stifled laugh. "Don't trip, she wasn't too bent out of shape. Huh, she cleared the table in record time and took off, counting her money."

"Good, let's head over to the bar," Dior suggested. "They're starting to move the tables back."

No sooner than Chandelle's behind landed on the wing-backed bar chair did Tony make another appearance. He hand-delivered a second bottle of chilled Cristal with three glasses. When she objected, Tony spread on the charm. "Chandelle, it's been years since I've seen you and there's no telling when you'll bless me with your presence again. At least do me the honor of having a drink with the prettiest woman I've ever been privileged to call mine." He watched Chandelle waffling under peer pressure. To push her over the edge, he dug deep into his bag of flattery and came out with an ace. "My mama still says you're her favorite. Yeah, she doesn't mind letting every sistah she meets know that too. She misses you almost as much as I do."

Chandelle read his face. There wasn't one sign of untruthfulness in his eyes, not anywhere. "How can I say no to your mama?" Chandelle answered. "Sue Ann did serve up dirt on you from your other girlfriends. I'll never forget that time your college sweetheart came home nosing around for you and Sue Ann ran her off with a broom, shouting how she was old news."

Tony's expression glowed against the candlelit lamp sitting on the bar. "Monise hasn't gotten over that yet. She came in here last month, loud and still salty. I was forced to tell her that you and I didn't make it. The worse part was you and I couldn't even hold onto our friendship either."

He poured two drinks but Dior placed a hand over her glass. "Uh-uh, Tony, you've already done more than enough and I'm driving, so maybe next time."

"Yeah, like I was saying," he joked, totally ignoring Dior. "You have someone, I respect that. Friendship like we shared doesn't come every day. To friendship," he said, raising his glass. Chandelle nodded her head, thinking back on moments better left in the past, where they belonged.

"To friendship," she agreed wholeheartedly. *He would have to be the finest friend a woman could hope for,* she thought. *My goodness, he still makes me feel like butter. Remember you are married, although not happily at the present. Hmm, Tony would have made an excellent husband if he weren't so driven. Success trumped his love for me. He made good on his dream after ours fizzled. I can't blame him. I wanted marriage and he needed to be somebody first. We both found what we wanted, so why am I sitting up here looking into his eyes and wondering how my life would have turned out had I committed myself to him like he did to his dream? Sue Ann said I was perfect for her son. Marvin seemed perfect for me. Whew, my head is spinning.*

When Chandelle emerged from her daze, she was seeing double. "Tony, where's Dior?" she asked groggily, "and why are there two of you?"

"Okay, let me find her for you," Tony offered, sensing she was sufficiently sauced and ready for the taking.

Chandelle's cell phone rang. She shook her head while feeling around in her bag for it. "Oh, here it is. Yes, uh . . . hello?"

"Chandelle, I am so sorry but that sick friend I was telling you about, well, he needs me right now." Dior explained. "I hated to run out but it's a serious matter. See if Tony can call a taxi for you. Sorry, I'll talk to you later. Bye." Once again she ended the conversation leaving Chandelle no choice and defenseless to reject her proposition.

"Okay, but that was not cool," Chandelle replied, after Dior had hung up the phone.

Tony, playing the concerned *friend* to the hilt, listened as Chandelle asked him to ring for a ride home. Of course, he wouldn't hear of it. He instructed the manager to lock up at closing time, then had the valet bring his car around.

The young man took a glance at Chandelle stumbling in her heels as he maneuvered Tony's black S-Class Mercedes to the front door. "Uh-oh, another fallen angel. With Mr. Jones she's liable to be a devil by morning." He handed the expensive sedan over to his boss and stepped back out of the way. "Have a *good* night, Mr. Jones."

"It's not like that this time," Tony answered without hesitation. "She's supposed to be my wife."

Chandelle giggled when she heard it. "Your wife, huh? When was all this *supposed* to happen, after you made it big? I never asked you for a dime and I didn't need you to be anything other than a man who'd put me above all he cared for. Where are we going anyway?"

"I was not going to let some stranger get you home safe tonight so I'm doing it myself," he answered, having memorized the directions Dior gave him in his office.

"Good, you're headed in the right direction. Keep on driving and make a right on Lake Highland. It's not too far from here."

Chandelle drifted off to sleep shortly after that, babbling about friendship, marriage, Marvin, and mayhem. Tony cruised along, glancing at her body nestled against the leather seat. Even intoxicated, Chandelle was irresistible. He often contemplated how his life would have been had she given him a bit longer to realize she meant more to him than the things money could provide. Now that Dior had delivered her, perfectly gift wrapped, Tony had a second chance to get inside her head again. He fig-

ured that getting into Chandelle's bed wasn't such a bad
way to connect their past and future with one steamy
night of unrivaled passion.

Chandelle fumbled with the key when they got to her
house. She stepped in to use her bathroom, passed out,
and threw up on herself. She had gone from sensually
sauced to dead drunk in the short drive to her house. Tony
tapped on the bathroom door after she'd been there over
ten minutes. "Chandelle, are you all right in there? Chandelle?" When he heard what sounded like snoring on the
other side of that door, he twisted the knob and opened it.
Chandelle had fallen asleep on the toilet. Tony did what
any man in his right mind would have done in an instance
that required precise execution during a difficult dilemma,
he peeled off every stitch of their clothing, held Chandelle
gingerly under a warm shower until she was clean, then
he toweled her off and climbed into bed.

Dior pulled away from the curb across the street from
Chandelle's house when she saw the lights go off in the
master bedroom. *Perfect, I knew Tony would come through
for me*, she thought. *It took him longer than I planned, but
done is done*. Dior glided through an intersection wearing
an impish grin. Within minutes, she arrived at Marvin's
apartment. She used the key she had neglected to return
after moving out. Within a few more minutes she wasn't
wearing anything at all.

Marvin had helped himself to a stiff shot of the cognac
she'd cleverly provided for such an occasion. He didn't
stir when she eased past him toward the bathroom. Dior
closed the door and flicked on the light. The bag she left
behind earlier in the day was still there, tucked under the
cabinet. She fastened on a wig with bobby pins, sprayed
on Chandelle's favorite perfume, and licked her lips. Anticipation guided her into Marvin's bedroom. She slipped

beneath the covers, began planting kisses on his chest, then lower. He murmured Chandelle's name and reached out for her, but Dior whispered insistently for him to relax. "No, baby, I've got this. Don't touch, don't move. Just be still and enjoy it." His hips gyrated when she placed him into her mouth.

"Ooh, that's good, Chandelle," he groaned. "I dreamed you'd use your key sooner or later."

"I know, I know," Dior answered, in a low, strained tone.

"I want you . . . I've missed you. Give it to me," he pleaded, growing in size and desire exponentially.

"Okay, move your hands," Dior ordered, when he made a second attempt to hold her by the waist. Unwittingly, Marvin complied. He shoved both hands under his pillow and let her satisfy him in her own way. Dior straddled his lap, forcing him inside her. Marvin's mouth watered. "Ohhh, it's good, Chandelle. Mmm, it's so good."

"Uhhh-huh," Dior moaned seductively, running her scheme at top speed. She smiled as Marvin's hips jerked erratically. This is what she'd been waiting for. "Come on," she whispered, with an exasperated breath. "Come on, I feel it. Let it go, daddy!" she screamed as he climaxed. His muscles contracted and most of him pulsated.

"Ahhh, something's wrong," he mumbled, trying to push Dior off. "Wait a minute," he said, reaching for the lamp on the nightstand. "Something's wrong," he repeated until the light exposed Dior and what they had experienced together. When it became apparent to him, he leaped from the bed with the sheet draped around his waist. "Dior? What the . . . What are you doing here?"

Dior moaned sensually while sprawled on the bed. "Don't you mean, what have *we* done?" she asked rhetorically. "Seeing as how my eggs are ripe, we probably just made a baby."

27

Too Hurt to Reason

After Dior shared her revelation, she spread her legs wider and laughed. "I knew you wanted it so I thought I'd let you have some," she said, mocking him.

Marvin paced around the bed like a caged animal, his room smelling of expensive perfume and cheap sins of the flesh. He clawed at his head, sweat pouring from it. His thick chest heaved in and out. Confusion held him hostage as he growled furiously. "You must be insane to think I wanted any part of this! You're sick, Dior, sick!" he shouted. "I know one thing, you're not taking me to hell with you. I'm reporting this to . . . to the police. Yeah, breaking . . . entering and . . . and rape," he stammered, wrestling on his underwear.

"Call the police!" she spat. "I'll tell them you raped me, and they love to beat black men half to death for violent crimes against women. Me rape you, ain't that a trip? First, I didn't hear you saying *No*. And you didn't have no problems with it when I was riding that big ol' thing of yours. Anyway, you were throwing it back just as hard, tryna get every little bit of this."

"You are crazy," he concluded. "I wouldn't have let you touch me if I hadn't thought you were Chandelle. I've got to do something about this." He scanned the room for her clothing. "Where are they, Dior, your clothes, where'd you hide them?" Marvin lunged at her violently. Dior kicked at him with both feet.

"Leeeave me alone!" she screamed. "Marvin . . . let me go." Dior whaled at him with her fists when he hoisted her from the bed. Tossed over his strong shoulders like a laundry bag, Dior's eyes bucked wildly. "Where are you taking me? Put me down!" He carried Dior's nude body into the bathroom, struggling to collect her dress, shoes, and purse as she put up a good fight to spring free. "You're hurting me, Marvin!"

"So, all you've done is hurt people who've tried to help you. Chandelle is your own cousin. She's your blood. She took you in, and this is how you repay her?" Marvin's eyes landed on the black nylon bag and bottle of perfume resting on the bathroom counter. "You're finally going to get what's coming to you. The games end tonight." He clutched her belongings in his left hand and held tightly to her with the other one. As he marched toward the front door with her draped over him, Dior panicked.

"Ohhh, no, you're not throwing me out after what we just did. Marvin, stop! Don't put me out there," she begged.

"Shut up!" he fired back. Marvin fought to pull the door open.

Dior was stomping mad, cold, and naked when he shoved her outside. "You're wrong for this," she asserted angrily, peering around to see who was getting a look at everything she had. "This is wrong, Marvin."

He threw her dress out on the sidewalk with her shoes and purse behind it. "Here, take what's yours and go. Don't ever come around here again or so help me I'll . . ." Marvin caught himself, well aware of the last time the police showed up at his apartment.

Dior tramped down the stairs after her clothing. "Go on and threaten me. I'ma tell Dooney and you know what he did to Kevlin."

"I don't care. Go on and *tell* Dooney," Marvin barked, insisting that he could give less than a flip if she did. "You think I'm worried about your brother? You'd better think again," he yelled, recognizing that Chandelle's opinion and feelings were the only ones that meant anything to him. Then, it hit him. If his wife had to hear about a sexual encounter with her cousin, it had better come from him. Marvin had the truth on his side, he figured, as long as Chandelle didn't hear lies from someone else beforehand. "Yeah, I told Chandelle you were trouble," he shouted at Dior. "Now she'll believe me." Marvin ducked back inside and slammed the door.

Dior slinked down the stairs and snatched her dress off the ground, cussing and ranting about not letting Marvin get away with putting her out like trash after having hooked up for the first time. She rammed her feet into her shoes and searched the immediate area for items that might have fallen from her purse. Boiling over with resentment, tears of anger spilled from Dior's eyes. "Ain't nobody gonna treat me like some of jump-off piece," she ranted. "Uh-uh, I've worked too hard to give up now." She threw her purse inside the car and hopped in the driver's seat. Dior was oblivious to the number of people spying from their bedroom windows, while she stared at her haggard appearance in the rear view mirror. "Putting me out after hitting it . . . I don't know who he thinks he is," she hissed to her reflection. She continued her tirade until she noticed Marvin hustling down the stairs from his apartment, dressed in jeans, an athletic jacket, and running shoes. Dior started her car and hurriedly backed out of the parking space, fearing he may have come out to cause her bodily harm. She lowered the car window and waved her middle finger in the air. "I'ma get you, Marvin. You'll see."

"Chandelle's going to deal with you," he answered, his tone dripping with confidence. He climbed in the SUV and whipped into reverse. Dior realized he was serious about telling the whole sordid story to Chandelle. Marvin was headed there to reveal her escapades at that very moment. Dior burned rubber out of the parking lot, spinning her wheels and spitting white smoke behind her.

Marvin gave chase, following her down back streets through dangerous intersections and red lights. He appeared at Chandelle's address just as Dior hopped from her parked car. It was odd the way she stood in the middle of the street daring him to expose what she had tried to get away with. Marvin thought she'd be halfway up the walk and shouting to the mountaintops about their romp, but she didn't. "What's up, you lose your nerve?" he grunted. "You're about to lose more than that."

He was so self-assured that the table had turned he didn't notice that there was a Mercedes parked in Chandelle's driveway. Dior hadn't missed it, though. She felt ambivalent about Marvin finding out about Tony, but quickly determined that it added leverage to her master plan, tearing Chandelle's marriage apart to give her unfettered access to her husband.

"Marvin, there's something else," Dior said, trailing behind him toward the front door. "You need to think about what you're doing. There won't be no way to get past it if you ring that bell." Dior darted in front of him as he approached the house. "Listen to me," she whined, slapping at his hand as he reached for the doorbell. "Ten seconds. Please listen for ten seconds."

"You ain't even worth that," he grumbled.

"Please," Dior said, as soberly as she knew how. Marvin huffed but agreed to lower his hand. "Marvin, before you ruin all of our lives, you need to consider everything. You think Chandelle will believe that you never knew it wasn't her in the bed with you. Think about it now. Marvin, you had to have known that what I put on you wasn't hers." Dior tried to read his mind by gazing into his squinted eyes. He had begun to give it serious consideration when the lights came on in the house. Marvin and the cunning manipulator stood on the porch, expecting Chandelle to investigate the noise, discover them when answering the door. You could have knocked Marvin over with a feather when Tony opened it instead.

"Dior, that is you?" Tony said, wearing damp slacks and an opened dress shirt. "What are you doing here this late?"

"Hey, Tony," she answered with a surprisingly keen grin. "Where's Chandelle?"

"She's upstairs sleeping," he replied slowly, eyeing Marvin's clenched teeth. "Who's your friend?"

"He's my husband," Chandelle said, appearing behind Tony wearing practically nothing at all.

Tony turned to Chandelle, then back at Marvin to size him up. "I thought he was in lockdown."

Marvin's hands contracted into two huge fists. "I was, but I'm out now," he said, glaring back at Tony.

Chandelle placed both hands over her face. "Dior, what did you tell him?"

"I didn't have anything to do with this," Dior offered.

"I didn't intend any of this," Chandelle said, her sad gaze fixed on Marvin. "This cannot be happening."

His eyes glassed over, filled with pain and betrayal. "Funny, that was the thing I was just thinking," he growled before nailing Tony with a stiff right jab. Tony's knees buckled as he fell back into the house. Marvin dashed inside to tear him apart, but Chandelle's terrified expression stopped him. He remembered his short stint in the county jail and the last thing the giant tyrant, who was due to stand trial for murder, said as the state corrections officer took him away in chains, "Don't ever let your love for no female get your freedom papers revoked, College Boy."

Suddenly, Marvin heard Chandelle screaming, he blinked several times and then peered up at the screwdriver he'd raised above his head. He had no idea how it got there, but he was so close to plunging it into a stranger's chest. During a blessed moment of clarity, Marvin got up and threw the sharp tool to the floor. He gathered how it must've looked, him standing over Chandelle's late-night houseguest. Dior and Tony were silent, both hoping he'd leave for obviously differing reasons. Chandelle's hand was holding her mouth closed, sensing correctly that in spite of what she said or how it came out, there was no remedy for what Marvin stumbled onto that night. The hurt ran too deep.

Tears ran away from Chandelle's eyes. "Marvin, please don't go," she cried, stepping over Tony to run after her man. "It's not what you think, Marvin! Baby, come back and we'll talk about it. You'll, you'll see that it's nothing!" she yelled. Defiant and disturbed beyond reasoning with, Marvin lit out as fast as he could.

Tony pushed past Chandelle on the front walkway as he hurried to his sedan. "Y'all deserve each other, Chandelle. You, him, and Dior, you deserve each other," he proclaimed bitterly, after seeing his past and future with Chandelle collide. "Dior, don't even think about getting me mixed up in something like this again. And if you ever come by the café, I'll have you arrested for trespassing. Believe that!"

"Come on in the house and put something on," Dior said, nudging Chandelle inside. "You're gonna catch a death of cold."

"What was Tony talking about, Dior? Did you get him mixed up in something?" Chandelle interrogated harshly.

"Nothing, I . . ." she tried to explain.

"Shut up!" Chandelle spat, poking her finger in Dior's face. "It's because of you Marvin came over here tonight. If you hadn't told him Tony was here, he wouldn't have known. How could you sell me out like that?"

"I . . . I . . . didn't say . . ." she stuttered, when confronted with too much of the truth to handle.

"Shut up!" Chandelle snapped again. "Everything that comes out of your mouth is bound to be a lie. Now you've ruined it for me. I hope you're happy, home wrecker. How does it feel? You got what you wanted. I didn't see it until you actually showed up on my doorstep with my husband. You're jealous of Marvin," she'd concluded wrongly. "It must really mess with you that I love him. Well, Dior, you need to grow up. I can't live for you and look after you like I've done since we were kids," she sobbed. "I want you to get out of my house." Dior's feet didn't move. She stood there undecided on what to say, if anything. "I said get out!" Chandelle hollered louder than before. "You're no longer welcome in my home. Marvin told me you were nothing but trouble. I should have believed him and chased you off like a rabid dog. Look at what you've done! It's over now. My marriage is over."

Dior made one last attempt to appeal to Chandelle's sense of family, but she had nothing else to say and desired to hear even less. Dior backed away and closed the door. She meandered down the pathway to the curb and was filled with mixed emotions. On the one hand, her well-devised plan had rolled off famously. On the other hand, she hadn't imagined ending up without Marvin or Chandelle in her life. Giving it a lot of thought, Dior spent the waking hours wondering what she was going to do next.

28

Knee Mail

November came and went without Marvin returning Chandelle's calls. She spent Thanksgiving with Grace's family, bouncing Nicole off her knee and loving every minute of it. Dinner was superb, but it wasn't the same as at home. The psychologist Chandelle had been seeing on a weekly basis told her to focus her energies on pushing ahead, charting the next twelve months, and preserving her sanity. While it sounded like sensible advice, there were too many stones that remained unturned. Chandelle's future was so uncertain that it was inconceivable to map out the next week of her life, much less try to forecast the following year. She was battling mounting stress and guilt stemming from her reactions to circumstances that had been initiated by Dior's meddling. Her mortgage and car notes were a drain on her bank account. Enduring the holiday season without Marvin to share her favorite time of the year placed an immeasurable strain on her heart.

When Chandelle finally realized she had nowhere else to turn, she made a conscious effort to look inward. She felt bad about flying off the handle when seeing Marvin with Kimberly, and having his furniture snatched from the apartment. Chandelle was even kicking herself for falling prey to good times and sweet love that too many happily married women took for granted. Her prayer life suffered incredibly because real life before Marvin's arrest had been so blissful that she'd forgotten to pay reverence to the one who had made it so.

Tears of sadness were transformed into tears of joy during a church service one Sunday morning as the minister's sermon on *God's knee mail* address made her dilemma evaporate into thin air. Grace, sitting in the same pew when it happened, leaned forward to catch a better look at Chandelle, who was holding her sides and giggling like it was going out of style. Peculiar behavior was at times commonplace from members of the congregation when their awakening refused to wait. Chandelle rocked back and forth, bursting at the seams as the choir belted out, *"I am resolved no longer to linger."*

Shortly after they took their seats, she strolled to the front of the sanctuary, with a congregation numbering 1,700 looking on. Normally too private and too proud to approach the masses in personal prayers, Chandelle stood boldly with the microphone in hand. She dabbed at her cheeks with a tissue, but it didn't affect the flow dribbling down her face.

"I'm Chandelle Hutchins, and I'd like to give honor to God, and my Savior Jesus Christ this morning. See, some of you may not know this, but I've always sat out there wondering why a person would come way up here and broadcast their business, but today I have my answer. Prayers of the righteous availeth much, says the Bible. While I believed that, I was scared to let anyone know I needed somebody to pray for me."

She fought back sniffles as the minister shouted, "Amen, sistah!"

Chandelle panned the area Marvin had shared with

her, but didn't see him. "Well, I'm up here, I am no longer ashamed. Y'all can talk about me all you want because my marriage is a mess, but that's not enough to stop me from asking my church family to pray . . . that my man comes back home. Thank you." Her testimony and frankness fortified several other women and a handful of men to go forward and bare their crosses publicly, each one in desperate need of prayers as well.

After the church service ended, Chandelle was barraged with married women who carried in their hearts similar words that hadn't reached their mouths yet, although she read it in their eyes clear enough. Feeling their pain convinced her that she was a lot like them, not hopeless or alone, just lonely, and that was a whole 'nother thing altogether. Grace passed her daughter to Wallace so that her arms could hold Chandelle tightly.

"You've finally caught on," Grace whispered. "Caught on to what you've been turning up your nose at. You don't have to go through anything by yourself. There is power in prayer for those who believe. Today you've humbled yourself and God requires that of us who follow him. You know what you'll get acting like you don't need to go to Him?" Chandelle shook her head slowly, insinuating that she didn't. "Nothing worth having," Grace answered. "Remember this, when you're down to nothing, He is up to something."

Feeling as if a ton weight had been lifted from her, Chandelle drew up the courage to do the one thing she'd asked others for but tussled with until that very day. She drove home, kneeled down beside her bed, and prayed like a child whose father had the power to respond to it. "God, I don't know how long it's been since you've heard my voice. Too long I know, but I'm here now, and despite not knowing the proper words to tell you how sorry I am, I feel it necessary to say it anyway. I'm asking your forgiveness for the harm I've caused myself and my marriage. You're more than familiar with my ways," she said, as a rush of emotion overcame her. "And . . . and you know my heart. I'm not used to asking for much because you've been so good to me already but . . . I'm praying not only today but every day that you mend my heart and tell Marvin how much I still love him and want him in my life. Father, I don't know if that's enough, but I do know you're listening. I pray that it be your will that my husband finds it within himself to see past the woman I am and recognize the Christian I'm trying to be. Father, please hear my cries, forgive my sins, and hold me close to you. In Jesus's name, I ask all things. Amen."

Chandelle slipped off her dress and climbed beneath the covers. Within seconds she drifted off to sleep. She dreamed of children playing in the yard, building a world around them, and making her house a real home. Blissful visions of a love deferred with a houseful of babies danced in her head and continued their ballet even as she awoke, refreshed and at peace for the first time in many months. However likely that the answer to her prayer would be a resounding "No," Chandelle was content on pouring it on until she got the answer she wanted. What she'd once taken for granted was worth pleading over, and she was more than willing to beg in order to get it back.

Dior was begging, too, in a passive please-don't-hate-me manner without actually having to speak it out loud. She'd sent a stack of *I'm Sorry* greeting cards, with hopes of persuading Chandelle to forgive her. None of the envelopes had been opened, but she couldn't deny the box of Godiva chocolates and the cutest black faux mink teddy bear on the planet that Dior had couriered to her door.

Chandelle held the stuffed animal closely to her chest every chance she got. The teddy came with a name tag, which Dior printed the word *Amnesty* on, thinking it just might help her cause to be granted sometime soon.

Chandelle tabled that idea to make an overseas phone call. She spoke with her mother, Maryland, who was a nomad by nature and retired military personnel moving from city to city while soaking up the culture and putting her government pension and relative health to good use. Maryland suggested that Chandelle not count on her making it home for Christmas again this year because a little village, in the south of France, had run amuck with handsome single men who thought she favored Diana Ross and she wasn't one to argue. She couldn't say when she planned on being stateside again but wished her daughter and son-in-law Happy Holidays. Chandelle didn't see any point of rehashing what she'd gone through, so she merely reciprocated her mother's good wishes and said good-bye.

"Frenchmen, huh?" Chandelle chuckled as the door-bell rang unexpectedly. It was Dooney going out of his way to stop in and see about her. "Hey, Dooney Bug," she sang, like she did while in her youth, when he'd shown up at just the right time then too.

"Ahhh, there you go," he said, smiling and laughing. "I haven't heard that name in a long time. You drunk?"

"No, silly, I'm high on life," she asserted. "Come on in here."

Dooney wiped his boots on the welcome mat. "High on life and what else?" he queried, eyeing his cousin peculiarly.

Chandelle took his wool peacoat and hung it in the hall closet. "You want some tea, Dooney Bug?" she hollered from the kitchen.

He dug around through a pile of empty candy wrappers in a virtually empty candy box that was resting on the coffee table. "Naw, I'll pass, but did you have to eat all the darn chocolates?"

She stepped into the living room, wishing she'd hidden the evidence. "Oh, that. I was hungry, skipped lunch and now you see the result. If you want me to put something on, I could thaw out a brisket."

"Thaw?" he objected. "I ain't got the time to be sitting around waiting on something to thaw out." He began to reel off perfectly edible items in his new house that did not need to be de-iced before sharing what he actually came for. "Yeah, Marvin talked me into getting a real place to lay my head. I'm glad he did too. It's not as nice as this, but it's mine. I got a chimney and everything, a room for my music, and a bathroom so big I can invite a special lady in the bathtub with me, know what I'm saying?"

"That's great, Dooney, but you shouldn't be having hussies running all up and through your house."

"And why not?" he asked, pretending to be alarmed that she'd ever suggest such a thing.

"Because it's not right," Chandelle said playfully, waving her finger in his face. "You need to pick one and settle down."

"Okay, it's time to go," he said, jumping up from the sofa.

"Dooney, sit your tail down. I'm not one to judge. I would like some nieces and nephews, though."

"Now I know it's time to bounce!" he shouted comically. "You want me to marry up and then conjure up some kids so you can play with them when you get ready?"

"Well, yeah," Chandelle laughed. "You know what the holidays do to me. Last year Marvin had a fit when I told him I had gone out and bought a dog."

"What dog?"

"Exactly," she replied on cue. "Marvin and I both knew we didn't need no dog."

Dooney glanced at Chandelle from the corner of his eyes. "It turns out you getting him fired was a good thing. He's got a great head for the real-estate business. Just thought you'd want to know."

"Yeah, I heard he was into that now. He's making it work with Kim Hightower," she sighed, feigning indifference. "I've seen the billboards with his name on them. I'm really proud of him." Dooney could tell that Chandelle wanted more than updates on his career, but he made her sweat it out for a minute. "Uh, how . . . how's he, Marvin . . . doing?"

"Who?" Dooney whooped with a straight face.

Chandelle tossed a throw pillow at his head. "Dooney, don't make me hurt you!"

"All right, all right, Marvin's good," he answered, ducking playfully, guessing other details she'd want insight on but assumed she wouldn't kick up the nerve to ask. "He's taking care of himself, working out and all that. He helped me paint my front room," Dooney informed her. "Uh-uh, he stayed with it all day and didn't even charge me a cent for labor. Look, cuz, a brotha like Marvin ain't gonna be out there single too much longer."

"What, did he say he was seeing somebody?" she asked with a nervous rise in her voice. If he'd stop avoiding her like she'd been avoiding Dior, Chandelle would have been up on a lot of what's going on in Marvin's world.

"Naw, nothing like that," Dooney replied. "He's a real rare dude, Chandelle. Marvin's the marrying kind. Don't ask me why, but that lifestyle suits him. He's the type to grow old with and all that other stuff white people usually do together, trips to the Grand Canyon, Yellowstone Park and such . . . boring stuff that women fall for."

On a whim, Dooney inquired about the details surrounding the night Marvin came over and found Tony opening a door to the house in his name. Chandelle mentioned that Dior had to have been behind it from the start whether she meant for it to go that far or not. Dior was the entity that put her and Tony in the same room, brought in the champagne, and then played Houdini until time came for the big finish. The event was too ugly to discuss any deeper than that so she let it go, demanding Dooney not bring it up to Marvin. He readily complied with Chandelle's wishes. However, she didn't say a word about going to Dior or Tony with a heavy hand and malice in mind.

Dooney left Chandelle's en route to Dior's apartment. Two blocks away, he saw her in the Big Cluck's fried chicken drive-thru. He hit a U-turn, swerved to miss a pothole, and then maneuvered around the back of the restaurant to ease up beside her.

"Hey!" he shouted with his window rolled down. Dior didn't notice him trying to get her attention right off so he honked his horn. With an annoyed expression, she waved him off. Dooney backed his Silverado pickup into a parking lane.

Seeing her brother upset was never one of her best memories of their childhood and adulthood wasn't any different. Dior banged on the small sliding window to hurry the cashier along. The young girl sneered at her as if watching the good-looking man stride toward her was more important. Dooney opened the car door before his sister managed to reach across and lock it manually. "Get out!" he ordered. "Get out right now!"

"Oh, you mean now?" she replied hastily, when he went to unfasten his leather belt. "I was just gon' get some wings first."

Dooney wasn't in the mood to watch her do anything other than get out of the car. His countenance suggested that he would carry out the perceived threat of whipping her behind right there in the Big Cluck's drive-thru.

"I'm out! I'm out!" Dior screamed from the cold concrete. Dooney slid in from the passenger side and crammed his legs over the console to get behind the wheel. Then he yelled for her to go over and stand near his pickup. As she backed out of way, the young cashier tapped on the car window to summon Dooney. He rolled the window down to see what she wanted.

"Here you go. This is yo' girlfriend's order," she said, with a flatter Southern drawl than his. "Hey, was you really gon' whoop her?" she asked excitedly.

"Why, you want me to *whoop* you next?"

"Huh, I get off at seven," she said with a seductive smile.

"How old are you, the truth?" he demanded, with an authoritative voice so she wouldn't likely try to front.

She leaned in closer to answer. "I'm legal . . . eighteen."

Dooney frowned. "I don't usually start whooping 'em until they're at least twenty-one. How old is your mama?"

"Oomph, she already got a man to do that for her on the regular. You're a trip," she said, sucking her gold teeth. "My boss is calling me. I gotta go." The upset cashier closed the sliding window and reluctantly returned to her duties.

Dior was shivering near Dooney's truck. "Heeello, I'm over here freezing and you're over there playing Sesame Street with high schoolers. Dooney, I want my wings," she ranted.

Wheeling the car to the right, Dooney parked it with the doors opened. He hopped out, staring at Dior the entire time. "Here, I'ma give you this, Gemini, and I'ma give you something else to take with you. I just came from Chandelle's. Uh-huh, and she's all jacked up about you bringing in her old dude on a deal to get her drunk. I heard she stood up in church and told all of those nosy heffas her business too. From now on, you are gonna do all that you can to get her and Marvin back together, *all that you can.*" Dior scowled with her hip cocked to the side defiantly. "Show out again if you want to. I'ma tell mama!"

"What? Nah, you ain't gonna tell Billie nothing because there's nothing to tell. Chandelle invited that man back to her spot on her own."

"That may be so, but it shouldn't have ever happened,"

Dooney charged. "Keep thinking I don't know about you ditching Chandelle and that other thing, the one you don't want her to know about." He didn't have additional dirt on her, but his bluff was solid. Dior promised to go above and beyond to square things between Chandelle and her Marvin, whatever it took at whatever cost.

29

Yesterdays and Whatnots

When Marvin woke up on Tuesday morning, he yawned and grinned. It was the first time since hearing Chandelle broadcast their marital woes in front of God and 1,700 other people that he wasn't shackled to a grueling headache banging the insides of his head. He couldn't believe she'd make a shameless public plea for prayers, but he secretly applauded her, after sneaking out of the service before the last amen. It was as if the words that went from Chandelle's mouth to God's ears had put a hex on him. The travel-size bottle of Excedrin he'd kept in his pocket served as a constant reminder when it rattled with every painful stride. Marvin had no clue what caused the block-party speakers in his brain to cease, but he thanked God regardless for seeing to it that someone pulled the plug.

Marvin whistled a happy tune as he showered, then hit the door to meet the day straight on. He didn't have to examine his daily planner for the first conference of the morning. It had been on his schedule for a week. Although he couldn't have guessed it then, breakfast at his favorite establishment promised to be one of the best ever.

The hostess at Java Hut greeted him with a cordial smile. She stated that someone was waiting at the corner booth. Marvin searched the busy breakfast den with an eager eye. "Yes, I see," he told her. "Thank you." His excitement grew as he approached an extremely familiar scene. "Super Dave," Marvin announced gleefully. "I see you still can't keep your nose out of the newspaper?"

"Morning, Marvin," the older man said, glancing at Marvin's charcoal-colored designer business suit. "I've got to keep track of who to be scared of next. I can't watch the TV news. It's way too violent for me."

Laughing, Marvin removed his coat. "Sorry I'm running late."

"Nonsense, I'm just running early," Dave answered, as he folded his periodical in half and then again. "You're starting to look more like your daddy every day. He wore his pants high on his waist too. Uh-huh, before his gut got in the way."

"Hmmm, you've never told me that before, Dave," said Marvin, glancing down to see just how he was wearing his slacks.

"That's because I ain't ever seen you in a suit of clothes since you've been fully grown. You've been smartly casual or in that rusty blue shirt they had you selling stoves in." Dave took a measured sip from his coffee cup.

Marvin snickered, sensing his friend was picking at him for a reason. "You know I sold more than stoves at Appliance World."

"But that was the only thing worth a plug nickel in that whole store," he replied. "I ought to know. My renters busted up all of the other appliances excepting for the stoves. I'm glad you got canned from that gig, or else I would still have too many irons in the fire, no pun intended."

"You sure?" Marvin asked, with his brow raised. He was waiting for the other shoe to fall.

"I'm just being ornery because it's my day off and I'm looking into the face of change but don't recognize too much nowadays," Dave went on to say while the waitress made her rounds and took Marvin's food order. "You might not know this, but I don't usually do business with black folk. Don't laugh now," he warned, as Marvin chuckled at his remark. "See, it used to mean something to give your money to one of your own. Back then, you knew they'd work until the job was done and, in turn, pass the money along to another fella's operation in the same neighborhood. Shoot, it's hard to find a Negro nowadays who stands behind his work. All they seem to do these days is get the money and pass the buck to the next fella, who wants twice as much to fix what the last knucklehead tore up trying to."

After Marvin studied Dave's demeanor a while longer, he came out with a burning question. "Are you sorry I helped you sell four of your rental properties and now you're feeling like a man with too little on his plate instead of too much?"

"Everybody hates a smart butt," was his answer. "You might want to remember that, Marvin."

"Dave, you've got more money than you need from the bar proceeds alone. Don't forget, I've seen your books. We've made the best use of your mutual funds, haven't we?"

"Yeah, but that's beside the point," he grunted like a stubborn child.

"What point?"

"The point that I've been avoiding since you sat down to this here table. Marvin, I'm afraid of having nothing to do. I'm supposed to take a vacation, one of them cruises where you pay upfront, then eat and drink all you want." Dave watched him raise his hands as if to ask what was wrong with that. "You're young still so I won't hold it against you. Ignorance, boy, it'll hide and then spring up like ragweed when you least expect it." Dave flagged for the waitress to come over. "Miss, could you please check around in the back to see if y'all got one of them dunce hats, the real tall kind, for my young friend here." She tossed a glance at Marvin, then humored Dave.

"That's why he's hanging around with you. I'm sure you can smarten him up a mite," she teased.

Marvin agreed with her wholeheartedly. "No doubt that's what he has in mind, ma'am." She moved on to genuine customer needs and left the fellows to themselves.

"I'll give you a heads-up on how it is to be an aging mature man," Dave said, to get Marvin's ear. "Most of my friends are dead and buried. Most of my teeth have been installed. Most of my body parts act up for the sake of it. Loving a pretty woman usually cost about a hundred bucks, that's in advance," he clarified, "and when you've got more money than time, Marvin, it just don't feel no kinda right. I've saved, made sound investments, and watched my bankers retire, one right after the other. I've seen their sons grow fat raising their kids. And I've seen a few other things, too, but you're not quite old enough for me to get into those with you. I will say that it cost a whole lot more than one hundred bucks, though." That brought a grin to his lips he didn't mind sharing before continuing. "Yeah, boy, good times. Then you wake up one day, and if you're lucky, you can start crossing off the things you wrote down on your list so long ago you forgot where you put it. I'll say this and move on, take a man's woman away, you break his heart, but if he loses his drive to get up in the morning, you've broken his spirit. Getting that new job didn't affect only you, I didn't plan on getting this far in life and watching the sunset all by my lonesome. All of a sudden, I'm getting tired of standing behind that bar six days a week and going home to a microwave and television reruns. I want to do a lot more, just not by myself."

Marvin looked into Dave's eyes, seeing something he hadn't before. The man was scared, scared of growing old and alone. "I'm sorry, Dave. I didn't know how much it meant for a man to stay busy. I'm spending all of my time trying to build something and that's all I know. Nobody told me what to do after it all pays off."

Dave rolled his eyes in utter embarrassment. "That's because you already had the other part figured out. I told your daddy I was gonna look after you as much as you'd let me. Don't make me out to be no liar, son."

"Okay, I'm listening. I've been listening, but you've been talking about your life, not mine," Marvin said, missing the point yet again.

Pretending to search frantically under the table for something heavy to hit Marvin with, Dave pounded his fist on the table. "Where's the lady I sent for that dunce hat? Marvin, I've been flapping my gums tryna tell you the best way I know how not to end up like me. Sure, I've got money, hand over fist, and I'm doubly blessed because I've still got my looks. But neither of them will do me a bit of good without the right woman to be glad about both of them with me."

Finally, Marvin understood Dave's roundabout way of warning him against making a dreadful mistake, having no one to witness his life with and his successes. He leaned back in the booth, staring into space. "I wasn't going to bring this up, but I almost killed a man, the one I caught coming out of Chandelle's about three in the morning." His eyes glassed over just as they did the night he decked Tony. The pain had resurfaced.

"I'm sho' sorry to hear that," Dave said matter-of-factly, seemingly not that shocked at the news. "What'd Chandelle have to say about it?"

"What could she say?" Marvin grunted. "The dude was buttoning up his shirt when I knocked on the door."

"See, there's two things wrong with that scene. You had to knock on the door of a house that belongs to you, and you didn't stick around to get the whole story when you should have. I know it looks bad, but things aren't always what they appear to be."

Marvin thought back to the hoax Dior ran on him. "You can say that again," he sighed wearily.

"Okay, you know I will," Dave said, to add levity to a tense situation. "If you can't come and go as you please in your own home, what were you doing on *her* lawn at all times of the night? Did she put you out for this other fella?"

"Naw, Dave, ain't nobody put me out of nothing," he insisted adamantly.

"Uh-oh, look at your chest swelling up. Did you get all ugly in the face when you had it out with the other cat? Don't tell me he came to the door wearing your clothes? I heard of stories like that before."

"Dave, you make it impossible for me to tell you how it is," Marvin fussed. "I didn't jump in your pot when you were cooking, did I?"

"You better not have either," Dave quipped. "I'll cut you." He went to checking his pockets for something sharp, since he couldn't find anything heavy earlier. "I'm old. I ain't got much to lose."

Marvin's entrée arrived but he'd lost his appetite. "Ma'am, could you put that in a to-go box please. Thank you." He pursed his lips and peered across the table. "Impossible" was the only word he could think of to describe how he felt about coming out of this conversation without wanting to strangle Dave.

"What's the matter with you?" the older man questioned, like he hadn't antagonized Marvin to no end. "I'm only sitting here having a chat with my godson."

"That's all?" Marvin heckled, obviously annoyed.

"Yeah, you didn't want to discuss why you had to knock and how this man shows up, but I'm ready to hear why you went over there looking for trouble?"

"Trouble found me. I—I was just . . . just," Marvin stammered. "I was in the middle of a quiet night. I was sleeping like a baby because I'd had a little too much to drink. I thought I was dreaming at first; then I felt her hands, so I knew it was really happening."

"I thought you were gonna tell me what you're talking about. You're going slow enough and I still can't keep up." Dave's eyes begged for plain talk in simple terms.

"Whew, I was sleeping when Chandelle's cousin let herself into my apartment and then climbed on top of me." That revelation caused Dave to whip out a handkerchief to wipe his mouth. He was drawn in too much to interrupt with foolish commentary and stall the juicy narrative. "I thought she was Chandelle coming back to me, but Dior had on this wig and perfume. It was a mess."

"Not so far it ain't," he debated. "What happened then?"

"Nothing, I mean, she said something Chandelle wouldn't say, not ever. She was going to work on me, then shouted, 'Let it go, Daddy.' Chandelle was molested by one of her mother's boyfriends who made her call him that so . . ."

"I see," Dave whispered, in respect to Chandelle's secret. "What did she say when you told her about the freaky cousin?"

"I was rushing over to tell her when the guy popped up at her place. Now I don't know how to handle any of it."

Having been around the block a few times himself, Dave examined Marvin before he submitted the question that needed to be asked: "Be honest, and not just to me when you open your mouth, did you know that wasn't your wife before you finished?"

"I didn't think so at the time, but the more I flash back . . . I can't be sure. It happened so fast."

Dave wiped sweat from his forehead. "Don't sound like it happened all that fast to me. Tell you one thing, though, you'd better sound a lot more positive if you're thinking on taking that story to Chandelle. I'm rooting for you and I find it hard to back your story."

"I know how it sounds and that's exactly why I've kept it to myself," Marvin explained. "She could be pregnant. I told you this was a big mess." He noted how Dave's eyes closed like he was trying to recollect or reconcile something in his mind. Within a few seconds, Marvin knew which one. It was a recollection. A memory tucked so far back in the recesses of his mind that it took some dusting off to come out fresh enough to spin.

"Ahh, I know where I've seen this tale play out before, live and in Technicolor. I was gonna take this to my grave, but it won't do no good down there. Some years ago, there was this certain man who'd fallen for two women at the same time. One he loved something awful and another he loved to be with more than anything. The woman he couldn't do without got herself into some trouble, that's what old folks used to say when a girl was having a baby without a husband, you understand. Well, by the time this fellow learned of her condition, he was two weeks from marrying his soul mate."

Marvin was mesmerized. It made his situation pale by comparison. "What happened? What did the man do?"

"That man was your father, Marvin. Don't think any less of him because he loved your mother with all his heart. He kept his mouth shut to her like he was supposed to and like I told him he'd better do. He cried though and I cried, too. If you're looking for something to call a big mess, *that* was it. As it turned out, several other cats in the neighborhood enjoyed the young girl's company as much as your daddy did. The baby wasn't none of his. The way it stands now, you're one up on him."

"How do you mean?" Marvin asked, while processing the revealing information.

"Because you're worrying over what we old-timers call an egg that ain't been laid. Marvin, first you need to double back and grill the hen. Hold her feet to the fire so she'll tell you what's what. You're a business man, get out there and handle your business . . . man. If Chandelle learns about her cousin's roadside ways and your uh . . . undetermined willingness to participate, better it be your tongue doing the wagging when she does. She's your wife. You owe her that much."

"I guess I do at that," Marvin agreed. "But hey, you didn't tell me what became of the girl with the baby."

Dave clasped his hands and smiled uncomfortably. "Well, I send the mother a little something from time to time to help her get by and my daughter Monique is a practicing dentist now," he answered, beaming wide to show off his daughter's handiwork. "She's making out just fine. Ain't nothing new under the sun, young blood. People have been trying to figure out what to do about life when it don't go according to plan since the dawn of man. You're not the first and don't think you'll hardly be the last."

"Wow, don't you think it's a lot to get over considering what I saw?" Marvin replied solemnly.

"That's a good question." Dave threw back across the table. "What did you see? I mean really? If Chandelle had walked in on you with her relative, that would be a whole 'nother issue." When Marvin couldn't say with certainty what had transpired before he arrived, the weathered veteran gave him a knot to cut his teeth on. "If you haven't learned anything else today, remember that things in this funny world are rarely what they seem. Do yourself a favor and find out for sure."

"Yes, sir, I will," Marvin said with the utmost sincerity.

Dave stroked his chin and chuckled heartily. "That's the smartest thing you've said all morning."

Marvin got up to leave. He shook hands and grabbed his coat. "Thanks for everything, Dave. What you've said means a lot to me, all of it. Uh," he said, to clear everything in his mind, "I'm confused about what you want me to do with your last two rental properties?"

"Oh those, why don't you take them off my hands? I'm willing to let them go *to you* at half the value."

"That's generous, but I can't accept that," Marvin objected.

"That's nonsense. Where's that waitress?" he joked, looking around the restaurant for her. "Marvin, you're the son I never had, but I'm as proud of you as if you were my own. Besides, you've been a good friend and haven't once asked me for a dime. Now go on and get the papers drawn, I've got to call a woman about a long boat ride."

Marvin stood longer than Dave figured he should have, so he glared at Marvin and then frowned. "Why didn't I marry Monique's mother when I should have? You didn't hitch your cart to a broken wagon back then. It took five years for me to discover I was the one who broke it. Shame stood in my way then. Now I'm flat out of excuses and Sadie has turned out to be a fine lady. I'm hoping it ain't too late for her to give me a second chance to do the right thing. In all honesty, I loved that girl more than your pops did. That was the real reason I cried so hard when he thought her baby was his."

Marvin walked out of the restaurant with his breakfast wrapped in styrofoam and his mind in a million little pieces. He'd gotten the lesson of a lifetime from a man who cared enough to pass down massive chunks of wisdom and a small portion of history for his benefit. Dooney was right about him. Marvin was the kind of man to take marriage seriously. Although he didn't know where to begin about sorting out the details that led him down a disastrous path, he realized there were now three obstacles standing in his way: the truth, a lie, and a maybe.

30

Something Worth Saying

Chandelle awoke at 5:00 A.M. She had dreamt of her first date with Marvin. The memory put a smile on her lips just thinking about it. The reservations he made at an upscale restaurant off the tollway impressed her, the hour-long wait despite their reservation did not. Chandelle, very hungry at the time, asked if it was all right with Marvin if she traded in her date at the fine restaurant for a bite at the first full-service snack shop they could find. What they found was an open table at a nearby Taco Bueno and had their fill for ten dollars and change.

Life was so simple then, Chandelle thought while flicking on the lamp on the nightstand next to her bed. She opened the top drawer and pulled out a notebook and an ink pen. *Since Marvin won't talk to me*, she reasoned, *maybe he'll let me talk to him this way*. Chandelle propped two pillows behind her back as she closed her eyes for a silent prayer to ask for the right words to convey the feelings she held so deeply, heavy with remorse and reconciliation. She took an exaggerated breath and began writing a letter she hoped he'd someday read.

Marvin,

I love you dearly and miss you even more than words can say. Every night I fall asleep wishing none of the things that have driven us apart happened, and each morning I wake up hoping this will be the day we find a way to begin putting them behind us. I've messed up, turned my back on you, and gone out of my way to hurt you. I'm so sorry for ruining what used to be a wonderful relationship and tearing down the best thing that ever happened to me, the love we once had. Your friendship meant a lot to me. Living without it is getting to be more than I can handle. Knowing that you have the right to hate me hurts just as much. I thought about us today, the us that we used to be and our first date that ended when the sun came up. You were the perfect gentleman, although I was secretly willing to make love and make you mine before you drove me home. Kissing you good night wasn't nearly enough for me, but it told me everything I needed to know about you, the patient man you were and how much you valued taking the time to cherish me. I called my mother that day and told her that I'd just spent the night with the man I was going to spend the rest of my life with. She said that you must have really put it on me. Well, you did. You put something on my mind, my heart, and my soul that I still wear proudly today.

Marvin, I'm not perfect, I've proved that time and again. I've handled things with my heart instead of with my head. Forgive me. I miss having you there to towel me off after a long shower. I miss rubbing your back when you've pulled a double shift. I miss you letting me cheat at cards when I'm losing. I miss the way you kiss me tenderly when I pout. I miss holding hands when we shop and the way people look at us, happy with our hands clasped together. Oddly, I even miss you getting on me about overpaying for things you say I don't need to make me more beautiful. I miss you holding me. I can't remember the last time I've heard you say my name, even though I swear I can hear your voice everywhere I go. You are a part of me, Marvin. The best part of me is you. I used to know exactly what love felt like, inside and out. I miss us, belonging together. I miss that most of all.

Chandelle

Chandelle placed the letter inside an envelope. On her way into the office, she wrote Marvin's name on it, and then slid it inside of the mail slot at Hightower Realty. She felt that he might be more inclined to read it if someone else handed it to him.

Marvin recognized Chandelle's handwriting the second he picked it up from the reception desk. Moved that Chandelle had the nerve to wander into unfriendly territory, Marvin couldn't wait to see what had inspired her.

On a lonely side road off the freeway, Marvin broke the seal on the envelope. Apprehensively, he pulled out two pages of yellow paper and unfolded them slowly. Looking at the ink bleeding through the paper in various spots, Marvin could tell that Chandelle had also penned the letter with her tears. "Marvin, I love you," he read aloud, thinking how long it had been since he'd heard that from her. He read further, only silently until he reached the part she'd written about the things she'd missed about him. "I miss toweling you off too," he said with regret. "And the way you rubbed my back. Working a double did have its rewards. You always cheated at cards and I loved kissing your pouting lips when you lost." Marvin's eyes watered as he read the rest of Chandelle's unabridged epistle of regrets, culpability, and love. He glanced out of his car windows, hoping no one saw him choking on emotion. "You miss holding me?" he whispered to the pages now stained with his tears as well. "I know what that's like. I miss you calling my name too." As he read her final words, he pulled a handkerchief from the breast pocket of his suit coat. "Whew," he sighed wearily.

Marvin wiped his face, then put the letter aside. He couldn't help but wonder whether Chandelle would develop a change of heart when he broke the news about his romp with Dior. After baring her soul, Marvin felt compelled to do the same, and tell Chandelle everything. As far as he could see, there was no way of getting around it.

Nervously, with knots bunched in his stomach, Marvin whipped out his cell phone. His first call went to Dooney at the barber shop, who provided a way to contact Dior. Marvin thanked him, then put in a call to her. She answered on the first ring, openly admitting how glad she was that he reached out to her despite all of the trouble she'd caused.

"I need to meet you right away," he told her. "Somewhere private."

"Okay, but isn't . . ." she started to ask until Marvin interjected.

"I don't want to talk about it over the phone. Meet me at the park next to the school on Whitehurst in ten. You know the place?"

"Yeah, I do. See you," Dior answered. She was anxious with questions and trepidations over seeing Marvin after having been with him under false pretenses. She'd promised to Dooney, under duress, to make good on helping to rebuild Marvin's marriage with Chandelle. Before she had the chance to talk herself out of it, Dior collected her keys and purse from the dresser in her bedroom. "I've got to go do this thing," she informed Kevlin, sadly. As she stepped into the designer jogging suit, which had been thrown onto the floor an hour ago, Dior returned his curious leer with a curt response. "Chill out, I'ma be all right. It's a family affair."

Marvin was already idling by the curb when Dior arrived at the playground. She pulled in behind him and left her car running too. A manufactured smile traced her lips. Marvin nodded "good morning" before the words came out of his mouth.

"Hey, Marvin," Dior replied, as she approached his relaxed stance against the SUV. "I know what you want to talk about, but meeting you here feels kinda like we're hiding something."

"It's more like plotting to uncover a cover-up," he answered, obviously looking for telltale signs of shifts in her weight. Dior folded her arms when she picked up on it. It was the first time she felt dirty when a man tried to undress her with his eyes. Perhaps it was the reason why Marvin peered at her that way that bothered her so much.

"I'm not having a baby, if that's what you're checking me out for?" she said, reading his mind. "Good thing too. It's hard out there hustling with a rug rat on your hip." Dior also noted Marvin's relieved expression morph into another question needing to be addressed. "Don't worry, I ain't gonna tell Chandelle. She's got enough problems paying for that house and the Volvo at the same time. I offered to kick in a few hundred, but she ain't on time for that or having nothing to do with me."

"Y'all haven't talked since that night?" Marvin asked, expecting to extort information about Chandelle and Tony if the opportunity presented itself.

"I've called and sent cards, but you know how she is, all prideful. She always was as stubborn as a mule."

"Hardheaded too," Marvin threw in.

"I'm keeping hope alive that she'll let me make it up for getting her busted out on her front porch. I could really use a break and my best friend back in my space." Dior pushed authentic tears from her eyes, not like the ones she produced to get out of jams in the past. These were the genuine article. "You got me up here boo-hooing and stuff," she spat playfully. "I can't stand for nobody to see me cry, never could." Dior accepted the handkerchief from Marvin. "Thanks. It's a little wet, though," she joked. "Ooh, I'ma have to keep a better tab of my sins. Done messed this up so bad for everybody. I miss Chandelle like crazy, Marvin."

"That makes two of us, Dior," he offered in a comforting tone.

"So, what do you want to do now? Dooney told me to mend my ways, but he didn't have to tell me to apologize to you. I'm sorry. It was me who got Chandelle and Tony together. Chandelle getting drunk on Cristal, that's on me too. And I pulled a fast one so he'd have to take her home."

Marvin couldn't believe his ears. He replayed Dior's sentence in his head. It was troubling to say the least, but he'd figured as much. The thought of having Dooney to deal with seemed more imminent now that his head was clear. "Wait a minute! You told Dooney about us, what we did?"

"Didn't have to, that fool twin brother of mine knows just about everything. You can't put nothing by him or over on him; trust me, I've tried." Dior laughed, though her merriment died a sudden death as another thought pushed the other aside. "He's got an old soul. Well, that's what this bag lady said, who roamed around the project where we grew up. She'd say, '*Dooney is a fine boy, the good twin,*' and then she'd turn her big nose up at me. '*And Dior, well, you ain't nothing but sinful. Dooney, he's the righteous child and you's what was left over in yo' mama's belly.'* Strange thing was, I believed her," Dior admitted honestly. "Sometimes I still do."

Marvin almost reached out to give her the hug he was certain she needed, but the image of Dior straddled over him and gyrating kept running through his mind. He quickly put that inclination to rest. "That's a cruel thing to say to a little girl," Marvin uttered, feeling sorry for her but wise enough to keep his distance.

"Who you telling? My mama heard that old witch going off on me, more than once, but she didn't think to argue." Dior turned away to clean her eyes with the handkerchief. "That seems like forever ago so it don't matter anymore. I'm all grown up now."

"You went through a lot of trouble to get between me and Chandelle," Marvin commented, thinking how she probably hadn't changed much from the bag lady's early assessments. "What made you do it, pulling the bait and switch in my bedroom that night?"

"I've seen how much you love Chandelle and care about her. Y'all were the only real love I've seen up close," Dior explained. "I wanted that dream to come true for myself. Huh, I used to think getting married was for old people and white folks."

Marvin had to remind himself that Dior's mentality often permeated the Black community, but he wasn't willing to let her off so easily. "Come on now, Dior, you're young and attractive. Why didn't you just hook up with a single brotha and get started on your own dream?"

Dior looked at Marvin as if he were an idiot in a fancy suit. "Man, please! What, do you think there's a gang of men coming home from college trying to fall in love and get married? Tell me when and where, because I want in. That sure was a dumb thing to say coming from such a smart man. Let a sistah know when educated black men start interviewing for something more than a booty buddy because that's what's up."

Honestly, Marvin had been the only man fitting Dior's criteria who wanted to be someone's husband. Only thing was, Chandelle got to him first and sealed the deal. It was excruciating for her to be close enough to touch it and too far away to enjoy. When the temptation grew too large to restrain, Dior wanted to do more than merely see what it looked like. She threw caution to the wind and got herself a taste.

That evening, Chandelle followed a group of associates off the elevator on the first floor. She had been second-guessing her decision to leave the envelope in the mail slot opposed to handing it over personally. *What if Kim discovered it and threw it in the trash, to get even for accusing her of man stealing and worse*, she'd pondered. When Chandelle exited her office building, a herd of what-ifs roamed through her head. So many that she couldn't keep them separated. *What if Kim gets the letter and throws it out?* she thought. *What if she gets the letter and reads it? What if it gets lost in the office mail? What if Marvin charges me with punking out for writing it all down instead of convincing him to hear me out face to face? What if he serves me with divorce papers?* she dreaded. As Chandelle rounded the building toward the side parking lot, a thought occurred that she hadn't considered all day. *What if he shows up with flowers, wearing a brand new suit and a beautiful smile?*

"Hey, you," Marvin greeted her, with a fresh bouquet of yellow roses.

"I take it you got my letter today," Chandelle said, smelling the flowers he'd given her.

"It would seem so," he answered. "I read it several times throughout the day. You were eloquent and inspiring. I've never known you to show that kind of vulnerability. A letter like that couldn't have been easy for you. Much props," he commended her.

"Thank you for the roses. They're beautiful. As for the props, you can keep those because I'm not looking for an 'atta girl.' I'm trying to get my man back," Chandelle aptly informed him. "I've been busy remembering a love written like a love song. I remember when you treated me like a diamond and didn't want me to leave your sight. I remember when you belonged to me too. Marvin, I want to stop depending on memories. I want to get back what was once ours, and I've been praying you'd soon feel the same."

Marvin's eyes scanned up and down Chandelle's legs, underneath her thin three-quarter-length jacket. He was awfully happy he caught her on one of Texas's unseasonably comfortable winter nights. "You look great by the way," he said, as he offered to discuss their future over a nice dinner.

Chandelle thanked him, blushed over his compliment, and then eagerly accepted his offer, but only if he agreed to dine at Taco Bueno. Marvin laughed, and Chandelle thanked God that her husband was not only interested in talking things over, he was also willing to do it at the very fast food restaurant where their lives together began. Chandelle felt great about following the spirit, which God used to move her. It didn't hurt any that He'd brought Marvin back around in record time either. She held her breath while en route to dinner, contemplating whether he'd care enough to stay there considering he hadn't brought up Tony, yet.

31

Dr. Bitter Betty

Dinner on the patio went off without a hitch. Neither Chandelle nor Marvin brought up issues that kept them divided during the past ten weeks. There was talk about Grace's baby girl and how hard Chandelle has had to work in Grace's absence. Marvin joked about Dooney contracting bids to get a brass stripper's pole put in the center of his bedroom, against his realtor's better judgment, of course. When Marvin explained how it could decrease the property value, Dooney couldn't for the life of him figure out why every man wouldn't want a brass sexual aid erected in the place couples needed it most. Marvin gave up arguing with him after Dooney decided he'd simply rip out the pole and take it with him if he ever decided to sell, if the buyers couldn't see the benefit in having one for themselves. It wasn't until Marvin and Chandelle went for coffee that the conversation reverted back to them.

"You should have seen those cops' faces when Wallace tossed the book at them," Marvin recalled. "I've never seen two grown men so afraid of their pasts catching up to them. Thank you for going to bat for me."

Chandelle reached across the small café table to place her hand on his. "I was standing up for my man," she replied with a subtle smile. "It was the least I could do after they practically put words in my mouth, then dragged you off like a runaway slave. I hope you didn't have to fight the men off you in lockup." Chandelle's statement wasn't rhetorical. She had heard stories about men being gang-raped as a part of a jailhouse initiation.

Marvin chuckled, realizing what she was getting at. "Nah, it wasn't that kind of party," he informed her. "Most of the guys in there weren't the types to get down like that. I can't say what they'll be like after serving their sentences, though. They say prison changes a man in more ways than one."

"Yeah, like turning them into women," Chandelle countered quickly. "Was that on your mind when you called Kim to raise your bail?"

Having had an abundance of time to think that question over since it occurred, Marvin shook his head. "Uh-uh, that was the furthest thing from my mind. I just didn't want to be there any longer than I had to. I was still hot at the way it played out at the apartment, angry with you, and mad at myself too."

"How could you feel bad about those cops busting in and hauling you off after they twisted my words?"

Marvin squeezed Chandelle's hand tenderly before answering, knowing his answer served as the real source of their problems. "Look, I should have told you this beforehand and none of the crazy stuff that happened to us would have occurred." He took a deep breath. "I was nervous about buying a home that we couldn't afford and just plain scared of losing it somehow and failing as a man. I mean my job is to provide and see to it that you had a roof over your head. You'd grown up in apartments your entire life. I knew how much having a house meant to you. I didn't want to risk dangling that in your face, and then let hard times steal it away from you."

"I thought you knew," Chandelle said quietly. "Sure I wanted a house, but anywhere you are Marvin, that's my home. They say home is where the heart is and I believe that. Being with you, even under a bridge, is better than having eight bedrooms and no man to share it with."

"You'd take me over eight rooms?" Marvin asked jokingly.

"Well, maybe six," she answered, behind a light chuckle. "I need you to understand something. I want us to be together, in love again. I never meant to hurt you."

"Then why'd you throw out all of my furniture, get me fired, and have my lights turned off?"

"Because I wanted to hurt you," she confessed, "but I was talking about that night you showed up and ran into Tony." Chandelle's eyes fell toward the floor, knowing how that must have torn Marvin's heart out. "Dior got me sideways with Cristal, then she disappeared on me. Tony owned the restaurant, saw me in bad shape, and offered to get me home safe." She said all of that without raising her eyes to note his reaction.

"Dior told me how it jumped off," Marvin replied calmly, too calmly for Chandelle's taste.

"And you're okay with that?" she questioned, not certain she wanted to know the answer.

"Not even a little bit. I keep trying to process it, with me ringing your bell and another man opening the door with his shirt opened. I've had nothing but bad dreams about you being with him and different guys, all laughing at me. If the DA could prosecute me for what I've done in my dreams, whew, I'd be serving four consecutive life sentences."

"Ooh, that's terrible," Chandelle groaned. "I promise I didn't know he was in the house. I was throwing up," she remembered, as the vision of them in the shower came to mind. She took a deep breath to compose herself so that Marvin wouldn't be the wiser to the parts she'd conveniently left out. "I heard the door, someone talking, and then there you were. For three days, every single time I closed my eyes, I saw that look on your face. I wish I could take it back. All of it."

It was Marvin's turn to hide his eyes then. He'd seen visions as well, sordid ones with him and Dior, their legs tangled and bodies slapping against one another. Images of Chandelle appearing at the door in her camisole rated a distant second. "I'm almost scared to ask, but I've got to know before I can go any further with this, with us." Marvin swallowed hard, resolved to end their relationship right then and there if Chandelle didn't come up with the right answer. However, if she opened her mouth and lied to his face, Marvin was willing to accept it. "Did you sleep with that man in my house?" he asked his wife in a slow, dry tone.

Chandelle's eyes floated up to rest on his. "I wish I could tell you the truth, but I honestly don't know." She couldn't believe herself, how she'd allow anyone to get her jammed up unwittingly. "It probably sounds like a tricky way to weasel out of what I'm sure you think I did, but it's not, Marvin. I was sick, tired, and I just don't know what else," Chandelle answered as best she could. "I've been by the restaurant to speak with Tony about it, but he had his security guards stop me on the sidewalk from getting in."

Hairs on the back of Marvin's neck stood on end. "You've been trying to get in to see the ol' dude? Shaming me once wasn't enough?" he barked scornfully. "I've heard it all now."

"No, you haven't, and that's why I'm laying it all out tonight," Chandelle asserted. "I don't want to go forward with you thinking I've been unfaithful when I . . ."

"Watch what you say, Chandelle. Some things are near impossible to take back once they're out of the bag," he warned. Marvin was beginning to feel disappointed about reconciling and initiating a meeting of the minds with his estranged spouse. He wanted to say how there was no reason under the sun to excuse cheating ways, but he couldn't. He wanted to say that Dior's mischief couldn't be held fully responsible for Chandelle putting someone else in her bed. There wasn't any sane justification whereby introducing alcohol to the equation would excuse a person's actions either. Marvin wanted to berate Chandelle for getting caught up, but he couldn't, because each of those played a role in him breaking the vows he'd also held so dear. Chandelle's indiscretion might have been hypothetical. Marvin's actually happened.

After what seemed like hours passed between them, Marvin noticed Chandelle was crying. Although she'd successfully muffled her voice, tears streaming down her cheeks were painfully visible. "I love you, Chandelle," he said finally. "I couldn't help it if I tried. You're my woman and my wife. I still need both of y'all to make me whole." He reached for his handkerchief, then remembered he'd given it to Dior. "Here, sweetheart, take this," he said, handing her a napkin from the table setting. "I never meant to hurt you either."

Marvin held Chandelle's hand as they sauntered to the parking lot. He placed a soft kiss on her lips, then pulled her close to him. "You were right. We do need someone who knows a lot more than we do about keeping our thing together." Chandelle sniffled as she nodded, her head on his shoulder. "Why are you crying?" he asked, when it appeared they were headed in the right direction.

"Because I didn't think you wanted me anymore. It looked like you've gone on about your life, all the new success in spite of the trouble I've caused, and I guess I thought you were going to say that you'd found someone else."

"I didn't have to be apart from you to know that was impossible," he assured her. "Your words said it better than I could; the best part of *me* is *you*."

The following day, Chandelle called to tell Marvin that she was going to her weekly session with her psychologist and how he could join her if he wanted. Marvin agreed that it sounded like a great idea, although he was apprehensive over giving someone else a peek into his rocky relationship. Throwing caution to the wind, he accepted.

The office of Betty Forrester, PhD, was situated in a house on the top of a steep hill. While it didn't appear that the one-level ranch-style home doubled as living quarters when he entered the light-colored brick building, Marvin felt like a stranger in someone's home nonetheless. The neat den served as a reception area. Just beyond the glass table with brochures on mental defects was a large room being utilized as an office. There was a small white sign hanging from the doorknob that read, SESSION IN PROGRESS. Since he was unaware of the protocol, he knocked.

The brown door opened from the inside. A thin-built white woman eased in front of him as if she were hiding someone on the other side. "Yes, may I help you?" she said, as if that was the furthest thing from her mind.

Marvin squinted at her, returning the same cold gaze she'd thrown at him. "I'm sorry to interrupt, but I'm Marvin Hutchins. I was wondering if Chandelle was back here." He noted the woman's dark-colored outfit clinging to her slight frame. Her pencil-thin nose tilted upward as she looked down it at him. She could have easily doubled as a school librarian in her spare time.

"Ahh, yes," she said, glancing over her shoulder and

behind the partially opened door. "Give us a moment, won't you?"

Not if I don't have to, he thought, as she closed the door rather abruptly. Marvin paced in the foyer as the moment she alluded to slowly lapsed into five minutes. When she did return, her demeanor hadn't changed one iota. "Come in, Mr. Hutchins," she offered begrudgingly. "Chandelle and I were going over some items from our last encounter."

Yeah, encounters of the third kind, he almost said aloud. "Thank you, ma'am," he replied instead, and then followed her into that room off to the side like a lamb to the slaughter. He was given a swooping motion to take a seat on the doctor's brown leather sofa. *What's with this chick and brown?* he thought. Chandelle was positioned on one end of it with her head in her hands and a stack of wadded tissue mounting on the wooden table in front of her. "Hey, Chandelle, sorry I'm late," he said, figuratively swatting at the tension in that room with a knife.

"Marvin," Chandelle grunted coarsely.

He stared at her, wanting to know what he'd done to warrant such a frigid response.

"Mr. Hutchins, I'm Dr. Betty Forrester, you can call me Betty, Dr. Betty, or Dr. Forrester if you like, but please don't call me Doc. I've always found it tacky and unprofessional."

What if I call you Doc-tor Seuss because this is about as crazy as the Cat in the Hat? "I'm cool with Dr. Betty," he replied cautiously.

"Good, then let's get started, shall we?" she suggested. Start doing what was Marvin's burning question. "I believe we all know why you're here. Now, Chandelle is a lovely woman, pleasant, polite, and traumatized. That brings us to you, Mr. Hutchins. Please enlighten us as to what has prevented you from giving her the respect and admiration she deserves?"

Marvin's mouth popped open. He peered down the row of leather at Chandelle, who refused to acknowledge him. "Huh?" he said, searching for something to say that wouldn't give her cause to summon the police.

"Huh?" Dr. Betty repeated arrogantly. "I have no problem believing that your Neanderthal-like response has contributed much in the way of Chandelle's instability. She has been here for several weeks, bawling her eyes out because you have allowed your lust for other women to run rampant over your beautiful wife's feelings."

Marvin was floored by her accusations and Chandelle's opposition to speaking up for him. With his eyes open as wide as his mouth, he said the only thing that came to mind. "Huh?"

"See there, just what I suspected," Dr. Betty huffed. She reached down inside her dress pocket and came out with a pack of cigarettes. "It's no wonder your wife finds it difficult to trust you beyond seeing you. It's men like you, Mr. Hutchins, who think they can simply run over women and come crawling back when they've sown their oats."

"Crawling? Huh?" Marvin grunted in sheer disbelief.

"Huh? Oh no, that doesn't cut it nearly enough, Mr. Hutchins," Dr. Betty huffed, this time along with a drag of nicotine. She blew a trail of smoke at Marvin, crossed her legs, and waggled her finger in his direction. "I'll tell you something else. If you were taking care of bid'niss at home instead of getting your groove on in the streets, Chandelle would be a much happier woman. Ever think of that? Trying a little tenderness?"

Chandelle finally spoke up when she saw Marvin blowing smoke from the top of his head. "Huh?"

Dr. Betty shooed her like a bothersome housefly. "Don't let up now, Chandelle," she hissed. "Men like this one are all about themselves, let me tell you." She hit her cancer stick again and began nervously tapping the toe of her shoe in midair. "Let them mistreat us and take us for granted; ohhhh-no, I ain't having it, girlfriend."

"Us?" Chandelle asked frantically.

"Uh-huh!" Marvin shouted. "She said y'all."

"I thought these sessions have been about me," Chandelle whined.

"I, me, us, whatever," Dr. Betty exhaled. "We women have to stick together."

"That's a good idea," Marvin barked, rising to his feet. "Chandelle, maybe you can deal with it, but I can't do this." He stormed out of the building in an uproar.

Chandelle chased after him.

"Don't say I didn't call it, but it looks like homeboy is making another dash," yelled Dr. Betty from the doorway of the house of horrors. "I told you he'd leave. They're all alike!"

"Marvin, don't you leave," Chandelle fussed. "You said you'd get counseling and you've already given up. I know Dr. Betty is a little high strung and that cigarette routine is new to me, too, but don't run out. She's a professional with certificates and everything."

Marvin climbed into his SUV and screamed, "*Huh*?" Chandelle stomped to the driver's side and banged on his window. "Get back!" he yelled. "I'm getting out of here!" Defiantly, Chandelle held on to the door handle. Marvin started the motor and gunned the gas pedal. "I'm counting to three, then I'm driving off. If you want your hand, you'll let go!" Chandelle released her grip while listening to Dr. Betty's *"All men are selfish cowards"* rant from the top of the driveway.

Marvin took off in one direction, unfamiliar with the neighborhood. Chandelle knew he'd have to come back the same way after realizing he was driving toward a dead end. He skidded to a blistering stop in the middle of a cul-de-sac.

Chandelle climbed behind the wheel of her car, ramming her key into the ignition. "You promised we were going to get some help with making up," Chandelle cackled. "And I'm not about to go home wondering if I'll ever get you back on that ugly brown couch." She parked her Volvo in the middle of the street, trying to block his escape.

He gunned the motor, his tires screeched against the cold concrete. The Four Runner burned rubber to get past Chandelle's blockade. She inched forward, leaving a few feet of road and the sidewalk. Marvin swung his steering wheel, faking to the right. He sped ahead hurriedly. When Chandelle didn't bite on his move, Marvin had nowhere to turn. He saw Chandelle throw her hands up to protect her face. The loud collision sounded significantly worse than it was. The SUV incurred barely a scratch, but Chandelle's bumper rocked noisily in the street. She climbed out to assess the damage. Marvin took one quick peek at her and laughed.

"That's what you get, road blocking me."

"Think that's funny? You hit me. Look at my poor car. It's dead. You killed my car. I'm filing against you. I hope your new job offers overtime, because your premium is about to have a fit." She marched back to her car, dug in her purse, and whipped out a cell phone. Marvin did likewise, calling the insurance company regarding a policy they were both still covered under.

Much to Chandelle's chagrin, Marvin reached an agent first. "Yes, this is Marvin Hutchins. Sure, I'll hold." He continued laughing at the fender, which appeared to have been ripped off by a wild animal. "Who? Mrs. Hutchins. Yeah, I know. I'm looking at her right now," Marvin clarified. "Nah, it's not a coincidence that she's calling at the same time to report another accident. She, we had the accident. What, no, I was driving and she was driving." Chandelle was glad that it wasn't she who was having the toughest time getting them to understand he wasn't with his wife, but rather he had hit his wife. "You know what, I'll handle it myself," he decided. "Forget it, man. I got it." He hung up, annoyed by Chandelle's riotous giggles. "What's so funny?"

"Look up the hill," she said, pointing at Dr. Betty's home office. The screwy marriage counselor was watching them from her window, puffing furiously on another cigarette.

Marvin sneered at the doctor, but she didn't budge from her vantage point. "You know Bitter Betty is crazier than a Bessie-bug, don't you?"

"I must be, too, for letting her jack up our reconciliation. Marvin, am I that bad a person that you'd try to run me over?"

"Nah, not hardly. I was trying to get back at you for all the things you must have told the doc about me. I wanted you shaken up as much as I was. I'm sorry to wreck your car."

Chandelle batted her eyes at him, just this side of sensual. "How sorry?" she asked shamelessly.

Marvin opened his checkbook, wrote on it, and then handed her an amount that should have easily covered the damage.

Reading the numbered figures first, then matching them against the written amount, Chandelle grinned heartily. "Five thousand dollars, Marvin?" she said suspiciously. "Are you trying to get me on a bad check charge, or will this thing really clear your account?

"If that's not enough, hit me back and I'll handle up on the difference." Marvin knew she was behind on her bills and having trouble with the mortgage. He also knew Chandelle wouldn't have admitted it to him after the way she claimed the house for herself after his release from jail.

"You got it like that?" she asked, fingering the piece of paper playfully.

"Yeah, somewhat like that."

"Hmm, you've never been this sorry before."

"Like you, I've been working at it some."

32

Brother to Brotha

Kim Hightower was sitting in Marvin's chair when he came in to work on the following day. He stopped midstride as she started smiling at him like she was about to burst. She leaned back in her tailored pantsuit like an alley cat taking a long stretch. Marvin stared longingly at her with a curious smirk. Sure, she was in great shape and easy on the eyes, but his gaze zoomed light-years past her outstanding attributes. "You're going to make me guess why I can't sit in my own chair?" he asked, avoiding her dangerous curves.

"Sorry, but this is no longer your chair or your desk. Little did I know that you've been beating some mighty tall bushes. I was kind of iffy about renting ad space on billboards, but it's gotten you more business than you can handle in your second month. That deal you made with the McClellans, buying her a new side-by-side refrigerator and him The Executive office cooler with a wood grain finish, in order for you to use photos of their home to seduce other Anglo upper-class buyers was a heady move as well." Marvin hunched his shoulders, in a so-what manner that made Kim laugh. "You have no idea how good you are at this business, do you?"

"Obviously I'm not too good because I don't have a place to sit," Marvin jested. "What's with the portfolio rundown? I hustle and eat what I kill. You taught me that."

Kim stood up from the desk and placed her hands on her hips, as if she were a *Price Is Right* game-show model. "Oh, silly man," she chided. "Some things cannot be taught; three of them are drive, determination, and good old-fashioned know-how. Marvin, you're a star. You've been nominated for Dallas Realtor of the Month by *D Magazine*." Kim picked up a copy of the latest issue from the desk and handed it to him. "Pages thirty-seven and thirty-eight."

Marvin sat his briefcase on the floor near his polished lace-up wing tips. "Let me see that. Page thirty-three, thirty-five. Here it is." He was looking down at the picture he'd taken with the McClellans the day they held a house-warming party. His face was plastered all over the page, with a story detailing how he'd jumped through hoops to get the family to move back within the city limits. "Marvin Hutchins of Hightower Realty made it a point to satisfy both needs of the . . . Managing Editor Butch McClellan and wife Sandy . . ." he read aloud. Marvin followed the next two lines of the piece having a difficult time comprehending how it was possible. "The Managing Editor? That's like the man, right?"

"Yes, he is, although humble and very prudent with his money," answered Kim.

"Yeah, that joker is cheap," Marvin agreed. "And he drives a hard bargain. After I had The Executive delivered to his office, he tried to get me to throw in a Backyard Bar-B-Q Smoker. I had to draw the line somewhere."

"And you've made one very important friend. His receptionist called about you last week, but you seemed distracted so I filled them in on how you didn't limit yourself to high-end clientele and how you have a knack for finding just what people needed." He moved to sit in the chair that no longer belonged to him, parked behind a desk he was no longer allowed to use. Kim leaped in his path. "Uh-uh, follow me."

Marvin held the magazine in one hand and his black briefcase in the other as associates observed without the slightest notion of what Kim was up to. She escorted him across the building to the other side, passing cubicles and work hutches along the way. He grew more excited with each step as they entered into uncharted territory. Marvin was entering the big money zone, where the big dogs ate, Kim had told him more than once. "There is your new home away from home," she explained, gesturing at the office space two doors from hers. "Here are the keys. We can't have upscale people reading that article, then coming here to do business in a cubicle. Besides, you deserve it."

"Four walls," he muttered, poking his head in. "I get my own four walls? Kim, I . . ."

"Take it, shut up, and get back to making good things happen for a bunch of good people. I once considered taking out an ad in that magazine, but now, thanks to you, I don't have to. Doing good things for good people, Marvin, that's you," she reiterated.

He poked his head inside of the nicely decorated room with leather chairs and real mahogany everything else. "This is very impressive," he said, getting used to his new digs. He inched his way to the oversized desk. "Wait 'til Chandelle sees how I'm living in my home away from home. I mean, it is cool if she comes by, right?"

"Sure, Marvin, I should have known that's what had you so preoccupied lately." Kim said gleefully. "I'm happy you're back together. Working things out is important, it builds character in a relationship." Marvin's awkward grin implied that not all had been restored in paradise.

After he ran down the story about the unbelievable Dr. Bitter Betty, Kim had a similar reaction to his. "Whuut?" she exclaimed, laughing her head off. "You're not going back to that quack?"

"No, I can't do Dr. Strange Love again. I'll wait for Chandelle to find another marriage counselor who didn't graduate from Koo-Koo U."

Kim was paged by the receptionist to take a phone call. As she was poised to leave her new golden boy, a thought came to her and it was a doozy. "Marvin, maybe the next session would go a great deal better if *you* selected the shrink next time around. Stranger things have happened."

"That's what I'm afraid of."

Chandelle was so excited when she received Marvin's message. She smiled when they met at the counselor's office days later, on the second floor of a church building. "This is really something," she said, as Marvin signed them in at the reception desk. "You did what most men wouldn't. I've got me an extraordinary man. I'm proud of you for looking this guy up and getting us in to see him. I hope he's a lot different from the last one."

Marvin joined her on the cloth-covered sofa and grinned, thinking that he couldn't lose with a black male psychologist, Malcolm Quincy, pitching for him. "I love you, girl, and if being extraordinary is what it takes, I'm down for that. Give me a kiss."

Chandelle leaned in and smacked him on the lips. "Yes, I've got a good feeling about this," she restated. "I saw the sign outside, Church of Christ. I'm not trying to have nobody slapping oil on me and if this man starts speaking in tongues I'm liable to laugh right in his face."

"Nah, I think that's another affiliation. I looked these people up on the Web. They call themselves a nondenominational Bible teaching church. I heard they don't allow mechanical music during worship, though."

Chandelle cringed. "No jamming in the pulpit? I couldn't do it. I need my music."

"Just remember that we're here to see about us. I need you," Marvin whispered, accompanied by another tender kiss.

Caught up in good vibrations, neither of them heard the second door open. "That's not something you see every day," said a thin forty-something white man, with a long pony tail to make up for a receding hairline. "Generally, I send a referee out here to keep things civil before the session begins."

Chandelle stood up and grabbed her purse. Marvin didn't move. *This white guy, wearing jeans and loafers, must have made a mistake*, he thought. "Uh, we were waiting to see Dr. Malcolm Quincy, a *brotha*," Marvin said, slowly rising to his feet.

"Good, then you've come to the right place. I'm Dr. Quincy, a *brotha* in Christ. Are you both Christians?" Chandelle's face lit up as she replied that they were. All Marvin could do was nod his head in the affirmative. "Thank God, that'll make our time together more productive. Come on in and we'll get started." Marvin dragged behind reluctantly, wanting to back out when he learned that the counselor was white.

"Chandelle, he probably don't even know a thing about black people," he whispered.

"I don't care as long as he knows something about married people," she argued. "Stop being silly. You picked him. Let's see what he's got to say."

Marvin plopped down in a leather chair, the same shade as the maroon one in his new office. He scanned the walls for degrees and certifications. There was no arguing about his education, the doctor had more skins on the wall than he thought necessary. "How long have you been doing this, Doc? It is okay if I call you Doc, isn't it?"

"Sure, I'm easy," Dr. Quincy answered, taking a seat behind his desk. "I have been working with couples for fifteen years and getting paid for the past seven." He waited for Marvin to come up with another question to discredit him. Marvin glanced at Chandelle's twisted lips mouthing "behave yourself" so he closed his mouth completely. The counselor opened a file with Hutchins written on it, hummed as he looked over it, and frowned. "Hmmm," he said, peering up at them from the paper on his desk. "Marvin, I listened to the automated questionnaire you answered over the phone and I must admit to being at a loss as to why you and Chandelle wanted to visit with me. You're a good-looking couple, you were smooching in the waiting room, and your body language indicates that you both really like each other."

Marvin smiled, relaxing his guard. Chandelle yielded the floor to her husband. "It's a long story that occurred in a very short time," Marvin answered. Again, Chandelle nodded her agreement.

The doctor clasped his hands beneath his chin. He sensed their unwillingness to break the ice so he did. "I have an idea. Let's begin at the beginning. Marvin, Chandelle, do you still love one another?"

Both of them blushed agreeably.

"With all of my heart," Marvin admitted.

"Like nothing else," answered Chandelle, her smile softening.

"Excellent, do you still want to be married to one another and be honest to me as well as to yourselves?"

Marvin cleared his throat. Chandelle reached for a box of tissues on the corner of the desk. "Doc, I don't want to imagine not being married to Chandelle. She's a good wife. We've just hit a rough spot."

"Marvin's right, I am a good wife," she seconded. "He's been a constant provider, financially and emotionally. I'm less of a woman without him. I'd like to keep him if I can."

Dr. Quincy seemed even more puzzled. There was no bickering and backbiting between them. He pondered whether they were putting on so as not to appear strained. He'd seen couples flat out lie to him in order to keep their troubles hidden and spare the other's feelings; those were the ones at risk for going postal. "Marvin, this rough spot you spoke of, why don't you tell me about it, as much as you feel comfortable? Chandelle, I'll ask you for your input in a minute, if there is a difference of opinion. Now, I'll ask y'all to respect the person with the cube." He handed Marvin a block of wood. "Let's work at sharing the cube and talking only while holding it."

As Marvin explained how he'd begun working more and giving Chandelle less of the quality time she needed, he told his wife how buying the house she wanted made him feel. He forgave Chandelle for the false arrest and commended her on getting it kicked. Dr. Quincy listened attentively, jotting notes here and there. After he'd started talking, Marvin shared *his business* so openly that it amazed Chandelle. She blotted the rims of her eyes as Marvin apologized for contacting Kim when he was incarcerated. "Anger was behind it," he said, "and my pride pushed me some too." He went on to bring up Chandelle's actions, but she reached her hand out for the cube, indicating that she wanted to speak for herself and publicly own up to her part in their moment of discontentment.

"I got my boss to go downtown with me," Chandelle said, staring down at the cube sitting on her lap. "When I heard that Marvin had been bailed out by another woman, I flipped. It was bad enough that she was the realtor who found that new home for us, then my cousin Dior told me she'd seen them hugged up when Kim dropped him off.

All I could think was that an affair had been going on under my nose. What else would motivate her to get Marvin out of jail? I believe him now that nothing went on between them, but I did some foolish things out of spite." Chandelle recapped how she gave the furniture to the Salvation Army, caused Marvin to be terminated from a job he liked, and then after getting a call from Dior, showed up at the grocery store to show her tail. While getting Marvin's electricity turned off was on her and her alone, Dior seemed to have always been around when the fireworks started. Marvin held Chandelle by the arm to comfort her as she reeled off details of the Tony Jones incident. She was fighting back tears and running out of tissues, but neither stopped her from telling it like it was. Of course, Dior's name came up quite a few times during her last bit of testimony.

Once Chandelle finished, she handed the cube back to Marvin. He gawked at it just long enough to allow visions of Dior's naked body lying on his bed to pop into his mind; then he tossed the cube on Dr. Quincy's desk like a hot potato. "Oh, my bad," he muttered as the block of wood skidded across to the doctor.

"It's quite all right, Marvin. It's my turn to talk anyway." Quincy leaned back in his chair and exhaled. "I must applaud your honestly and the lengths to which you've gone to demonstrate the love you apparently share. However, there are two issues I'd like to work on starting next week. One is getting you to agree on a COC—Code Of Conduct—to follow when things get a bit heated and learning methods to resolve them without being destructive. As Marvin discovered, masking feelings usually lead to dangerous outcomes. Chandelle, hopefully you'll think back on the things you've done to Marvin and recognize that there are some anger management concerns to be dealt with." Dr. Quincy pulled out two business cards while flipping through his calendar. "God runs a faith-based program and so do I. Bring your Bibles next week on the eighteenth, then follow up if necessary."

"Whoa, Doc!" Marvin objected. "You're going to kick us to the curb after our next session? I thought you said we had *two* things to hash out. I think we're making headway."

"You are correct, Marvin, that's why I don't anticipate seeing you that often. I make it a point not to become the third wheel in my patients' marriages. You'll have to resolve things between yourselves. I'm only providing the venue and direction. You two love and respect each other, a child could see that. My client roster is littered with men who've molested their daughters, mothers who've sat by and let it happen; I've had women who've been raped and their husband's unwillingness to touch them afterward, or brides who can't stop talking about how beautiful their wedding was long enough to participate in the marriage. There are couples with dependency problems, and some who really have no business being married to each other. I want to say this, you are lucky to have one another, so don't forget that the next time you lose your temper or get your feelings hurt." The doctor stood and circled the desk, then presented them with his cards. Marvin accepted one and passed the other to Chandelle before giving the doctor some soul brother dap.

"Thanks, Doc. I knew that something led me to you and I'm grateful."

"It didn't happened to be the Holy Spirit and the way my name sounded?"

"Yeah, you got me, but I am not sorry for it."

"Me neither," said Chandelle, shaking the doctor's hand firmly. "You're really good at this, making people loosen up and see things clearly."

"That's why I have another couple waiting," he replied, to hurry them along.

"Okay, Doc, we're going, but you said two things. I'm

with the code of conduct and showing the love, but what's the second one?"

"Don't listen to Dior," Quincy answered casually.

Chandelle whipped her head around. "What do you mean?"

"It appears that most of your challenges have occurred because of something she said or did. Take it from me, friends and family can ruin a good thing faster than infidelity. Oh, it's okay to have them around. Just don't put any stock into what they tell you about your spouse unless you've had the chance to check it out for yourself. Now, you have to go. Call me if you're going to cancel."

"Oh no, that's not happening," Marvin contended, already looking forward to that session.

On their way out, holding hands and genuinely happy to be weathering their first big storm, Marvin pushed the door open to ask the doctor for additional business cards. He quickly lurched back when it came to him that he'd opened the wrong one. He was about to close it when he spotted he and Chandelle's old counselor, Dr. Betty, sitting on pins and needles next to a man who acted as if he'd rather be any place other than there with her. Marvin chuckled quietly. "I knew it, the blind leading the blind." He pulled Chandelle forward to see what he'd discovered through the cracked door.

"Who? Ooh, that is her," she uttered to him. "I'm getting my money back."

"Why don't you let her make it on this one? By the looks of it, she's going to need to take out a loan for Brotha Malcolm Quincy to straighten out all of her issues."

"And what makes you think it's her who's got their marriage twisted?" Chandelle asked facetiously. "You're right, she's going to need every penny."

33

If It Kills Us

The elevator door opened on the ground floor. Marvin and Chandelle strolled out of it casually, hand in hand, a vast difference from after their other counseling adventure. There were no insulting tirades to contend with or snotty, smoke-blowing man-bashing episodes either. They had found a sensible facilitator who cared about his client's welfare and had utilized methodologies to bring about positive change. Chandelle enjoyed the thought of involving scriptural study to help assist them in piecing their relationship back together. That reminded her of Marvin's zeal and respect for the Word when he approached her on day one.

"Marvin, you did good, baby, choosing this Dr. Quincy," she said tenderly, on the sidewalk outside of the church's office plaza. "I've heard preachers say how much easier it is to get men and women to do right when they stay in the Bible for support. Remember how we used to have a weekly study, on Wednesday nights, nothing too heavy, but thirty minutes or so reading chapters to each other?"

Marvin nodded, smiling as he thought back. "Yeah, I

sure do. I grew up watching my folks shutting it down to put the outside world aside on the regular. Maybe that's why I rarely heard them going off. You can't read about God's blessings, and then turn around and act a fool. Well, I couldn't."

"When we met, you were so witty, charming, concerned about doing right and being a Christian example that I didn't know how to take you. I didn't know what a *Christian example* was or know of any brothas willing to take me out for dinner and pass up on the dessert, if you know what I mean. Before I met you, I figured every man was alike, thinking a woman owed them something after they paid the check."

"Wait a minute now, I wasn't perfect nor was I trying to be," Marvin clarified immediately. "Don't think it was easy for me to take you home when my man-man was begging me to close the deal," he joked, glancing down at his zipper. "We both wanted to do some things to you, get you involved in some wickedness."

"Yes, but you didn't, that's what drew me to you upfront. You didn't press or make my feel obligated."

"All this time, I thought you were feeling me because I was fine," Marvin said, fishing for a compliment.

"Uh-uh, that's what made me want to get at some of that wickedness you were talking about. I'm saying how it was refreshing that you knew Jesus but weren't freaky and annoying about it."

"Those are the ones you have to be worried about," he agreed, "when you can't help wondering if they're trying to convince you or themselves. Wolves in sheep's clothing is what my mama used to call them."

"Huh, wolves in wolves' clothing if you look closely enough," she said knowingly. "God knew what he was doing all right. When I met you, I was searching but didn't know it. Remember the time you invited me to attend church? I was so scared. Didn't have church clothes, and

I was afraid that I'd say or do something wrong. Nervous of being found unworthy, I guess."

Marvin leaned in closer to show his compassion. "Unworthy? Unworthy of what?"

"The invitation for a church date and a man like you," she answered, before digging up skeletons from her past. "I wasn't accustomed to men opening doors for me, saying thank you and please, showing that they cared about me without expecting the panties to drop. I became selfish, scandalous, and out for mine. Funny, I thought that graduating from college would somehow change me, make me more of a lady. I had a diploma in my hands and still too much street in my heart. Lies are what I lived by. Game is what I understood. That's why I kept avoiding you in the beginning. I wouldn't let myself trust your words even though you gave me no reason not to." Marvin wrapped his arms around her. Chandelle laughed to keep from crying. "Where do you think Dior got all of her bad habits? She grew up watching me doing dirt and perfecting mine. Yeah, I'm still paying for that today," said Chandrelle.

Marvin gritted his teeth and looked toward the sky, thinking that Chandelle had no idea how right she was about that. "We all make mistakes that haunt us, baby. That's life," he uttered, speaking for himself as well.

"Teaching my little cousin the ways of the world, that's my cross to bear. I programmed the girl and she's running wild. I'm the one responsible, and I'm the one who's duty-bound to take her in for some serious soul scrubbing. You don't cut for her, I understand why, but she's my blood, my family, and I can't have her out there like she doesn't have any." During their long embrace, Chandelle tilted her head back to look in her husband's eyes. "Marvin, you showed me a whole other life I didn't know existed outside of what I saw in the hood and what white folks put on television. Being married to you was like liv-

ing a dream with my name on it. Dior was just jealous of
our relationship," she assumed, correctly although mis-
guidedly. "I heard what the doctor suggested. He's right.
I'll check her on sticking her nose into ours, but I've got
to get Dior some help, if it kills me."

What if it kills us? he wanted to say but didn't. "Hey,
cheer up," he cooed in its place. "I have my arms wrapped
around you and I'm not ready to let you go. Can you
swing an extended lunch? There are some things I want
you to see."

"You kidding? All I have to do is call and tell Grace
that I'm with you and she'll give me a pass." Chandelle
did phone Grace, who hadn't too long ago returned to work.
When she heard a lift in her friend's voice, Grace told
Chandelle to take all the time she needed, just as predicted.
"I told you she was rooting for us," Chandelle chuckled
gleefully.

"I'm down for us too," Marvin said, searching the
nearly empty parking lot for Chandelle's Volvo, forgetting
that he'd smashed the grill the week before. "Where's
your car?"

"You are funneee," she snickered. "I almost laughed."

"Oh snap, it's in the shop?"

"Uh-huh, *in the shop*," Chandelle answered, bobbing
her head up and down, as if she wasn't sure how to take
him forgetting how he'd plowed into it. "It'll be *in the
shop* for three more days and eighteen hundred dollars'
worth of repairs."

"Ahh, yes, it's getting clearer now," he said, wincing in
jest. "Then that's you in the white Neon over there?"

"If you keep cracking on my replacement whip, I
might not write you a check for the difference. Let me get
out my checkbook right now and do that." Chandelle un-
zipped her purse, hoping that he'd stop her from returning
$3,200 she'd planned on reallocating for overdue bills.

"Sweetheart, don't. I gave that money to you because I

wanted you to have it. Why don't you put it on something else you need?" That's exactly the response Chandelle was working on. She quickly zipped her bag, then smacked Marvin on the lips.

"He still loves her," she moaned sensually.

"He cares for her too," Marvin added.

"Told you you was gonna want me back," Chandelle teased.

"You think I ever stopped?" he questioned. "Nah, my mama didn't raise no fool. Let's take my ride. I don't see me fitting in yours."

"Ha-ha, another crack? That was almost less funneee than your last one. Congratulations."

Marvin had scheduled midday errands to run. Having Chandelle along seemed more than ideal, considering they affected her as much as him. Every five minutes she asked, "Are we there yet?" like an impatient child on a road trip. Marvin laughed each time she did it, realizing how much he had missed her sense of humor and their perfect pairing. Chandelle dropped hints about him leaving the apartment to join her in the house. Marvin caught each one but refused to tackle that conversation, which encompassed a great deal more than him changing his address.

"Oh look, we're here," Marvin said, as he drove his eight-year-old vehicle into the Toyota dealership.

Chandelle looked around curiously. Marvin had taken excellent care of his SUV and enjoyed four years without having to pay a monthly note. She couldn't see him parting with it, at least not the old Marvin. "Do you have a client here?" she asked from the passenger seat.

"I'm here to get your opinion," he said, straight-faced and plainly. "I test-drove a Sequoia the other day. It's a step up from my Four Runner."

"A step up?" she questioned. "It's not like you're interested in buying one. Are you?"

Marvin opened the glass door and ushered Chandelle inside the motor-plex. The white lady, wearing a headset behind a partially obstructed desk, smiled and waved at him. "Hey, Marvin, you here for another spin?" she asked.

"I do like that new car smell," was his response. "Is Lawrence in today?"

"Yep, I'll tell him you're back."

Chandelle tugged on Marvin's sleeve. "On first-name basis with the staff? Just how often do you come by here?"

"Just a couple of times, but I've test-driven several of these," he told her, motioning toward the SUVs in the showroom. "I'm kinda like a mascot now. Hey, check out this blue one," he said, opening the passenger side door to a mammoth vehicle. Chandelle stepped on the running board and climbed in.

"Wow, Marvin, this is so big," she marveled. "And look at how long it is."

"Thank you," he replied, lewdly implying her inference was regarding his features.

"You are so nasty," she giggled. "I was about to say how much bigger this one is than yours."

"Oh," he said, feigning disappointment.

"Marvin," announced the slick-dressed salesman, approaching from behind him. "You keep coming by and I'm going to have to tell my wife about us," he jested. Chandelle bit her lip, trying not to laugh when it appeared her husband had worn out his visitor's badge at the dealership.

"Hey, Lawrence, this is *my wife*, Chandelle," Marvin said, greeting him with a firm handshake like an old friend.

"So, you do like girls, after all?" the chubby blond man cracked wise, knowing Marvin could handle it. "I just lost twenty bucks."

Chandelle's mouth flew open when a loud burst came flying out. "Hello," Chandelle said, extending her hand to him. "Now, that was funny! Pleased to meet you, Lawrence."

"She's beautiful and recognizes talent when she hears it? Marvin, I'm giving you my home number so Chandelle can talk to my wife, maybe smarten her up a bit."

"Look before you leap, Lawrence. Chandelle might take you up on it," Marvin answered. "You do not want my woman in your wife's ear. Trust me."

"Marvin?" Chandelle objected lightly.

"So, are you test-driving again today?" Lawrence asked, seemingly annoyed with people who wasted a lot of time without making a purchase. "You know, I could give you a brochure and that would cut out a lot of this back and forth."

"Yeah whatever," Marvin said, dismissing him quickly. "Chandelle, which of these do you like best? There's the beige one over there we could try out. It's got cloth seats, six-disk CD changer, and a navigational system. That's a black one, with leather seats and a flip-down TV monitor. Oh, that silver one comes with leather, the CD changer, the navigational system, and seat warmers."

Chandelle's eyes widened with excitement. "Seat warmers?"

"Uh-huh," Marvin answered. "They'll make your booty hot."

"Let's check that one out," Chandelle replied, like a little kid at an amusement park.

"Lawrence, you heard the lady. Open the door and get me the keys," Marvin demanded with a crooked smile. The salesman hunched his shoulder and shook his head.

"Okay, Marvin, I've got your photo ID on record. You know the rules better than I do. No speeding, no car chases, no stunts, no hitchhikers, *and no stunts*," he reiterated for the sake of making Chandelle laugh. After his mission was accomplished, Lawrence smacked his thigh. "I keep telling my wife that I'm funny. Hold on, I'll get 'er opened up, but this time you bring it back with some gas in it."

"Man, just get me the keys," Marvin demanded, grinning. "I'm leaving you mine for security. It's got two hundred and sixty-seven thousand miles racked up, that's barely broken in good and I'm trusting you with it."

Soon enough, the large glass windows slid back. The salesman strutted out and handed Marvin the keys. "We have to stop meeting like this or people will start to talking about me too," he said, winking at Chandelle. When she snickered again, he gloated. "I still got it. Chandelle, enjoy the ride. Marvin, be safe out there and put some gas in it!" he hollered as the vehicle inched down the sloped exit.

"Ooh!" Chandelle squealed with delight. "I'm sitting so high up. This is really nice, baby."

"It is nice, huh?" he said, pressing the button to activate Chandelle's seat warmer. "Hold on, I forgot to get something." He stopped directly behind his vehicle, got out, and returned with a briefcase. "Is it hot yet?" he questioned, leering at her seductively.

"Uhhhh-huh," Chandelle moaned, playing alone. "I'm digging it too." She ran her fingers along the leather seats and wood grain finish on the console. "I wish you could afford this, Marvin. No wonder why you keep showing up and bothering Lawrence. I'd hate to take this one back."

"Good, because we're keeping it," he revealed casually. "All I needed to know is that you liked it."

"You're serious?" Chandelle asked apprehensively. "I saw the sticker price and I'm in shock that you would ever contemplate paying that much. If you just bought this, why didn't he have you sign the papers?"

"Lawrence had me approved the first time I walked into the building a week ago."

"Hmmm, if this is yours . . ."

"Ours," Marvin corrected her.

"If this is really ours, I can take off my clothes and roll around in all this leather?"

"Do I need to stop the car? I'd pay to see that." Marvin pulled onto the shoulder of the road to watch, but Chandelle was only bluffing.

"Not that I believe you, but why would you trade in your truck for a new note? Huh, tell me that?" Marvin reached in the backseat behind Chandelle for his briefcase. After opening it, he retrieved a copy of the magazine praising his real-estate savvy and brilliant customer service skills.

"Flip it to page thirty-seven."

Chandelle didn't know what to think as she thumbed through the pages. When she saw his picture and the article, she started screaming and hopping up and down on the heated seat. "Oohhh! Oohhh, baby! This is you! This is you!" she shouted, celebrating his accolades. "What did you do?" she asked, reading the first paragraph.

"I'll need a better vehicle if I expect wealthy clients to take me seriously. I got lucky with the guy who runs that magazine. I hooked him up with something he and his wife both liked, saved them money, drive time, and . . . there you go, page thirty-seven."

Marvin merged back on the avenue as Chandelle read the entire article. "Hutchins, previously working as an assistant manager for a private major appliances company, has proven that the will to go above and beyond easily crosses industry boundaries. His knack for exploring out-of-the-box possibilities for clients at the Hightower Realty agency has put him atop this magazine's list of outstanding realtors. In as much as two months, Hutchins has utilized the company's First-Time Buyer program while outlining the benefits of home ownership to a young entrepreneur who runs a successful barber shop." Chandelle looked up from the page. "Dooney? They're talking about Dooney."

"Yeah, Kim gave them the scoop. I didn't suspect a thing. Dooney gets his freak on and I get the credit, I guess."

"Additionally, Marvin Hutchins exhibited a wealth of

cognitive resources," she read on, "when he convinced an older gentleman to liquidate his rental properties in order to enjoy his good fortune by traveling more and concerning himself with working less." When Chandelle stopped reading, she glanced at Marvin.

"Super Dave had way too much going on to be fooling with renters and the upkeep of six houses," he answered her inquisitive expression.

"Why are we here?" she asked. "What's in this neighborhood?"

"Those two houses," Marvin answered proudly. "The one with the red trim and this one, with the huge bay window, I . . . we bought them both from Dave. I sold another one to Dooney and the others went fast."

Chandelle closed the magazine as her head fell forward. "I'm proud of you, Marvin. So proud," she said softly, her eyes cast toward her lap.

"Then what's wrong?"

"Nothing," she lied, because the truth hurt too much to say.

"It doesn't look like nothing from here," he debated. "From here, it looks like a big something. Chandelle, you never could lie to me, so you may as well spill it." She wagged her head slowly, then mumbled her answer.

"All of this stuff. All of this good stuff happened to you in spite of me," she said. "Look at everything. You're balling now and I wasn't around to help you do any of it. Maybe you are better off without me. Here I was thinking how we might spend Christmas together, in *our home,* and you've already bought two of them for yourself."

Marvin allowed Chandelle's feelings to sink in. He'd been too busy moving and shaking to give what she had or hadn't been a part of any real consideration until then. He realized that she was right and wrong at the same time. "Chandelle, all of this stuff happening to me has more to do with you than you think. If I hadn't been arrested, I'd still be happy at Appliance World. If you hadn't talked Mr. Mercer into firing me, I'd still be happy at Appliance World. If I hadn't called Kim Hightower to bail me out, I'd still be happy at Appliance World. Dooney wouldn't own his first home. Dave wouldn't be taking time off work to live instead of living to work. By the way, he sold these houses to us at half price . . . both are valued at over one-hundred gees apiece. That's the only reason I qualified for them. Kim makes money on the back end of every buy and sale, so she came out pretty good on hiring me. Just think if you and Dior hadn't jacked me up . . ."

"I know, you'd still be happy at Appliance World."

"It's funny when you think about it, huh?"

"No, it's funny the way you explained it," she answered. "You know, I could get you busted again and we can see how your luck is running then?" Chandelle offered disingenuously.

"Thanks, but I'm gonna pass on going back to county. God put us through a lot to get us this far. I'd hate to mess with that."

Chandelle sighed, then leaned over the console to kiss Marvin. "Grace said He had plans for us. He sure did. And I thought Dior was just getting in the way."

Marvin put the SUV in drive, thinking how God didn't have anything to do with Dior managing to get herself more than just in the way.

34

Two Shoe Boxes

Chandelle puttered down the road in her rented Neon. It was a far cry from the comforts of Marvin's new Sequoia SUV. No CD disc changer, leather, or cozy seat warmers she'd already developed an affinity for. The tiny two-door she drove reminded her that her life in general was smaller by comparison with what Marvin had amassed in her absence. Although Chandelle couldn't help but applaud his recent triumphs after pushing her away, she wasn't as thrilled about what Dior must have been up to since she did the same to her.

As soon as she arrived home, Chandelle collected the stack of greeting cards Dior had sent her. With Amnesty, the adorable chocolate-hued teddy bear, on her lap, she read the cards and their inscriptions one by one. Most of them shared the same sentiment, asking for forgiveness, understanding, and yet another chance to recapture their friendship. Chandelle correlated Dior's pleas to just how much she wanted Marvin's attention and absolution. Anger and jealousy had both played such major roles in all three of their lives, and Chandelle was tired of letting them decide how and who she'd let in. Certainly Dior's shortcomings were practically of urban legend proportions and those were only the stories she'd heard about. Regardless, Dior was family, which Chandelle could not or would not dismiss. After reading the last card begging adamantly for her oldest friend to at least resume communication in fear of the door to their future being closed forever, Chandelle had made up her mind to overlook her cousin's devilish acts and the evil spirits that led her to pulling them off. "Come on, Amnesty," she said finally, nuzzling with the stuffed animal. "Let's call Dior and have a long talk about keeping her nose out of other people's bid'ness, especially mine."

For two days, Chandelle dialed Dior's home and cell numbers to no avail. Praying that she wasn't missing, Chandelle called Dooney. Despite not having seen his sister since that day he embarrassed her at the Big Cluck's fried chicken drive-thru, he suggested that Dior was somewhere doing her own thing. "If you need me to run by her apartment and snoop around, I can handle that when I close the shop," he offered.

Chandelle read her wall clock, then determined there was a better solution. "No, Dooney, I'll go over and see if she's there myself. You've got money to make without worrying about Dior."

"I know that's right," he quickly concurred. "But look here, if she's not at home and you want in, call the maintenance man Harold Gulley. We go way back to my hustling days."

"This Harold Gulley, he's an ex-con too?" Chandelle questioned. "Because I'm not trying to get caught up in anything."

"Gulley is good people. We did a short stretch together over this little misunderstanding between his baby's momma and her pimp. We pulled his collar and let him know she wanted out of the game. One of his other girls sold us out to the law. Ol' dude was smart enough to keep his busted mouth shut when time came to testify. That old playa rolled into the courtroom in a wheelchair shivering like a wet dog," Dooney cackled, "but we only did what was necessary. Gulley is harmless otherwise. He'll do what I tell him."

Chandelle took Gulley's digits and called him. He complained about being tied up until he heard Dooney's name; then he wasn't so busy, after all. Gulley agreed to help her immediately.

Standing by a faded Ford truck with an aluminum ladder attached, Gulley smiled nervously as an attractive woman stepped out of a car that didn't fit her nearly as well as her blue jeans, sweater, and boots. "You Chandelle?" he asked, careful not to do anything that could in any way be misconstrued as disrespectful. He was there when Dooney crippled the loud-talking defiant pimp.

Chandelle narrowed her eyes, squinting at the hefty built dark-skinned laborer. "Yeah, I'm Chandelle. Thanks for meeting me on short notice. I really appreciate it." She knocked at the door but no one answered.

"Uh-uh, don't say another word about it," he cowered. "Any friend of Dooney's is cool with me." The metal loop of keys rattled in his hands when opening Dior's apartment door. "You need me to hang around until you're through?" he asked, wanting eagerly to get as far away as he could from Chandelle, that apartment, and the debt he owed for his baby's mother's safety.

"No, thank you, I'll be fine," she answered, feeling sorry for the man who looked to be seconds away from wetting his pants. "I'll lock up when I'm done. Oh, and I'll be sure to tell my cousin Dooney you were very helpful."

"Thank you, thank you, sistah," he answered graciously, backing away. "Thank you." In the blink of an eye, Gulley was gone.

Chandelle closed the door, locked it, and turned on the lights in the living room. Clothes were scattered here and there, the way Dior liked them when she was coming and going too much to bother with keeping house. The answering machine resting on the end table displayed the number 17 in the new messages field. Chandelle moved through the house slowly from room to room, looking for anything that remotely resembled a clue to Dior's whereabouts. She saw an assortment of dirty clothes piled up in the bathroom, another of Dior's bad habits. Clutter had always reassured Dior that she was too busy to care about sorting things out.

Something told Chandelle to look underneath the bed, where Dior was known to hide her most private possessions. When they were kids, it was a diary. Now Chandelle had the opportunity to peek into what Dior had been up to lately. She found two shoe boxes. One contained a myriad of herbs and pills, intimate toys, and flavored body oils. Chandelle knew that bad girls played hard, since she was once one of them, so the contents in that box didn't alarm her. However, she was startled when removing the second box lid.

The sight of cold steel shook Chandelle. A black revolver stretching out on a bed of tens, twenties, fifties, and big-faced Benjamins warranted a closer look. There was a small black book hidden beneath the money. Chandelle was shocked by the number of bills in the box because Dior was often worse off financially. Somehow, she'd come upon some fast cash since her near eviction. Chandelle began flipping through the black book, which turned out to be Dior's daily planner. The first three entries Chandelle read from the previous month explained why Dior wouldn't carry it around with her. If picked up by the police for high-priced prostitution, that book would have served as her own undoing.

Chandelle passed several dates in search of the most recent entries. Fortunately for Dior, she skipped by the passages detailing notes of Marvin coming out of Kim Hightower's house after 10:00 P.M. She also glided past documentation of the well-devised plan to share a drink with Marvin, get him plastered, and later share his bed.

"Let me see, Friday . . . Friday the thirteenth," she mumbled quietly. An eerie feeling swept through Chandelle when she said the date. Not that she was superstitious, but that date was tied to tragedy in the minds of most people so she couldn't shake it. "Okay . . . a nooner with the Judge," she read aloud, in Dior's handwriting. "Nooner . . . judge?" she repeated anxiously. "Eight o'clock birthday threesome at the Jennings . . . Special Occasion . . . Take enough Viagra? Ten-thirty dessert with Giorgio, Aristocrat Hotel. No Viagra, bring toys," Chandelle exclaimed disapprovingly. "Ohhh, Dior."

Chandelle racked her brain trying to remember the woman's name who had Dior pent up in the fitting room stall at the boutique. "What was that loony white chick's name? Rose, Rosey, Rhonda, Rona, Rhoda . . . Rosalind! That's it, *Rosalind* Jennings!" Chandelle remembered Dior saying how she'd served as a nanny for the Jenningses before her work had turned to play. The couple was into some kinky stuff, dangerous sexual activities. It didn't help that Rosalind exhibited addictive and possessive personality traits. Chandelle reasoned that the woman's husband was likely just as mentally defective so she picked up the phone and dialed information. "Yes, I need a number and address for a Rosalind Jennings, in Plano. Yes, I'll hold." The operator returned with bad news: The number was unlisted.

Chandelle tore through Dior's dresser drawers in the

bedroom, then made her way to the kitchen, rifling through papers, unopened bills, and old check stubs. "Jennings . . . Jennings," whispered Chandelle. "Paul and Rosalind Jennings! I got y'all now." She shoved the pay stub into her back pocket and hurriedly headed for the door. "It's seven forty-five."

Chandelle locked the door and sped off toward I-75. She hooked a right on the service road and then another one into a Kinko's parking lot. Friday night guaranteed the place would be virtually dead with plenty of available PCs. Chandelle sat down at the computer farthest in the back. She slid her credit card in the slot, waited, and then clicked on the Internet Explorer icon. Within sixty seconds, she was printing off the driving instructions to the Jennings's residence.

"Dior had better be all right when I get there," she growled, while maneuvering through sluggish traffic in her rental. "I know that much! Birthday threesomes for the man who has everything, huh?" Chandelle felt around on the passenger seat, as she darted in and out of sluggish lanes toward the Park Avenue exit. "He's about get a birthday surprise too."

When Chandelle found the house, Dior's tricked-out Escort was sitting next to the curb in front of it. She beat on the door like the police, loud and insistently. Moments later, Chandelle began kicking the heel of her boot against the door more violently. "I said, open this door!" she shouted and banged, drawing attention from neighbors walking their overcared-for pooches. Eventually, a half-dressed white woman, the same one who'd been stalking Dior, answered frantically.

"Go away, you must have the wrong house," she persisted, with the chain on the door. She tried to close it, but Chandelle jammed her boot against the frame.

"Dior is coming with me so you might as well open up," she howled boldly.

"Dior isn't here, I tell you. Now go before I call the police."

"I'll give you something to call them about," Chandelle threatened as she burst into the house. She stomped around downstairs behind the kitchen in the maid's quarters. "Why are you standing there looking at me? I thought you were calling the law?" Chandelle spat, once discovering Dior's purse and jacket on the washer in the utility room.

Rosalind glanced at the cutting board near the kitchen isle. Chandelle knew what she was thinking. "Go ahead on," she dared, pulling a straight razor from her purse. Dooney taught her to use one in self-defense before she went off to college. "We can let the police pick up the pieces after their next donut break. I'd bet your neighbors would love that."

"What if Dior doesn't want to go with you?" Rosalind submitted, with her arms folded.

"Like she has a choice," Chandelle barked. "Where is she, up there?" Not waiting for an answer, she raced upstairs, searching the rooms until she discovered Dior tied up like an animal, bound and gagged. Chandelle gawked at Mr. Jennings, who was naked except for leather riding boots. He lunged toward her, his soft frame jiggling. She raised her knee and kicked him in the gut.

"You're in here whipping her? Slavery days been over, and if you ever come around my li'l cousin again, I'm gonna make a few calls and see to it that some of the biggest black men I know free you from that saggy bag hanging between your skinny legs. Believe me, you don't want to mess with us. What you've been getting from Dior ain't worth it. Whatever you're paying her ain't either."

As Chandelle ripped the gag off Dior's mouth, she coughed and sputtered. "Uh-uh, Chandelle, you've got it all wrong. You gave up on me so I'm doing what I'm good at. These people pay lots of money to be with me. This 'plantation mammy' thing they like goes over big out here in the burbs. Just pretend you didn't find me, and then leave us alone."

"Dee, get your clothes on and shake any idea of ever doing this again from your empty head," Chandelle demanded while untying Dior. "You have shamed me and every black woman who ever lived. Now, get your stuff before I beat you myself and spare our ancestors the embarrassment. The games these kinds of people play are dangerous. People have died being restrained like this." Dior hesitated a second too long for Chandelle's liking so she began dragging her down the hall. As they neared the steps, Dior screamed.

"All right! All right, let me up!"

"Fool!" Chandelle kept an eye on Rosalind and the top of the staircase in the event Paul gave another shot at getting his birthday threesome wish. "Hurr'up, Dior. I don't like this place or these nasty friends of yours."

"They ain't friends, they used to be paying customers," Dior grumbled, while zipping her dress in the back. She yelled angrily at the way Chandelle wrestled her to the door by her hair. "You ain't got to be handling me this way. I said I was going."

"And I'm making sure you keep your word." Chandelle was glad that there weren't any neighbors looming about to witness the outcome of her thunderous entry into the Jennings's home. "Dior," she said, shoving her into the compact car. "What were you planning to do once those people had used you up and thrown you out?"

"They were just getting some kicks. Ain't nobody tryna to use me."

"Don't be a fool your whole life. That man was about to ride you like a birthday pony with his wife watching. That whole scene is triflin', and it won't ever turn out like you thought. I've got too much on my mind to go casket shopping for you over some hot mess." Chandelle was seething. She roared out of the subdivision with her tires smoking. "And don't think for a minute that this ends here, Dior. Get out your cute little flip phone and call to cancel your ten o'clock with Giorgio. One Viagra pill-popping white man a night ought to be enough." ·

"Giorgio don't do pills and he ain't white, he's I-tal-ian," she fussed, with her purse sitting on her lap. "Any-way, how'd you find me, how do you know about my ten o'clock, and what is up with the itsy-bitsy car?"

"Do not even comment on the car, all right. It's going to get us home, I hope." Chandelle felt Dior's eyes piercing holes in her side. "Oh, and I found the black book of yours, the one you had hidden under your bed," Chandelle answered. "I saw the loot, too, but I won't go into that. What's done is done."

Dior froze. "The book? What . . . you read my stuff?"

"Yeah, I read it, had to. How else was I going to find you before some pervert went too far?"

"What else did you read . . . in the book?" Dior asked soberly.

"Don't stress, I read about the judge, too, but that's not as bad as this," she replied, guessing she was afraid of the judge's affair getting out. "Oooh, Dior, you make my head hurt. Nobody's perfect, but you don't have to be stu-pid. And oh, you're going to church with me too."

Dior smacked her lips in direct opposition. "No, I'm not!"

"You want to bet? You can go standing up or like I found you, tied up with both hands behind your back. But you are going, if I have to drag you in by that raggedy weave of yours."

"Chandelle, quit playin'. You've done your good deed, but you can't make me go to church. You ain't my mommà."

"You're right, I'm not, but since she's doing a bid and

can't help straighten you out, I'm going to step up and put my two cents in until she gets released. You could use a dose of house arrest."

"Humph, you're trippin'," Dior smarted off.

"And you're coming to church with me on Sunday."

That's what she thinks, Dior said to herself. *We'll just see about that.*

35

It's Complicated

The following morning, Dior opened her eyes to a strange room. She popped up in the bed, looking around to gain her bearings. *Oh, I'm at Chandelle's*, she realized, then leaned back to finish resting her head. It felt good, thinking of all the trouble Chandelle went through to find her, acted in what she considered a highly overprotective manner, and later refused to let Dior out of her sight. She almost laughed at the way Chandelle had marched her up the stairs, cranked on the shower, and forced her to wash the filth off her body before allowing her to sleep in the bed. Then Chandelle set the house alarm, dared her to attempt an escape, and slept at the foot of her own bed to discourage any further foolishness.

Dior found herself wondering where Chandelle was now. Certainly Chandelle didn't think that the sunrise was enough to stop Dior from leaving if she really felt like it. Unbeknownst to her, Chandelle had her own issues to contend with.

"Chandelle," Dior called out from the bed. "Chandelle! I'm hungry!" She swung the cover aside to climb out of bed, wearing a borrowed flannel nightgown. "It wasn't that cold last night," she huffed, shrugging it off. Dior opened the second dresser drawer but found a collection of flattering panties. "Ooh, I like her style, but where does she keep the T-shirts?" When she looked in the top drawer, Dior discovered a white plastic bag from a local pharmacy. She stood on her tiptoes and craned her neck to search inside without disturbing it too much. "What the . . ." she muttered, trying to calm her voice and surprise. Inside of the bag, Dior counted three Early Pregnancy Test kits; only one hadn't been opened, the other two read positive. "Chandelle's gonna have a baby," she sighed nervously. She plopped down on the bed in a strange daze, unable to be joyous because of the situation she'd manipulated with Chandelle's old boyfriend Tony. Dior's mouth felt dry. She leaped up, pushed the bag closed, and snatched a shirt from the drawer. As she wrestled it over her head and exited the bedroom, she heard a peculiar sound coming from the other side of the closed bathroom door in the guest room. "Chandelle?" she said, leaning against the door. She tried to twist the knob but couldn't. It was locked. "Chandelle, what's the matter with you?" No one answered but Dior heard more of the gargled groaning like before. She began pounding on the door. "Come on, Chandelle, I can help you." Dior didn't know how to feel—torn, helpless, or guilty, but elated wasn't one of them. She took a fast step backward when the toilet flushed. "I know you're in there," she yelled, growing increasingly impatient. Water from the wash basin ran for a while before the door opened.

"You didn't have to bang on the door," Chandelle replied finally. "There are two other restrooms." Dior didn't move when Chandelle took a calculated step to get past her. "Move, Dior, I must be coming down with something, maybe it's the flu," she said, with her eyes half closed and a lie fully exposed.

"You're coming down with a baby," Dior said, with sad eyes that were a close resemblance to Chandelle's. "I saw the EPTs, both of them." She watched as Chandelle turned an odd shade of green as she clutched at her stomach and then bolted for the toilet again. "I didn't mean to snoop but . . . you saw mine last night and now I've seen your secret too." Dior pulled a washcloth from the cabinet. She ran cool water over it, and then placed it on the back of Chandelle's neck as she spat up violently. "Go on and get it out," Dior said, like a doting sister. "We'll go to the doctor today. I can tell by the way you're hiding things that you haven't been."

Chandelle shook her head sorrowfully and pointed at the vanity area. "The cup," she said painstakingly. Dior filled it halfway but felt fully responsible for Chandelle's plight despite just having learned about the pregnancy. Dior watched her rinse from the cup and spit into the bowl repeatedly.

"What are we gonna do?" Dior asked, offering to be there every inch of the way.

"You act like you know something I don't," Chandelle whispered, with her back against the wall.

"I know something you haven't told anybody and why it's so hard to admit it to yourself," she answered. "You haven't told Marvin because it might not be his child. You haven't told me because it could be my fault. I'm not stupid just because I do stupid things." Dior stared straight ahead, distressed more than Chandelle would have ever predicted. "Girl, I know exactly how you feel."

"How could you even fix your mouth to say that?" Chandelle whined, feeling another surge rumbling in her stomach.

Dior licked her dry lips and hunched her shoulders hopelessly. "I can say it because I'm pregnant too." Chandelle's eyes bucked as she pounced toward the toilet bowl for the third time. Her body shook as she began to cry. Dior went to her aid, like she promised. "It'll be all right. You'll be all right. I'll get you something to eat and we'll talk about it."

"This is a mess, Dior," Chandelle said sorrowfully. She idled on her knees with her head lowered, her mind racing laps in her head. It wasn't long before she remembered the shoe box filled with money, the appointment book, and notes regarding Viagra and sex toys. "Uh-uh-uh . . ." she sighed, trying to exhale away the thought that made her want to cry all over again. "Do you know . . . who the daddy is?"

Dior cracked a labored half smile. She knew with one hundred percent certainty. "Yeah, but it's complicated. Just my luck, he's already in love with somebody else." Chandelle threw her arms around Dior and held her tightly, rocking back and forth.

"Ahhh, Dior, you're concerned about me and you're in a jam too," Chandelle cooed, unaware of what a jam Dior's pregnancy potentially placed her in as well. "I wanted to tell someone but couldn't figure out how to say I'm having a baby but I'm not sure if it's with my husband." They sat on the floor, empathizing with one another. Chandelle looked like death warmed over. Dior felt like it on the inside.

"That's why you haven't gone to the doctor?"

"I'm scared," Chandelle admitted. "I'm scared that of all the times Marvin and I tried to conceive, a one-night mixup might have beaten us to it."

"The doctor could tell how far along you are," Dior suggested, secretly having visited one herself recently.

"Yeah, but what if the dates don't add up? Marvin and I still have the same insurance policy. He could find out before . . ."

"Before you decide if you're keeping it," Dior answered for her when the words got stuck in her throat. "Well, you can't keep walking around getting sick like nobody's gonna catch on."

Chandelle closed her eyes, wishing she had the answers. "I've driven by a public health clinic three times this week, but I didn't have the nerve to stop."

"I'll drive you," Dior offered, holding her cousin's hand. "You don't have to make any decisions, but you do have to find out how far along you are. All of this crying might be for nothing."

"Nothing? Have you forgotten that you're practically in the same boat? You should be crying too."

Dior's labored half smile made a second appearance. "Who said I haven't been?"

After finishing off two bowls of Cheerios, Dior convinced Chandelle to nibble on a slice of cinnamon toast before accompanying her to a clinic she had learned was open on Saturdays. They packed it into the rental car and set out on a very difficult journey, which actually didn't begin until they reached the oatmeal-colored brick building off the interstate. Dior proceeded in first. Chandelle lingered behind a few paces, still not wanting to commit one way or the other. The black woman who asked them to fill out a form attached to a brown clipboard smiled briefly. However, it quickly faded when she noticed that Chandelle was about to lose her breakfast.

"It's right over there, sweetie," the woman informed her, motioning toward the women's restroom. Chandelle rushed inside, bent over at the waist, and hurled into the public toilet. She washed her hands, then rinsed her mouth with two handfuls of water from the sink, all the while looking at herself in the mirror. Not so much that most people would notice, Chandelle's face had begun to change ever so slightly. Her cheeks appeared puffy and the sharp angle of her chin was beginning to round. She didn't know who she was any longer, standing there debating whether she would go through with it if it happened to be Tony's DNA commingling with hers instead of Marvin's. There had to be another way out, but she couldn't see one through the fog.

Eventually, Dior came in to check on her. "Hey, I was filling out the paperwork, but they're asking all kinds of stuff about you that I don't know. Like about allergies and stuff."

"I'll be right out," Chandelle answered, taking one long, lasting look at motherhood in its earliest stages. She stared at her reflection, smiled wearily, and placed her hand on the hand in the mirror. "What are you doing?" she asked, but the reflection simply returned her curious expression. "You don't know either, huh? That makes us even."

Chandelle exited the restroom, feeling weak. She took the plastic chair next to Dior's. "Let me have that," she said, reaching for the information form. "I don't see why they need all of this to get in to see a doctor. I'm not allergic to anything that I know of. I haven't been sick a day in my life, and it really isn't anyone's business when my last sexual encounter was or how many I've had in the past six months."

Dior was glad no one was asking her those questions. She would have had to guess anyhow.

"And look at this, sexually transmitted diseases, none. Blood type? How am I supposed to know?" Chandelle was growing more agitated with each mounting question. "Dior, I'm going to ask that woman how much of this paperwork I need to fill out before I change my mind altogether. This is ridiculous." She stood up too fast, took two steps, and fainted on the spot. The last thing Chandelle remembered was being carted off in an ambulance.

* * *

Dior was frantic. She dialed Marvin's cell number. He didn't answer so she left a message explaining that Chandelle was at the Riverdale Clinic when she passed out and was now being taken to Texas General Hospital for some tests.

Dior paced outside the clinic, dialing Tony's number and hoping she was doing the right thing. If he was the father, he needed to be with Chandelle, she reasoned. It was clear that she was not going through with an abortion regardless.

Tony answered, with loud chattering going on in the background. He didn't want to have another conversation with her, but she made him listen. After she told him Chandelle was having a baby, he said to leave him out of it, then hung up in Dior's face.

On the way to the hospital, she did something that she hated more than anything. Dior called Dooney and asked for his help.

"What you done did now?" he asked, with a barber shop busting at the seams with customers.

"You know I wouldn't be calling you, Dooney, unless I had to," she wailed.

"I would have figured you'd gotten yourself thrown in the clink, but you're calling from your cell?"

"Nah, I'm straight this time," she answered hurriedly. "It's Chandelle. She's on her way to the emergency room at Texas General Hospital."

Dooney burst into his office and closed the door, leaving a man in his chair with a partial haircut. "What? The hospital? What you done did to Chandelle?" he shouted loudly.

"Why you always got to be blaming me? I ain't done nothing to her!" Dior explained how she'd taken Chandelle to the clinic to see about her pregnancy, hoping Dooney wouldn't put that one on her too. Sure enough he did. "Shut up and let me tell you why Chandelle needs you. She's been trying to get with the guy I set her up with, but he had her kicked out of his restaurant when she went to speak with him. I just called him, told him what I told you, and he said he didn't want no parts of it."

Dior counted down from three. By the time she reached one, Dooney was asking her where to find this Tony who had slept with his cousin, then had her strong-armed afterward. Dior gladly revealed his whereabouts and his cell number in case he had a mind to move around. With Dooney on Tony's scent, Dior revved up the motor in the Neon and whizzed onto I-75 like a stock car driver going for a checkered flag.

"Where's Chandelle Hutchins?" she yelled frantically to yet another receptionist at the emergency department check-in area. The white woman was moving too slow for Dior's taste, so she prompted her again. "Hey, stop stalling and tell me where my cousin is. Chandelle Hutchins, they should have brought her here a minute ago." Annoyed that Dior thought she deserved preferential treatment, the receptionist rolled her eyes.

"Quiet down and I'll check for you," she said, picking up the phone to dial another extension. "Did y'all just admit a Hutchins, Shandrelle?"

"*Chandelle*," Dior corrected her. "You're tryna be funny."

"Oh, I see," replied the woman to something said over the phone. "I'll pass it on. Thanks."

"Pass what on, what?"

"Ms. Hutchins is being seen to now," she advised Dior.

"That's *Mrs.* Hutchins," Dior spat nastily. "Some of us black women do have husbands."

"We are talking about the woman who was brought here from the Riverdale Clinic?" the receptionist debated to make her point.

"Yeah, and . . . it's complicated," Dior snarled.

"I'm sure it is. *Mrs*. Hutchins will be a while so you can take this clipboard and sit over there until it's been filled out."

"Again with the clipboard," Dior huffed. "Give it here. Her *husband* is on his way."

"Her husband is right here," Marvin grunted, standing directly behind Dior. The way he was grinding his teeth made the white woman giddy inside. He was overwhelmingly upset and she didn't doubt that Dior had something to do with it.

"Hey, Marvin," Dior greeted him, in a voice so soft she didn't even hear it come out of her mouth.

"Don't *hey Marvin* me. I was breaking my neck to get here when I realized where you said Chandelle was when she passed out. What was my wife doing at an abortion clinic?"

"She—she . . . I—I," Dior stuttered to the delight of the eavesdropping receptionist. "It's like this," she started saying, when a black supervisor thundered over and demanded they keep their voices down.

"Ma'am, I'm just here looking for my wife," Marvin argued. "Chandelle Hutchins, have you admitted her?"

"Uh-huh, she's in the back with the doctor now," replied the black woman, with graying temples and attitude to spare. "If you don't want to be escorted out, keep it down."

"Yes, ma'am," answered Marvin, scratching his head. "Will somebody please tell me what she was doing at Riverdale?"

"See, I woke up this morning and Chandelle was throwing up. I started telling her how she needed to tell you that she was pregnant and . . ."

Marvin's chest heaved out when he heard the word *pregnant*. "Chandelle's pregnant?"

"Uh-uh, I told her that everything needed to be out in the open."

"What else did you tell her, Dior?"

"Nothing about us, I swear."

The receptionist snickered then. "Maybe y'all need to go into the conference room to discuss what wasn't said. These walls have ears," she warned.

Marvin took her advice. He pulled Dior into a glassed-in room with a long table and comfortable chairs. "Now, tell it to me slow," he said. "All of it."

"I don't know too much because Chandelle doesn't. I promise I don't, Marvin. She's going through it right now. There wasn't going to be an abortion, she just wanted to know how deep in it she was. I swear that's all."

The expression on Marvin's face could have stopped a clock. The muscles in his jaws flexed mightily. "So, she *did* sleep with him?" he stated in the tone of a resolution.

"You don't know that," Dior contested, as the voice of reason.

"I know that you made it possible for him to get with her, though. How did it come to this?" Marvin rose to his feet, then turned his back to Dior. He couldn't stand the sight of her. "Chandelle should have told me."

"She almost lost you once," Dior reminded him. "Can you blame her?"

"Nah, that's all on you," Marvin ranted, "you and him." Dior glanced out of the wall of glass. She saw Dooney leading Tony up to the check-in desk. She wanted to disappear when the receptionist gladly pointed her and Marvin out to them.

"I guess it's on now," she whispered, about as terrified and ashamed as she could be. "Don't go back to jail, Marvin. I'm not worth doing time over. Whatever the outcome may be, it's my bad."

"Who you telling," Marvin agreed, as Dooney marched Tony into the conference room. Tony hesitated when he recognized Chandelle's husband. Dooney shoved him in the back to prod him along.

"Get on in there, dude," Dooney urged him. He glared at Dior, then nodded hello to Marvin. "Hey, Kinfolk."

"Dooney," Marvin answered, staring a hole in Tony. The red bruise on the side of Tony's face implied that he had needed some convincing in order to come with Dooney, but it didn't stop Marvin from wanting to put in work of his own. "Who told you to do that?"

"Mr. Tony did when he insulted my people. I just went down to that Café Bleu of his to talk to the man, but naw, he wanted to loud talk me and holler for his boys. Don't stress, they didn't like the odds." Dooney raised his jacket, revealing a chrome-plated automatic handgun. "Now we get along just fine. Ain't that right, Mr. Tony?"

There was a light tap at the door. A tall black man pushed it opened and stepped in. "Sorry to interrupt. I'm told that you all are here for Chandelle Hutchins."

"Yeah, we the family," answered Dooney, the only visitor who wasn't too overwhelmed to speak.

"Good. Chandelle is doing fine. Her blood sugar is low, but we're giving her an IV to correct that. All I need to do is get this form signed by the co-parent of her child, then you can see her in about an hour." Initially, no one moved. The doctor looked at Marvin as a suitable candidate, but Marvin looked away in disgust. Next, the doctor appealed to Dooney. "Sir?" he asked, holding out the form for his signature.

"Uh-uh, Doc," he declined. "Talk to one of them."

"Sir, then you must be the baby's father," the doctor assumed, via process of elimination, but Tony shrugged his shoulders.

"Baby?" he shouted. "Don't look at me," he objected as every eye in the room glinted at his. "What? Is that what all of this is about?"

Dooney sucked his teeth rudely. "I thought you knew, podner."

"That why Chandelle's been bugging me?" he said, biting his lip angrily.

"Watch your mouth, man. I done told you once already about snapping on my people," Dooney reminded him. "You might want to think twice."

After the physician looked at his watch, he realized he'd wasted enough time. "Look, I don't have all day. Are you accepting responsibility as the father or not?"

Tony straightened his jacket and slid both hands inside his pockets. "I can't take responsibility for something I didn't have anything to contribute to. Me and Chandelle didn't hook up that night or any other night since she got married. Yeah, I wanted to, but she was lit and hysterical about her separation. I couldn't take advantage of her after she tried to drown her sorrows with champagne. Besides, she's still in love with him." Tony tilted his head in Marvin's direction. "Even a fool could see that," he remarked sarcastically. "The only reason I stayed that night was to look after her. That's it. If I hadn't been so stubborn and had taken her calls this wouldn't have happened, huh?" He stroked the cheek that Dooney had tattooed with a stiff forearm.

"Congratulations, you're going to be a father," the doctor announced as he handed the document to Marvin for his John Hancock. "Chandelle will be up and running in no time. Just make sure that she keeps on a proper diet."

Marvin extended his hand to Tony, thanking him for doing right by his wife at her weakest moment. "Man, I . . . uh, much respect for staying with her. A lesser man would have . . ." His voice trailed off, merely contemplating the alternative. "I don't know whether to hug your neck or beat you down for being there in the first place."

"Oh, I'd beat him down," Dooney chimed in his unsolicited two cents.

"Can I go now?" Tony asked, pandering to Dooney.

"Yeah, man, but the next time a woman calls you, talk to her. As least see what she wants before you dismiss her."

"Point well taken," he replied on his way out of the conference room. "Well taken, indeed."

Dooney was happy to do his part, as usual. When he saw Marvin wiping his eyes and smiling, he frowned at Dior. "What's going on in here? I know why Kinfolk's boo-hooing. He's got an eighteen-year food bill in the oven, but why is your face all torn up?"

"Because I know what I have to do now. Ain't no question about it. Thank you, Dooney, for showing up like always." Dior hugged her brother for such a long time that he suspected she had gotten in way over her head in some other aspect.

"Dior, you straight?" he asked, using her given name.

"Yeah, thanks to my big brother." She rubbed her tears away with the back of her hand. "I'd like to call you tomorrow if that's all right. I want to talk to you about Billie."

"Yeah, okay then," answered Dooney. "I'm going to see her for Christmas."

"I know . . . and it's about time I went with you."

"Mama would really like that," he told her, softening his tough-guy bravado.

"I would too."

36

My Cross to Bear

Saturday night, the clouds opened up and rained down a flash flood. Tremendous downpours without warning were common in Texas, but this one rated off the charts. Marvin had continually checked on Chandelle in the master bedroom every half hour since the doctor released her earlier that day. She was panic-stricken after learning that Marvin knew about the abortion clinic, her indecisiveness, and the reluctance to share the news regarding her pregnancy. Marvin refused to discuss any of it and insisted that she rest while he looked for something in the kitchen to prepare for dinner. Chandelle slept so soundly for hours that he made the most of his time alone in the house, her house and his.

The décor in the living room was charming and inviting, the sofa and love seat were made of a tan synthetic material he swore was genuine suede with a contemporary flare. The formal dinner table was redwood, very expensive and carved in the shape of a narrow rectangle to stimulate intimate conversation among future guests. Chandelle's taste seemed to have matured during her spiteful period of anger and ambivalence.

Marvin felt like a stranger in the house, a man whose presence wasn't expected but was welcomed. His first trip up the staircase was an arduous climb. He'd turned the corner in the fully furnished home, then put Chandelle to bed probably in the same manner Tony had, and that jostled him where he stood. The thought of replacing the king sleigh bed with another, free from some other man's fingerprints, occurred to him, but that was a discussion for a different time. He had so much more to think about and be thankful for. His wife was having his baby, Dior wasn't having anyone's child as far as he knew, and he was very close to moving in. The house Chandelle had to have and the one he dreaded paying for had become the perfect size for raising a family, with ample room for a home office he could write off at tax time. All in all, their blessings were falling from the sky in buckets like the rain outside the kitchen window. He thanked God for allowing his marriage to endure the strain of almost certain ruin. It had been tested beyond his wildest imagination and thus far weathered the storm successfully, forging a stronger bond between them.

There was just one other item that needed to be addressed. He felt obliged to tell Chandelle about Dior and the night they slept together. Hopefully, their relationship had grown strong enough to sustain itself afterward. Dior would have to understand his rationale. It was his family he had to protect, and his alone.

Marvin realized that when Chandelle floated down the stairs with a certain glow in her eyes. She rubbed her eyes and dragged her feet like a drowsy adolescent who'd awaked from a long dream that ended the way she wanted. "I'm so tired," she said, pressing her face against his chest. "Thank you for letting me sleep as long as I needed to.

You must have a million questions about the house and about me."

Marvin kissed her on the forehead tenderly. "Not a one, either way," he answered sweetly. "You're okay and that means I'm okay. I'm going to be a daddy and that's icing on the cake."

"You are going to be a daddy, a good one too," she predicted. "Grace's daughter, Nicole, will have a playmate."

"Grace, we have to call her," he suggested. "Her and Wallace, you can't do any better than them as friends. Let's do something nice for them."

Chandelle nestled her nose against Marvin to warm it. "Hmmm, like what? They've got crazy money."

"We'll think of something they need, like a lifetime babysitting service for whenever they want a night out on the town. Kim said she has canceled dates because of problems getting a sitter."

"Now that's another person I need to add to my Christmas list. I've been so wrong about her, Marvin, and she's done nothing but have our back. Will you tell her I'm sorry for the way I acted?"

Marvin chuckled and then kissed Chandelle again. "That apology would mean a lot more coming from you."

"Yeah, it would at that," she agreed.

"I know what I'm going to do," he said assuredly. "Since I owe her more than money could say and good ol' Tony for taking care of my woman in my stead, who knows, Kim might dig him, maybe not, but I'm introducing them the first chance I get."

"*Good ol' Tony*, when did all this happen?" she asked, with a surprised glimmer in her eye.

"I'm just saying that in a strange way, I'm in his debt," Marvin answered. "He's on my short list of stand-up brothas, a very short list. I'll figure out a way to pull a Dior and take Kim to the restaurant for a bite, and then

leave them to figure out what's what." He laughed when
Chandelle opposed the idea.

"Humph, you let good ol' Tony work his own angle.
He and Dior . . ." she began to say before something told
her to button up and let it go. "Well, I'm staying out of
other grown folk's affairs. That reminds me, I didn't hear
Dior upstairs. I thought I'd find her down here trying to
tell you how to season meat like she did at the apartment.
Let the girl throw together a couple of decent meals and
she's Julia Child."

"Dior probably would be fussing about this and that if
she was here, but I haven't seen her since we left the hospital."

Chandelle loosened her embrace when a wall of worry
fell on top of her. "I saw the rental car in the garage when
you pulled in. That means she's been here. She does not
need to be running the streets in her condition. It's really
coming down out there."

In what condition? Marvin wanted to ask but dared
not.

"I wasn't supposed to say anything but you are my husband and I'm tired of keeping things from you. Dior's
pregnant too. She told me this morning." When Marvin
held his comments, Chandelle assumed he didn't want to
add insult to injury. "But please don't mention it unless
she brings it up."

Again, Marvin was speechless. He couldn't have said a
word if he wanted to. His heart had jumped out of his
chest and lodged itself in his throat.

"Thank you, honey, I knew I could count on you to
keep a secret. So, what's for dinner?" she asked casually.
"Something smells great."

Marvin told her to have a seat on the sofa while he
made her plate. He motored around the kitchen trying
to stay out of his own way, but the third time he
dropped a dish Chandelle asked if there was anything

wrong. He had to come clean. She'd been honest with him and she deserved the same, he kept telling himself. He couldn't shoulder living with the burden of carrying Dior's lie any longer. After dinner, he'd open his mouth and come right out with it. There was no telling when she'd spring it on Chandelle and turn his wife against him, he feared.

Marvin's hands trembled as he set the dinner tray in front of Chandelle. She muted the volume on the television while awaiting Marvin to say grace over the meal. "Dear Lord . . . Jesus wept. Amen," he said in short, choppy breaths. Chandelle stared at him for the shortest prayer ever.

"Wow, you've been on the quiet trip ever since I told you about Dior having a baby. Don't fret, she is not coming to live with us or raising it here. She said the baby's daddy has a main thing, meaning he's likely married. He'd better have his money right because she's gonna jack his . . ."

"What?" he asked, hanging on every word. "What did Dior say she was planning to do?"

"Nothing," she replied in a hushed, bewildered tone. "That's her car on the news. Right there, on the news, that's Dior's car." Marvin picked up the remote control from the serving tray where Chandelle had placed it. She couldn't move, gazing at a white newsman standing beneath an umbrella on the front lawn of the Jennings's house. "Ohhh no . . . Dior. I know you didn't go back there after yesterday." Marvin found the volume button and pressed it.

"As I said a moment ago, this is breaking news from Plano, a Dallas suburb, where the local police are tight-lipped but neighbors have reported a host of strange activity originating in and around this house behind me," the newsman reported. "They say that as recent as yesterday, two conspicuous females were seen leaving after heated words with the owners. Now, the couple who lives here is going to be charged with homicide. We don't have the name of the victim, but we have confirmation that she is a young black female." As the Jenningses marched out in handcuffs and perp-walked from their home, the cameraman zoomed in on their faces. "As you can see, Paul and Rosalind Jennings have been taken into custody. The cause of death is sketchy at best, but it is known that a black woman has died inside of their bedroom. There has been sex paraphernalia found at the crime scene and foul play is suspected."

"Turn it off, Marvin. Marvin, turn it off!" she shouted unnervingly when he didn't respond the first time. "I'm sorry for yelling but I can't listen to any more of it. I told her. I told Dior to stay away from those types of people."

"Chandelle, it might not be her. Let's call the police. Let me . . ." his voice trailed off when someone knocked at the door. Reminding his feet to move, Marvin shuffled slowly toward it. He brushed the curtains aside to see out front. "There's a police car," he said, as if it were death itself parked next to the curb.

Chandelle covered her mouth with her hand as Marvin turned the doorknob. A uniformed police officer removed his hat like they do in the movies, as a prelude to delivering horrible news. Chandelle heard herself gasp when he asked if they were related to Dior Wicker. Marvin nodded with grave distress. The cop turned and motioned to another one still sitting in the car. Chandelle sat her tray down and then stood up from the sofa.

"What happened?" she asked, afraid of the answer. "Where's Dior now?"

"Ma'am, there's been a terrible tragedy," he said, watching Chandelle fold like paper.

Marvin raced over to hold her up. "Dior is my wife's cousin." he explained. "They were very close."

The second policeman appeared, holding a standard black umbrella over someone Marvin presumed to be the department's designated bearer of bad news. As they drew up the walkway, he saw something else. He shook Chandelle softly to get her attention. Sobbing sorrowfully, her eyes found Dior, standing in the doorway shrouded in a yellow police raincoat. She was shivering and soaking wet with streaks of mascara staining her face.

"I'm so sorry," she cried, her teeth chattering.

"Here's a dry blanket," the second cop said, removing the raincoat from her shoulders.

Marvin ushered Dior into the house, covering her with the navy blue cloth. He'd never been sorrier for anyone in his whole life after she started rambling uncontrollably.

Chandelle listened intently as her wayward cousin babbled on like a sinner needing to repent. "I had Kevlin take me by there to pick up my car and get my things from yesterday when I saw the police cars," Dior muttered pitifully, her eyes glassy and red. "The ambulance was taking her away, Chandelle. They killed her."

She threw her arms around Dior to comfort her. "Who, Dior? They killed who?"

"Isis, my friend," she answered as if they should have known. "The Jennings killed her. They've been calling me all day, but I wouldn't pick up. Instead, I called my friend. She said she could use the money. Pray for me, Chandelle. I have to change. I have to. I could have died tonight. Now another girl is dead because of me."

"Don't say another word," Marvin insisted. "Is Dior under arrest?" The officers explained that she wasn't involved in the actual incident but the DA would be expecting her to come in on her own to give a written statement on Monday morning. Marvin promised them she would appear and cooperate as long as she wasn't being charged as an accessory. He'd learned that tidbit of lawyering from watching countless episodes of *Law & Order*.

"Are you her attorney?" the other policeman asked.

"No, I'm her family. Her attorney will be there with her on Monday to make sure she doesn't get dragged into this mess on the back end. Thanks for bringing her home, officers. We'll take it from here." The cop who escorted Dior from the patrol car handed Marvin a pink plastic bag with Riverdale stenciled on it. He didn't get the meaning but Chandelle did at first glance.

As Marvin closed the door, Chandelle pursed her lips. "When they leave, I need you to do something right away," she told him, with a determined expression. "I'll get Dior in some dry clothes and off to bed. She can't be left alone, not tonight." Chandelle helped Dior stay on her feet as they ascended the stairs.

"Ohhh, God, help me!" Dior clamored miserably. "Pleeease help me! Pray for me, Chandelle. Pray for God to forgive me. I need Him to forgive me."

"I'll pray for you, Dior . . . and He'll fix this. He'll fix it. It's not your fault."

"Isis is dead, Chandelle," cried Dior. "She ain't coming back. The lead detective said they tied her up and choked her to death. He said the Jennings went too far just like you told me they would."

"I know. Hush now. I know."

Marvin felt a chill scale up his back. He wanted to believe it was caused by the draft from having the door open too long but couldn't convince himself of that. He understood what Dior was going through, wading up to his neck in guilt. He was relieved when the officer knocked at the door before the other one brought Dior from the car. He was ashamed to have given her up for dead so easily. Now it was next to impossible to expose his motives to Chandelle and his conscience was kicking him in the stomach.

Unable to shake the chill, he lit the fireplace and wrung his hands near the flames. Chandelle startled him. He flinched anxiously. "Ahh, I didn't see you there."

"I'm sorry, Marvin. I know you're taking this hard too," she said, estimating that to be the cause of his nervous reaction. "These are the keys to Dior's apartment. Do you remember how to get there? Good. This is what I need you to do." She explained in detail where to locate the shoe boxes in the bedroom. "Bring them here and don't touch anything else. I'm not in the mood to be putting my trust in police these days. In case they go back on Dior and try to pull a fast one after she rats on those murderers, there won't be anything for them to build a case with for some other stuff she's done."

Marvin shrugged on his leather jacket and baseball cap. "She stepped into the fire, huh?"

"She must have been coming from the abortion clinic when she learned about her friend," Chandelle enlightened him. "That's what was in that pink bag the cop handed you, an after-care kit." She kissed Marvin on the cheek, and then asked him to be careful. "Don't forget. There's a box of money with a gun. Ain't no telling where she got it from or what crimes it can be connected to. You know Dior buys everything hot. And there's also a black book, a daily planner with all of her dirt from the past eight weeks or so. I read the names of some very powerful people in there. Bring it back here. I know what to do with it."

Marvin used the keys and found the shoe boxes where Chandelle said they would be. He kept a sharp eye out for anyone tailing him. Curiosity got the better of him along the way home. He turned to the date where he expected to find his name. There it was in bold ink: *Marvin's bedroom tonight. No Viagra, no toys necessary*. Shock didn't begin to describe what zigzagged through him when he read her entries outlining how she'd followed him and reported fictitious and highly inflammatory information to Chandelle. Everything made sense then, why his world had fallen apart in a matter of days. Dior had single-handedly orchestrated it and used his wife's jealous streak as the fuel. He'd seen thousands of movies before but nothing that held a candle to Dior's diabolical plan. There was no denying it, the painful reality that Dior's sinful ways had sucked him in unwittingly. Thanks be to God and God alone that he survived by the skin of his teeth.

As soon as Marvin returned home, Chandelle met him at the door. She asked him to hide the gun and money until she figured out what to do about them; then she held out her hand for the daily planner. Marvin hesitated briefly, tempting fate with every second he delayed. "Well, you did get the black book, didn't you?" asked Chandelle.

"Yeah, I got it." He raised his jacket and reached into his waistband. "Here it is." Chandelle held it with both hands, opened it, and then began tearing out the pages. She tossed them into the blazing fire one by one. The glowing embers reflected in Marvin's eyes.

"Are you positive you know what you're doing?" he asked, as if it pained him to do so.

"I'm doing what I should have done the day I discovered it. I'm putting an end to this foolishness, once and for all. If Dior is going to get a break, it starts here and now. Poor thing was upstairs talking in her sleep as soon as you left. Kevlin took her to the clinic after she told him the baby was his. Men are so gullible. Just because she told him that didn't make it so." Chandelle looked at Marvin knowingly, and then smirked at him as the last page floated into the fiery furnace. "I don't ever plan on discussing this again, you understand me?"

"Oh, of—of course not," he answered uneasily.

"And I'll expect you to be all moved in by the end of next week. Agreed?"

"Uh . . . uh . . . agreed," he stuttered, realizing then that it had been revealed to Chandelle who the father was.

"I told you that I had a cross to bear for teaching Dior the ways of the world. Less than an hour ago, God strapped it down to my back extra tight to remind me," she said, pecking him on the lips. "Good night, Marvin. Lock the door on your way out."

1

Penny Worth
o' Blues

Three months deep into 1947, a disturbing calm rolled over St. Louis, Missouri. It was unimaginable to foresee the hope and heartache that one enigmatic season saw fit to unleash, mere inches from winter's edge. One unforgettable story changed the city for ever. This is that story.

Watkins Emporium was the only black-owned dry goods store for seven square blocks and the pride of "The Ville," the city's famous black neighborhood. Talbot Watkins had opened it when the local Woolworth's fired him five years earlier. He allowed black customers to try on hats before purchasing them, which was in direct opposition to store policy. The department store manager had warned him several times before that apparel wasn't fit for sale after having been worn by Negroes. Subsequently, Mr. Watkins used his life savings to start a successful business of his own with his daughter, Chozelle, a hot-natured twenty-year-old who had a propensity for older fast-talking men with even faster hands. Chozelle's scandalous ways became undeniably apparent to her father the third time he'd caught a man running from the backdoor of his storeroom, half-dressed and hell-bent on eluding his wrath. Mr. Watkins clapped an iron pad lock on the rear door after realizing he'd have to protect his daughter's virtue, whether she liked it or not. It was a hard pill to swallow, admitting to himself that canned meat wasn't the only thing getting dusted and polished in that backroom. However, his relationship with Chozelle was just about perfect, compared to that of his meanest customer.

"Penny! Git your bony tail away from that there dress!" Halstead King grunted from the checkout counter. "I done told you once, you're too damned simple for something that fine." When Halstead's lanky daughter snatched her hand away from the red satin cocktail gown displayed in the front window as if a rabid dog had snapped at it, he went right on back to running his mouth and running his eyes up and down Chozelle's full hips and ample everything else. Halstead stuffed the hem of his shirttail into his tattered work pants and then shoved his stubby thumbs beneath the tight suspenders holding them up. After licking his lips and twisting the ends of his thick gray handlebar mustache, he slid a five dollar bill across the wooden countertop, eyeing Chozelle suggestively. "Now, like I was saying, How 'bout I come by later on when your daddy's away and help you arrange thangs in the storeroom?" His plump belly spread between the worn leather suspender straps like one of the heavy grain sacks he'd loaded on the back of his pickup truck just minutes before.

Chozelle had a live one on the hook, but old man Halstead didn't stand a chance of getting at what had his zipper about to burst. Although his appearance reminded her of a rusty old walrus, she strung him along. Chozelle was certain that five dollars was all she'd get from the tight-fisted miser, unless of course she agreed to give him something worth a lot more. After deciding to leave the lustful old man's offer on the counter top, she turned her back toward him and then pretended to adjust a line of canned peaches behind the counter. "Like what you see, Mr. Halstead?" Chozelle flirted. She didn't have to guess whether his mouth watered, because it always did when he imagined pressing his body against up hers. "It'll cost you a heap more than five dollars to catch a peek at the rest of it," she informed him.

"A peek at what, Chozelle?" hissed Mr. Watkins suspiciously, as he stepped out of the side office.

Chozelle stammered while Halstead choked down a pound of culpability. "Oh, nothing, Papa. Mr. Halstead's just thinking about buying something nice for Penny over yonder." Her father tossed a quick glance at the nervous seventeen-year-old obediently standing an arm's length away from the dress she'd been dreaming about for weeks. "I was telling him how we'd be getting in another shipment of ladies garments next Thursday," Chozelle added, hoping that the lie sounded more plausible then. When Halstead's eyes fell to the floor, there was no doubting what he'd had in mind. It was common knowledge that Halstead King, the local moonshiner, treated his only daughter like an unwanted pet and that he never shelled out one thin dime toward her happiness.

"All right then," said Mr. Watkins, in a cool calculated manner. "We'll put that there five on a new dress for Penny. Next weekend she can come back and get that red one in the window she's been fancying." Halstead started to argue as the store owner lifted the money from the counter and folded it into his shirt pocket but it was gone for good, just like Penny's hopes of getting anything close to that red dress if her father had anything to say about it. "She's getting to be a grown woman and it'd make a right nice coming-out gift. Good day, Halstead," Mr. Watkins offered, sealing the agreement.

"Papa, you know I've had my heart set on that satin

number since it came in," Chozelle whined, as if the whole world revolved around her.

Directly outside of the store, Halstead slapped Penny down onto the dirty sidewalk in front of the display window. "You done cost me more money than you're worth," he spat. "I have half a mind to take it out of your hide."

"Not unless you want worse coming to you," a velvety smooth voice threatened from the driver's seat of a new Ford convertible with Maryland plates.

Halstead glared at the stranger then at the man's shiny beige Roadster. Penny was staring up at her handsome hero, with the buttery complexion, for another reason all together. She turned her head briefly, holding her sore eye then glanced back at the dress in the window. She managed a smile when the man in the convertible was the only thing she'd ever seen prettier than that red dress. Suddenly, her swollen face didn't sting nearly as much.

"You ain't got no business here, mistah!" Halstead exclaimed harshly. "People known to get hurt messin' where they don't belong."

"Uh-uh, see, you went and made it my business by putting your hands on that girl. If she was half the man you pretend to be, she'd put a hole in your head as sure as you're standing there." The handsome stranger unfastened the buttons on his expensive tweed sports coat to reveal a long black revolver cradled in a shoulder holster. When Halstead took that as a premonition of things to come, he backed down, like most bullies do when confronted by someone who didn't bluff so easily. "Uh-huh, that's what I thought," he said, stepping out of his automobile idled at the curb. "Miss, you all right?" he asked Penny, helping her off the hard cement. He noticed that one of the buckles was broken on her run over shoes. "If not, I could fix that for you. Then, we can go get your shoe looked after." Penny swooned as if she'd seen her first sunrise. Her eyes were opened almost as wide as Chozelle's, who was gawking from the other side of the large framed window. "They call me Baltimore, Baltimore Floyd. It's nice to make your acquaintance, miss. Sorry it had to be under such unfavorable circumstances."

Penny thought she was going to faint right there on the very sidewalk she'd climbed up from. No man had taken the time to notice her, much less talk to her in such a flattering manner. If it were up to Penny, she was willing to get knocked down all over again for the sake of reliving that moment in time.

"Naw, suh, Halstead's right," Penny sighed after giving it some thought. "This here be family business." She dusted herself off, primped her pigtails, a hairstyle more appropriate for much younger girls, then she batted her eyes like she'd done it all of her life. "Thank you kindly, though," Penny mumbled, noting the contempt mounting in her father's expression. Halstead wished he'd brought along his gun and his daughter was wishing the same thing, so that Baltimore could make him eat it. She understood all too well that as soon as they returned to their shanty farmhouse on the outskirts of town, there would be hell to pay.

"Come on, Penny," she heard Halstead gurgle softer than she'd imagined he could. "We ought to be getting on," he added as if asking permission to leave.

"I'll be seeing you again, Penny," Baltimore offered. "And next time, there bet' not be one scratch on your face," he said, looking directly at Halstead. "It's hard enough on women folk as it is. They shouldn't have to go about wearing reminders of a man's shortcomings."

Halstead hurried to the other side of the secondhand pickup truck and cranked it. "Penny," he summoned, when her feet hadn't moved an inch. Perhaps she was waiting on permission to leave too. Baltimore tossed Penny a wink as he helped her up onto the tattered bench seat.

"Go on now. It'll be all right or else I'll fix it," he assured her, nodding his head in a kind fashion and smiling brightly.

As the old pickup truck jerked forward, Penny stole a glance at the tall silky stranger then held the hand Baltimore had clasped inside his up to her nose. The fragrance of his store-bought cologne resonated through her nostrils for miles until the smell of farm animals whipped her back into a stale reality, her own.

It wasn't long before Halstead mustered up enough courage to revert back to the mean tyrant he'd always been. His unforgiving black heart and vivid memories of the woman who ran off with a traveling salesman fueled Halstead's hatred for Penny, the girl his wife left behind. Halstead was determined to destroy Penny's spirit since he couldn't do the same to her mother.

"Git those mason jar crates off'n the truck while I fire up the still!" he hollered. "And you might as well forget that man in town and ever meeting him again. His meddling can't help you way out here. He's probably on his way back east already." When Penny moved too casually for Halstead's taste, he jumped up and popped her across the mouth. Blood squirted from her bottom lip. "Don't make me tell you again," he cursed. "Ms. Etta's havin' her spring jig this weekend and I promised two more cases before sundown. Now git!"

Penny's injured lip quivered. "Yeah, suh," she whispered, her head bowed.

As Halstead waddled to the rear of their orange brick and oak, weather-beaten house, cussing and complaining about wayward women, traveling salesmen and slick strangers, he shouted additional chores. "Stack them crates up straight this time so's they don't tip over. Fetch a heap of water in that barrel, bring it around yonder and put my store receipts on top of the bureau in my room. Don't touch nothin' while you in there neither, useless heifer," he grumbled.

"Yeah, suh, I will. I mean, I won't," she whimpered. Penny allowed a long strand of blood to dangle from her angular chin before she took the hem of her faded dress and wiped it away. Feeling inadequate, Penny became confused as to in which order her chores were to have been performed. She reached inside the cab of the truck, collected the store receipts and crossed the pebble covered yard. She sighed deeply over how unfair it felt, having to do chores on such a beautiful spring day, and then she pushed open the front door and wandered into Halstead's room. She overlooked the assortment of loose coins scattered on the night stand next to his disheveled queen sized bed with filthy sheets she'd be expected to scrub clean before the day was through.

On the corner of the bed frame hung a silver-plated Colt revolver. Sunlight poured through the half-drawn window shade, glinting off the pistol. While mesmerized by the opportunity to take matters into her own hands, Penny palmed the forty-five carefully. She contemplated how easily she could have ended it all with one bullet to the head, hers. Something deep inside wouldn't allow Penny to hurt another human, something good and decent, something she didn't inherit from Halstead.

"Penny!" he yelled, from outside. "You got three seconds to git outta that house and back to work!" Startled, Penny dropped the gun onto the uneven floor and froze, praying it wouldn't go off. Halstead pressed his round face against the dusty window to look inside. "Goddammit! Gal, you've got to be the slowest somebody. Git back to work before I have to beat some speed into you."

The puddle of warm urine Penny stood in confirmed that she was still live. It could have just as easily been a pool of warm blood instead. Thoughts of ending her misery after her life had been spared fleeted quickly. She un-buttoned her thin cotton dress, used it to mop the floor then tossed it on the dirty clothes heap in her bedroom. Within minutes, she'd changed into an undershirt and denim overalls. Her pace was noticeably revitalized as she wrestled the crates off the truck as instructed. "Stack them crates," Penny mumbled to herself. "Stack 'em straight so's they don't tip over. Then fetch the water." The week before, she'd stacked the crates too high and a strong gust of wind toppled them over. Halstead was furious. He dragged Penny into the barn, tied her to a tractor wheel and left her there for three days without food or water. She was determined not to spend another three days warding off field mice and garden snakes.

Once the shipment had been situated on the front porch, Penny rolled the ten-gallon water barrel over to the well pump beside the cobblestone walkway. Halstead was busy behind the house, boiling sour mash and corn syrup in a copper pot with measures of grain. He'd made a small fortune distilling alcohol and peddling it to bars, juke joints and roadhouses. "Hurr'up, with that water!" he shouted. "This still's plenty hot. Coils try'n'a bunch."

Penny clutched the well handle with both hands and went to work. She had seen an illegal still explode when it reached the boiling point too quickly, causing the copper coils to clog when they didn't hold up to the rapidly increasing temperatures. Ironically, just as it came to Penny that someone had tampered with the neighbors still on the morning it blew up, a thunderous blast shook her where she stood. Penny cringed. Her eyes grew wide when Halstead staggered from the backyard screaming and cussing, with every inch of his body covered in vibrant yellow flames. Stumbling to his knees, he cried out for Penny to help him.

"Water! Throw the damned . . . water!" he demanded.

She watched in amazement as Halstead writhed on the

ground in unbridled torment, his skin melting, separating from bone and cartilage. In a desperate attempt, Halstead reached out to her, expecting to be doused with water just beyond his reach, as it gushed from the well spout like blood had poured from Penny's busted lip.

Penny raced past a water pail on her way toward the front porch. When she couldn't reach the top crate fast enough, she shoved the entire stack of them onto the ground. After getting what she went there for, she covered her nose with a rag as she inched closer to Halstead's charred body. While life evaporated from his smoldering remains, Penny held a mason jar beneath the spout until water spilled over onto her hand. She kicked the ten gallon barrel on its side then sat down on it. She was surprised at how fast all the hate she'd known in the world was suddenly gone and how nice it was to finally enjoy a cool, uninterrupted, glass of water.

At her leisure, Penny sipped until she'd had her fill. "Ain't no man supposed to treat his own blood like you treated me," she heckled, rocking back and forth slowly on the rise of that barrel. "Maybe that's cause you wasn't no man at all. You' just mean old Halstead. Mean old Halstead." Penny looked up the road when something in the wind called out to her. A car was headed her way. By the looks of it, she had less than two minutes to map out her future, so she dashed into the house, collected what she could and threw it all into a croaker sack. Somehow, it didn't seem fitting to keep the back door to her shameful past opened, so she snatched the full pail off the ground, filled it from the last batch of moonshine Halstead had brewed. If her mother had ever planned on returning, Penny reasoned that she'd taken too long as she tossed the pail full of white lightning into the house. As she lit a full box of stick matches, her hands shook erratically until the time had come to walk away from her bitter yesterdays and give up on living out the childhood that wasn't intended for her. "No reason to come back here, Momma," she whispered, for the gentle breeze to hear and carry away. "I got to make it on my own now."

Penny stood by the roadside and stared at the rising inferno, ablaze from pillar to post. Halstead's fried corpse smoldered on the lawn when the approaching vehicle ambled to a stop in the middle of the road. A young man, long, lean, and not much older than Penny took his sweet time stepping out of the late model Plymouth sedan. He sauntered over to the hump of roasted flesh and studied it. "Hey, Penny," the familiar passerby said routinely.

"Afternoon, Jinxy," she replied, her gaze still locked on the thick black clouds of smoke billowing toward the sky.

Sam "Jinx" Dearborn, Jr., was the youngest son of a neighbor, whose moonshine still went up in flames two months earlier. Jinx surveyed the yard, the smashed mason jars and the overturned water barrel.

"That there Halstead?" Jinx alleged knowingly.

Penny nodded that it was, without a hint of reservation. "What's left of 'im," she answered casually.

"I guess you'll be moving on then," Jinx concluded stoically.

"Yeah, I reckon I will at that," she concluded as well, using the same even pitch he had. "Haven't seen much of you since yo' daddy passed. How you been?"

Jinx hoisted Penny's large cloth sack into the back seat of his car. "Waitin' mostly," he said, hunching his shoulders, "to get even."

"Yeah, I figured as much when I saw it was you in the road." Penny was one of two people who were all but certain that Halstead had killed Jinx's father by rigging his still to malfunction so he could eliminate the competition. The night before it happened, Halstead had quarreled with him over money. By the next afternoon, Jinx was making burial arrangements for his daddy.

"Halstead got what he had coming to him," Jinx reasoned as he walked Penny to the passenger door.

"Now, I'll get what's coming to me," Penny declared somberly, with a pocket full of folding money. "I'd be thankful, Jinxy, if you'd run me into town. I need to see a man about a dress."

Look For These Other
Dafina Novels

If I Could
0-7582-0131-1

by Donna Hill
$6.99US/**$9.99**CAN

Thunderland
0-7582-0247-4

by Brandon Massey
$6.99US/**$9.99**CAN

June In Winter
0-7582-0375-6

by Pat Phillips
$6.99US/**$9.99**CAN

Yo Yo Love
0-7582-0239-3

by Daaimah S. Poole
$6.99US/**$9.99**CAN

When Twilight Comes
0-7582-0033-1

by Gwynne Forster
$6.99US/**$9.99**CAN

It's A Thin Line
0-7582-0354-3

by Kimberla Lawson Roby
$6.99US/**$9.99**CAN

Perfect Timing
0-7582-0029-3

by Brenda Jackson
$6.99US/**$9.99**CAN

Never Again Once More
0-7582-0021-8

by Mary B. Morrison
$6.99US/**$8.99**CAN

Available Wherever Books Are Sold!

Check out our website at www.kensingtonbooks.com.